ECHOES OF THE FALL

ECHOES OF THE FALL

AN EARL MARCUS MYSTERY

Hank Early

CROOKED
LANE

NEW YORK

Published in the United States by Crooked Lane Books, an imprint of The Quick Brown Fox & Company LLC.

Crooked Lane Books and its logo are trademarks of The Quick Brown Fox & Company LLC.

Library of Congress Catalog-in-Publication data available upon request.

ISBN (hardcover): 978-1-64385-181-5
ISBN (ebook): 978-1-64385-182-2

Cover design by Melanie Sun
Book design by Jennifer Canzone

Printed in the United States.

www.crookedlanebooks.com

Crooked Lane Books
34 West 27th St., 10th Floor
New York, NY 10001

First Edition: November 2019

10 9 8 7 6 5 4 3 2 1

For my family—Becky, Joy, Luke, and Bop Bop.

Part One
The Fall

1

With what felt like superhuman effort, I turned and faced the bright morning sun.

The world moved beneath me while it burned me from above. My head hurt and my eyes felt sealed shut. Worst of all, my mind was a blur of memory, sensation, and sound, all of which conspired to create a glaze of hazy dread.

My entire being was a question mark, a mystery, a painful knot I could not untie.

Then the screaming started.

I recognized the whiskey-soaked drawl immediately. It hardly mattered that he'd amped it up to a place where the dial didn't turn. It was Rufus. Why was he screaming at me like the goddamn world was on fire?

I tried to open an eye, but the glare was too bright. I closed it again, willing the confusion to stop, hoping to find something solid enough to hold onto. That was when my mind clicked back to the last thing I remembered. Nighttime, high in the mountains. Backslide Gap, the smell of afternoon rain still wet on the grass. My bare cheek scrubbed raw against the splintered wooden planks of the suspension bridge where I lay with the bottle of whiskey, daring a strong wind to tip me over into the ravine, into that long and inevitable fall. But that strong wind never came, only a soft breeze that rocked the bridge so gently, it might as well have been a lullaby, while the North Georgia night sky remained a still life framed raggedly by pines, basswoods, and oaks as old as the very dirt from which they grew.

Now—back in the brutal now—the world was moving, alive with kinetic energy and jarring possibility. There was wind for sure, and behind the constant screams from Rufus, I heard the snarl of an almighty engine, tuned for maximum menace.

"Stop," I managed at last. To the world. To the engine. To Rufus who was still screaming at me.

Neither the world, the engine, nor Rufus stopped. Hell, Rufus didn't even slow down. That was when something rough and wet touched my face. Goose. It had to be my dog, Goose, licking the dried whiskey from the corners of my mouth. I tried to open my eyes again. The light made me wince in pain.

Pain. Shit. I remembered the pain. It was physical. Some of it, but not the worst parts. "Let me alone," I said. "Let me die."

"Fuck dying," Rufus said, or maybe I imagined he said it. It sounded like something Rufus would say. He was stubborn. The world could scramble itself into a thousand different variations, but that would never change. He was immutable, a dark mountain hollow in human form, a legend whispered on the wind come to life. He continued to scream at me, his voice nearly as loud and as rough as the engine rumbling beneath us.

My head swam, my consciousness trying to stabilize, to find a rock to hang on to in a sea of treacherous waves. It was daytime, summer in the Georgia mountains. I smelled blackberries and honeysuckle and something dead, boiling in the unrelenting heat. I was blistered, sunburned. I forced one eye open. My other seemed stuck shut. The light felt like pain, pure and hot.

Reflexively, perhaps instinctively, I reached for a bottle. Where was the whiskey? I flailed my arms around and felt nothing but hot . . . steel? Aluminum?

My other eye snapped open, and I saw the sky above me, sliding smoothly past the tops of the trees. It was blue and clear and I didn't understand how it and my misery could exist in the same world, at the same time.

That was when I finally glimpsed Rufus in my peripheral vision. He was sitting near me, his mouth working hard, chewing his words, spitting them out, all of them incomprehensible. I concentrated hard and heard, "You ain't quitting on me." The snarl of the engine seemed to echo him, like a hype man whose voice had been shot through a cement grinder and amplified by the world's most ineffective muffler.

"If I want to, I will," I said, but was pretty sure my mouth didn't move. Where was the whiskey?

And then something new. Something overpowering. Something in my gut. It jerked me to my knees and gave me my first glimpse of where I was, what was happening. I was in the back of Ronnie Thrash's pickup truck, going fast up a mountain road, dense trees gliding past in a blur of branches and leaves and vines. I grabbed the side of the truck bed, leaned my head out over the dusty road, and vomited. I was still vomiting when the truck came to a stop beside Ghost Creek, not far from the old church my father had built. Rufus grabbed my arm. "Come on, Earl," he said. "It's time to get born again."

*   *   *

Ronnie, who'd been driving the truck, helped drag me over to the same creek where Daddy had baptized me so many years ago. They stood me up and made me stare down into it.

"On my count," Rufus said.

"What's going on?" I asked. This time the words came out loud and clear. They tasted like bile and whiskey and maybe blood, and they tasted like defeat.

"Full immersion," Rufus said. "We're going to dunk your ass."

"He's still pretty drunk," Ronnie said.

"Good. Maybe he'll scream less."

"You might drown him."

"*Might* ain't a useful word here. He might never stop drinking neither. He might just kill himself. Might, might, might. The word I need is *got*. As in, he's my friend, so I got to do something. Now, are you with me or aren't you?"

"I'm with you," Ronnie said, and I was just sober enough to understand that even Ronnie was worried about me. That didn't speak well for my condition, considering that Ronnie's lifestyle could best be described as falling somewhere between a backwoods hoedown and a crime spree.

"I'm not," I groaned, and tried to pull away. Going into the creek seemed like a terrible idea to me. Just looking at the brown water made me feel sick again. It wasn't far from how I'd felt as a kid with Daddy's big hands behind my head. I'd felt out of control then, subsumed by the whims of a tradition I didn't understand. I couldn't ignore how this moment seemed to be the final culmination of the promise of my first baptism. Religion had cut me deep, and now either I was going to drown with it or

God would raise me back up again for more misery and purposes unknown.

They slung my rag doll body into the creek, and one of them—Rufus, I guessed—drove me down toward the bottom with both hands. My face slapped mud, and I tried to breathe.

Didn't work.

Nothing worked. Nothing had ever worked.

Except Mary.

Her name lit up my brain, bringing it all back, every last detail that had led me to Backslide Gap and the suspension bridge, to the very place my daddy had predicted I'd go one day to die if I didn't ever get right with the Lord.

Mary, goddamn it. Mary. Except that wasn't right. Mary wasn't the one who was damned. That was me.

She'd been the only good part of my life. Without her, I didn't work. Without her, I sputtered and broke. Without her, moving forward felt impossible.

Water rushed into my mouth, my nose, and I was a kid again, shivering in my father's arms, desperate for the warmth of the sun on that cold spring day.

Hands clutched my shirt, hauling me back up into the now. The hot summer air felt glorious in my lungs. Rufus turned me around until I was facing him. His eyes were savage and dull. They saw nothing and everything at once.

"This," he said, "was the creek your daddy baptized you in. I watched him dip you under from that bank over there. I remember thinking you was somebody special even then. I thought you were the only one in these whole mountains who had it in him to eclipse your father, to eclipse this whole place. I wasn't wrong neither. Nope." He slammed me down in the water again. He held me long enough to make my lungs burn before pulling me up.

"Now look at you," he said. "Crying over some damned milk you yourself spilt."

"I'm not crying," I said. "I'm drinking."

"Yep," he said. "That's 'cause you like to drown. Well, I'm going to show you where all that whiskey is going to get you."

He shoved me down again, this time harder than ever. The back of my head hit the muddy bottom and cut a groove between two rocks, either of which might have knocked me out if I'd hit them straight on. He held me there, increasing the pressure on my chest, in my lungs. I clawed at his wrists, his arms, but I wasn't as strong as Rufus, and my weakness was doubled because of the oxygen I lacked. I knew he didn't want to kill me, but I was afraid he was going to do it anyway.

My father had held me gently at first, as he stood waist deep in the frigid creek water. The banks on either side were lined with members of the congregation he'd worked so hard to build. They hung on his every word, and had become so caught in the high beams of his personality that they could no longer see what was right in front of their face. Daddy kept one hand under my head and pressed the other into the small of my back. I wiggled my bare feet in the water, trying to gain some purchase, but I was so small I couldn't touch the bottom even in this shallow creek. Daddy spoke, saying the words he was always saying. Heavy words. Words that fell out of the sky instead of his mouth. This time the words were about me. He was praying for my life, for God to turn a watchful eye on me, to keep me safe and to never let me stray.

The hand slipped away from the small of my back, but somehow he kept me above water. I was floating, suspended somewhere between heaven and earth, between the God my father made his appeals to and the man I called Daddy. For a moment, I saw the sky in a new way, and I felt God in my heart. I believed he would take care of me, because in so many ways Daddy was God made flesh, and if Daddy believed in me, so would his father in heaven.

Then the dunk came. Daddy's big hand covered my forehead as the other hand fell away. The bracing water beneath me, so cold in the early spring morning, vanished, and I fell.

I fell through the years of struggling to come to terms with the broken promise my life had become. I fell through the years of learning to live with myself and the memory of my father, through the years of believing he was dead and the year when, at long last, I found out he wasn't. I fell through the more recent years of having Mary beside me, of believing I could live and die with something approaching dignity because I'd been to the mountaintop, I'd emerged whole from the first cold immersion in this creek. I'd made it, I'd survived. I'd been redeemed.

But then I fell some more, and Mary was gone. I was alone with the bottle. My days turned to nights, my mornings became eternal, the drunken moments of pleasure all too brief, forever running away from me like a memory of the past I could never quite reach.

When I finally hit the bottom, I found myself back in the moment, Rufus's hands holding me down, baptizing me again, since the first one so many years ago clearly didn't take. Now I lay on the bottom of the muddy creek and forgot about breathing and instead inhaled the long-lost feeling of my childhood, the feeling of wanting to be saved, to be redeemed by something or somebody. Full immersion, the water cool and silky around me. Maybe, I thought, the only way to be redeemed was to do it myself.

But how?

I couldn't help but think if Rufus had held me down longer, I would have known. Or maybe I would have died. There is always a fine line between secret knowledge and death. But he let go, and I floated back to the surface, to the world of the living where I had no choice but to breathe again.

2

Who can say where mysteries begin?

Perhaps they don't even have temporality but exist instead in a timeless cycle, a spoked wheel, endlessly spinning, buffeting strange winds in all directions.

Or maybe their starting points are definite, but because mysteries are nothing if not dark mountains constructed out of darker hollows, those beginnings are ultimately as furtive as their solutions.

I'd spent most of my life chasing mysteries, following them up and down mountains in Georgia and North Carolina, tracing them as far as I could to their origins in order to better understand their endings and hopefully catch a glimpse of their solutions. This latest mystery had tendrils that reached into aspects of my unexamined life and would bring me to that point on the bridge, and ultimately to my second baptism. In many ways it was a mystery that had begun at Backslide Gap, where I'd played as a teenager, hanging from the suspension bridge over the long and tantalizing fall into nothingness, believing the equally tantalizing lie of my own immortality, and it was this mystery that had followed me toward the inevitable break with my father and his fundamental and stifling church to the cold beds of women I barely knew in an effort to find comfort, and then to my long love affair with the bottle. I left the mountains of North Georgia, thinking the answer to the mystery might be found elsewhere, like some boon at the end of an epic quest, only to find nothing but vaporous dreams and half-remembered visions of home. I was haunted. Not just by my past, but by my inability to piece it together with my present and envision a future that might act as some small salvation before my time

9

here was finished. All of this to say that my mystery had many beginnings, but there was only one that hadn't been obscured by the passage of time and the deficiencies of memory. One moment that opened the door to my past and my future.

And that was the moment I discovered the dead man in my yard.

* * *

I'd been on my way home from a disturbing night out with my best friend, Rufus Gribble. Rufus had been upset by something he wouldn't share with me. Normally, a night out with Rufus at Jessamine's, the area's best honky-tonk, would involve us both drinking to the point of having to crash in my truck, but not on this evening. Instead, we had a few beers, I asked him what was bothering him, and he shrugged muttering something about how he hadn't been sleeping well. Not much more happened. Just some drinking and monosyllabic grumbling about inconsequential topics.

We left the place at nine, only slightly inebriated, and I drove Rufus home, letting him out at the doors of my father's old church, where he'd been squatting for the last five or six years. I glanced across the creek at the old moonshiner's shack where Ronnie Thrash had lived before heading to the state penitentiary the previous January. He was doing time for manslaughter but had recently contacted me to tell me he was coming home soon. There were quite a few extenuating circumstances that had helped lessen his sentence, not the least of which was that the man he'd killed was a member of a white supremacist organization that had abducted Mary Hawkins, a black Atlanta police officer and my girlfriend.

Rufus left without saying much that night, and I watched him pick his way toward the doors of the old church, amazed as always by how easily he moved, how deftly he avoided obstacles despite his blindness.

I was probably three minutes from my own house when I heard what I felt certain was the report of .22-caliber rifle.

My reaction wasn't instantaneous. Maybe it was the alcohol. I wasn't drunk, but I'd had enough to take the edge off.

At first I thought it might be a hunter, but it wasn't hunting season, and the only person who lived up this way was me. The sound was close.

Close enough to make me wonder what occasion would have caused somebody to head up this far into the mountains. Other than the abandoned trailer down the ridge from my place, there wasn't anything up this way except trees and rocks—and some of the best views you could ever imagine.

By the time I reached the last rise before the ridge I lived on, I'd all but dismissed it as some rando who'd decided he wanted to kill a six-pointer and had followed it a little too far up the backside of the mountain. Occasionally hunters did wander up this way, though I had to admit I'd never encountered one in July before, much less at this hour. There were also the Hill Brothers to think about. I'd seen them both before, several times, cutting through my yard, moving like ghosts from some mythical past, floating by the big oak tree where I parked my truck, their expressions somewhere between solemn and hangdog. They lived together in some undisclosed place in these mountains and made their way on foot through the darkest hollows, rarely speaking, never smiling, like spirits of long-dead men who lived feral and hard and with a kind of silent pride that bespoke violence and desperation as well as a strange and hard-worn nobility. I thought they must have been called the Hill Brothers because no one knew their real names, and they stalked these hills like panthers hunting for God only knew what.

I pushed my truck a little faster over the last rise. Immediately I noticed a dark sedan in front of my house. My headlights canvassed it, and I thought it might be a Ford or Chevy, fairly new. I cut my wheel onto my gravel drive, and my headlights picked up a shadow sprinting across the yard, toward the back of my house where I had a tool shed and lawn furniture and some cornhole boards set up. Beyond that were trees and higher elevations overrun with caves and gullies and boulders that made the terrain nearly impassable on foot. There were sheer drops that could make a man dizzy just thinking about them.

The shadow—I can hardly call it anything else—vanished behind my house. I floored the gas, planning to go around the other vehicle and squeeze between the massive oak tree and my little house to head the intruder off before he made the woods.

It might have worked if I hadn't hit something first.

I saw it at the last second, far too late to stop.

It was a body; I knew when I heard the distinctive, and unmistakable crunch of bone beneath my tires.

I swung the truck around, completely forgetting about the intruder, who was surely to the woods by now, and aimed my headlights at what I'd just run over, hoping against hope it was a coyote and not my dog, Goose.

When my headlights illuminated the body, it was clear. That was no coyote or dog. It was a man.

3

Goose, I eventually remembered, was inside the house. Before heading out to pick up Rufus, I'd decided to leave him in because it looked like rain. The rain never materialized, but in its absence something worse did.

The dead man in my yard was young, somewhere in his twenties, I guessed, broad shouldered and thickly muscled. Best I could tell he had sandy-blond hair and surprisingly dark features. His eyes seemed too large for the rest of him, each frozen pupil fathomless and somehow haunted. His face revealed a strange tangle of emotion: revulsion, surprise, melancholy. Below that, there was a hole through his neck, and the blood—massive amounts of it—had drained off toward the ground along the underside of his left earlobe. As revolting as it was, I felt a small measure of relief because the wound made it pretty clear he'd been dead before I'd run over him.

I saw all this under the glare of the penlight I kept on my key chain, and when I couldn't take looking at it anymore, I switched the light off and sat down in the grass, thankful for the comfort of darkness.

I wished I was drunk. Too drunk to care about this kid I didn't know. That had certainly been the way of things for me lately, reaching for the bottle a little earlier each day and stumbling toward bed a little more reck-lessly every night. But the one night I needed to be three sheets to the wind, I was closer to sober than I'd been in a while.

I thought of Mary. She and I were still together, though the seeds of our dissolution had already been planted. We were doing the relationship "long distance" now because she'd decided to move out to Nevada to be with her brother and her five-year-old nephew who'd recently been diag-nosed with leukemia. Her brother, Jeremy, had just gone through a terrible divorce, and it was absolutely the right thing for her to do. What's more, it was absolutely the *Mary* thing for her to do. Still, I'd taken it hard, too hard. It wasn't like it was the end of us, but somehow, in a way I couldn't properly explain, it felt like it was just that. The end.

And now I had a dead man in my yard.

I flicked my penlight back on and went to retrieve my phone from the truck. I was running on instinct now, and every instinct I had was telling me to call the authorities. It wasn't until I had my phone in hand that I realized I was about to make a huge mistake.

The problem with calling the authorities about the dead man in my yard was this: the newly elected sheriff of Coulee County didn't like me much. Nope. That didn't quite do it justice. The sheriff, Preston Argent, would probably relish nothing more than charging me with this murder. He wouldn't be overly concerned about evidence—well, not any more concerned than he needed to be to plant it.

Not only had I lost to Argent in a hotly contested race for sheriff just four weeks earlier; he was also beholden to the one man who hated me more than anyone else. His name was Jeb Walsh, and he was a stain on this county that wouldn't come out. Despite taking down the white supremacist organization Walsh ran last fall, I hadn't been able to touch Walsh or Argent. Not only that, but Walsh was growing more powerful with each passing day as he raised more money and support for his House of Representatives bid in the fall. According to all the reports I'd seen, he was expected to win in a landslide. God help us all if they were right.

No, calling Sheriff Argent would be like presenting myself to him with my hands already cuffed. There was no way he wouldn't see this as an opportunity to, at the very least, hassle me. More likely, he'd confer with Walsh, and they'd arrest my ass. Once that happened, I might sit in the jail until doomsday without a trial, bail, or representation. Argent and Walsh saw me as a thorn in their side, one of the few in the whole county. There was Rufus, of course, but as irritating as he could be, he was still somewhat of a pariah in this area. People tended to think he was just some crazy mountain man, which was true, of course, but what people missed about Rufus was how smart he was, not to mention how determined. Argent and Walsh hated Mary too, but she was in Nevada for the foreseeable future.

Besides, they'd already tried to take advantage of her once, and it hadn't gone very well for them.

Bottom line: Argent and Walsh would use this body against me. Even if they didn't get a conviction, they'd make sure a prolonged court battle ruined my life and my reputation.

Even now, replaying it all in my mind, I'm pretty certain I would do the same thing all over again.

What I did was stand up, dust the dirt off my blue jeans, and head to the house. Goose was still inside and would be wanting out by now. I was glad it was relatively early in the evening, not yet ten thirty. I had plenty of time before daylight to figure this out. My first instinct was to call Mary, but I resisted. The last thing she needed was to be pulled into something like this. Her hands were full with her nephew and brother.

Next, I considered heading into the woods behind my house to look for the man I'd glimpsed on my property. Perhaps I could find him tonight and put an end to this nightmare. But something kept me from pursuing him. He'd be long gone by now, somewhere on the backside of the mountain where there were trees and caves and places no sane man would go at night.

I started to call Rufus but then hesitated. Calling him would only satisfy my need to confide in someone. He'd want to help, but I couldn't see how a blind man would be useful to me right now, other than the advice he might offer. I was pretty sure I already knew what that advice was going to be, and there was no way I was calling the authorities. Like Mary, he would help, but it didn't seem fair to inflict this on him just for the sake of my own deep-seated need to talk to someone.

That left Ronnie, who was still at Hays State Prison. He'd help me hide the body in a heartbeat if he could, but not having him around to help me in this moment felt like a relief. He'd already stuck his neck out for me once, and look where it had gotten him. There was no way I could ask him to get involved in this.

So, in reality, that left me. Yet, I was still sitting here, doing nothing. I needed to wake up. Get moving.

I sighed and went inside to grab a pair of latex gloves from under the sink. I needed to search his pockets. Maybe I'd find a wallet with some form of identification. Goose greeted me at the door, more subdued than usual, almost cautious. He could sense something was up. Maybe he could even smell the body. I knelt and patted him on the head, speaking to him in a soothing voice. He wagged his tail, licked my earlobe, and eased past me into the dark yard. He lifted a leg, pissing and sniffing the wind. When he finished, he lowered his nose to the ground and started toward the body, but I whistled at him sharply. He seemed relieved to come back inside the house with me.

Once I had the gloves on, I walked to the body and shined my penlight at his face, checking again to see if I recognized him. A sense of unreality washed over me, and for a brief second I believed I did recognize him. It was vague but undeniable, the way you might hear a snippet of a song you loved as a child and know it but not quite be able to remember all the words.

The moment passed, and the man's face was unfamiliar again, a stranger. But a sliver of doubt had wormed its way into my subconscious, and I wondered at the likelihood of a stranger meeting his demise way up here in these mountains, just a couple dozen feet from my front door.

4

This is what I found in his pockets:

His car keys, three dollars—most of it in change—a piece of lined paper, folded into a neat square, and a bookmark from a place called Ghost Mountain New and Used Books. I unfolded the paper and laid it out in the grass under the glare of the penlight.

It was a letter, written in a tight cursive script.

Dear Joe,

I have continued to try to reach out to you. Your situation is very much like my own, except you seek rebellion instead of understanding. Rebellion only works when it is righteous. Please reconsider this course of action. As you can see, going to the authorities isn't going to work. The authorities believe in the same tenets we do, tenets as old as time and as unshakable. If you insist on pursuing this present course, I do not know how it will end. Well, that's not completely true. I have an idea how it will probably end. These are powerful forces and not to be trifled with. Though they may, at present, seem evil to you, I assure you that they are on the side of good.

I hope you will come talk to me. We can work this out. God never creates a situation we can't handle. Call me—706-308-9495
Dr. Blevins

I put the paper down on the ground. What was I supposed to make of that? Dr. Blevins? What the hell? And what was the talk of rebellion and going to the authorities? I read the letter again, this time more slowly, letting the words take hold in my mind. There was a lot that wasn't being said

17

here. In fact, I felt pretty confident after the second read that the entire letter was a veiled threat. So, was coming to see me the "course of action"
he'd been asked to reconsider? The letter claimed he'd already tried the
authorities and hadn't received any help. *The authorities believe in the same
tenets we do.* Two things struck me about that line: one, using the word *we*.
It meant that this Dr. Blevins was only a spokesperson for a bigger group.
The second thing that stood out to me was that word *tenets*. He seemed to
suggest a set of rigid religious beliefs.

I didn't think it was a stretch to assume he'd been coming to me for
help and someone had stopped him because they believed I might actually
be able to help him.

I looked at the bookmark again. I'd actually heard of the bookstore.
My friend Susan had recommended I swing by and meet the manager, as
she was supposed to be somewhat of an authority on the Fingers area and
apparently eager to help me solve cases. The Fingers were the five mountains that surrounded the little town of Riley, and they had their own legends, lore, and history. I knew a lot of it from growing up here, but being
away for thirty years had created some gaps in my knowledge.

As a general rule, I tended to stay away from people who wanted to
help me solve my cases. Too many folks considered themselves armchair
detectives these days, and it was far too easy to imagine some old lady who
had read a lot of cozy mysteries and thought she was the next Miss Marple.
But now it looked as if I'd be introducing myself to her after all.

I put the bookmark and the letter into my back pocket and grabbed the
man's keys. Maybe I'd find a phone in his car. Hell, maybe even some identification beyond his first name.

The doors were unlocked. I dipped my head into the vehicle on the driver's side and saw no wallet or phone. Just a McDonald's cup in the center cup
holder. I lifted the cup, shaking it lightly. There was still ice in it, which
meant he must have been by the McDonald's in Riley before coming up the
mountain. I wondered if that was before or after his stop at Ghost Mountain
Books. I opened the center console, continuing to search for a wallet or
phone, but found nothing but some change and fast-food receipts.

That was all. No phone, no wallet. I opened the dashboard and found only
the car manual. I was stumped. Who drove without their wallet or phone?

Nobody, that was who. The answer, I realized, had to be that whoever
had shot the man in the throat had also taken his wallet and phone.

I was about to get out when I heard something buzzing in the driver's seat. A cell phone. He was getting a call. But where was the phone? I looked everywhere—the floorboard, the back seat, the dash—but couldn't find anything. The buzzing stopped.

I got out of the car, slid the driver's seat all the way back, and spotted a slim iPhone. Somehow it had fallen down under the seat. If it hadn't buzzed, I doubt I would have found it. I picked it up and pressed the home button. The lock screen came up, revealing the number of the last call. I pressed the button again, and it asked me for a six-digit code.

Damn.

I let the screen go dark again, and this time when I touched the home screen and the phone number came up, I recognized it as the same number on the letter. So Dr. Blevins was still calling him, right up until the end.

I noticed the phone was about to die. I didn't have an iPhone, so I looked around the car for a charger I could use to keep it going and found nothing. I slipped Joe's phone in my pocket and opened the letter again. I dialed the number on my own phone, making sure to enter *67 before the rest of the number to keep my number anonymous.

It rang four times before a man answered. His voice was cold and suspicious. "Hello."

"Dr. Blevins?" I asked.

"Who's this?"

"Someone who wants to know what happened to Joe."

"I don't know any Joe."

"You called him. And wrote him a—"

The line went dead. No surprise. Him talking to me had been a long shot at best. What now?

I looked at the body again and realized with a sharp chill that what I did in the next few minutes, the decisions I made, might be the difference between spending the rest of my life behind bars and remaining free. If Argent caught even a whiff of this situation, he'd be on the phone to Jeb Walsh in a heartbeat and be here to arrest me just as fast. The thorn in their side would be gone.

The worst part was that there was nobody I could call for help. Not Rufus, Mary, or Ronnie. Certainly not the police.

I was going to have to do it alone.

5

worked quickly, taking down my shower curtain and wrapping the body up before heaving it into the back of my truck. I wore gloves, of course, and was careful not to let any blood get on my clothes or skin. Once Joe (God, knowing his name made it so much harder) was in my truck, I went to my shed and got out my lawn mower. I gassed it up and put on the grass catcher I'd never used. Then I rolled it around to the spot near where his body had been. I turned my headlights on and mowed the entire yard on the lowest setting.

It took me nearly a half hour before I felt like I'd done all the mowing and collecting of gore I was likely to do. Morning would tell the story of how much I'd missed, but for now, I had to call it quits. I pushed the mower into the shed and started around to my truck, carrying the grass catcher. I stuck it in the passenger's side floorboard, shut the door, and turned to consider the man's sedan.

I'd hide it for now. Getting rid of it was important, but not as important as getting rid of the body. I drove it into the woods behind my house, guiding the front end slowly into some pines until the entire vehicle was completely out of sight.

From there, I went to grab Goose, and he jumped into my truck, excitedly, before noticing the bag of grass and blood. He whined and sniffed at it as I started the engine.

Just as I was about to pull away, I heard the sound of a vehicle approaching. That was one of the advantages of living on the top of a mountain. I usually had plenty of time to prepare for visitors. I could hear an engine powering its way up the steeper inclines a mile or more away. And the last half mile to my place was a doozy of twists, turns, and sharp rising hills that could take an inexperienced driver as much as ten minutes to navigate.

But now this knowledge put me in a quandary. If I started down, I'd pass whoever it was, and on the off chance it was a sheriff's deputy, I might be pulled over for questioning. That wasn't something I was prepared to deal with while I was carrying a dead body in the back of my truck. I eased the truck forward, between the two live oaks where I liked to park. I kept going, nudging the front end over some small brush and into the trees until most of the truck was hidden in the woods behind my house, not too far from where I'd parked the sedan.

I killed the engine and the lights and waited, patting Goose's head reassuringly. A long time passed, but I could still hear the sound of the engine revving as it worked its way up the mountain.

I thought of the whiskey I kept under the seat. A nip would go a long way toward easing my nerves. I picked up the bottle, wishing it wasn't here with me because, as any drunk will tell you, having alcohol nearby is a sure way to make sure you drink some. I unscrewed the lid and took a sip, just enough to wet my lips and tongue, just enough to feel the sweet burn.

A light appeared in my rearview. I turned and saw a Coulee County sheriff's Durango cresting the ridge. The bottle went to my lips and I took a real swallow, the kind that wasn't a tease. The warmth spread out across my body, all the way to my fingers and toes, and I felt steadier, more clear-headed than before.

The Durango came to a stop and the lights blinked off. Two doors opened and two men stepped out. One was in a deputy's uniform and the other wore a pair of blue jeans and a leather jacket. Based on his imposing size, the former was a deputy named Hub Graham. The man in the leather jacket was Preston Argent. I could tell just by the arrogant way he walked. Hub tossed a cigarette butt into my yard and they looked around. Not seeing anything of interest, they walked to my front door. I lost sight of them, but I imagined them standing there, knocking, waiting for somebody to answer. Would they notice anything amiss? I didn't think so. The murder had been surprisingly clean, and I felt like I'd hidden the blood well enough, at least in the dark. Besides, Argent had had no real experience in law enforcement before winning sheriff, and as far as I could tell, there were actual police dogs smarter than Hub, whom Argent had clearly recruited for his intimidating size and brute strength.

Still, it was nerve-racking not to be able to see what they were doing. For all I knew they were in the house now. I'd taken care to clean up after myself, but what if I'd left a glove out or something else that would give them pause, make them look a little closer until they noticed my truck parked out underneath the pine trees?

A few minutes later, I let out a long sigh of relief when the men came around the corner. Both of them were smoking now. And laughing. I watched them, sure they were headed for the Durango, but they surprised me. Instead of returning to their truck, they turned and headed toward my shed. I was parked maybe five yards away. One of them was bound to see my truck.

As they approached, I could hear their voices through the open window.

"Jeb don't care for his friend, neither, that blind joker, Rufus something or another." That was Argent. I'd recognize that slow, willfully uneducated drawl anywhere.

"Traffic accident," Hub said. "That's the way to do it."

"There's lots of ways to do it," Argent said. "The secret is doing it clean. Jeb don't like to rush shit. Besides, that's too impersonal for Jeb."

"Impersonal?"

Argent grunted. "Most people don't know, but Jeb's not immune to getting his hands dirty. Especially with the real assholes like this one."

"Well, shit. He needs to get on it, then. I'm just saying. If you want somebody gone, get 'em gone. Don't make an ordeal about it. Where the fuck is he anyway? I mean at this hour?"

"Probably at the African Queen's hut down in Atlanta."

I squeezed the steering wheel so hard, my knuckles turned white.

"Shit, you can't tell me you wouldn't hit that, Sheriff."

"Of course I'd hit it, but that don't mean I'd date it."

"I'd date it," Hub said, "as long as she let me hit it whenever I wanted."

"Open that shed door and shut up," Argent said, shining his flashlight at the shed.

Hub yanked the shed door open much too hard, nearly pulling it off its hinges. Argent shined the light in. "I'd kill to find something illegal in here," he said.

"You could plant something," Hub suggested. "Wouldn't be much to it."

Argent didn't respond but instead waved the flashlight around, looking into the shed.

"You hear me, Sheriff?"

"I heard you. Listen, do you really think you're going to come up with a way to deal with this asshole that Jeb ain't already thought of?"

Hub shrugged. "Just trying to help."

"You wanna help? Just do what you're told, and don't try to be smart. You ain't smart, okay?"

"Whatever."

"Shut it back."

Hub slammed the shed door and said, "You reckon that woman really heard a shot from up here?"

"I doubt it. She was so drunk she wouldn't know a fart from a gunshot. Let's go. He's probably neck deep in dark meat right about now."

They walked to the Durango and pulled out of the yard and onto the gravel road. A few minutes later, their taillights were gone and the sound of their engine had nearly faded away. I wiped sweat off my brow and cranked the truck. I put it in reverse as Goose licked my hand on the gearshift. I patted his head, and he smiled that open-mouthed smile some dogs have. He seemed to intuitively know we'd dodged a bullet.

*   *   *

I drove over to Ghost Creek Mountain, where I'd grown up and where my father's original church had been. I took the long way to the hidden meadow in order to avoid the church, but not because of the bad memories. Well, not *only* because of the bad memories. The main reason was that I wanted to stay as far away from Rufus as possible.

Because of Rufus's blindness, he'd learned to recognize the sounds of vehicles. He was never surprised when I showed up at the old church to pay him a visit. "I recognized the sound of your truck," he'd say. So I didn't want to pass too close to his place at the risk of him wanting to know why I was in the area, especially considering I'd dropped him off just a short time ago. Then I'd either have to tell him about my present clusterfuck or lie, and I'd never been much good at lying to my friends.

I went up the backside of the mountain, following an old logging road overgrown with weeds. Twice I stopped the truck to move fallen branches out of the road, and once I came to a complete stop, not sure I could go any farther because the road was so narrow. On one side of the road was a creek and on the other a sheer drop. Fifty feet of free fall that ended in a field of boulders and green moss.

I ended up putting two tires in the creek and working my gear shift to gain purchase until the road widened. From there, the drive mostly went straight up. I switched to second and then first, then prayed my truck wouldn't flip. Hell, there was a moment or two when I felt like I'd gone nearly perpendicular to the pull of gravity, and I was sure the dead man was going to fly off the back of the truck and down the mountain. But he didn't, and I eventually eased over the last rise and into the hidden meadow where Daddy had once tried to plant tomatoes and okra. There was no sign of any gardening now, just a flat stretch of tall grass waving darkly in the night breeze. The meadow was broken by a half dozen scattered trees. I aimed the nose of my truck toward the largest of these, a massive oak whose branches seemed to overspread the whole field.

Once parked, I took a look around. Dark woods surrounded me on three sides. As far as I knew, nobody came up this way anymore. This land was owned by the power company but protected from exploitation by some government regulations. I had a hard time keeping up. The important thing was it would be a long time before anybody came up here to do any serious digging.

I got right to work, breaking a sweat despite the cool air. My hip started to hurt nearly immediately, but I pushed through the pain, my mind already obsessed with what had happened and what I was going to do about it.

There was always the Wild Turkey option, but as enticing as that sounded, it felt like a betrayal somehow. Not of my values or my own life, but rather of the man I was about to bury. Joe. He'd come to find me. *Me.* God knew why exactly, except he'd already tried with Argent and had obviously been turned away. If I just buried him and returned to my drunken fog, what kind of man would I be? How long would I remain haunted by the questions his presence in my life posed? Did I know him from some dark place in my past? Hell, did I even know myself, for that matter?

The other option was to take his case. It was something I'd done hundreds of times in the past, but I'd rarely taken on a case with this little information. Or for a dead client.

A phone number, a bookmark, and a letter scribbled on a piece of folded paper.

It was a mystery. Who knew where it started or how I was involved? I only knew, for better or worse, that I was a part of it now, that the dead man's mystery and my own had become intertwined.

6

While I was burying the body, unbeknownst to me, Rufus was dealing with his own crisis. He had not slept in three days, and now he sat alone in the sanctuary of the old Holy Flame, his hands clasped together in what might have appeared a prayerful posture to someone who didn't know that Rufus had been an atheist for years. The position of his hands might have been an unconscious nod to his religious past. He certainly wasn't aware they were clasped together under his chin.

He *was* aware of the shaking that wracked his body. He was also aware he was acting like a child, like the same kid who'd been too scared to go into his mother's room after she screamed about the "witch" because he thought he'd see what his mother saw, and then he'd never be able to stop seeing it.

He hadn't been completely wrong about that. When he was a child, his mother had explained her nightly terrors with mountain folklore as colorful as it was ignorant. According to her, she was simply getting "rode by the witch."

"Once she finds you, she don't never let you go," his mother used to tell him on those rare occasions her breathing was slow enough to allow her to talk.

Each time he heard her scream out during the night, he came to her (after an elaborate ritual to "psych himself up," which included saying the Lord's prayer and turning on her light the second he flung the door open) and sat at her bedside, a towel in his hand, ready to wipe more sweat from her brow. Usually she wouldn't talk. Usually she was breathing too hard, gasping and crying, squeezing his hands until they hurt. But sometimes she lay awake and told him what she'd seen, how it happened.

"She starts at the foot of the bed," his mother would tell him. "She's a little twisted thing. Her back's all . . . it's all buckled up like maybe it stunted her growth some. She's got missing teeth, and her voice is always a whisper, but I can hear it loud like she's right in my ear. It don't take long for her to start creeping."

"Creeping?" he'd said.

"That's right. Creeping up to my chest. She gets there and just sits and talks to me. I can't move. No matter what. I just have to listen to her. And feel her. I can't close my eyes. That's the worst of it. I can't even look away. And one of these days, I know she's going to kill me. She promised me she would."

"I'm sorry, Mama."

"Pshaw. That ain't the worst."

Rufus remembered thinking *how could it be worse?*

"The worst is when she told me who she was."

"The witch?"

"Yeah, the witch. She said she was Madeline."

"Who?"

"Your aunt Madeline. She died when she was eight or so. I was supposed to be watching her out at Backslide Gap, and I got distracted, got to daydreaming about some boy, not your father, and when I checked to see where she was, she was standing over on the side of the gap, near the swinging bridge. I screamed at her, but that just made her laugh. She wasn't never right in the head and sometimes took to laughing the minute other folks took to being serious. I got mad at her because I was fifteen and, Lord, I thought I was the queen of the holler and I didn't need nor want to be looking after some little brat who didn't even have the sense to know when her sister was getting on to her. Oh, Lord forgive me."

Rufus wiped her brow with the towel and kissed her forehead. He'd always been the good son. At least until he couldn't do it anymore. Maybe that was why he'd found the witch too. Maybe it was punishment. Hell, it was definitely punishment.

"I told her she was a stupid little kid and that made her laugh even harder. So hard, I guess she lost her balance. She fell all the way to the bottom. Took your grandfather half the day and night to get down there to her body. He said she hit a rock at the bottom, twisted her up real bad."

"It's just a bad dream," Rufus remembered telling her.

She sat up and grabbed his chin with one hand. "No. Never say that. Dreams end. This never ends. It comes back over and over again. And I swear I'm wide awake. She's here in the room with me when it happens."

That was the first time his mother had ever told him about "getting rode by the witch," but it wasn't the first time he'd come to comfort her in the middle of the night. He did what he always did. He waited for her to make room for him and he crawled into the bed next to her.

He wished someone were here to do the same for him now. But it was just him, though the tingling on his scalp made it clear he wouldn't be alone for long.

* * *

The tingling had returned a few days ago. He'd been without it for at least twenty years now. Since being blind, he hadn't had a single visit from his "witch." But before he'd lost his sight, the tingling was always the sign. She was coming again.

Even though he knew by now that the real, scientific name for what his mother had dealt with was sleep paralysis, it was no comfort to Rufus. Maybe it had been once, right up until he'd experienced it himself. Then he realized his mother's term had been better, and all the scientific knowledge in the world couldn't alleviate the terror that came with being rode by the witch.

Like his mother's witch, Rufus's was also female, but unlike his mother's, she didn't show her face. Rufus thought of her simply as the shadow girl, because she had no features and in many ways appeared to be no more substantial than a shadow.

Each visit began the same way. Rufus would see the door to the barn where he'd once lived blown open by the wind (at the time, he'd occupied a barn belonging to a local farmer on the east side of the county), and the shadow girl would slip inside. At first, she only stood at the door, seemingly watching Rufus. Rufus couldn't close his eyes while she was there, and he couldn't move. Sometimes he felt like he couldn't breathe, but then all at once his breath would return. The shadow girl never moved beyond the edge of his doorway, but that didn't make it any less frightening. Hell, in some ways, Rufus wanted her to move. He wanted to get a better look at the shadow, to see her face.

This all began during a particularly turbulent time in Rufus's life. He'd just left the church in rather dramatic fashion and shortly thereafter found himself working for a man he simultaneously admired and loathed. He was trying to figure out who he wanted to be and what he believed.

The shadow girl didn't help.

But he kept it under control in the early days. She came often, but she always kept her distance. The episodes were harrowing but didn't threaten his sanity. At least not at first.

The shadow girl drew ever closer, but she never revealed her face. It hardly mattered. Rufus soon figured out who his "witch" was. Her name was Harriet Duncan, "Harry," as she had been known at the school. Ironically, she'd killed herself in much the same way his aunt had died. The difference was that Harriet had meant to do it. She'd jumped from the top of Two Indian Falls on purpose. Her body had been swept away by the river and never found, but she was dead. Rufus had watched her make the leap. And he'd done nothing to stop it.

What he'd done after she was gone had been even worse.

7

I ended up taking the car down to the cornfield known as the Devil's Valley. It was the perfect place to hide something you didn't want found because of the high stalks of corn that grew as far as the eye could see. I drove around the outskirts of the huge cornfield before finding a small opening in the corn large enough to drive the car between. When the gap narrowed, I kept on driving, plowing over corn, digging deeper and deeper, until I decided it was far enough. I parked the car and got out. The dark morning was already too hot, the air charged somehow with something more than just the threat of the impending sunrise. There was a heaviness in it that made me feel the weight of the past on the present as a tangible thing. I wiped sweat from my brow and looked around. Just eight months ago, I'd been chased by an entity known as Old Nathaniel through these same rows. I'd been sure at the time that he was just a regular man wearing an old burlap sack, but had discovered the truth wasn't so simple.

He'd actually killed me with his own bare hands a few miles from here on the banks of the Blackclaw River. I'd been dead somewhere between seven and ten minutes, depending on who you talked to. According to Mary, who had waited by my side, trying to revive me, it was ten, maybe more, but if you asked medical experts, they'd tell you it couldn't have been more than seven. More than seven wasn't possible. Fifty-three years on this earth had taught me that a lot of things that "weren't possible" seemed to happen anyway. I'd seen men manipulate whole communities with nothing but raw conviction and a pretty voice. I'd seen lightning pulled from the sky because of the depravity of belief, and I'd watched my father defy death—at least for a little while.

This cornfield had a way of hiding the truth, like it had hidden Old Nathaniel, and the place out in the center where the skulls of his victims were. Maybe it would do the same for this car. At least until I figured out more about the dead man named Joe, and why he'd been in my front yard.

It took me a full twenty minutes to get back out to the road. Once there, I turned south and started home toward the Fingers, looming in the distance. About an hour later, I thumbed a ride from two nearly mute middle-aged men who made me think of the Hill Brothers, except these men seemed more benign, less desperate.

The men said they were cousins from South Carolina, but other than that offered little explanation for why they were in the middle of rural North Georgia. I didn't blame them. There were some things that just didn't bear explaining.

*   *   *

Finally free of the man and his car, I decided to call Mary.

"Better, actually," she said when I asked about her nephew, Andrew.

"That's great!" I had to resist the urge to ask her if that meant she would be coming home soon.

"Yeah, he's far from out of the woods, but the last round of tests showed the disease isn't as far along as the doctors had thought."

"What does that mean?" I asked.

She was silent.

"Mary?"

"Sorry. It's just . . . well, it's good news, but it's the kind of good news that only puts the bad news off. Forget it. Can we talk about something else?"

"Sure. I'm sorry."

"Something else, okay?"

"Okay. I miss you."

"I miss you too. Oh! I just remembered. My brother is supposed to be getting a week off from work soon. When he does, I'm coming back to stay with you. For the whole week."

"What about your work?"

"They won't know unless I tell them, and I'm not going to tell them."

"When?"

"That's the thing. I don't know. It could be next week or a month from now."

"Let me know as soon as you find out."

"Nah."

"What?"

"I thought I might just show up. Surprise you."

"Oh, please don't do that."

"It will be great. Can you imagine how you'll feel when you see me standing at your door?"

"I guess," I said. This was one of the few things I didn't like about Mary. She loved to build a moment up, to make it better than it would be otherwise. One of the ways she did this was with the element of surprise, something that didn't bother me except when it came to my relationships. I hated not knowing what to expect.

"How are *you*?" she said.

Her voice was filled with something unmistakable. Not pity. Mary was far too empathic for that. But maybe concern. I understood she was worried about my generally fragile mental state without her. And probably curious as to how I was taking losing the sheriff's election.

"All good here," I lied.

"Yeah, right."

"Why do you doubt me? I'm fine. Got a new case," I said, and immediately wished I could take it back.

"Oh, tell me about it. I'd love to help, if I can."

I winced, trying to decide what to say. "It's pretty boring."

"Well, I'm pretty bored. Tell me."

"I'm looking for a guy. A man. He came up to the Fingers and vanished."

"What? That doesn't sound boring at all! What's his name?"

Shit. "Hey, I got to go. Let me call you back later, okay? There's someone at the door. I think it's about the case."

"Oh, go. Take care of that. I'm glad you have something to keep you busy. Be safe, and remember I love you."

"I love you too."

I ended the call and pushed myself back in the recliner and closed my eyes.

When I woke, it was afternoon and Goose was barking at something in the yard.

I went to the kitchen window and saw the Hill Brothers, shimmering ghosts in the midday heat. They were on their way down the mountain and had taken a shortcut through my yard, as they often did. I found myself wondering if they were twins. They both had dark complexions and long, fragile faces. Their eyes didn't move; they *flitted*, never lingering on anything long. They ignored Goose as he barked at them and trudged on through the shade of the oaks, out into the open sun. They were dressed in dark T-shirts and ripped blue jeans split open at the ankles to fit around their oversized boots. One brother's hair was longer than the other's, and he was thinner too, lending him the appearance of a strung-out rock star. The other one looked more like a character from a Flannery O'Connor short story. He had short hair, cut as if he'd worn a bowl for a crown and gone to work with the scissors himself. He was the taller of the two and walked with an easy athleticism, chewing a blade of grass as he moved past the house and toward the dirt road connecting me with the rest of the world.

Before thinking it through, I went to the front door. I opened it up, whistled at Goose to stop barking, and then called out to them.

"Could I ask you boys something?"

The long-haired one turned to look at me, his eyes sliding over my face as if he already knew what I was going to say and had no patience for it. The other brother didn't even acknowledge me.

I jogged over to them, trying to catch up with their long, relentless strides.

"Did you boys hear any shooting up this way last night?"

This time the short-haired one with the piece of grass looked at me. His expression was wilder, more feral, like a dog kept in a cage for too long that can't wait to get out to bite someone, anyone.

"No," he said, his voice soft but ragged with something that might have been scorn.

I stopped, a little stunned by the animosity I felt from him. I'd heard stories that they'd both been born addicted to drugs, that they'd never known either of their parents and had grown up more like animals than people. I should have known better than to try to engage them.

They disappeared onto the dirt road and over the rise. I watched the dust gather in the wake of their passage, and I wondered at how many mysteries these mountains could hold.

And if any of them could ever truly be unlocked.

8

Susan Monroe was the library director and my go-to for information about the area. She was also one of the nicest people I'd ever met. In her midfifties, she'd been single since her husband died a decade before and had never remarried because, in her words, "the men in this area couldn't hold a candle to David." I didn't know David, but I figured he would have had to be a good man to deserve Susan.

"Let me guess," she said, grinning at me as I approached her near the front counter where she stood behind a stack of hardback books. "You've got a case."

"How did you know?" I reached over the counter and gave her a side hug. She squeezed me back tightly.

"Well, I could say it's the only time you ever come to visit me, but I'm too nice for that. So, I'll just say you've got the look."

"The look?"

She moved her hand across her face, waggling her fingers. "It's in the eyes, and maybe the cheekbones. You look perplexed."

I laughed. "That's one way to put it."

"So I was right?"

"You were right."

"Well, let's go to my office."

I followed her through the stacks toward her office, where just last fall I'd sat with Rufus and Ronnie's niece and nephew, trying to figure out how we were going to bring down Jeb Walsh. That still hadn't happened. In fact, he had a better foothold in the area than ever now that Argent was sheriff. Suddenly, I felt more down than I had in a while. We'd accomplished nothing. *I'd* accomplished nothing. Not only that, Mary was on the other side of the country *and* now I had a dead man to deal with.

Susan sat down at her desk and motioned for me to do the same. "You look down."

"Is it that obvious?"

"You don't hide your emotions well, Earl. You never have."

I shrugged. I didn't like this line of conversation. The truth was, as much as I liked Susan—or maybe *because* of how much I liked Susan—she always made me a little nervous. She was an attractive woman, and I'd be lying if I said I hadn't noticed some spark between us. Or maybe that was just my ego talking. It had a helluva mouth sometimes.

"It's Mary, right?" She didn't wait for me to answer. "You must miss her terribly."

"I'm okay."

She gave me a searching look as if trying to read what was behind my eyes. "Long-distance relationships are always hard. Are you sure you're doing all right?"

"I'm sure. We talked this morning. She's coming for a visit soon."

"Oh, that's good news, Earl. I'm so excited for you."

"I'm pretty excited myself."

"So, how can I help you?"

I told her I'd found a phone while hiking and was trying to get it back to its owner.

She wrinkled her nose at me. "That doesn't sound too interesting."

"Sorry. My life is pretty boring right now."

"Give it time," she said. "Danger always finds Earl Marcus."

"Yeah, can't wait." I said it sarcastically, but there was more than a grain of truth in her words. If danger didn't find me, I usually found it. It wasn't so much for the thrill of it as it was the pure adversity. I'd never been very good at the mundane tasks of day-to-day living.

She laughed and asked to see the phone.

"Oh, I didn't bring it. It's at the house. See, I'm trying to find out a little bit about the person who last called the phone."

She looked confused. "Why?"

"Well . . ." I said, not sure how best to handle this.

"Never mind. I'm prying."

I smiled at her. "I wasn't going to say anything."

"I'm sorry. Listen, if I ever start being nosy, just tell me, Earl. Sometimes . . ." She trailed off, her eyes going distant. "Sometimes I forget myself and treat you like I treated David." She reached over the desk and touched my shoulder. "I'm not trying to be weird."

"It's okay." The thing was, I believed her. She wasn't flirting. If she knew it sometimes seemed like flirting to me, I was pretty sure she would have been mortified.

"I'm assuming you tried calling the number?" she said.

"Yes. I even know his name. Dr. Blevins. I'm trying to find out the scoop on him. Who he is, where he works, that sort of thing." I winced and shook my head. "I suppose I might as well tell you this is a *tad* bit more complicated than just finding the phone."

"I picked up on that. And say no more. I've got a meeting in thirty minutes, but after that I'll see what I can come up with. You going to stick around?" She looked hopeful, but I had to disappoint her.

"No, just give me a call when and if you find out anything."

"Will do. And Earl?"

I was already making my way out of her office.

"Yeah?"

"I hope things work out with you and Mary. You two are so good together."

I didn't know exactly how to respond to that, so I just smiled and walked out.

* * *

She called me later that evening. I'd spent the afternoon scouring the front yard for any evidence of the shooting. I found nothing except some more blood in the grass, which I took care of by mowing again, mulching the grass over and over until all traces of the blood were invisible to the naked eye. I was sitting near the ridge where Mary and I had set up some chairs to enjoy sunsets together. It was still hot, and the day didn't want to let go. Dusk got tangled up in the sunset, and it was probably the most gorgeous thing I'd seen in a long time.

When she called, I was drinking a beer and trying not to think of the dead man's face. There was something in his countenance I found disturbing, something all too familiar. As long as I could think of him in the abstract, as a mystery and not a man, I was okay, but when I remembered his face, I felt a kind of aching loneliness I couldn't shake.

He was dead and buried, and nobody but me and the killer knew it. Whoever he'd left behind didn't know where he was or if he was ever coming back. Didn't they deserve more than that?

"Thanks for getting back to me," I said to Susan.

"No problem. I didn't find a ton. This guy has absolutely no social media footprint, but he's made the papers a few times, so that helped."

"The papers? For something bad or good?"

"Both, actually. In 1984, he was named the Coulee County teacher of the year."

"Teacher?"

"Science, apparently."

"Okay, what's the bad news."

"He was fired in 1988 after allegations of sexual harassment came to light."

"Against students?"

"The article isn't clear. It just says sexual harassment during . . . let me see . . . the 1986–87 school year. The principal at the time went to bat for him, but it says a suit was filed and he was ultimately let go from his job."

"Interesting. Were you able to access the court filing?"

"Tried, but this is Coulee County, you know? I don't need to tell you that when Hank Shaw was the sheriff, paperwork was not a priority. Apparently the county courts followed his lead. They said there was a room with some boxes that I was welcomed to peruse . . ."

"That's all right. You've done plenty. I'll look into it at some point if necessary."

"I don't mind. I mean, for all we know he's innocent. Or, even if he's guilty, there are all kinds of levels of that sort of thing, not that they aren't all gross, but I think the key is to know whether he was harassing a student or an adult."

"Yeah, that makes a pretty big difference, but I'd hate to ask you to do that. Where did you say he taught?"

"Coulee County High."

"Okay, I wonder if anybody around there would still remember him."

"Maybe, but I have more."

"You do?"

"Yep. Apparently, he used the time off to get his doctorate in abnormal psychology, which he then parlayed into another job here in Coulee County."

"Yeah? Where?"

"The Harden School."

"Never heard of it."

"Well, you haven't been paying attention. It's been around for a while. It's a reform school on the eastern side of the county, not far from Brethren. Apparently, now he's the behavioral therapist and science teacher there."

"Interesting. Do you have an address?"

"Yeah, but Earl, you should know this school has come under some fire in the last few years."

"What kind of fire?"

"It's vague, and I get the feeling there's been an effort to cover it up. I can only find a few articles that mention it, but there's been some lawsuits filed by parents against the administration's discipline methods."

"That sounds about right. Do they have a website or something?"

"You're still limited to your phone, right?"

"Like that's a bad thing," I said.

"Well, computers do have larger screens."

"Yeah, but if I had one of those, I'd feel obligated to turn it on occasionally."

She laughed. "Facebook is not coming for Earl Marcus anytime soon."

"God, I hope not."

"I'm going to text you the website address. You can find the physical address on the website. Are you going to pay them a visit?"

"Probably."

"Well, be careful. I've heard rumors about Randy Harden, the school's founder, for years."

"What kind of rumors?"

"Well, women talk to each other, you know. Especially about men like Harden. He's a predator, Earl. Definitely not the kind of man who needs to be working with kids."

"Got it," I said. "Thanks, Susan."

"You're welcome."

"You're the best."

I ended the call. Goose nuzzled his snout against my knee as I clicked on the link Susan had sent over.

It was a pretty sparse affair. The home page showed a photo of the school, which looked more like an antebellum plantation home. The headline read *The Harden School: Excellence in Alternative Education Since 1984*. I clicked the *About* link and was taken to a separate page with a short blurb.

The Harden School is a boys only school created specifically for young men who lose their way and require discipline and therapy in order to rediscover themselves. Our curriculum is based on traditional Christian values, and our educators and administration believe strongly that these values form the bedrock of a young man's life. We also affirm the Biblical admonishment of "spare the rod, spoil the child," while still embracing cutting edge therapeutic techniques designed to unlock the true "male" instead of the watered down version too often popularized in our modern, increasingly pagan culture. To discuss your boy's unique circumstances, call for an appointment.

A phone number was listed below along with the address.

I decided to make an appointment. What did I have to lose?

9

There are some people you meet who you connect with immediately. Claire of Ghost Mountain New and Used Books was one of those people for me. She was my age, or maybe a few years younger, and had the kind of engaging personality that could light up a room. Her eyes were somewhere between blue and the color of cold steel. There was an air of subdued intelligence about her, a sense she knew more than she was letting on, and that was one of the things I liked best about her from the beginning. Maybe I'd spent too much time with men like my father and men like Ronnie, who threw it all on the table as soon as you met them, leaving it up to you to sort through what was worthwhile and what wasn't. At least in Ronnie's case, I'd found there was a lot that was worthwhile. My father, unfortunately, had been made of bluster and unchecked ambition, and there was nothing about his life or legacy that didn't make me feel ashamed.

"Earl Marcus," Claire said, with just the slightest emphasis on my last name. She said this even before I introduced myself.

"That's right," I said, hesitating as I tried to decide how to best explain that I was nothing like my father.

I never got the chance. "I've read about you in the papers." She beamed at me. "In fact, I even voted for you. Too bad you didn't win. The one we got is an asshole." She covered her mouth. "Oops. Sorry. I forget myself sometimes."

"No worries. I appreciate the vote and agree with you one hundred percent."

She continued to beam at me. "To what do I owe the pleasure of this visit? Did you come to buy books, to browse, or to talk?" She leaned in conspiratorially. "Between you and me, I'd love to just talk. Gets a little lonely in here sometimes."

I smiled and looked around, taking in the store. The bookshop was a renovated old home just down the street from the library. The entire first floor was the bookstore, and I appreciated that the owner hadn't knocked down any of the walls to create a larger space but instead had just made each room a kind of surprise. We were standing in what I believed had once been the dining room. There were three tables and several bookshelves, all loaded down with used books. *Mystery/Crime and Thriller Room*, the sign on the wall read. How appropriate.

I picked up a James Lee Burke novel I hadn't read. "I'll buy this, but I would like to talk too."

"Best of both worlds. Come with me to the kitchen and I'll ring you up. Then we can have coffee."

I followed her down a hall flanked on either side by smaller rooms, each one overflowing with books of every sort. There was one room that focused on transportation and seemed to contain both nonfiction and some fiction. We passed an "occult" room with stacks of books about magic and weird studies. There was a small table dedicated to H. P. Lovecraft and some other authors I'd never heard of who obviously wrote in that same vein. Two other rooms went by in a blur before we reached the kitchen.

This was the only room without books. Well, that wasn't exactly accurate. There was a shelf of books behind the kitchen table, but on the wall above the shelf was a sign that said *Not for Sale*. Claire sat down at the table by an iPad and an old cash register.

"Cash or credit?" she said.

I gave her a ten and told her to keep the change.

"How long have you been working here?"

"About a year, but I don't want to talk about me. I want to talk about you. And hopefully something juicy you're working on."

The bell in the front room rang as she spoke, and she shook her head as if to tell me not to worry, she wouldn't let a customer interrupt what I had to say.

"Well," I said, "I did want to check in with you about something I found recently."

"Oh, goody," she said. "I've always wanted to help solve a mystery."

"Well, it's not too exciting." I held out the bookmark. "I assume you give these out to customers?" As soon as I asked the question, I realized she hadn't given me a bookmark.

"No. Well, I did at one point, but I ran out."

"When did you run out?"

"A couple of days ago. The owners are supposed to print some more soon, but with a different design." She made a face. "This one makes me want to vomit. Where'd you find it? Was there a criminal in the bookstore?"

"I'm not sure about that, but I am looking for the man it belonged to."

She moved a strand of blonde-gray hair from her eyes and tucked it behind her ear. "I can look at the credit card receipts and give you a list of names."

"That would be amazing. Would you mind?"

"Not at all. I'll have to figure out how to do it, of course. And it's not going to work if he paid cash."

"Sure. I don't mind waiting."

"Oh, I can't do it now. I'll have to talk to the Robinsons. They're the owners. They handle the technical stuff. I'm just a glorified clerk." She laughed.

"Can you run checks too?" I asked.

"We don't take personal checks."

"Not a bad policy around these parts."

"Hey," she said. "I have an idea. Why don't we make a dinner date to discuss it further?"

She fixed me with a penetrating gaze that made me look away. I realized suddenly that I found her attractive.

"I'm actually, uh, spoken for," I said.

"Ugh, please forgive me," she said. "I'm not usually like this. I feel like a jerk."

"No problem. You had no way of knowing . . ." I felt myself blushing a little and wasn't sure why.

"Well," she said. "This is awkward." A floorboard creaked out in the front of the store, and I remembered we weren't alone. "I'll get that information to you soon, Mr. Marcus. Can you just leave me your number?"

I lowered my voice a little, keenly aware someone else was in the store. "Call me Earl. And sure, you got a pen?"

She reached for a pen, and I scribbled my name and number down on a yellow legal pad.

"Would you mind telling me a little bit about the case you're working on? I'd love to help."

A floorboard creaked again out front, and I smiled at her. "Do you need to check on that customer?"

She cupped her hands to her mouth and hollered hoarsely. "You need any help?"

No one answered.

"Gone," she said.

"But . . ."

She waved her hand, dismissing my concern. I wasn't ready to let it drop. "How many ways out are there?"

"Just one, but you never answered my question."

I had to admire her persistence.

"You mean about the case?"

"That's right."

"Well, let's just say it's a case of secret identity. I'm trying to find out who a man is."

"The man with my bookmark?"

"That's right."

"Is he dangerous?" I swear I thought I saw excitement in her eyes.

"No," I said. "Hate to disappoint."

She frowned. "I suppose that's good."

"Yeah. It's good. I do have one more question for you, if you don't mind?"

"Please."

"Do you know much about the Harden School?"

"I've heard of it. Reform school, right? On the eastern edge of the county. It seems like there was a tragedy there in the eighties, or maybe it was the early nineties."

"Tragedy?"

She smiled. "I remember bits and pieces of things. I'll have to look it up."

"If you find anything, can you please let me know?"

"Of course. I'll be in touch."

I stood up and reached across the table to shake her hand. She smiled at me as we shook, and I felt a little better, the awkwardness gone.

43

"I hope you succeed," she said.

"Thank you," I said, and headed out of the kitchen, down the hallway. I glanced in the rooms off the hallway as I passed each but didn't see anyone there. Once I reached the front room, I looked around but didn't see anyone there either. Perhaps the customer I'd heard come in had left. But I had a way to test that theory easily enough. I walked to the exit and pushed the door open. The bell rang loudly.

10

I tried three of the rooms before I understood what had happened. Or at least before I felt comfortable considering my theory of what had happened.

In the fourth room, which consisted of local history, true crime, and westerns, I found a window partially ajar. I raised it and leaned out, noting that the shrubs just below the windowsill had been mangled. I squinted past the shrubs, looking for a footprint in the small patch of soil, but didn't see anything. Probably because whoever had climbed out had made the short leap to the concrete after getting tangled briefly in the shrubs.

Closing the window, I rushed to the front of the store and peered out one of the windows. My truck was the only vehicle in the lot. Shit.

So, what did it mean? I wasn't sure, but my best guess was I'd been followed here. Whoever it was had decided to also follow me inside the bookstore. While eavesdropping on our conversation, he or she had hidden out in the true crime/western room before escaping out the window in time to avoid being seen.

All of that seemed reasonable enough. The problem I couldn't get my head around was why. Why would someone would be following me? I'd told no one about the body I'd found. Unless, of course, the killer himself was following me, trying to make sure I didn't trace things to him.

I felt a chill. What exactly was going on here? It was like being on the outside of a large house filled with secret doors and rooms. Until I could get inside, I was essentially in the dark, missing too much information. That was what was happening, I realized. Somebody wanted to make sure I didn't find a key to get inside the house.

There were a lot of questions, and I didn't have any suitable answers. I headed for the western/true crime room to look around again.

"I'm still here," I called out to Claire.

"Oh, that's fine. Take your time."

The room consisted of two tables, where books lay faceup, and three bookshelves. I glanced at the bookshelves first to see if there were any gaps and didn't find any. The tables likewise appeared undisturbed. Something caught my eye on the floor beneath the table. I knelt for a closer look and saw a small black piece of plastic. I picked it up and turned it over. On the other side, I saw a tiny flexible aberration on one end of the plastic. It looked like the battery door for a small electronic device.

Could someone have been taping my conversation with Claire? It seemed highly unlikely, but the piece of plastic seemed almost certainly to have come off the back of a mini recorder. It wasn't difficult to imagine the intruder deciding to split quickly and knocking the device against the window frame as he or she climbed out.

"See anything good?" Claire said.

I jumped, shocked by her voice, the nearly soundless way she'd approached.

I turned and smiled, trying to play it off. "You lose this?" I held up the plastic.

She eyed it suspiciously. "No. Where'd you find it?"

"Underneath this open window."

"Open?" She stepped closer for a better look. "Why, I didn't leave it open."

"I think we had an eavesdropper on our conversation." I nodded at the plastic battery door. "And maybe whoever was here wasn't just listening. Maybe they were taping us too."

She scratched the side of her face, perplexed. Her eyes did something curious then. They seemed to go nearly blank, or at least clouded over, losing their focus. I felt as if she were riffling through all the knowledge she'd tucked away over the years in order to fit these possible events into some kind of decipherable framework. "Weird," she said at last, as her eyes came back into focus. "Just very, very weird."

* * *

I thought it was weird too. More than weird. I couldn't help but go back to my brief conversation with Blevins. Had he taken it upon himself to investigate me? How could he, since I'd blocked my number? But maybe there was something I'd missed? He clearly had some connection with Joe's murder. Maybe he'd sent someone to follow me to make sure I didn't connect the dots.

On the way up the mountain to my house, I watched the rearview mirror nearly as much as I watched the road in front of me. Sure enough, I saw a pair of headlights once or twice when the long, winding mountain road straightened out behind me like a bullwhip before curling back into its sinister coil.

When I reached my house near the top of the mountain, I saw Goose trotting over to the truck, beating the wind with his big, bushy tail. I'd saved him from a rattlesnake not too far from the spot where he stood now. That had been over three years ago, and he'd already managed to return the favor, not just by saving me, but also through his boundless enthusiasm for my presence. I parked under one of the large oaks that stood like sentries on one side of the small house and got out, immediately kneeling to let Goose lick my face. I patted his head and neck and rubbed his belly until he flopped onto the ground with a contented sigh. Then I rubbed him some more, just the way he liked, until his back leg twitched uncontrollably and this upper lip stretched out, revealing his dark gums.

"Keep an eye out," I said. "Something ain't right in the world." I patted his belly once more for good measure and headed into the kitchen to open a new bottle of whiskey.

11

Rufus came by that evening, wanting to hang out again. He seemed a little out of sorts and tired. His usual gaunt face was positively hollowed out. Once again, he wouldn't say what was bothering him, and when I pressed him on it, he changed the subject to his favorite whipping boy, Ronnie Thrash.

"He's back," Rufus said.

"You're kidding?"

"Nope. Asshole showed up today. That piece of shit he calls a truck nearly blew out the doors of my place, and I knew he was back."

"Well, shit. He didn't even call me."

"He's probably still mad at you," Rufus said.

"Nah, I visited him a few times and we worked it out. Ronnie can't stay mad at me."

"Eight months?" he said, shaking his head. "For running a man down in that truck? A man lost his life because of that asshole. Don't seem much like justice to me."

We were sitting in the two wooden chairs near the ridge. From here, I could see nearly the whole southern valley—the lights of Riley, the endless trees on the ridges below, the peaks of the nearby mountains, the way the stars circled them like halos adorned with space dust—and beyond that I could see vast fields fading into a horizon still bleeding purple from the resonance of a recently vanished sun.

"The man he hit was a violent white supremacist. He was participating in the kidnapping and torture of a police officer. Ronnie was there purely to help put a stop to that. He didn't intend to kill anyone. If you ask me, the punishment was too harsh."

"Nobody asked you," Rufus scoffed.

I chuckled. "Jesus, what's wrong with you?"

"Just pass that bottle."

"Anything you want to talk about?"

"Nope. I'll be okay. Just pissed off that out of all the places in these mountains, that piece of steaming shit decided to live twenty fucking yards from me."

I wasn't stupid. I understood Rufus didn't like Ronnie, but I also understood Ronnie was just a punching bag right now. Something else was definitely on his mind.

"Did you get any sleep last night?" I asked him. Based on the bags under his eyes, I thought the answer was probably no.

He didn't bother answering. Instead, he tilted the bottle back and took a large swallow. "I'm going to sleep tonight."

*   *   *

We both did. Right there in our chairs, overlooking the ridge, we fell asleep. It took me a while because Joe and his connection to Dr. Blevins and the Harden School were weighing heavy on my mind. I'd considered mentioning it to Rufus several times, but then stopped short. Not only did he seem to have enough on his mind at the moment, but I also felt hesitant to bring up the issue with Rufus because he'd proven so unfailingly sharp at seeing through me in the past. Opening that door would almost certainly allow him to figure out the secret I was hiding about Joe. And the last thing I wanted was Rufus knowing what I'd done. Knowledge was implication, and I meant to make sure no one else but me had a chance of being implicated.

When I did finally fall asleep, rest was short-lived. Something woke me up in the early dark of the morning. Sounds from the ridge below. A car engine, country music floating through the night, the sound of a door creaking open.

I opened my eyes, found the dark sky, gone cloudy now, the moon in silhouette, its pale fire surreal and dreamlike.

A voice on the ridge below almost got me out of my chair. It was female, something low and sexy in the tone. She was murmuring, the way Mary murmured sometimes just before sex. God, how long had it been? Weeks, going on a month. Too long even for my old ass.

But I still didn't get up. I closed my eyes again, fading into blackness like the moon, like all of those stars that had seemed to vanish from earlier. The woman's voice from the ridge below walked into my dreams, and now it was Mary's voice. She'd come to the house like she'd promised. A total surprise. Except she'd only been home a short time before we were thrown into turmoil. The dream didn't make anything clear except the emotions. A bitter despair settled over me.

Then I woke, the sun shining in my eyes. I sat up. Rufus was gone. How long gone, I wasn't sure. Maybe he'd walked home in the darkness the night before, or maybe he'd waited until morning. Either way was the same to him.

I walked over to the ridge for a piss. I'd already started when I remembered the voice from last night. I looked down and saw that the vacant trailer that had been there since I'd moved in now appeared to be occupied. A Toyota Corolla was parked out in the grass in front of the trailer. Inside, I saw someone move past the open door. I turned around so that I was peeing on the ground in my yard instead of out over the ridge. When I finished, I zipped up quickly and turned back to see if anyone had been watching me.

As soon as I did, a woman stepped out of the trailer. She walked over and stood beside the driver's side of the car, pausing to light a cigarette. She smoked it for a moment, just standing there, her hair an electric gold in the morning light. Despite the distance, despite the odd angle from above, I was struck by her. There was an energy about her, a kind of attitude that drew me. I felt a sudden attraction but tried to repress it. It was just going a month without sex that caused it, I told myself.

Then something happened, something I hadn't been expecting. She looked up. I felt like I'd been caught and started to back away from the ridge before realizing how foolish that would be. Instead, I stayed put and lifted a hand awkwardly.

"Hello," I said.

She blew out some more smoke, her face upturned, her features nearly invisible, lost to the harsh light of morning.

"I can barely see you," she said, squinting up at me.

"I'm up here. On the ridge. We're neighbors."

"That right?"

"Yes. My name is Earl. Earl Marcus."

"Hey, you were running for sheriff," she said.

"That's right, but I didn't win."

"Good for me," she said.

I waited, expecting more, some explanation of the cryptic comment, but she said nothing else.

"Well," I said. "If you need anything . . ."

"I'll holler," she said, and opened the car door and climbed inside. I watched her pull away from the trailer and onto the rutted dirt road. It wasn't until her taillights had disappeared that I realized she'd never told me her name.

12

The next morning, before heading over to my appointment at the Harden School, I decided to give Ronnie a call to see if he wanted to join me. At least that was my plan. I didn't actually get to ask him the question. Ronnie was—to put it mildly—excited about hearing from me. And he couldn't wait to fill me in on how prison had changed him.

"Got a vision inside the joint, Earl. Well, I got lots of visions, actually, but they all told me the same thing. You know what they told me?"

"What?"

"You gotta guess."

"Okay, let me see. Maybe they told you it was time to get your life together?"

"Close, so fucking close, Earl. No, they all told—well, actually they all *showed*—me the same thing. They showed me it was time to get the band back together."

"The band?"

"Yeah, you know I play guitar."

"Actually . . ."

"Sure, you knew that. Anyway, I'm building a fucking studio, and I've already gotten in touch with my old drummer and bass man. We're going to cut an album. DIY, baby. Fuck the labels. Hell, you want to get the production credit, Earl? I'll give it to you. Imagine that, 'produced by Earl Marcus.' I like it. We got three songs I wrote in jail, and Hunter's got two of his own, and—"

"Ronnie?"

"Yeah, Earl?"

"I'm on my way over, okay?"

"Sweet. I'll throw on some steaks for you and the boys."

"The boys?"

"You ain't been listening, have you?"

"I'll see you in a few."

"Hell yeah," Ronnie said. "Ain't nothing like being a free man again."

* * *

The truth was, as soon as Ronnie had said he was going to get the band back together to build a recording studio, I had sort of tuned out. It wasn't as if I hadn't heard this kind of shit from Ronnie before. Not too long ago, he'd been running a "siding" company. I'd never seen any indication he knew the first thing about siding. Before that it had been a tattoo parlor, and before that he was going to run Rufus out of business by opening his own churchyard maintenance service. At least Ronnie had tattoos. I wasn't sure if he'd ever even pushed a mower or held a weed trimmer.

So imagine my surprise when I pulled up to his place and saw that he and some of his buddies had already framed out most of the recording studio. I'd taken no more than a few steps toward the studio before Ronnie tossed me a beer from a cooler and grinned. "Earl, meet the band."

Two other men, both older than Ronnie, stared at me. One of them looked high; the other one just looked stupid.

"This is Hunter Rawlins, but you can call him Easy. Best drummer this side of the Mississippi." Easy held out a hand. He was the high one, but when he shook my hand, his grip was firm.

"Ronnie's told me a lot about you," he said. "I guess you could call me a fan."

I waved him off. "Don't believe his shit."

"I'd never lie about the great Earl Marcus."

I laughed. Ronnie liked to build me up to his buddies. I'd never understood exactly why he thought so highly of me, but I'd finally come to realize it was genuine. Hell, once Ronnie decided he liked you, and once you liked him back, even a little bit, he was a totally different person. That was what I couldn't get Rufus to understand.

"I liked how you stood up to that preacher daddy of yours," Easy said.

I turned to the other man, because this sort of adulation always made me uncomfortable. "And I guess you play bass?"

"That's right," the man said. He had dark facial hair somewhere between a five-o'clock shadow and a beard, and tiny, nervous eyes. "Daryl Roan." He held out a hand.

"You boys are making some progress," I said, taking his hand.

"We should be up and practicing by sometime next week," Ronnie said. "Soundproofing the walls is going to take a little bit, but once that's done, we're going to get our songs down and hit the road. We already got a gig at Jessamine's in a couple of weeks."

"Got a name?" I asked.

Ronnie smiled broadly and glanced at Easy. "Tell him."

"The Bluegrass Mountain Cult."

When I didn't react, Ronnie shrugged. "You know, like the Blue Öyster Cult, except hillbilly style."

"Right," I said. "I can't wait to hear it."

"You're going to love it, Earl."

I didn't think so, but what did I know? Hell, I'd never have guessed Ronnie and I would be friends, so that showed pretty clearly I didn't know much. And here I was, coming to him to ask for help once again.

"Can we talk for a minute? Alone?"

Ronnie grinned. "Holy hell, you got us another case, don't you?"

"Take it easy. I just want to talk to you."

Easy patted him on the back. "Lucky."

Ronnie shrugged. "I told you I helped him, didn't I?"

"You sure did," Daryl said.

* * *

Inside Ronnie's house—if you could call it that—I told him what I was planning on doing. He grinned the whole time. When I finished, he nodded. "Cool," he said. "I can do that."

"Now remember," I said. "We're not trying to go overboard. We just want to see the school, maybe meet some teachers, get a feel for the place before we decide to move all the way from Arkansas."

"What's my son's name?"

"You decide," I said.

"I want to call him Leroy."

"Leroy?"

"Sounds like a boy who'd be up to no good."

"Fine. Just stick with it. And remember, if somebody approaches us, I'm Bob Jenkins, the granddaddy, and you're the father, Bobby Junior."

"Right. One question, though."

"What?"

"Why are we doing this?"

"It's part of a case."

"I got that, but what's the case, what are we trying to figure out?"

It was actually an excellent question. I would do well to figure it out myself. The only thing I knew for sure at this point was I wanted a look at "Doctor" Blevins. "There's something up with the school. The description on the website made my skin crawl."

"You mean they might be abusing the boys or something?"

"Maybe. That's what I'm hoping to find out."

Nearly thirty minutes later, we'd made our way through Riley and over to Brethren, as far as a person could get from the Fingers and still be in Coulee County. To get to the Harden School, we had to follow a long, winding road up a mountain I wasn't familiar with. When we finally saw the school in the distance, we also saw the fence surrounding the grounds. It was at least twelve feet high with barbed wire at the top.

"Shit, they don't want nobody coming in, do they?" Ronnie said.

"I think it's the other way around."

"Huh?"

"They don't want anybody getting out."

"Oh . . ."

I pulled up to the gate. There was a call box, and I pressed the button labeled *Main Office.*

"Just stick to the story," I said.

There was a beep, and then a voice said, "State your name, please."

"Bob Jenkins," I said. "I've got an appointment with Mr. Harden."

"Just a minute," the voice said. It sounded like the secretary named Mindy I'd spoken to on the phone earlier.

The intercom crackled. "Okay, Mr. Jenkins. You'll need to show your license at the front desk, so please have it ready."

"Oh," I said. "Me and my boy are here from Arkansas, and it's been a long day. I hate to tell you that I left my wallet in the damned hotel room.

Maybe you could let me in this one time? I just got to figure out something for my grandson. We flew over just for this meeting. Harden is supposed to be the best."

"It's okay," she said. "Maybe just bring it the next time you come?"

"Will do," I said.

The gate opened and I pulled through. Here the road turned from dirt to paved and the trees had been cut back from the road a little. The road went on for at least a half mile before the trees cleared completely and I saw the falls. Great flumes of whitewater tumbled over the gap in the mountains at a furious pace. I watched, mesmerized. The spectacular view seemed matched only by the inevitable danger that would come as I drew closer to the rocky bluffs. I looked away and punched the gas, guiding my truck around another bend and up a final rise. That was when the school came into view again, and this time I got a good look at it.

It was made of faded red bricks and large shuttered windows. A great white portico dominated the front of the massive four-story building. The lawn was pristine, an odd thing to see in the middle of such wilderness. As we drove up to the small parking area to the left of the school, I saw a couple of boys trimming the hedges. They were both sweating profusely, and their faces wore molten expressions of pure misery.

I parked, and Ronnie and I walked to the front door. One of the boys glanced at us. I nodded at him and smiled. He shook his head and turned his glare away, back to the shrubbery he was working on.

The door wouldn't open, but I saw a button to the left and pressed it. The same female voice came over the loudspeaker. "Mr. Jenkins?"

"That's right. And my boy Bobby Junior's here too."

"I'm opening the door. Please see me at the front desk to sign in."

I heard a click. This time the door opened when I turned the handle. We stepped into a large lobby. It was—to put it mildly—spectacular. Marble floors, a giant chandelier, and leather furniture conspired to give the space a deeply luxurious feel. There was no way, I realized, a person could step through that door and not take the school seriously. Even if—like me—you were predisposed to having a bad opinion about the place.

On the far side of the lobby, I saw a counter with a young woman behind it. She smiled at us as we made the long walk across the expanse of polished marble.

"I'm Mindy," the girl said, still smiling. I took her in. Young, brunette. Pleasant demeanor.

"Bob," I said, and jabbed a thumb at Ronnie. "And Bobby Junior. It's his son we're here about."

"Nice to meet you both," she said. "We're excited that you're considering the Harden School." She pointed to a sheet for us to sign in.

"So, do the boys handle all the yard work?"

"They do, under Coach Blevins's watchful eye."

"Coach Blevins?"

"Well, that's what they call him. He's actually a doctor. Really smart, they say, but I've also heard he's . . ." She shrugged sheepishly, almost apologetically.

"What were you going to say?"

She shook her head. "Nothing, I should have kept my mouth closed."

"But you didn't, and now I'm wondering if I should be concerned about sending my grandson here?"

I saw something like doubt creep across her face. "Absolutely not. Everyone says Dr. Blevins is the best. I'm sorry. He's just . . . unorthodox."

"Well," I said, trying to buy time, hoping she'd say something more. Often it was easiest to let silence bait the hook. Most people simply couldn't abide it.

"What's your son's name?" she said, smartly changing the subject.

I pointed at Ronnie and said, "Bobby Junior."

"No, not him, the one you want to talk to Harden about."

"Leroy," Ronnie said. "He's about as wild as a buck."

"Leroy," she repeated thoughtfully. "How old is he?"

I hesitated, giving Ronnie time to answer again. He seemed like he had a vision for this.

"Fourteen and hell on skates."

"It's a tough age," she said.

"Yep, he thinks he's got the world figured out, but he ain't got nothing, not even a clue. He believes he's the damned cock of the walk now that his balls dropped." Ronnie snorted. "Truth is, he ain't nothing but a little banty rooster."

Mindy made a face I couldn't quite read. Concern? Not exactly. More like surprise, but why would she be surprised? Surely this story wasn't uncommon. Maybe it was just Ronnie's colorful language she wasn't prepared for. Her next statement went a long way toward clearing up my confusion. "I will add him to our prayer list at church. I've seen God change kids. It's not his will for them to be like that."

"It sure isn't," Ronnie said.

"So," I said. "Does the school serve boys and girls?"

Mindy shook her head. "No, just boys. I've heard they had a girl here a long time ago and it didn't go well."

I pointed at a sofa in one corner of the giant lobby. "Okay if we wait over there?"

"No need to wait," came a booming voice from the other side of the lobby. I turned and saw a well-dressed older man smiling at us. He was handsome, the kind of man who, despite being in his seventies, was still likely to get second looks from younger women. He was muscular and trim and had a roguish quality about him that belied the suit and shiny shoes he wore.

Striding across the lobby, he held out a hand. "I'm Randy Harden."

"Bob Jenkins," I said. "From Little Rock. My boy, Bobby Junior."

"Nice to meet both of you fellows. Let's go to my office."

13

Harden's office was a clean and spartan affair, with decor that looked like it had last been updated in the 1970s. His bookshelves were filled with great tomes about military history and religion. Interesting mix, I thought, but not surprising. In Coulee County, religion and violence were always close bedfellows.

Behind his desk were some photos of Harden with what I assumed were former students. In all of them, he stood in front of a concrete maze lined with plants, flowers, and hedges. The students smiled, while Harden posed as the proud father whose hard work had finally paid off.

"Those are my success stories," he said.

"You've only had ten successes?" Ronnie asked.

It was actually a good question. I had been thinking the same thing. Harden, for his part, took the question in stride. "When I say successes, I mean *successes*." He swiveled in his chair and pointed at a photo of a smiling red-haired kid. "That's Jimmy Lawson."

I waited for more.

"You boys don't know Jimmy Lawson?"

"We're from Arkansas," I said.

Harden laughed. "Well, that explains it. Jimmy's the new county prosecutor. He came through here in ninety-three. That kid was messed up. But I'm going to tell you what he needed."

Ronnie and I both waited as Harden drew out the moment.

"He needed somebody to tell him no, and mean it. That's what I did. I told him no. You'd be surprised how many boys crave that."

I nodded, trying to decide exactly how to play this. I needed him to believe our boy was a good fit for the school, at least long enough to show me around, to let me meet the teachers, particularly Blevins, and get a feel for the place.

"My cousin lives in the area and she told us about the good work you do here, Mr. Harden. We've flown out from Arkansas to check the place out. I'd very much like to hear about your philosophy and maybe see the place. And meet some of the teachers."

"Hold your horses," he said. "This school ain't for everybody. I'll need to hear a little about your boy. And I'd like to meet him, of course. Why don't you start by telling me why you believe your boy would benefit from a program like this. Did your cousin tell you what we focus on here?"

"She said you had a way of straightening boys out. That you'd been here for a long time and got the job done. My grandson, Leroy, he's into drugs and guns, and recently we found out he got some girl pregnant. A middle-schooler. I'm ashamed to tell you these things, Mr. Harden, but I assume you've heard worse."

Harden was silent for a moment. From somewhere outside, I heard some boys shouting, chanting something.

"What's that?" Ronnie said.

"Just morning exercises," Harden said. He stood and shut his office door. The sounds went away.

"I'm flattered that you've made such a long trip because of the good things you've heard about our school, but I'm going to be up front with you. I'm going to have to see if we have room. We've had an influx of new students lately."

"Well," I said. "I'd like to hear a little more either way. We've got to decide if this is the best place for Leroy. Like I said, meet the teachers and whatnot."

Harden picked up the phone on his desk. "Mindy, can you ask Dr. Blevins to come to my office?" He hung up and smiled at us. "Excuse me," he said. He walked out of the office, shutting the door behind him.

"What do you think that's about?" I said in a low whisper.

Ronnie shrugged. "Why are we checking this place out again?"

"Abuse."

"Right." He nodded. "He's the type."

"What do you mean?" We were both still whispering so he wouldn't be able to hear us right outside the door, but another possibility struck me.

What if he was recording us? What if I'd said something that let him know I was here for reconnaissance and *not* for my grandson?

"I mean, he's got that look. You know, handsome but a little creepy. Full of himself. Like your daddy."

"Yeah," I said, realizing there was definitely something about Harden that put me in mind of my father. I thought it was the air of confidence he exuded, the sense that he'd carved out his place and that even when the world around him changed, he'd just drag the old world with him, using it to insulate himself from the changes and requirements brought on by the new one.

The door opened up and Harden came in, followed by a large, bald man with a big smile. The bald man seemed almost boyish in his manner, like a big, goofy kid who'd found himself in a man's body. He wore black sweatpants and a T-shirt that said SCIENCE IS ALWAYS CHANGING in large green block letters.

"This is Dr. Timothy Blevins," Harden said. "We call him Coach. He teaches science and handles the coaching."

"You have teams here?" I said, hoping he wouldn't recognize my voice.

Dr. Blevins shook Ronnie's hand and then mine, meeting my eyes with his own big brown ones. "No, not like that. I coach the boys on how to behave like men. I teach them to get in touch with who they are, who God made them to be."

"I see."

Blevins's expression changed slightly. He looked less boyish and a little more crafty, like a kid who'd figured out he could steal bubblegum instead of paying for it. "Do I know you?"

"Maybe. You got ties to Arkansas?"

He seemed to relax. "No, my people are all from right here in North Georgia." He beamed. "God's country."

"I have to admit," Ronnie said, "it is pretty."

An awkward silence followed.

"Well," I said. "What kind of things do you teach the boys?"

I was talking to Blevins, but Harden was the one who answered. "I don't think that will be necessary. Sorry to say, Mr. Jenkins, but I think we're full at the moment. If you'd made contact just a week or two earlier, we would have had a spot, but . . ." He shook his head and held out his hands apologetically.

"Full?" I said.

"That's right," Blevins said. "Not a single room. We should be graduating some boys next spring, if you want to check back then."

"Well, I sure do hate to hear that," I said.

"It sounds like your grandson isn't as bad off as some we have here," Blevins said.

"He's in pretty bad shape. What do you have here, murderers?"

I couldn't miss the quick look Blevins and Harden exchanged. Then Harden smiled. "We're just full. I think what Coach means to say is you seem like the kind of man who can figure this out. You got your son here. That's two male role models, Daddy and Granddaddy. Hell, most of the boys we have haven't had a single decent male role model in their life before they came here. Just stay on him. Discipline is key."

"And don't forget that the love of a father is crucial. Boys have to make a connection with male role models before it's too late," Blevins said. The way he said it made it clear he'd recited that line over and over again.

"I'll keep that in mind," I said.

We shook hands all around, and Harden opened his office door to let us out. "You can find your way out?"

"Sure," I said, thankful they weren't walking us to our car. I wasn't done yet.

"Can you distract the girl at the desk?" I whispered to Ronnie.

"Sure. Easy."

"Do it. I'm heading to the stairs. After I'm clear, get the truck"—I handed him the keys as we made our way down the hallway—"and meet me out by the gate."

"When?"

"Give me twenty minutes."

"What if you're not there?"

"I'll call you if something changes."

"Okay, got it."

When we made it to the desk, I turned toward the exit but walked slowly. Ronnie went toward the front desk. Once I heard him talking, I veered toward the stairs, moving quickly and quietly. I opened the door and disappeared into the stairwell.

14

I had no idea what I hoped to find upstairs. If anything, I just wanted a closer look. For some reason, Blevins had called the dead man's phone *and* written him a letter, and I would be damned if I could let that go. They were literally the only two things I had to go on—other than the bookmark—and I meant to look into them as exhaustively as possible.

The second floor was made up of classrooms. There seemed to be only one class in session. An elderly man wearing a sweater vest sat perched on a stool in front of eight boys—all dressed in the same blue jeans and blue shirts—mumbling something about a proof. The boys looked extremely bored, but they didn't look particularly troubled. Well, that wasn't exactly true. They all looked troubled, but they didn't look like trouble*makers*. Maybe it was because they were all dressed the same, but none of them looked the least bit threatening.

I wandered into one of the empty classrooms. Based on the writing on the chalkboard, I assumed it was Blevins's. The chalkboard read *Check your facts . . . Climate Change is a THEORY not proven science.*

Yep, I was still in Coulee County.

I looked at his desk, the computer sitting there. The screen saver said *Let boys be boys today and they will be men tomorrow.*

I wiggled the mouse and his desktop came up. Maybe I could find some record of Joe's attendance at the school. I had to assume that he'd once been a student. Otherwise, why the connection with Dr. Blevins? I made a quick scan of the files on the desktop. There were only four, one labeled *junk* and three labeled *untitled.* I clicked on one of the untitled folders and found it filled with documents. I skimmed the list. Each document was titled with an initial and a name. I clicked one of them at random.

> *Doug Knowles*
> *11/3/00*
> *Age: 17*
> *Status: Floor three*
> *Parents: Marjorie Knowles*
> *Status: Supportive*
> *Complaints: One call, 3/6/18. Asked about rumors with Josh H.*
> *Response: H. returned call. Discussed how we are aware of said*
>   *rumors but are handling it with therapy.*

Below this were two photos of Doug. One showed a happy kid, his hair dyed green, laughing at a football game with some of his friends. The second showed him dressed all in blue, not smiling, standing erect, his head shaved, his eyes filled with a sadness that jumped through the computer screen and gripped me somehow. Jesus, what were they doing to these kids?

I heard someone coming down the hallway. Hopefully it would be someone who hadn't seen me yet. If it was Blevins or Harden, I was screwed. Worst case scenario, I could hide under the desk, fight my way out if necessary.

I closed the file, scanning the rest of the names. One near the bottom caught my eye.

E. Walsh

My mouth fell open. Surely not. It couldn't be. I opened the file and saw it was much more expansive than Doug's. That was all I had time to see before the footsteps drew even closer.

I fumbled with the mouse, trying to close the window and get under the desk, but I was too late.

"Who are you?"

It was a kid, dressed like the others I'd seen except for one difference. The collar on his shirt was white. He seemed a little older than the other boys I'd seen, too, which led me to believe he was some sort of prefect, or maybe an RA.

"Tech support," I said, reaching for the front of my shirt where an ID badge might have been hanging. "Oh, forgot my badge."

"We've never had any tech support here before."

"Well, Dr. Blevins asked me to come up and look at his computer. He's downstairs if you want to talk to him."

The kid eyed me suspiciously. "What's your name?"

"Preston Argent," I said, without missing a beat.

He nodded. "I'm going to go check with him right now."

"Go ahead. I wanted to ask him something about his computer anyway. So send him on up, if you don't mind."

The kid walked out, moving purposefully down the hall. I opened the Walsh file and read from the top.

Edward Walsh
1/3/03
Age: 15
Status: Floor four
Parents: Jeb Walsh / Eleanor Walsh—divorced
Status: Father supportive / mother combative
Complaints: Multiple calls, log below
Response: See log

I scrolled down past paragraphs that were simply labeled *Notes*. I found a chart listing the date of each of his mother's calls and visits and how they had been handled. Most of them had been handled in the same way—*contacted Jeb*.

Only two were different, and they'd come recently, just last month. *Referred her to Sheriff Argent.*

I tried to see what the complaint was, but the section of the chart under *Complaint* said the same thing all the way down— *General*.

I knew my time was limited, so I closed the file and headed out into the hallway. Just then the elevator at the end of the hall dinged. I ducked back into the classroom and jogged over to the bank of windows on the far wall. I opened the first one I came too and pushed the screen out. It fell into the garden below.

And what a garden it was. Every manner of plant and flower grew below, each contained within a planter or its own little walled-off section. There were fishponds, benches, stone pillars, and brick walkways that formed a labyrinthlike pattern among the plants.

Leaning out the window, I saw I was looking at about a twenty-foot drop into one of the fishponds. It was hard to tell how deep it was, but I didn't have time to worry about it. The footsteps were drawing closer.

Swinging my feet up through the open window, I held onto the window frame with both hands as I eased myself down as far as I could before letting go.

When I did let go, the speed of the fall took my breath away. I had just enough time to look down and see I was indeed going to hit the water before I was there, stabbing through the dark pond, feetfirst. I braced myself for impact, and it came, but the water was deep, deep enough to slow my descent. My boots hit the bottom, and the impact rocked my knees and my hips, but nothing felt broken or too badly injured. I swam up, toward the sun, and reached for the pond's edge. I pulled myself out and began to run toward the back of the garden. I ran through the gate and kept going onto a broad expanse of green lawn. Several boys stood to my left in straight rows while a young man spoke to them. I kept running. Only the boys saw me, as the man's back was to me.

A line of trees lay in front of me, and I didn't stop running until I'd broken through the tree line and lost myself in the woods.

I walked for a while, just trying to listen. I figured if anyone was pursuing me, I'd hear them coming. But the more I walked, the more a new sound filled my ears. It sounded like a roar, a droning and endless roar.

Five or ten minutes later, I emerged from the trees to a spectacular scene. The waterfall I'd glimpsed earlier was just a few feet away now, looming over a tower of flat rocks. The waterfall and the river below cut a path through the land, creating a deep ravine that stretched as far as the eye could see. I walked to the edge for a better look at the river hundreds of feet below. The distance to the other side of the ravine was surprisingly close, almost close enough to cause a man think he could make the leap across, but he'd have to be a fool to try. To my left some rocks had somehow landed atop each other in a stair-like structure that led up to the waterfall. I followed them, feeling the heat of the sunbaked rocks as

I climbed. The heat was so intense my clothes were almost dry already. At the top was a single flat rock, nearly fifteen feet wide and just as long, that was the perfect spot to view the waterfall and the ravine below. From here, I was mere feet from the waterfall, and its sun-colored spray cooled me as I stood, taking it in. It was loud. So loud it was nearly impossible to hear anything except the droning roar of the falls. I moved to the edge of the flat rock and looked down. A narrow ledge lay directly below me, about ten feet or so away. It couldn't have been more than three feet wide. I wondered if it would be enough to break someone's fall or if the force of the impact would just carry a person on over, toward the bottom of the ravine and an almost certain death.

A wind blew from behind me, strong enough to make me fear that I might be about to find out.

Enough of this. I needed to call Ronnie and figure out how we were going to get out of here.

15

We got out without further incident. I skirted the interior of the fence that ran around the school grounds until I made it out to the gate, where Ronnie picked me up. We used a call box to contact Mindy at the front gate. She didn't seem to know about my second-floor leap and let us out, wishing us a great day. The gate swung open and we pulled away, free of the school. Immediately I felt myself relax a little. I'd been too pressed while on the property to truly appreciate it, but there was something deeply troubling about the school and its students. Somehow I had *felt* their despair while inside.

Ronnie chattered the whole way home, but I was barely listening. Instead I spent the ride trying to process what I'd seen on Blevins's computer. First and foremost was the discovery of Edward Walsh, son of Jeb. I supposed I shouldn't have been surprised Jeb's son was at a reform school, but it still seemed meaningful. Anything Jeb Walsh was connected with needed to be scrutinized carefully. Not that Blevins's connection wasn't enough to keep me interested.

Still, I couldn't help but think I was missing some major pieces of information. It was like putting together a puzzle, but you didn't know what the puzzle would show because too many pieces were still missing, and each new piece seemed to suggest a completely new puzzle rather than fitting into the current one.

As Ronnie continued to talk (he was on to the band now, telling me again how they were going to play their first gig in a few weeks at Jessamine's), I ran through what I knew for sure:

A man had been shot in my yard. His name was Joe. He looked to be in his midtwenties, which meant he would have been at the school about seven or eight years ago.

He'd clearly been coming to see me, most likely to hire me. But for what? Could he have wanted me to investigate the Harden School all along?

And why had the letter warned him to stop pursuing his course of action? The "course of action" had to be coming to me, didn't it? Was that what Blevins had wanted him to stop? Now that I knew about Jeb's connection to the school, I wondered if he wasn't the "powerful force" the letter mentioned.

This last piece might have been the most intriguing, suggesting a complex and vast picture that could actually mean something good for this whole county if I could assemble it and use it to somehow bring Walsh down.

What else?

There were the notes on the computer I'd found in the classroom. I couldn't help but think complaints were pretty commonplace at the school if Blevins kept such detailed notes on them. Then there was the part about Jeb's ex-wife eventually being referred to Argent. What was that about?

"You ain't been listening to a damn word I've been saying, have you?"

"Huh?" I realized we were almost to Ronnie's place. The old church was in sight.

"I was telling you about the weird stuff I witnessed in front of the school."

"What weird stuff?"

Ronnie blew out a long sigh. "Jesus H. Christ, Earl, you are as bad as a child sometimes. You mean to tell me you ain't heard *none* of what I was saying?"

"I heard . . . some of it," I said.

"About the band?"

"Oh, I got that."

"So where did you stop listening?"

"Right after you talked about the band."

He gave me a sharp look as if to say he knew I was lying, but he'd let it go for the moment.

"So, when I got in the truck and started to pull off, there was some kid standing there. He had a Weed eater and was working on trimming the grass near the driveway. He waved me down. I wasn't going to stop, but I swear he was going to just let me hit him if I didn't, and well, you know

I already done time for that." He stopped to snort a bunch of snot up into his nose and wiped some leaking out on the back of his hand, which he promptly rubbed on my seat. I said nothing, not wanting to delay where this was going even a little bit.

"Anyway, I stopped, and the kid kills the Weed eater and comes over to the window, motioning for me to roll it down. It takes me a minute to figure out your truck, but I get it down and he leans inside. 'Mister,' he says. 'Yeah?' I say. He gives me this look, all puppy-dog eyes, not what you'd expect from a boy in a place like this, and asks me to take him with me."

I grunted, not surprised. I'd gotten the definite sense, despite all Harden's victory photos of changed lives hanging behind his desk, that the reality was a lot messier and didn't lend itself to being captured inside a snapshot.

"I told him that was a no-go, but he didn't want to hear that for an answer. He reached in the damn truck, Earl. He grabbed my arm and started begging me."

"Jesus. Did he say why he was so upset?"

"He was crying, saying something about the Indians and his sister."

"Indians? His sister? None of that makes sense."

"It was fucking crazy."

"So what happened?"

"I saw the front door to the school open up. That smiley-faced doctor asshole came out in a dead sprint, shouting at the kid to stop. The kid let go of my arm and fell down on the grass crying. I drove on off."

"You think Blevins noticed I wasn't in the truck with you?"

"Maybe not. He didn't get too close."

We made it to the church, and Ronnie eased my truck across the creek. I saw Rufus standing out beside his firepit, looking forlorn. He wore his overalls but no shirt underneath. He was sweating, and I saw he'd been working in the small garden near the cemetery.

"That asshole was up all night last night. My first night back, I would have liked to get some sleep, but no. He was out here, rummaging around in the garden, splashing in the creek."

"Give him a break, Ronnie. Something's up with him."

"I'll say."

Ronnie parked my truck at his place. His bandmates were gone and the studio still stood unfinished. Ronnie seemed a little down about it, but I reminded him they had a gig coming soon, whether it was finished or not.

"Indians and his sister?" I said again. "Anything else you can remember?"

Ronnie lit a cigarette and sucked on it like it held the very essence of life.

"Nah, but he was scared of something. More scared than anybody I've seen in a while. I don't know what's going on there, Earl, or why you can't talk about it, but you gotta do something to help them boys."

I knew he was right. What I didn't know was what to do next. The puzzle was laid out, but too many pieces were still missing, leaving huge chunks of nothing at all.

16

The previous night, unbeknownst to me, Rufus had not fallen asleep in the chair at all. Instead, he'd risen silently, finished the last of his whiskey, and headed for the old church.

Rufus didn't mind walking. He'd been doing it since he'd been blinded almost twenty years now. Sometimes he lost his way, but it happened less and less these days. He couldn't explain it exactly. People said he had a sixth sense. Over the years, he'd come to think they might be right. In the beginning, he'd just pretended to have a sixth sense, using tricks and information people didn't know he had to fool them, to create a kind of persona, but after a while those tricks had become a part of who he was and he was able to skip some of them or not even realize he was using them. Or hell, maybe he'd just taught himself how to be psychic, how to "know" what was there without being able to see it. He wouldn't rule it out. Not in this crazy world.

He made it home without incident, still angry, still out of sorts over the tingling he'd felt the previous two nights and his inability to even drink himself to sleep, so he decided he'd do the one thing that never failed to relax him. He found the creek bank and stripped out of his overalls and briefs. He shrugged off his T-shirt and tossed it on the ground where he felt like it would stay dry. Now, totally naked, he reached for the water with one of his feet, letting the sharp coldness sting him with the knowledge that his body would soon adapt.

Slipping his entire body into the creek, he felt the water engulf him and lift him, creating a kind of dark balance where all things could be internalized and held. Somehow he felt the stars, their pull. Sometimes that happened, especially when he was in the creek, no clothes to separate him from the wider world. Being blind helped him feel a part of things, as if he were any other living organism that lacked vision but still possessed a deep connection with these dark hollows: a tree, a rock, a creeping vine, hell, even an old shack like Ronnie's place across the creek. Rufus believed if something had been in one place long enough, if it had heard the rain and the thunder and the swelling of crickets and the lonesome night birds, that thing—be it house or fence or bone—became something else. That it too became a part of these mountains' great and secret history.

His head touched the soft mud at the bottom. His nose and mouth were clear of the waterline, but his ears were inside, so he could hear the pulsing of the creek as it flowed across rocks and carved its way down the mountain. He felt his eyes open, not the ones burned by acid so many years ago; those were closed forever. Instead, he felt the eyes of memory opening. His breathing slowed. A fish slipped over his belly, and it tickled as its wiggling body grazed the flesh just above his navel. The water was silk, the stars were pinpricks of heat, there were rocks beneath his hands, cool against his rough palms.

He saw the girl, Harriet. She wasn't really a girl, Rufus realized, but that was how she'd seemed. In reality, she'd been closer to a woman, too old for the school, and also the wrong gender. It didn't matter, though. Harden wanted her there, so she was there. He saw now she'd been like him, unsure of herself, trying to feel her way through a cruel world, looking for a way out that was hidden inside the deepest traditions and fears of the South.

Nobody called her Harriet except Rufus. To everyone else she was Harry or just "the dyke" because, unlike her twin sister, Harriet couldn't hide who she was. In fact, she'd confided in Rufus once that other people had known she was a lesbian before she did.

"I just knew I was different," she said. "I'm still different, I guess."

Harden had made it clear her being "different" was unacceptable. He was a man who valued brutality and grudges, and the young staff looked up to him because he never had issues with the boys. They all responded to his gruff and commanding presence. All except Harriet. She was an outlier in more ways than one. Not only was she female and gay, she was also a good kid, not a criminal or troublemaker like the boys who'd been sent there for various crimes and transgressions at their regular schools. Harden never had a problem exposing the boys for the sniveling weasels they were. Of course, exposing people was what Harden did. His personality was like a light; when he turned it on you, you had to either shy away, shield your eyes, or stare into it straight and risk being blinded.

Rufus's body shook with laughter, disturbing the intricate path the water had formed around him. It was funny because of the irony. He'd lost his vision because he'd turned away from Harden, because he'd been too afraid to stand up for what was in him, because he'd still been looking for a savior, someone or something outside himself to validate him, to force the world to make sense.

Maybe he was still looking for one now, too. Maybe it was time to stop.

* * *

Years ago, on the day Rufus had finally mustered the courage to leave the Holy Flame, he'd been looking for a savior too, except then he'd finally been forced to look inward. And what he'd found inside himself had been enough. If only he'd been able to hang on to it. But like so many of the important things in life, it had proved fleeting.

He'd waited until Easter Sunday, until the very moment he was supposed to fetch the new spring snakes. Every Easter, the church "renewed" its commitment to faith by bringing new, wild snakes into the church. They were called "spring snakes," and it had long been Rufus's job to bring them one at a time from their cages in the back of the sanctuary. He'd hand them each to the preacher, who would hold them up and proclaim Satan had no power in this church before slipping them into the snake pit near the altar.

When the time came for him to bring the first snake, the preacher, Brother RJ, as they called him, motioned to Rufus. Rufus stood and skirted past his mother, who patted his back, her way of showing her pride for what he was doing. He used to crave that touch, that sense of accomplishment, but for the last few years her touch had come to represent something else entirely.

He slipped out into the aisle. RJ stared at him, a smile playing on his lips. It was almost as if he knew Rufus was planning something. It was almost as if he was enjoying it, as if he had a preternatural sense of what was coming and did not believe Rufus would have the courage to go through with it. But Brother RJ was wrong, and the knowledge of this spurred Rufus on, the courage welling up inside him as he stood eye to eye with the preacher, not withdrawing from the older man's hardened countenance. Rufus turned to get the snake from the back. All eyes watched him as he made his way down the aisle. Even then people thought him weird, different in ways great and small. He wore the same black suit that had been his father's before he made his own exit nearly fifteen years earlier, and as a young man he liked to spend his time out in the churchyard, staring at the headstones, wondering at the bodies beneath the ground and where their souls were, how they'd slipped their skin and flown upward to a heaven the preacher said was in the clouds and filled with delights unimaginable to the mortal mind. He was a quiet young man, diffident and prone to always being on the edge of the other young men, skulking along the periphery of their tight-knit circle, always feeling alien and—yes, he would admit it—slightly superior to them. Likewise, though he found many of the young women utterly fascinating, he suspected he'd barely registered on their radar. He was persona non grata, the young man who sat up front with his mother and gave the good girls creeping skin when and if they ever happened upon his face in a dream or a random thought. Or maybe that was wrong. Would he even have realized it if a young lady had found him interesting, attractive? Maybe just mysterious. No, he felt sure he wouldn't have.

What a fool he'd been in so many ways.

But not then, not at that very moment, in the sanctuary aisle, every eye on him, every mind fixed on what he held in his hand, a writhing cottonmouth, the same type that had struck Earl years before, nearly its twin, and Rufus found that appropriate. He held it tighter, higher, thrusting it forward as the faces on either side of him drew back in surprise and admiration.

No, he hadn't been a fool then. He'd been redeemed then. He'd found the door to heaven and blown it open wide, except it didn't take him where he expected to go. It didn't take him to any shining city with gold walkways and silk flags blowing in the perfect breeze. There were no colors unimaginable to the human mind as the preacher had promised. If there was a God there at all, it was a God who was hard to know, a God who kept his eyes closed to avoid seeing the carnage the world had wrought in his name. But Rufus felt something as he walked forward, and instead of handing the cottonmouth to Brother RJ, he threw it into the air, aiming it at the stained glass that filtered the sunlight into the church like religion had filtered God into the world, discoloring and weakening it, trapping it, *using* it until it became a thin veneer, ready to break at the least impact.

The snake hit the stained glass above the alter, cracking it, just a sliver, just enough for real light to stream into the church. It fell on Rufus's face, lifting him, cleansing him, redeeming him, and he felt the great eyelids of God begin to open.

"This is all lies," he said. He had no more spoken the words than he realized they were the first ones he'd ever spoken in front of this church that were his own—not the preacher's or his mother's or some scripture memorized by rote. These were his words, goddamn it.

"He's a liar, and we're all too weak to call him on it. Not anymore. I'm done."

And that was all. He didn't need to say anything else, because to do so would be to whittle a wooden key past the point where it fit perfectly into the lock.

He'd been redeemed. He felt God's eyes open upon him for the first time. As he walked out of the church, he prayed it would not be the last.

17

The next day, I looked up Eleanor Walsh online and found her number. I wrote it down on a sheet of yellow lined paper and laid it out on the table while I was eating breakfast. Calling her shouldn't have been a difficult proposition. Based on the records I'd seen on Blevins's computer, she was the logical next step. I needed to find out why she'd been referred to Argent and what he'd told her.

Yet . . .

I shook my head and touched the paper with my right hand, sliding it away from me slowly. Part of me wanted to just let this all go. So far, I'd heard nothing about the young man I'd found in my yard. No one had come looking for him. No one seemed to even miss him. I'd checked headlines on my phone each night before going to bed, and I had yet to see anything. Wasn't the hard part over now? His body was gone, his car hidden. Wouldn't it be easier to just let it ride? Keep my nose out of whatever nonsense was brewing over there at that school?

The reality of the situation was clear to me. The more I pushed into the school and tried to connect it to the dead man in my yard, the greater chance I'd have of being implicated in the murder, or at least the cover-up of a murder. I'd been burned by Jeb Walsh before, and as much as I'd have liked to finally take him down, and as much as I'd have liked to help those boys (there was obviously something not right at the school), I felt compelled to consider the wisdom of just letting it go.

I picked up the notebook paper and balled it up, tossing it aside. I didn't need this. Hell, I'd already put up my best fight against Walsh and Argent when I'd run for sheriff. I'd lost. Maybe it was time to admit that.

I pushed my bowl of cereal away and made some coffee. When it was finished, I poured a few fingers of whiskey into it and walked outside to the ridge.

The morning was still relatively cool, which for this time of year just meant you could walk outside without starting to sweat immediately. I sat down in one of the chairs, ready to stop thinking about the school, about Walsh, about anything except slowly getting drunk.

But I couldn't. My mind—of its own accord—turned back to what Ronnie had shared with me in the truck. Something about Indians and a boy's sister? I also thought about the weird kid who'd caught me on Blevins's computer. Something had been off about him. Come to think of it, something was off about all the boys I'd encountered there. The ones in the grass out back, in the classroom, all of them. They didn't seem like the kinds of boys you'd expect to be in a place like that.

I knew from experience that stereotyping criminals was a mistake. They came in all shapes and sizes, colors, and genders. But nearly all the ones I'd known carried the same angry chip on their shoulder that was hard to miss. Sometimes it manifested itself in the way they walked. Other times it was in the way they kept their heads down and would not meet your gaze. Most of the time, you could see it in their eyes. Eyes could never lie. The rest of the body was always capable of deceit, but the eyes were different. They always told the truth.

Finishing my coffee and whiskey, I pulled out my phone and called Mary. She didn't answer. Probably too early out there for her. I stood up and walked to the ridge, peering down at the trailer that I noticed was looking a little better now. The woman had cleared away a lot of the kudzu that had been growing on it and gotten rid of some of the junk from the front yard. Her car was there, and I wondered what she was doing right now. Eating breakfast? Still asleep?

At just that moment, the door to her trailer swung open. She came out, dressed in a pair of cutoff blue jeans and a blue, tight-fitting T-shirt, cut low enough to reveal the tops of her freckled breasts. She was carrying a round red water cooler.

I watched as she walked to the road and started up it toward my place. Not wanting her to know I'd been watching her, I returned to my chair and sat down, picking up my empty coffee cup. I tried to look contemplative.

"Hey," she said.

I feigned surprise. "Morning."

"You said if I ever needed something to come on up. I don't have a well yet. They're supposed to come next week to dig it, so I was hoping I could fill this up?"

"Sure," I said, standing up quickly. I smiled at her, trying *not* to look at her breasts, but damn, it wasn't easy.

She grinned at me knowingly. "I'm Daphne, by the way."

"Earl," I said.

"I know. You told me the other night. You like to spend a lot of time on this ridge, don't you?"

I shrugged. "When it's nice out."

"Well, I guess I better remember to keep my blinds closed when I'm prancing around naked, huh?"

I froze, not sure how to respond to that. She gave me an intense look, so hard to read but not hard to *feel*. There was something deeply sexual in her gaze.

"I haven't ever . . ."

"I'm kidding, Earl. Lighten up. Besides, I'm not one of those feminist types or nothing. I like to be appreciated by a man."

I'll bet you do. I almost said it. But I managed to stop myself. That would have been the wrong thing to say. All of this felt wrong suddenly. In fact, I felt a little dirty just being in her presence, but I had to remind myself it wasn't her fault I felt like that but my own.

"Well, let me get you the water," I said, and reached for the cooler.

She pulled it away from me.

"Do you have a girlfriend, Earl Marcus?"

I swallowed hard, hesitating. Why was I hesitating?

"Yeah. Her name is Mary."

"Where is she? I don't see her?"

"She's . . ." Shit. Did I really want to tell her Mary was across the country? But why lie? Why was I afraid to tell her the truth? Was I that fucking weak?

"She's in Nevada for a while."

Daphne nodded. She had green eyes that knew how to look at a man, how to gaze and pout and flash. Shit. She was trouble. No, I reminded myself. *I* was responsible for my own actions. I was the one who was trouble. Always had been. With Mary I'd managed to keep myself on the straight and narrow. But now she was gone. I was down. *Way* down.

"I think I'd better get that water for you," I said.

"Sure thing, Earl," she said, grinning the kind of grin that makes a man feel things he probably would be better off not feeling.

* * *

After Daphne left, I went to the trash and found Eleanor Walsh's number. Sure, it would have been easy to let it go, but I was pretty sure I needed something to keep me moving, to keep my mind occupied. As much as I dreaded dealing with Jeb Walsh's ex-wife, I'd never been too good at life without danger. The danger had a way of blotting out all the pain and doubt inside me, the stuff that broke me over and over and made me feel like a failure. I'd take my chances doing what I'd always done: trying to make a difference, even if it meant beating my fists against the door of an empty room.

18

Eleanor Walsh was a surprise. Knowing Jeb Walsh like I did, I'd expected a former beauty queen with a mean streak, but instead I found a pleasant, middle-aged woman, who frankly seemed a little frightened by me and the clandestine nature of our meeting.

We met at an old gas station not too far from Backslide Gap and its shaky suspension bridge.

"I appreciate this," I said, climbing into the passenger's seat of her Volvo. "I hope we can work together to help your boy."

She nodded, taking me in with a cautious yet hopeful gaze. "I'd like to know what this is all about," she said.

"Let's drive, and I'll tell you."

She nodded and eased the Volvo forward. It was a nice vehicle, all leather, the latest technology, good air conditioning. I appreciated that last one, especially on a day like this.

I pointed at the lake on our right. "When I was a boy, my daddy took me fishing over there. We camped out up on the top of that rise. I hadn't thought about it much until I came out here to meet you today, but I'm pretty sure it's one of the best memories of my life."

"What does this have to do with Edward, Mr. Marcus?"

"Maybe more than you think. See, I have a soft spot for boys who disappoint their fathers, especially boys whose fathers are demagogues."

I tried to read her face, to see how she felt about me referring to her ex-husband as a demagogue. Ex-spouses could hate their former partner one minute and the next feel beholden to defend them. After all, nobody wanted to admit they'd been foolish enough to marry an asshole, much less a demagogue. Her expression remained neutral, so I decided to press on.

"In the course of another investigation, I came across some records indicating you'd made some complaints against the Harden School, and eventually they referred you to Sheriff Argent. I wanted to follow up with you about that. I think your situation might not be unique at the Harden School."

She slowed the car, making a right onto an overgrown side road. "Jeb was right about you," she said.

"How's that?"

"He said you were the kind of man who couldn't hear a sound in the middle of the night without getting up to see what caused it. He said you were broken, that you weren't the kind of man to let other men live their lives."

I thought that through for a moment. It sounded like an indictment, but I wasn't so sure I saw it that way. Hell, I wasn't so sure *she* saw it that way. What kind of man would I be if I let Jeb Walsh and men like him do what they pleased? Sometimes, I thought, if it wasn't for men like him, I'd have no purpose at all, no reason to exist save for getting drunk and the pleasure I felt being near Mary Hawkins.

And maybe there was a kind of brokenness in that. Maybe. But I thought we were all broken in one way or another. It was one of the truths of existence, like gravity or aging. Death or taxes. Both.

"Guilty," I said.

She watched the road. It seemed to narrow as we went deeper into a part of the Fingers I hadn't been to in years. It was a shady part, covered with layers of trees and dense foliage that seemed thorny and alive. I knew this road would eventually lead us to Backslide Gap, where I'd played as a young boy, where my father claimed all backsliders went to die.

He'd once promised me that it would be my fate too. And the thing about it was, I'd never for a second doubted him.

"Can you tell me about Edward?" I asked.

The only sound was the road crunching beneath the tires, the wind against glass, the tireless pitch of time outside the car. I saw the dead man in my yard, his car sliding neatly between the rows of corn in the Devil's Valley. I saw my father standing in front of the congregation, about to hand me the cottonmouth that would ultimately bite me and change my life, an endless journey of time in the twitch of a synapse. All of it winding down to this. What could I do to make my life meaningful, to fulfill the promise of hope I'd once felt before I'd seen the corrupt underbelly of the world?

"I'll tell you," Eleanor said, at last, "but you have to promise me you'll find a way to help him, even when you hear how impossible it is."

"I promise," I said, knowing there were some promises you made because you had to and not because you thought you could keep them.

"Edward told me he was gay when he was twelve," she said, keeping her eyes on the road. "I knew before that, of course, but I dreaded the day when he figured it out. When he accepted it himself. I actually prayed that the day would be delayed, that it would dawn on him in his twenties sometime after he was far removed from his father's control, but none of my prayers have ever been answered. That's probably why Jeb and I aren't married anymore. I mean, sure there was some abuse and the affairs, but I knew that was part of the deal going into the marriage. I wanted to believe Jeb was onto something greater, that even if he was a flawed man, he was right about something bigger. I wanted to believe he believed in God, that he was a sinner, sure, but also a man who aspired to more." She slowed the car around a sharp bend, and I took a moment to try to process what I'd heard. Edward was gay? She said this as if this bit of news was already understood, as if it were common knowledge.

"Anyway, when he told me, I tried to keep it a secret from Jeb, of course. We were already divorced at the time, but still in constant contact because of the two boys and the alimony payments he was always trying to stiff me on. I kept my mouth shut and encouraged Eddie to do the same, but when Eddie turned fourteen, he had a boyfriend, and he wasn't shy about it at all. I mean, he knew not to bring him around his father or even to act 'gay' around him." She made a face. "That probably sounds terrible, but Eddie does act the part sometimes. He plays it up. Fine. Wouldn't bother me except for the possibility of his father finding out, so I tried to encourage him to tone it down. He wouldn't do it unless he was around his father. But eventually, word got back to Jeb. You know how these things work in small towns."

I nodded. I did indeed.

"Jeb lost it. I mean, he *really* lost it. He showed up at my place, demanding to see Eddie. I thought he was going to kill him, so I told Eddie to lock his door. Jeb broke it down. I called the police, but Jeb called them too. He told them not to come. Can you believe that? He told them not to come and they didn't."

I could believe it. If I had my timeline correct, this would have all happened under the last sheriff, a man named Doug Patterson, a man who'd found himself quickly and easily corrupted by Walsh's influence.

"The only good thing that came out of me calling the police was it calmed Jeb down a little. When he went back to Eddie's room, he just ranted and raved. He told him being gay was a myth, that it was my fault for babying him too much. He said he'd fix it. And then he left."

"So he sent him to a reform school with a bunch of other boys? Did he really think that would fix him?"

"You're not serious, are you?"

"What?"

She shook her head but didn't explain. We'd come to a sharp rise in the road, and she dropped the Volvo into second gear. A small ramshackle building with a crooked sign hanging out in the front window lay at the end of a dirt drive. The sign said *Open, Come on in.*

"What's this?"

"A place Jeb used to bring me when we were dating. After the divorce, I started coming here again. It's quiet and the beer is cold." She looked over at me. "You do like beer, right?"

I nodded, once again amazed by all the hidden places there were in Coulee County. For such a small area, it was brimming with secret places, like a cabin you find in the woods whose cellar opens up into a cavernous and subterranean world. It was one of the only places I could think of where a man could lose himself and still be within ten miles of everything else.

She parked, and I held the broken screen door for her as we went in. The place had plank wooden floors and wooden siding covered with old paintings of fishermen and hunters in cheap plastic frames. A small bar jutted out from one wall and had room for exactly three stools, two of which were occupied. One man sat, nursing a nearly empty glass of beer. He was somewhere north of sixty, I guessed. His skin was thick with wrinkles and his jowls were heavy, giving him the appearance of a man tortured by his own age. Two seats over sat a young slip of a man dressed in a dark suit at least a size too large. His blond hair was slicked back, revealing large blue eyes framed by red cheeks. He looked too young to be drinking, but he had a can of Miller Lite sitting in front of him, and when he saw me looking at him, he picked it up and drank half of it, his eyes never leaving mine.

The bartender was an obese, middle-aged man who didn't bother to look up from his magazine as he said, "Cans are two-fifty, bottles three. A glass is extra."

Eleanor looked at me. "Can or bottle? Glass or no glass?"

"Can, no glass," I said, and reached for my wallet.

"It's on me," she said. "Sit down somewhere. Maybe near the back?"

I found the table closest to the restroom in back. Of the three men in the bar, only the youngest seemed interested in us, and his interest seemed confined to me. He continued to give me what I could only call challenging looks as I settled in.

I ignored him and tried to think through what Eleanor had told me in the car. Had Jeb's reaction to Eddie's sexuality driven Eddie to act out in some way, landing him at the Harden School? Or maybe Jeb had used the school as a way to hide his son, to send him away so he wouldn't be an embarrassment. My bet was on this second option.

Eleanor returned with two cans of cheap Mexican beer. "It's my favorite," she said. "Drinks like cold water but packs a little punch. Nothing better on a hot day."

I thanked her, and we both opened the beers and drank deeply. I was aware that the young man at the bar was still eyeing me aggressively. What was it with young males, so many of them always looking for a fight? I couldn't help but wonder how he'd react if I stopped ignoring his intensely aggressive gapes and stood up, walked right over to him, and looked him in the eye.

Instead, I turned to Eleanor. "Neat place."

She lifted her can. "The beer's always cold, and I like the memories. I suppose it's strange to treasure memories with a man I can't stand now."

"I don't think it's so strange," I said.

"I figured you'd be a nice guy," she said, and I thought from the look in her eyes that maybe the alcohol was already getting to her.

"Why's that?"

"Simple. Jeb hated you so much. It got to the point he'd become so twisted that he loved evil and hated good. The worst part of it was that in his own mind, he believed it was the other way around."

"Most men tend to believe they are working toward the good. It's human nature. Some men just have the capacity to fool themselves more than others."

"I thought that too, at first. But not anymore. He's not fooling himself. His eyes are wide open. He knows what he's doing and he likes it. That's the very definition of evil, if you ask me."

I couldn't disagree with that either but wondered why we were spending so much time on Jeb. "I want to go back to Edward," I said. "You seemed surprised a moment ago at my description of the school. What was that about?"

She gave me an odd look. "What do you think the Harden School is?"

I shrugged. "Reform school. A place where they try to straighten bad boys out, I guess."

"That's what it used to be. But then Jeb changed it."

"Excuse me?"

Well, Jeb didn't change it single-handedly, but he did help fund the change. The school was losing money in the late 1990s. Apparently, there weren't as many 'bad' boys. Or something. Whatever the reason, it was going under, and Harden came to Jeb with an idea. Change the mission of the school."

"Why would he come to Jeb?"

"They've been friends for years. And, more importantly, he knew if he could get Jeb on board, everything would go more smoothly."

"Okay, so what was the new mission?"

"Reparative therapy."

"What's that?"

"Conversion therapy. The Harden School specializes in converting gay boys. Trying to make them straight."

I drank the rest of my beer and put the empty can down on the table gently. Conversion therapy? I'd heard of such places, but they'd always seemed far away in states like Kansas or Arizona, not right here in Coulee County. But the more I thought about it, the more I realized I shouldn't have been surprised. Coulee County was, in many ways, the ideal spot for something like this.

"So, Dr. Blevins—"

"He's the therapist, the man they brought in to fix these kids. And because of his reputation, which is somehow good, people keep sending their boys there, and the school is now making a lot of money. And I do mean a lot."

"So . . ." I said, trying to piece it together. "You said Jeb helped change the mission of the school. So he loaned them money?"

"That's right."

"And now that the school is successful, I assume he's getting repaid several times over?"

"That would be my guess. Is there anything you can do to help Eddie?"

"Maybe. Tell me more."

I had to force myself to focus as she began to talk. The problem was my mind kept going back to Joe. Maybe I'd finally stumbled upon the connection. One line from the letter that was lodged in my memory told me I was right: "The authorities believe in the same tenets we do, tenets as old as time and as unshakable."

Joe had been a former student at the Harden School. And if my instincts were correct, he'd been a former student with a story to tell.

19

"At first, I told myself it wouldn't last. That they would see they couldn't break Eddie. I swear I don't know where he got it from, but Eddie is tough, and he's determined, and he knows the difference between right and wrong. Ain't that something? A daddy like Jeb Walsh, and he *still* turns out to be a great kid."

I smiled. "Sometimes the apple *does* fall a long way from the tree."

"And sometimes it doesn't," she muttered. "Our other boy, Andy, is evidence enough of that."

"So what happened?" I asked. "Did they break him?"

She shook her head. "Not yet, but I swear they're determined to. There's only so much one person can take."

"Have you thought about going to child services?"

"I have. In fact, I spent nearly a month on the phone with them trying to get someone from their office to the school. The problem is they don't find me credible."

"Why not?"

"Jeb has spread lies about me being on drugs and spending time in a halfway house." She closed her eyes and kept her face still, as if she were trying to endure a great pain. "The drugs are a lie. I did have a breakdown earlier this year, but it was over Eddie. It wasn't a halfway house. I simply checked myself into a psychiatric care center. They put me on some medication. I'm doing better. But nobody ever wants to hear that part. All they hear is Jeb telling them in that 'aw-shucks, I'm just a simple country boy' voice he's fucking mastered how his wife went crazy and his youngest child is at reform school because she wasn't a good parent and let him run wild."

"I'm sorry."

She waved me off. "I should be apologizing to you for the way he treated you. I'm not even married to him anymore, and I got an earful about what kind of a special liberal snowflake you were."

I shrugged. "If being a snowflake means taking care of others, I'm fine with it."

"Exactly. My thoughts as well."

I glanced over at the kid at the bar in the bad suit. He was still darting glances this way. None of them were friendly.

"About three months ago, Eddie called me. They get to make one call a month. Can you imagine that? One call every month? Hardened criminals get more than that. He'd told me before how he and another boy had hit it off. They were friends, but I knew by him saying friends, he meant they were thinking about being more than that. A month or so later, he called and said they were 'dating.' What that meant at a place like that, I have no idea. But I was happy for him. I just told him to stay out of trouble. I told him there was no way he could let anybody find out. I wanted to tell him to stop immediately, but I hadn't heard him sound so happy in months. I couldn't bear to do it."

I didn't like where this was going. I felt myself getting tense just listening to her talk now, and the next time I glanced over at the kid, he was glaring at me with a kind of naked hatred that made me want to punch him in the face. It was one of my flaws. Injustice made me angry. Anger made me violent. I was working on it.

"So, the last time he called—this was three months ago, in March, maybe early April—he was in tears. It took a while for him to tell me what was bothering him because he was crying so much. When he finally got it out, I was stunned. 'Mama,' he said, 'they killed him.' I just started crying right there on the phone with him."

"Wait," I said. "His boyfriend was murdered?"

She shrugged. "He's dead. The school claims he committed suicide. There's a waterfall behind the campus. They call it—"

The screen door swung open. I turned and saw two men enter. The Hill Brothers. As interested as I was in Eleanor Walsh's story, I couldn't focus on her words. Instead, I sat transfixed as the two men approached the bar, both of them crowding around the kid who had been looking for a fight. Neither man acknowledged him as the taller one leaned against the bar and said something to the fat bartender, still slumped in his chair. The bartender's face changed when he saw the brothers, and he pulled out two bottles of beer, twisting off the caps before passing them over. No money exchanged hands as the two boys took the bottles and scanned the small, hot room. The long-haired brother lifted his bottle and touched it to the side of his hairy face. As he did, his shirt rode up to reveal a scarred midsection and the top of a pearl-handled revolver protruding from the waistband of his blue jeans.

Their eyes never stopped, never rested, flitting around the room like there might be an attacker lying in wait among us and they'd need to be ready. They still stood too close to the young man in the suit, and his anger had shifted away from me toward them.

I turned back to Eleanor. "Hold that thought," I said softly. "I want to see this."

The Hill Brothers had finally given the kid some space, as one of them stepped toward the door and the other one settled in against the far wall. It seemed odd to see them like this, still at last, their ceaseless motion finally stopped. Whenever I'd seen them before, they had always been on the move, and their long, dogged strides had become almost a part of their character. Now I saw a different side of them. Now their attitude was somewhere between *fuck this place* and *we're going to stay for a while.*

Just when I was about to turn back to Eleanor, the kid said something under his breath. When no one reacted to his words, he said it louder. "Assholes come in like they own the place."

Neither Hill Brother acknowledged him. Instead their eyes went from their beer bottles to the windows, back to me and Eleanor at our table, an endless cycle, like each stop was a note in a song with its own curious tempo.

"Hey," the kid said, looking at the taller Hill Brother, the one with the bowl cut. "I'm talking to you."

Bowl Cut looked at the kid briefly before setting his beer bottle on a table and pulling out a pouch of tobacco. He reached into the pouch for a huge hunk of dark leaves and stuffed it down deep into his jowls. He sucked on it for a while, then opened the window behind him and leaned out to spit.

"Livingstone!" the kid cried. "You gonna let him chew tobacco in your place?"

Livingstone sat up in his chair behind the bar. "He ain't hurting me."

"And what about paying for them beers? I want a free beer too."

"They got a tab, Slim. You better just mind your own business."

Slim slammed his beer can on the bar, and for the first time I realized he wasn't *just* drunk, he was also filled with something else, something that had found him when he was a young man and stuck inside him, something that managed to drive him and move him and imprison him all at once. There were places in these mountains where they say bad water messed with young people's minds and made them insane, incapable of living in polite society. Maybe that explained what we were witnessing.

"I don't think it's right!" Slim said. He stood up and stepped in front of Bowl Cut, jabbing a finger in his face. "You need to take your uneducated asses back to the woods."

Bowl Cut lifted his beer bottle to his lips and drank it empty. Then, instead of putting it down on the table, he turned it over in his hand until he held the bottle by the throat, the fat end jutting out from his grasp like a baseball bat. With a sudden and terrifyingly efficient motion, he slammed it into Slim's head. The bottle exploded, glass flying all over the small room. A piece landed in my hair, and I brushed it out as I stood up, reaching for my .45. Two things happened before I could get it out. Slim hit the plank floor with a hollow thud. The other Hill Brother pulled out his pearl-handled .38 and aimed it at my face. His eyes settled on me, still for the first time. There was nothing in them. Nothing to make me think he wouldn't shoot me, nothing to make me think he'd care if I was dead or alive.

I raised my hands in the air.

"He's going to need a doctor," I said.

Bowl Cut's eyes fell on me before flitting to Livingstone. "Two more for the road," he said in a voice that might as well have been the mountains themselves speaking, it was so dusty and deep and unused.

Livingstone snapped to, grabbing four beers instead of the two Bowl Cut had asked for. "On the house," he said.

Bowl Cut dropped the neck of the broken bottle he was holding and scooped up the new beer bottles. He nodded to his brother, who lowered the gun. Bowl Cut stepped over Slim and followed his brother out the door. I went to the screen door and watched as they headed through the tiny dirt lot and into the trees, disappearing like shadows at dusk.

20

It took the paramedics so long to get to the hidden beer bar that Slim woke up, put some ice on the gash in his forehead, and elected to go home rather than wait any longer. He was a different man upon waking. Instead of looking at me with that burning gaze of hatred, his eyes were softer now, uncertain and filled with gratitude when I offered him a hand.

"Do you need a ride?" Eleanor said.

"No, ma'am. I'll be all right. I been hit harder than that before," he said, some of his former bluster returning. He straightened his cheap tie, which had now turned red with his blood, and walked on rubbery legs toward the exit. He paused just before opening the screen door. "Who were them boys?"

I shook my head and deferred to the bartender, Livingstone.

Livingstone opened his big meaty hands to the roof. "They come in every now and again. I learned a long time back to just let them have their way. Give 'em a wide berth. Seems to be best."

"Well, goddamn, next time I'd appreciate a warning," Slim said. "I still can't see straight and my head feels like it's got glass stuck up inside it."

"You need to see a doctor," I said.

He was fully back to himself now. He glared at me. "Fuck you, old man. I wouldn't never take advice from a man such as you that let a lady buy his beer."

I laughed. What else was there to do?

Slim snarled at me and walked out, letting the screen door smack the doorframe and echo away into the deep heat of the midafternoon.

*   *   *

I asked Livingstone what else he knew about the brothers.

"Not much," he said. "They usually come in with this woman. Don't know her name, but she doesn't really fit them."

"What do you mean, *fit* them?"

"I don't know. She seems educated, maybe. Smart. It's almost like they're her hired bodyguards."

"Can you describe this woman?"

"She's about your age." He glanced at Eleanor. "She's . . ."

"Go on."

"A looker. Turns heads."

"Hair color?"

"Varies. She's always dying it."

"Height?"

"Maybe five six. Average, I'd say. But when she wears that red dress . . ." He shook his head and then remembered Eleanor again. "Sorry, El."

"It's fine. I think I've seen her before too. She's hard to miss."

"So, do you have any idea where she's from, what she does for a living?"

He shook his head. "You run a little out-of-the-way place like this for your livelihood and you learn not to ask too many questions and forget all the rumors you hear. Like I said, she seems to be with them brothers, so I go out of my way to mind my own business. Keep everybody happy, you know? Them boys don't function too well in polite society. It's a damn lucky thing they didn't just kill Slim." He glanced at Eleanor. "I apologize you had to see that, El."

"It's okay. I'm not going to stop coming. You know I love this place, Ralph."

He nodded and looked at me. "You're the one who lost sheriff, right?"

"Yeah," I said. "That's me."

He pulled out two more cans of Mexican lager. "These are on me. One for the lady because she had to witness that, and one for you, sir, for having the guts to run against her asshole of an ex-husband."

I thanked him and briefly considered correcting his statement. I hadn't run against Walsh. I'd run against Preston Argent. But what was the point? In some ways his statement was actually more truthful. I really *had* been running against Walsh and his political machine. Argent was just the tool Walsh used to tighten his already viselike grip on the county.

"You know," he went on. "I can't think of a single person who voted for that Argent fellow. You ever think of investigating the election results?"

I shook my head. "I think that would be an uphill battle, but I do appreciate your vote."

"Enjoy the beers," he said. "And I apologize for all of that stuff."

"Not your fault," I said. "Might help if you could get some police presence up here."

"I called them," he said. "But I ain't holding my breath."

"Shit," I said, looking at Eleanor. "We better boogie."

"Yeah. If Argent does come, he'll be on the phone to Jeb as soon as he sees my car."

We took the beers with us and headed for her Volvo. She drove fast so as to get off the small dirt road before we had a chance to meet Argent or one of his deputies coming the other way.

Once we made it to the main road, I popped open the beers and handed her one. "Here's to the one good thing about Preston Argent being sheriff. You can get away with damn near anything."

She bumped her can against mine, and we drove out toward the county line. The sides of the road were lined with trees and sometimes old filling stations in various stages of decay. Other times burned-out houses flew past us like memories a person once held and then forgot. Eventually all was clear and there was only flat land and old fencing, dragged down by time and gravity, spindles of barbed wire disentangled and dead beneath a sun whose power seemed eternal.

"You were telling me about the boy who died," I said. "What was his name?"

"Weston Reynolds. He was seventeen. They say he snuck out of the dorms, or whatever you call them, one night and made his way to the waterfall that edges up against the school property. There's a rock there the boys tell stories about. They say he climbed up on top of it and flung himself off into the river below."

"But you don't believe it?" I asked.

She shook her head. "I don't. I'm not saying it *couldn't* have happened. Sure, it's possible. Eddie doesn't think so, of course. He swears Weston would never do anything like that. He says they killed him because they couldn't change him. A lot of the boys, according to Eddie, pretend to be straight so they can get out. Makes sense. I even encouraged Eddie to do it, but he won't. He says it would be disrespectful to Weston's memory to do that. Can you believe it? I mean, I don't believe in genetics anymore. There's no way that boy is Jeb Walsh's son."

I was less shocked about the whims of genetics than she was. People had long wondered how I could be my father's son. Except, in most scenarios, I was the one who'd been born wrong and he was the one who was innately good. What a screwed-up world we tried to navigate. No wonder it was so hard.

"So, you went to Harden about this?" I asked.

"Multiple times. I demanded to know what had happened. He said the police had looked into it and determined it was suicide. End of story. Except it wasn't the end for me. I wanted to know if they'd driven him to it. Eddie told me there was a rumor they made some of the boys have sex with some woman."

"What?"

"That's right. It was like a test. There's some woman they know that meets the boys out by the waterfall to, you know . . . have sex with them. According to Eddie, it was Weston's turn to meet her. He didn't want to go, but if you didn't show up, they'd make life really hard on you. So he went. He never came back. Of course, Harden and Blevins deny all of this, and Jeb does too. They say it's just the boys making up stories." She shook her head and looked for all the world like she wanted to cry.

"Take it easy," I said. "I'm going to help you."

"That's the thing," she said. "You can't help. No one can help. Now that Argent is sheriff, he told me the next time I called the school about anything, he'd have me arrested for harassment. He said things would get harder on Eddie, too. What can you do when there's no law willing to help you?"

It was a good question, just one of the many I didn't have a satisfactory answer for.

"We'll figure something out," I said.

She sighed. "And until then?" she asked.

"Stay in touch with Eddie and keep your distance from your ex-husband."

She gave me a look that suggested she'd been hoping for more from me. I resisted telling her that it was okay. I knew exactly what it felt like to expect more from Earl Marcus than he'd ever been able to deliver.

21

Later that evening, I pulled out the letter I'd found on Joe again and laid it open on the kitchen table. Goose lay under my feet as I reread it. My eyes continued to be drawn to the greeting. The name Joe was so common as to almost be useless, but maybe if I could combine it with another search term . . .

I opened up my phone's search app and typed *Joe, Missing, Georgia.*

I got nothing. Frustrated, I tried again, this time typing *Joe, Missing, Tennessee.*

Again nothing. I repeated this process with South Carolina, Florida, and finally Alabama before I got a hit.

I cursed out loud when I saw the headline of the third result under the *news* tab. *Local Reporter Seeks Answers in Partner's Sudden Disappearance.*

According to the article, his full name was Joseph Timmons. He was an intern at the *Birmingham News* and had been dating Chip Thompkins, a full-time staff writer, for nearly two years. Thompkins said Timmons had been "distant" in the days and weeks before his disappearance. When Chip has pressed him on what was going on, Joe had told him he was trying to "tie up some loose ends" from his abusive childhood. Chip didn't elaborate on what kind of abuse this had been, and the article wasn't clear about whether Chip even knew the extent or nature of the abuse.

The article went on to say that police had been investigating the disappearance but at this time didn't have any leads.

Shit.

I took a deep breath, walked to the refrigerator, and reached for a bottle of whiskey from the top. I opened it and drank deeply straight from the bottle. I felt a little better, though nothing would ever be able to make me feel good about what I was about to do.

*   *   *

Half a bottle later, I called the number listed on Chip Thompkins's staff profile at the *Birmingham News*. I was pretty drunk, but years of practice being drunk had made me a pro at handling my business while intoxicated.

I didn't really think he'd pick up his office phone at eight o'clock in the evening anyway, but he not only picked up but barely let it ring before answering eagerly.

"*Birmingham News*, Chip Thompkins."

"I've got some news on Joe," I said.

"Who is this?"

"A friend. Name is Earl Marcus, and I'm a private investigator over in Georgia. Coulee County."

"Never heard of it."

"Well, Joe has."

"Do you know where Joe is?"

"No," I said, "but I know he's in some trouble."

He was silent. I waited, not sure what I was doing or what to expect.

"Have you contacted the authorities?"

"See, that's the problem. The authorities here . . . well, it's complicated."

"Explain to me exactly what you know about Joe."

This was the part I hadn't prepared for, the part that surely would have prevented me from calling if I hadn't had so much bourbon. I needed to make something up and fast.

"Do you know about the Harden School?"

"The private school Joe attended for a few years? Sure."

"But do you know what they did there?"

Chip was silent. "What are you talking about? I'm assuming they did school there."

"Not exactly. The Harden School was—well, *is*—a gay conversion clinic."

"What?"

Now came the hard part, the part where I was just running on instinct. "He didn't want to tell you because he knew you'd freak out. He didn't want you to worry." This sounded plausible to me.

"How do you know these things?"

"He came to me for help. He laid out the whole thing—well, at least as much as he knew at the time. He wanted to hire me. We had a conversation a couple of days back, but now he's dropped off the radar. I can't find him. Have you heard from him?"

"No. It's been over a week. Do you think someone has hurt him?"

I knew it was best to hedge here. On the one hand, I needed Chip to feel optimistic or he'd likely go to the authorities himself. On the other hand, I wanted to start preparing him for the sad truth that Joe was already dead.

"I don't know, but based on what he told me, I have some concerns."

"Have you called the police?"

"No. See, that was the other thing that Joe understood. The police here in Coulee County . . . they're useless. No, that's not even true. They're worse than useless. They're crooked."

"Why should I believe you?"

"Because Joe came to me. He trusted me. You should too."

"I don't even know who you are."

"I understand. I'm going to ask you to trust me, though. The Harden School is backed by one of the wealthiest and most powerful men in the South. He has every reason to protect the school's interests. He's also in bed with the sheriff in Coulee County. He's a very dangerous man. Maybe you've heard of him."

"I doubt it. I don't even keep up with small-town politics in Alabama, much less Georgia."

"His name is Jeb Walsh," I said.

There was silence from Chip's end. I knew why, of course. The reason was simple: you'd have to have been living under a rock to not know who Jeb Walsh was. He was followed closely by the mainstream media, as his racial bigotry was well known. He'd also been closely tied to the alt-right over the last few years, and really just about everyone had an opinion on his divisive politics.

"You're kidding," he said after a moment.

"No. Jeb's son is at the school now. And I have reason to believe Jeb himself may have orchestrated a student's apparent suicide."

He was silent again.

"Chip?"

"I want to go to the police."

"I understand, but that's not going to end well for anyone if you do. I actually reached out for two reasons. One was to see if you'd heard from Joe. I'm deeply worried about him at this point. Two, I think there's a way you can help me."

"Me?"

"Yeah, I need someone who'd be willing to write all of this up. An exposé centered on the school and Jeb Walsh."

More silence. I could tell he was overwhelmed. How could he not be?

"Chip? I want you to know I'm going to figure out what happened to Joe. If he's alive, I'm going to . . ." I winced at the deceit. "I'm going to find him."

"I need some time to think about all of this. Can I call you back?"

"Sure." I gave him my number and tried to convince him how important it was not to go to the authorities. "I've been dealing with Walsh a long time now. He'll win if we try to do it through the police. He's too powerful." I hesitated before saying the next part. The words felt horrible coming out of my mouth. "Powerful enough to hurt Joe. Powerful enough to hurt all of us, which is why we have to operate on the down-low. Do you understand?"

"I'll call you back," he said.

22

There are some quirks of personality that seem ingrained in our very natures, and no matter how much we might try to get rid of them, they continue to influence our decisions and desires. I knew a man in Charlotte who constantly fought against his innate irritation with people.

"Earl," he told me once, "you're one of the only people I can hang around."

"Why's that?" I asked him.

"Because you don't get on my nerves."

"Was that why you divorced your wife?" I asked him, half joking.

His response was deadly serious. "Actually it was. I loved her too. But I couldn't stand to be in the same room with her because everything she did irritated me."

I always remembered that friend when I thought about how we are prisoners to whims of our genetic makeup.

The flaws that came along with Earl Marcus were simple but had proved nearly impossible for me to overcome. I sought to self-medicate, and I used two methods: alcohol and women. After talking to Eleanor Walsh and lying to Chip Thompkins, I felt the need to self-medicate like I hadn't felt in a very long time.

I couldn't explain why my conversation with Eleanor Walsh had affected me like it had. For some reason, it made me feel helpless and hurt all at once. Maybe a part of me identified with Eddie Walsh. Not being gay, but just being a disappointment in the eyes of a father who cast a long shadow. That was the part of me that hurt. The part that felt helpless was born out of the realization that I'd tangled with Walsh before and failed. What made me think it would be any different this time?

I also identified with Joe. He'd obviously seen an injustice and tried to do something about it. There was always a risk in doing the right thing. And, too often, it felt like the risks outweighed the benefits.

Not to mention that doing the right thing was a far cry from what I'd done in that phone call with Chip.

All of that made me feel pretty miserable, so I just kept drinking. I was pretty drunk and close to calling it a day when I heard the knock on the door. Who knows how it would have all turned out without that knock? Maybe Mary and I would still be together.

No, that's bullshit. Nothing conspired against me. Except maybe some deep part of myself that was afraid of the future, afraid that deep down inside me I wasn't worthy of anything, especially not happiness.

When I heard the knock, I glanced at the clock over the oven. Nine thirty. Not late exactly, but late enough for me to wonder who it could be. Not Ronnie, that was for sure. I would have heard his truck coming from miles away. Rufus? Maybe, but he tended to burst in rather than knock.

I rose from the table on unsteady legs. The knocking came again. "Coming," I said, and then realized I might want to grab my gun just in case.

Goose was growling low as I went to my bedroom for my .45. The knocking continued.

I tucked the pistol in my waistband and went to the window. Daphne was standing outside my door in a bathrobe.

I felt . . . how can I describe this? Something like a tingle of anticipation, almost pleasure, but also pain. I felt as if I were stranded alone, on a precipice, waiting for the slightest breeze to knock me over and into the longest fall of my life, a fall that would only end when I hit bottom.

The bottom.

Once I'd believed I'd been there, but that was before I learned the truth of human misery. There is no actual bottom; there is only the falling. The landing never comes, which might seem like a blessing, but it most definitely was not.

Don't open the door. The voice was loud and strong and clear. My own voice, the voice of experience and reason. I ignored it. I almost always ignored it.

Maybe if Mary hadn't been gone, if I hadn't just lied to Chip Thompkins, I wouldn't have opened the door. But I still had a chance, right? I was just opening a door. I'd done nothing wrong.

Yet.

Daphne stood there in nothing but a bathrobe that barely covered her ass. She was grinning as the smoke from her cigarette drifted up toward my face.

"I need another favor," she said.

I just stared at her legs. There was so much of them, so little of her bathrobe.

"I need to borrow your shower. Would you mind?"

Tell her no.

"Wouldn't mind at all."

She beamed at me as she came in, not bothering to put out her cigarette. I didn't care. "Thank you so much. I promise to be quick."

"Uh, do you need a towel or something?"

"A towel would be perfect."

"Just a sec." I left her standing in the kitchen and went to my bedroom, thinking how this was a bad idea. Just all the way around. A bad, bad idea.

Only if you make it bad, Earl.

That was true. Finally, the voice of reason. I'd go outside. Simple enough. I'd go outside while she showered and avoid all temptation.

I grabbed the cleanest towel I could find, taking a minute to sniff it in a few places just to be sure. It smelled all right.

When I returned to the kitchen, she was standing beside the table, her back to me, giving me a glimpse of upper thigh that was enough to make my legs go weak.

"Here you go," I said, my voice deeper than normal, like a croak, really. Shit, I was acting like a damned teenager.

She jumped, and her bathrobe fell open. And when it fell open, it fell off. Completely off. So fast it was as if her body had repelled it.

One hand went to her breasts and the other to her crotch. Neither hand did a very good job of covering anything. And she didn't seem particularly embarrassed about it in any case.

I turned away. Hell, it took me long enough.

"Oh, I am so sorry," she said.

"Nope," I said. "I'm sorry. I'll just wait outside."

The trouble with waiting outside was I had to go past her to get to the door. A quick glance told me she hadn't even picked the damn robe up yet, much less put it on.

"This is awkward," I said. "I've got a girlfriend." I kept my eyes on my refrigerator. A photo of Mary and me we'd taken in downtown Riley this spring stared back at me.

"You keep saying that, but I can't help but wonder what kind of girlfriend would leave her man alone so much."

"Listen," I said. "I think this was a bad i—"

I stopped. Her breath was on my shoulder, the heat of her right next to me. I turned slightly, and her mouth was on mine. I smelled the nicotine and the cinnamon and something fruity. Her lips brushed mine. My tongue found hers, and she sucked at it while hers swam free in my mouth, and her body pressed firm and urgently against me.

Later, I'd tell myself I was overwhelmed, surprised, not fully aware of the situation, but I knew that was bullshit. The truth was much uglier: I'd been fully cognizant. Fully aware. I'd just decided to enjoy it. I'd decided to not think about anything and let the moment be the moment. It was to be a moment that would haunt me for the rest of my life.

* * *

When it ended, I felt like something had crawled inside me and clamped down on my heart. It hurt with every beat. At any moment, I felt like it would stop beating forever. Daphne lay next to me, panting.

"That was good," she said.

I nodded, not feeling anything now but the fist around my heart, the slow thudding of my lifeblood being squeezed into a future that was beginning to feel a lot like oblivion.

23

What followed after leaving the church was a series of events so dismal and damning, Rufus lost all faith in anything other than himself. It started only a few months after he left. He'd been living on the east side of the county, in a little town called Millerville, where he worked on the farm of a man named Paul Bushman. Bushman liked Rufus's work ethic, the way he was quiet and kept to himself, the way he didn't seem to make friends with the others, always keeping his distance. Now it seemed a strange thing for a man to like about another one, but time had made Rufus reconsider if Bushman really *liked* anything about him at all or if instead he saw an opportunity in Rufus's diffidence. Whatever the reason, he asked Rufus to stay after work for dinner one evening. Rufus halfway wondered if he was being set up with some girl and worried about being underdressed, with only his work clothes on as he sat down at the dinner table.

When an older man showed up and Mrs. Bushman served them and quickly exited the room, Rufus understood there was something different happening.

"Rufus Gribble," Bushman said, "meet Randy Harden."

Harden was a tall, lean man with broad shoulders and a mustache that made him seem like he'd come from a different time and place, perhaps 1850s California or 1920s Alabama. He sat erect at the table, as if he'd had some military training. Rufus could not guess his age, not with any accuracy, anyway.

Harden didn't waste any time. He shoveled his food down, making no small talk, something Rufus would soon learn the man disdained. Rufus had disdained small talk too, and it caused him to take an immediate liking to the man.

When he finished eating, Harden pushed his plate away and leaned back. "Tell Rachel that was an excellent meal," he said.

"Well, tell her yourself, Randy. She'll be back in with coffee."

He held up his hand. "I'll have to pass on that. No coffee for me after four. It's something new I'm trying. Coffee—a cup or two—in the morning is good for a man. Too much is not. It's like whiskey or anything else. Moderation. You're the one that walked out of the Holy Flame, ain't you?"

It took Rufus a moment to realize Harden was speaking to him. It was something he'd get used to over the next year or so—the man's random shifting from subject to subject, from one person to another.

"Yes, sir."

"I always thought RJ Marcus was a fraud, myself. I like a man who can see straight. Clear. That's in short supply these days. You agree?"

Rufus told him he supposed he did.

"Well, Bush tells me you're a good worker, and I was already impressed by what you done. I want you to come work for me." He put both palms flat on the table and looked at Rufus. The door from the kitchen swung open, and Mrs. Bushman stood there with three cups of coffee on a tray. Harden raised a hand. "Not now."

Mrs. Bushman nodded and slipped back into the kitchen, letting the door close behind her.

He was staring at Rufus intently, waiting. Rufus wasn't sure he'd ever met a man like this, and even though he found himself put off by the man's intense gaze and abrupt manner, he was also curious about the man's confidence. What kind of man dismissed RJ Marcus like that?

A hundred times over the next year, Rufus wished he hadn't wilted under the man's gaze. A hundred times he wished he'd told him he'd think about it or at least asked a few questions. Hell, he didn't even know what kind of work Harden needed done. But none of that seemed to matter in the moment. The truth was, everything that had come after his moment of redemption in the church had felt like a letdown. He was lost, looking for something to cling to. For his entire life, the preacher had been the source of all rules, structure, and knowledge in his life. Often he still heard the preacher's booming voice echoing in the back of his mind: *If the Bible doesn't say it, I don't believe it!* Rufus had gotten over that hurdle; he'd decided the preacher's interpretation of the Bible wasn't true, but he'd yet to find anything to replace it. He was looking for a philosophy to live by, not just one to reject.

"Okay," he said.

Harden grinned, a crooked thing, filled with broken light. "You living in the bunkhouse?"

Rufus nodded. He'd been staying a half mile away on Bushman's property with some of the other field hands.

"Pack your bags tonight. I'll be by at first light. First day of school starts tomorrow. Afterwards, you'll be staying with the Duncans."

"The Duncans?"

"That's right. My sister's family. Three daughters. Maybe you'll find a wife."

Harden stood, and he and Bushman shook hands.

"Excuse me, what am I to do? I mean what kind of work?"

"You're an educator now, boy."

An educator. He liked the sound of that. On the walk through the woods to the bunkhouse that evening, beneath a moon so large and bright and a sky so clear, Rufus wondered what he would teach. Courage, he thought. I'll teach them how to be brave.

In the end, though, he didn't teach anything, and he was the only one who learned.

* * *

Harden picked him up early the next morning like he'd promised. The sun wasn't even up when Rufus heard the banging on the bunkhouse door. Rufus rose, zombielike, and pulled on his blue jeans and boots. He walked to the door, and Harden was standing there awash in the headlights of an old pickup truck.

"You overslept," Harden said. "Not a good start. These boys we're going to be working with need role models. They need to see a young man who has his shit together." He put his hand on Rufus's shoulder and guided him to the truck. A door opened and a man climbed out, holding the front seat up so Rufus could climb into the back.

"This here is Steve Deloach," Harden said. "He's second in charge behind me. He's what they call 'old school.' Grinds his coffee fresh every morning and still rolls his own cigarettes. Treats the kids like kids and expects them to treat him like an adult. You would do well to follow his lead."

Deloach—who had a cigarette in the corner of his mouth now—nodded at Rufus. "You don't remember me?"

"Why should I?"

"I remember you. I went to the Holy Flame before me and my wife split up. Loved that church. Brother RJ is the kind of preacher the world needs more of."

Rufus wondered at that moment if this was a mistake. Did he want to get involved with a man who believed RJ Marcus was a good preacher? But then Harden patted him on the back and said, "It's one of the few things me and Steve disagree on. I already told you I thought Marcus was so full of himself he was about to pop."

Rufus slid into the back. A girl not much younger than him was seated on the far side. She appeared sleepy but nodded at Rufus. "And that's Harry," Harden said, opening the driver's side door and climbing in.

"Harry?" Rufus said.

"Harriet Duncan," the young woman said. She reached for Rufus's hand. "Ignore Uncle Randy. He likes to make jokes."

Harden pulled the truck out through the trees and onto the little logging road that led to Highway 52. "Harry there used to sneak into my brother-in-law's closet and get into his dress clothes and cologne when she was a girl and play like she was a man. I come over one time and saw her dressed up like a firefighter. Now what kind of young lady wants to be a firefighter?"

Harriet shook her head and turned her face hard to the window. Rufus saw her sad countenance reflected in the dark glass.

Deloach laughed. "She's got to learn to appreciate men is all. Could learn a thing or two from her twin sister, Savanna. That's the one you'll be interested in, Rufus."

"Her daddy's a little worried Harry here might be one of those lesbians. Asked me and Steve to work with her a little bit. I've been studying up on how to deal with these kinds of situations," Harden said. He seemed pleased with himself, as if he had agreed to donate to an exceedingly worthwhile charity.

Rufus had no idea how to respond. He'd grown up in a community that felt the same way about gay people, but he'd never—to his knowledge—actually met one before, and now that he was sitting in the back seat with Harriet, he wasn't sure how he felt. Before, gay people had seemed slightly unreal, more of an idea than a reality. Now that he was actually sharing the back seat with someone who might be gay, he felt conflicted.

"What about your daddy, Rufus? He still around?"

"No," Rufus said, but wouldn't Deloach know this already?

"Right. I remember now. He didn't take kindly to Bible teaching. Left you and your mama hard up. I always thought only a snake could do such a thing to his family."

"Let him be," Harden said.

"What?" Deloach shot back, his voice high-pitched and whiny.

"Just let him settle in before you start riding him, all right? His daddy probably left that church because the preacher thought he had the inside track to Christ Jesus himself."

Deloach was silent then, and they drove through the dark morning. In the east, Rufus saw first light. It scoured the sky in a rust-colored halo, spreading up and out with a slow resolution Rufus found himself envying. It would simply be what it was, when it was. No need to rush, no need to worry, no need for anything except the pure heat it generated.

"You planning on being a teacher?" Harriet said.

"Excuse me?" Rufus felt jolted out of a dream. The thoughts he'd had seemed silly, hard to even put into context suddenly.

"I figured you might want to be a teacher because of working with kids. Last fellow we had was like that."

"Oh Lord," Harden said. "Not Bryan again."

Harriet closed her eyes and sank into the dark corner of the truck.

"Me and Randy think Harriet had a thing for Bryan."

"Bryan?" Rufus said.

"He was the man who worked before you. Good man. But we think Harriet there had a crush on him."

"I didn't," she said.

"Well, I reckon that's true, Steve. Considering she only likes other girls."

Rufus looked at Harriet again. If you believed Brother RJ, the "gays" were perverted abominations, bent on turning good Christians to the devil. Harriet seemed normal. Nice, even. Maybe they were just giving her a hard time, anyway. Maybe it was all a joke.

"I wish I had my teaching degree," Harriet said. "I'd be gone in a heartbeat."

"A teaching degree is the last thing you need," Harden said. "Hanging around all those women. Hell, you need to spend some time around men, get an appreciation for what they can do for you. You need to stick with us until you start seeing the world a little straighter, okay?"

Deloach giggled a little and turned in his seat. "You don't like dicks do you, Rufus?"

"No, sir."

"You sure about that?"

"Yes, sir."

"What about assholes?"

Rufus shook his head.

"One more question. Now, I know you was brought up right in RJ's church, but I gotta ask anyway. What do you think about a woman or a man who would lay with his own kind?"

Rufus felt his face go red. He didn't know what to think. He didn't *think* anything. He more *felt* it. It was fear, maybe pity. It was a feeling of despair because the whole thing made him sort of sick to his stomach, not so much just the physical thing, but the hate that seemed to come with it, the sense that such a man—or woman—would be forever doomed to walk outside the circle of fellowship Rufus himself so badly craved. But he didn't feel like he could say all of this to Deloach, at least not in a way that would make sense. Instead, he said, "I'm not sure what I think."

"Oh shit," Deloach said. "Not another one."

Harden slowed the truck. "I'll make it simple, okay, Rufus?"

"Okay?"

"Would you want your son to be gay?"

"No, sir."

"Would you want anyone to be gay?"

"No, sir."

"And would you associate with someone who is gay?"

Rufus glanced over at Harriet, her eyes open wide now. They were staring at him, expectant. Maybe sad. Maybe a little hopeful.

He swallowed.

"Hey, Rufus?"

"Yeah."

"Answer the question."

"No, sir, I wouldn't want to associate with someone who's gay."

As soon as he said it, he dropped his head and didn't look over at Harriet for the rest of the trip.

24

You can fill in the rest.

When Daphne left, I got serious with the bottle. I quickly lost track of time as I attempted to numb my pain, just me and a night tormented by winged creatures fluttering through the trees, scratching and clawing. They were my sins, my past, all of me that was incomplete, now returned to haunt my present.

I picked up the phone to call Mary at least a dozen times before putting it down and grabbing the bottle instead. In my drunken state, I had a notion I should just tell her, and by telling her I would absolve myself, and by absolving myself, Mary would understand and absolve me too. It had been a mistake, a single moment of weakness. It didn't change my love for her, and it wouldn't change her love for me either.

Except, even in my drunken state, I didn't really believe that.

I wasn't exactly sure when or why it occurred to me to go to Backslide Gap. In truth it was an insidious thought, one that seemed to flash within my consciousness like lightning, sudden and fierce, but unlike lightning, the thought lingered.

Drinking more made the night go soft around me, like a quilt or a warm bath. Bourbon became some arcane form of magic, Goose my familiar, me the wizard of regret.

I thought again of Backslide Gap. Perhaps it was an indictment of my parents that the one place we played as kids more than any other was the suspension bridge that stretched across it. According my father, an authority on the area and the ceaseless folklore of its geography, Backslide Gap had earned its name when a couple of boys went feral and gave up on their

Christian upbringing, choosing to embrace their natural, sinful selves. Maybe that was what drew us to the area. Here was the physical embodiment of what we were all a little too afraid to do, to become. The implicit danger of the place only added to the appeal. We could, in our imaginary games, feel those two boys' fall from grace without actually possessing the courage to slide away ourselves.

The old bridge was made of ropes and wires and wooden planks that had nearly rotted away from years of rain and neglect. Not content with simply wading out onto the unstable bridge, we soon developed a way to take even greater risks. By carefully twisting the ropes around one ankle, we could dangle headfirst out into the open space, hands free and empty, supported by only the tension of the twisted rope. It was ridiculously foolish, but at one time or another, we all tried it, tempting fate, daring God to take us or to save us, wishing perhaps for some sign from that great "Provider" our parents were so obsessed with. After hanging for a while and realizing no sign was forthcoming, we'd begin what came to be known as the "swing." Waving our arms to create some momentum, we'd eventually get our torso and hips involved until our bodies swung back and forth like one of those pendulums that never stops. When the momentum was finally great enough, we would be able to put our other foot on one of the wooden planks and reach for the opposite rope with both hands, stopping the momentum and snapping our trapped foot free. It was a neat trick, and for the life of me, I couldn't remember who'd been brave enough to do it for the first time, but by the time I was thirteen, it was a rite of passage, something that both my brother, Lester, and I did far too often. When I thought about it now, I wondered if it was possible we'd had some kind of death wish. It certainly would seem that way, but as I grew older and more reflective, I was more inclined to believe it was just the opposite. I believed we had a "life" wish, that it was only in experiencing such vicarious rebellion that we could truly know the potential of living a life without constraints or boundaries.

Maybe when Daddy had promised I'd die there one day, he'd just been speaking in metaphor after all. Maybe I didn't believe him because I didn't know how to hear him. The fall was just my life, the flames weren't a literal hell but something worse, something I carried inside me, something I'd swallowed a long time ago and never been able to expel.

Goose jumped into the back of my truck, and I slid into the cab with two bottles in hand. There was a good chance I'd pass out before I even made it there, or maybe I'd run my truck off into some gully somewhere, sleep it off, wake up the next day and still be in hell. Or maybe I'd make it to the gap, maybe I'd hang off into the breach one last time, feeling possibility, feeling something. And after that . . . well, I wasn't sure there would be an after that, and this knowledge did not bother me.

The truth was, I couldn't imagine going on without Mary. She was my ledge, the one person I'd been able to grab to break the long fall.

I turned the key and the truck roared to life. Goose whined from the truck bed. I slid the gearshift into drive and started down the hill into a night lit by the fires of my past.

* * *

Backslide Gap was unchanged. All these years, it had just been sleeping, waiting for my return. The suspension bridge still held resolutely to the two sides of the gap, like a Band-Aid stretched across a wound it would never quite cover.

I ignored Goose's whining and climbed out of the truck, leaving the keys inside. I walked on unsteady feet toward the bridge. It rocked gently, blown by the softest breeze. The light was fading, and what was left of it felt strained and empty somehow. Dusk had come again. It was always dusk here. Goose followed me, still whining, and somehow in my drunkenness I wondered at the loyalty and wisdom of dogs. He knew what was happening, and he'd be damned if he let me do it alone. I stopped and patted his head, murmuring that he was a good boy, but he couldn't go out on the bridge with me.

He wagged his tail and whined again when I let go of him and turned to the bridge. I held the bottle of Wild Turkey in my left hand and used my right to grip the old double-braided rope that served as a guardrail on the bridge. I stepped forward into the gap and felt the bridge already trying to twist around on me. I was keenly aware of the imbalance of my body and the breeze blowing up out of the gorge. When I reached the middle of the suspension bridge, night had come, and I was as blind as Rufus. I knelt on shaky legs, put the bottle down on the wooden planks of the bridge, and stared off into the dark void.

I was afraid. Not of jumping and crushing my body against the bottom of the gap, but of falling and realizing too late that there was no bottom, that a man's fall could last forever and redemption was just a whisper on a long forgotten wind.

I would let God decide. I let go of the rope and lay down on the wooden planks. Without holding on, any disturbance could cause me to pitch over the side and fall. I folded my hands across my chest and looked up at the stars, waiting for something—anything—to happen.

Part Two
The Nets

25

After Rufus and Ronnie baptized me in Ghost Creek, I felt numb, which I supposed was better than feeling miserable. I mostly sat in my front yard with Ronnie and drank coffee, trying hard not to think about anything, especially not Mary. After bringing me home, Rufus had made Ronnie collect all the hard stuff I had in my kitchen, and together they'd poured every bottle out onto the grass. I didn't try to stop them.

He also told Ronnie to get my keys from the truck and give them to him. That sort of pissed me off, but Rufus didn't care.

I was sitting in the front yard, my headache finally cleared, when he told me he'd be back to check on me in a couple of days.

"Call Mary," he said. "You have to tell her."

I'd already decided to do just that. Maybe some folks would have been able to get themselves together, psych themselves up, and just move forward, letting the mistakes of the past remain there. But not me. I had to call her. Not doing so would have caused me to explode.

"Yeah," I said. "I get that."

Rufus cocked his head in surprise. "You do?"

"Yeah. I do. Just give me a chance to figure out what I'm going to say."

"I'll check back in a couple of days. We need to talk."

"About what?"

Ronnie cleared his throat and stood. "Sorry, buddy." He walked into the house.

"What's going on?" I asked.

"Your boy Ronnie told me you were wrapped up with something at that school."

"And?"

"We need to talk about that."

"You know something about the Harden School?"

"I do."

"Well, what are you waiting for? Talk."

He nodded. "Two days. Get your shit together. Handle the thing with Mary. Then we'll talk."

I started to argue, but he was already walking away, toward the trees. I shook my head and turned back to face the ridge. It was a gorgeous day, cooler than it had any right to be. It should have felt good sitting outside, being sober, having a second chance. I just wasn't sure I wanted one without Mary.

* * *

As it turned out, I never had to call her. She showed up the next day. Daphne had been by once, the night before, and I'd done my best to get rid of her. She seemed disappointed but eventually left. When Mary's car pulled up, Ronnie was sitting with me in the yard.

"Oh shit," he said when he saw the rental car. "Want me to leave?"

"Maybe just go in the house," I said.

He nodded and waited long enough for her to get out of the car. "Hey, Mary," he said, solemnly.

"Hi, Ronnie!" she chirped, obviously in good spirits. "How are you?"

"Making it," he said, and slipped on inside, leaving me alone with Mary and the slow death I knew was about to begin.

I'd tried to convince myself not to tell her, but the secret guilt of what I'd done would only linger inside me and taint every moment we had together from now on. Only by coming clean did I have any hope of moving on, of living something like the life I'd hoped for. But would she be able to forgive and forget?

"Earl? What's wrong?"

I stood up. I could feel my face breaking, the tears starting to fall.

She came to me, wrapping me up in her arms. God, it felt good. She was so beautiful, so perfect, and yet I'd been willing to throw away perfection for the smallest salve. I needed salvation, not a salve.

Now I had neither.

I told her about the man in my yard first. I told her about lying to his boyfriend, about the school and what I suspected was going on there. I wasn't too proud to offer this context before I told her the rest.

She held me tightly as I talked, whispering in my ear. It felt like I was a young boy again and my mother was holding me, telling me it was going to be okay. It felt like I was young enough again to believe her. Is there any secret more potent in this world than the secret that all men seek to find the comfort of their mothers again? The comfort of their warmth and reassuring voice against a cold and viscerally aggressive world, against the evil inside their own hearts? My own mother had been so far from perfect, but she'd at least given me comfort and love. Even in my state of utter brokenness, I was thankful for that.

"There's something else," I said, and immediately I believed I felt Mary's arms begin to loosen around me. She felt my betrayal already.

By the time I'd finished speaking, she'd let go of me completely. The message was clear. I was on my own now. Alone again like I'd been for so much of my life.

I looked at her, tears in my eyes. "I'm sorry."

"I don't know what to say."

"I don't either."

"Who was she?"

"Nobody. Just some woman. She hit me at a moment of weakness."

"Your whole life is a moment of weakness, Earl. What was her name?"

"It doesn't matter."

"Goddamn it, Earl. Tell me her name."

"Daphne. I don't know her last name. She moved in on the next ridge down. She's been back. I turned her down."

"Am I supposed to be impressed by that?"

"No."

She stepped back, toward the car. "I came all this way for this? Well, maybe it was worth it. At least I know the deal now. You're willing to throw away everything for some floozy willing to suck your dick."

"Mary," I said, reaching for her. The look in her eyes made me stop short.

"I would prefer you never to touch me again."

"Mary . . ."

"How in the hell did you think this would go? Did you really think you could fuck some woman while I was in Nevada taking care of my family, casually mention it to me, and have me forgive you? You probably imagined we'd be having makeup sex about right now, didn't you?"

"No."

"Of course you did. You're Earl Marcus. The put-upon, the scarred, the abused kid who just can't get over his daddy issues. I'll bet you've already forgiven yourself, haven't you. Probably blamed it on your daddy."

"Mary, please."

"Oh, goddamn it, Earl. You blew it this time. You really blew it."

"Come inside. I'll send Ronnie home. We can try to start over."

"You've been starting over your whole life, Earl. Seems like just a few years ago you were 'starting over.' You were going to make a new life. You had me to help you. Now you don't. Good luck pulling yourself out of this one with nobody."

"Please, think this over."

"Nothing to think about."

"If you leave me, I'll be nothing."

"See, that's what you don't understand, Earl. I *have* to leave you. You've spent your whole life looking for somebody to save you. I don't want to be anybody's savior. Maybe you've got more in common with your father than you thought."

"Please," I said. "I'll be okay if you just stay. Without you . . ." I shook my head. "I'm not anything. I'm a failure."

"Once I might have argued with you," she said. "But not anymore."

26

Ronnie refused to let me self-medicate. There was no bourbon, and when I told him I was going to walk down the mountain and buy some, he took my wallet and threw it onto the roof of my house, and I didn't have the energy to climb up there to retrieve it.

I went to bed, slept for six hours, and rose again to find Rufus sitting out in the yard with Ronnie. Twilight again. Eternal dusk, the light lingering, mingling with the invading dark.

Rufus nodded when he heard me coming outside. He still looked about as bad as I felt. The hollows in his face more pronounced, his lips dry and chapped red, his hair standing up in a cowlick that made me think he hadn't showered in days.

"We need to talk, Earl."

"About what?"

"About the Harden School."

"Okay, but so you know, I'm off that case."

"Since when?"

"Since all this. You do know Mary left me, don't you?"

Rufus was silent, but I didn't like the expression on his face. Somehow, it seemed to say he was not at all surprised. But there was more, wasn't there? He was angry.

"You got something you want to say about that?"

"Yep," he said. "I sure do."

"Say it then."

"I can't believe it took her so damned long."

"What's that supposed to mean?" Normally I would have punched him over that, but I felt like a hollow man, devoid of energy, just skin and bones holding in hot air, no blood to boil, no muscle to fight.

"It means a woman like that shouldn't have ever had to hold your old ass up."

His words hurt me, but I could hardly argue with him. He was right. Somehow I'd lost my way. Or maybe I'd never found my way. It was as if after escaping the clutches of my father and his suffocating religion, I'd been lost to the wilderness of the real world. I'd believed I'd vanquished my father when I'd watched him fall to his death three years earlier, but now I saw that his legacy still haunted me, that it dogged my every step and had imprinted itself upon my very DNA. Damnation had found me, just as he'd predicted.

"Did you come just to ridicule me?" I asked.

"Nope. I came because Ronnie told me you've been looking into the Harden School. I've got some experience with that place."

"I told you. I'm done with that."

"The hell you are." Rufus stood up. I could tell he was trying to locate me.

"I'm right here. You going to punch me?"

"Maybe."

"Bring it on."

Ronnie cleared his throat. "Why don't you two boys have a beer?"

"I'd rather take a drive," Rufus said.

"We can do that too," Ronnie said.

"Not you. Just me and Earl."

"Fine," I said. "Let's got for a ride. You can tell me about how much of a loser I am."

"Nope," Rufus muttered. "Going to tell you about how much of a loser I am."

I hadn't expected that. Suddenly, the mood changed. The sun seemed to lift a little bit, to return a piece of the afternoon that had been lost. The idea of Rufus making mistakes seemed to offer me some hope. He had his shit together now. He was clearly a force for good in the world. Wasn't he?

* * *

Once in my truck, I asked him where we were headed.

"Down the mountain," he said. "Over toward the east side of the county. There's a farm there. It's where I went after I left the church."

"You never told me how you left the church," I said.

He smiled. It was a genuine smile this time, the kind that could lift any amount of weight from the past, the kind that broke his face in half before reassembling it into something that was pure joy.

"That was a good moment for me," he said. "A real good moment."

"I can relate. The day I left the church is still the best moment of my life."

"Yep." He laughed again. "Ain't we something. A couple of old timers reminiscing about the good old days when we stuck it to the man. I thought I was well on my way then."

"What do you mean, well on your way?"

"Just that I had life by the balls, that I'd stood up to fucking RJ Marcus, and that meant I could stand up to anybody. But that was a mistake. You don't never take life by the balls. It's always got you." He shook his head. "And the world never runs out of men like RJ Marcus. Evil men, you know?"

I did. "Jeb Walsh?" I offered.

"That's right, but sometimes the most evil men are the ones who know they've got something you want, and they know how to lord it over you just so."

"Well, Daddy did that," I said.

"Sure. I guess so. With you, especially. With me, it was more about my mother, about not wanting to disappoint her."

"Understood. So where are we going exactly?"

"Stay on Fifty-Two. It's a ways. Just relax and listen, okay?"

I tried my best. Truthfully, relaxing just wasn't an option. Distraction, though, had potential. I focused on trying to think about what Rufus might be able to show me. If it could have any bearing on the mystery of the Harden School. What had happened to the kid, Weston? Was I going to give up on that? And what about Joe? Didn't I owe it to him to finish what he'd started?

Not to mention that giving up on things had never been my style. I'd made a career out of solving mysteries, and I'd done it mostly through sheer force of will. Determination had been a far greater ally in getting to the bottom of problems than talent, smarts, or even luck. I tended to just wear a case down, or short of that, I simply used brute force to break it wide open.

I could still do that much, couldn't I? If the answer was no, I wasn't sure who I was anymore.

There was also Eddie Walsh and the other boys at the school to think about. They were depending on me. I couldn't forget Rufus either. Despite his current easygoing manner, I still felt like something was off with him. There was certainly a physical element to my feeling: he was gaunter than usual. Pale and haggard, the way I used to look in the mirror after three or four nights without sleeping because of a case. It was probably how I looked now, too. I wasn't sure because I hadn't been able to bring myself to look in the mirror since I had cheated on Mary.

"When I left the church, I went by my house for my fishing pole and twenty dollars I'd stashed away. Didn't know where I was going. I just started walking. Went to Ghost Creek, followed it up the mountain to its source, and slept there for three or four days, fishing the creek. From there, I moved down the backside of the mountain, into the valley. I'd stop when I found a pretty spot by some water and make camp for a few days. I must have wasted a few months doing this very thing until I woke up one night shaking from the freezing cold. I knew I had to at least head to town to buy some warm clothes, but I was pretty sure I didn't want to go into Riley, because that was where I was most likely to see somebody from the Holy Flame, so I made the hike east toward Brethren. At the time, Brethren wasn't much more than a couple of churches, a post office, and a gas station that also doubled as a general store. It was there I bought a winter coat and some new shoes. I didn't have enough cash to pay for it, so the owner agreed to let me work it off on his farm. Wasn't long before I'd paid the jacket off, and he hired me full-time. He let me sleep in a bunkhouse with the other workers. I was fairly happy. Didn't even know it at the time."

I was on 52 now and was afraid Rufus had forgotten that I didn't know where to go. "Do I just go all the way to Brethren?" I asked.

"Not quite. There's a farm right before the town where I want you to stop. Where are we now?"

"Just passed Jessamine's, about to hit downtown."

He nodded. "Still got about ten minutes before you need to start looking for it."

"So how did you hook up with Harden?" I asked.

"I'm getting there," he said. "Do me a favor?"

"What?"

"Pretend you are a patient man. It's important for me to tell it my way."

"Sure."

He nodded and cleared his throat. He adjusted his shades on his nose and continued. He told me about being happy at the farm, about rising early and having his coffee in the morning dark before beginning work in the field each day. He told me about the work he did on the farm, and how the landowner said he wanted Rufus to come to dinner at his house one evening.

"I sort of expected he might be about to set me up with his daughter. Only problem was he didn't have one." Rufus grinned at the memory. "No, he wasn't setting me up with no girl. That came later. He was setting me up for another job, a bigger and better one."

He went on to tell me how Harden came by for dinner, how he talked to Rufus directly, man to man, and how Rufus found himself wanting to please the man despite his misgivings. I understood. It was exactly the way I'd always felt around my father.

"Next thing I knew," he said. "I was working at the school. They said I was a counselor, which meant I didn't get paid much, but Harden believed I would be a teacher there one day, so I believed it too." He fell silent, as if silently debating the internal logic of believing anything Harden had told him.

"Was Dr. Blevins at the school then?"

"Who?"

"His name is Timothy Blevins. He's supposed to be some kind of conversion therapist."

"You mean like converting kids from gay to straight?"

"Yeah."

"Jesus. It's gotten worse, then."

"Worse?"

"Where are we now?" he asked, ignoring my question.

I told him we'd passed through the city and into the open part of the county, where the valley spread out briefly before turning to hills again, and finally mountains.

"There's an old farmhouse on the right. Be on the lookout for it and pull over when you get there."

I saw it a few minutes later. It was old, all right. Years of neglect had taken their toll on what might once have been a nice place. There was certainly plenty of land and two large barns, both of which were in better shape than the house.

I pulled off the road into the overgrown grass of what passed for the front yard.

"We're here," I said.

"What's it look like?"

I described it to him, taking time to mention the way the woods behind the house seemed to be creeping toward the structure and would likely overtake it in the next year or two if somebody didn't cut them back. I mentioned the wild roses that bloomed in an irregular pattern on one side of the house and the broken shutter hanging crookedly from a second-floor window.

"What about the barns?" he asked.

"There's two. The bigger one is red, but it looks like it's faded to almost pink. It needs a new roof. The door's open."

"And the other one?"

"More of a shed, I guess. It's in decent shape. Not pretty to look at, but it would probably keep you dry in a rainstorm."

"I want to go in."

"The house?"

"No, the barn. The smaller one."

"Why?"

He sighed. "This is where I lived when I worked at the school. Harden arranged for me to stay with his sister, a woman named Leah Duncan. Her husband was a farmer in the area, and one of the all-time assholes you would ever want to meet. They lived here with their three children. All girls. The youngest two were twins. They were both a little younger than me. One was named Harriet and the other was Savanna."

"You lived in the barn?"

"That's right. The smaller one."

I killed the engine and we got out of the truck. I grabbed Rufus's shoulder and turned him until he was facing the smaller barn. "Straight line," I said. "Clear path."

He nodded. "Sorry about earlier."

"Why? You were right. Just because I'm miserable doesn't mean I shouldn't help others."

"I'm miserable too," he said.

"I'm beginning to sense that. Do you want to elaborate?"

"I think I'm about to." And that was all he said on the matter until we came to the smaller barn.

"Is it locked?" he asked.

"We'll find out." I reached for the sliding doors and pulled one of them to the right. It felt stuck. Not locked. "Give me a hand," I said, and guided him to the door. Together we pulled it open. When it slid back, a sweet, old smell rushed out as if it had been waiting to escape all of these years. Without waiting on me, Rufus stepped inside the old structure. He stood there in the half-light, inhaling deeply. His face changed then. Instead of gaunt and worried, it expanded with something like light. But the light was soon dimmed by deep furrows forming above his black shades. Lines of sorrow, I thought as he began to speak.

27

"The twins were interesting to me from the very start. They had a connection I'd always missed. Hell, I didn't have any family besides my mother, and by then, I didn't even have her. I had no friends. I'd never had a girlfriend. Savanna. That was her name. The sister. Of the two, she was the more confident one. She seemed to be the dominant one in their relationship. She was always sure of herself, never timid, but she still made you feel important, like she genuinely cared about you. It's how she treated everyone." He shook his head. "Crazy, but it was the sexiest damned thing I'd ever seen. If only it had been real."

He laughed and turned his head up to the rafters, breathing in the scent of the place again. "Of course, she could have acted just about any old way and still been sexy to me. I was hard up by that point for female companionship, and she was like sex on wheels. Long, blonde hair, legs that never ended, a smile that lit me up. When she showed it, I felt like somebody was flipping a switch inside me. My pecker went hard as a two-by-four and nearly as straight. You ever been just sick for a girl before, Earl? When she's all you can think about, all you can see? That was me."

I started to explain that's how it was with Mary, but I never got the words out. It wouldn't have sounded believable after the shit I'd just pulled. He pressed on, his head still turned toward the rafters. I followed what his eyes would have been looking at if he'd still had the use of them, and I saw there was a loft up above. No way to access it, but it was there nonetheless, and I wondered if it had been the site of some memorable romantic encounter with Savanna.

"The only thing that kept Savanna from being absolutely perfect in my mind was something I couldn't put my finger on. These days I know more and could name it. Then, there just seemed to be something slightly off about her. I didn't see it as much as Harriet complained about her. According to Harriet, she was cruel. Everyone thought they were close, with a connection only twins could have, but in reality Harriet just wanted to get away from her. I suppose that should have been enough to warn me, but I was so smitten by her beauty, by the attention she eventually began to show me. You know . . ." He trailed off, shaking his head. His eyes seemed filled with light, and for a moment it was as if he almost focused on me directly. He did that sometimes. He could figure out just where a person was in the room and track them. It was uncanny, but almost everything about Rufus was uncanny. This whole story he was revealing seemed almost the stuff of legend. I looked around, trying to imagine him sleeping in this old barn, tried to imagine a young Rufus freed from the shackles of my father's church, couldn't quite do it.

"You know," he went on. "The way she fooled me isn't too unlike the way your father fooled me, the way Randy Harden and Steve Deloach fooled me. They all saw my weakness. I was a kid who knew nothing about the world, a kid who needed human connection, but even more I needed to understand how everything worked, how it fit together. I found out all right."

"You okay?"

"Sure. It's just . . . Well, shit. You know enough about regret to understand what it can do to you. It's like carrying around that old millstone. Just gets a little heavier year after year."

"Yeah," I said. I did know about regret. I just didn't know about *his* regret yet. I hoped I would soon, though. I felt myself getting a little impatient with his slow and detailed delivery.

His eyes seemed to find me again. For a moment, I believed he really saw me, or maybe I was the one seeing him for the first time. It was a different Rufus. Not the old blind version that liked whiskey and politics and being a grumpy wiseass, and not the choirboy version of himself he'd been when I'd known him a long time ago before his blindness, before he'd decided to be an atheist and, ironically, a better Christian than just about anybody I'd ever known. This was none of those men, and yet somehow all of them. This was the Rufus who'd broken free of the shackles of one institution only to find himself ensnared in something even more powerful. It was a Rufus I'd never known, one who'd had to create himself out of nothing, just as we all had to do. That he'd become such an original, such a distinct vision of himself, was a testament to his doggedness, his creativity, and his "fuck all" individualism. The version I was seeing of him now was not these things, not exactly, but rather the *potentiality* of these things. The version I was seeing now was timeless, at once a ghost from his past and a man haunted by his present and all possible iterations of his future.

"Before I go any further, I need to tell you about the waterfall near the school. Have you ever seen it?"

"Yeah. When I went out there with Ronnie a few weeks ago. It's beautiful."

He grinned, seeming to remember it in his mind's eye. "That it is. Do you know why they call it Two Indian Falls?"

"No, but I'm going to guess two Indian lovers jumped to their deaths there."

"Wrong. The story says two boys challenged each other to see who could jump across to the other side."

I remembered standing on the large rock a few weeks ago. So much had changed in that short time. I'd learned about Eddie Walsh and Weston Reynolds. I'd lied to the significant other of the man I buried. Jesus, just thinking of Joe's face did something to me I couldn't put into words. It felt like I'd been betrayed, except somehow I was the one who'd betrayed myself. That was exactly what I'd done when I'd slept with Daphne. I'd betrayed Mary and myself. And now Mary was gone. And here I was standing in the past with Rufus. I thought about the chasm near the falls. I thought about what a monumental leap it would be to make it to the other side. Monumental, but maybe not impossible.

"The story says a bunch of people gathered to watch, and the two boys both prepared to jump. One of the reasons the boys wanted to do it was no one had ever been to the other side before. There's no way to get to it short of being dropped in by a helicopter. The Native Americans believed there were answers to be found on the other side. Answers to great mysteries. Who knows where. Maybe they were written on the inside of some caves that could only be accessed by jumping across."

It was a tantalizing thought, but if acted upon, I couldn't imagine it *not* ending in disaster.

"The boys waited until dusk, because there was some legend that said there was a wind at sunset that would blow you across. The first boy paced off his steps, standing on the broad flat rock that juts out into the falls. He backed up as far as he could and sprinted toward the gap. They say he jumped too high, and not far enough. His hand slid down the rocks on the other side as he tried to gain purchase, and he fell to his death. The crowd went wild with grief. They begged the other boy not to try it, pleading with him, telling him how foolish it was and that the first boy was faster and stronger and he hadn't even come close. But the story says the second boy was honorable, that he told the gathered crowd he had no choice but to honor his friend's death by keeping his word.

"'To not jump,' he said, 'would be to die.'

"An old woman broke free from the crowd and clambered up on the rock beside him. She blessed him, saying a prayer to the spirt of the wind, that it might guide him across. Then they helped her down, and the second Indian was alone.

"He paced off his steps, once and then again, and then held his hand up, checking the wind. There was none. He waited for some time for the wind to return, but it seemed as if it had given up for the evening. The sun was gone; a darkness held sway over the land. The story says a quarter moon hung in the sky, but its light was dimmed by heavy clouds.

"Soon, the people began to chant his name, which was Yaholo. It means 'one who shouts,' because Yaholo was known for his great cry while playing with the other children. Over and over, they chanted it, and all the while the sun disappeared over the horizon.

"When he finally made the leap, no one could see. They heard his signature yell as he flew over the waterfall, and some claimed to see a dark shape make it across to the other side. Several people described seeing him in midair, and others swore he fell through the dark gap between the bluffs. No one could agree. The next day, when the men went down to the bottom of the waterfall, all they found was the body of the first Indian. They never found the second one."

28

Rufus heard the story of the second Indian told so many times in his first few weeks at the Harden School, he found himself wondering how it had even survived so long, and how much of it was true. Every time he heard it, some of the details were different, but the essential mystery of the story stayed the same: no one knew whether the second Indian had lived or died. And that left the possibility of making the leap across an open question. Not only an open question, but a tantalizing one.

Rufus quickly discovered all the kids in the school had one thing in common: they wanted out. The campus was surrounded by a twelve-foot-tall fence with electric barbed wire along the base and the top, making it a dangerous proposition to attempt to climb over or dig under. The gates were under constant surveillance, and rumors of cameras were prevalent. All visitors were closely monitored and vetted. That left the falls, and the single flat rock that was open to any and all of the more adventurous teens to stand on and to wonder if perhaps one of them had what it took to make the leap. As far as what the students believed about the second Indian, they were mostly split. Some swore he'd made it, while others expressed a well-earned cynicism.

For his own part, Rufus wasn't so sure. He often spent his break time standing on the rock, trying to judge the leap. He was of two minds about it. First, it was probably technically possible for a man in good shape, with good timing, and a good wind to make the leap. Second, anyone who tried it would almost surely be committing suicide. There were just too many factors that had to go exactly right.

It was on one of these breaks, standing there, thinking about the Indians flying across in the dusk so many years ago, that Harriet approached him.

Rufus wasn't completely sure where she fit in at the school. She was about three or four years older than any of the other students and did not attend classes. In fact, he rarely saw her but had heard that Harden and Deloach forced her into special sessions daily in which they counseled her in how to be heterosexual. The rumors about these sessions were as wild and varied as the rumors about the falls. She was servicing both men. She wasn't a lesbian at all but instead a nymphomaniac who simply had to have it every day. Others claimed they were making her watch videos of women performing cunnilingus while making her bathe in the blood of dead pigs as a means of aversion therapy. The less radical rumors held that she was simply being counseled on the error of her ways. Rufus tended to believe this last one, but he still didn't like it. He'd increasingly come to wonder why it was any of Harden's or Deloach's business if she was a lesbian or straight. Yet he lacked the courage of his convictions to do anything about it. Hell, he was still Harden's—and to a lesser extent, Deloach's—lapdog. He wasn't sure why he wanted to please the two men so much, but he did. Their praise seemed to fill up a hollow place inside him, much like the old preacher's had done before he saw the lies the man told, the deceit on which his whole ministry had been founded.

Since Rufus had arrived at the school a month or so earlier, he and Harriet had had minimal contact. Rufus was a classroom aide, which meant he was to help ride herd on the boys when they acted obnoxious during lessons. There were only two real teachers at the school—Deloach and an old man named Irvin. Deloach didn't need the help, but Rufus was told to go to his classes anyway to pick up tips about discipline. Irvin was close to eighty and going blind, so Rufus found himself very busy in that classroom. It was a shame, because when the kids did settle down enough to listen to Irvin, he was a hell of a teacher. Looking back on it now, Rufus realized being in Irvin's classroom, listening to him teach history, was one of the only good things to come out of his time at the Harden School. At least one of the only good things that lasted. But neither room allowed Rufus to see Harriet, because she wasn't permitted to attend classes with the boys.

"Hey," Rufus said when Harriet climbed onto the rock.

She was upset. That much was clear. She didn't speak; instead she just sat down on the edge of the rock, her feet dangling off over the river.

"You doing okay?" Rufus asked.

"I hate this place."

"Well, maybe you won't have to stay too long."

"Yeah, I could leave tomorrow if I wanted to. Today even."

Rufus couldn't tell if she was kidding or not. He sat down beside Harriet. "What are you talking about?"

"It's real simple. My father wants me to be something I'm not. If I want to leave, all I have to do is go to Harden and tell him his stupid therapy worked, that I'm normal. I'm a real woman. I want to go clean the kitchen and keep my mouth shut except when it's time to stuff a dick in it."

Rufus winced. He'd never heard a woman speak like this.

"Well," she said. "What do you have to say to that?"

He shrugged. "I don't think that's how you become a real woman."

"Okay, then tell me. How do you do it?"

He shook his head, confused. "I think you already are a real woman, Harriet."

She opened her mouth, as if to argue with him, and then his words seemed to register. "Oh. Well . . . damn right I am," she snarled. "But don't tell that to my father or to Harden. You know Harden has all of the boys calling me Harry, right? They all do it. How is that supposed to 'help' anyone. Not that I need any of their fucking help."

"Don't listen to them."

"That's easy to say, harder to do. It's all I hear. Besides, I'm not the one who needs the help."

"I'm sorry," Rufus said. He didn't know what else to say or do, so he just sat there, looking down at the river a hundred yards or more away. He could see the whitewater, moving fast over the rocks. It was moving on its own accord, oblivious to the whims of the foolish and inescapable human world.

"It's true, you know," she said after a time.

"What's true?"

"Are you stupid?"

Rufus flinched, a little hurt. He was trying to be a friend. And now he was stupid?

"I don't understand."

Harriet shook his head. "The only person that knows the truth about me is Savanna. Everyone else is just assuming the thing that makes it easiest to hurt me." She closed her eyes, as if the next part was especially painful. "I think this was her idea."

"Wait. Her idea? You mean to send you here?"

Harriet nodded, her eyes still closed. "It had to be. I mean, she was the only one I'd ever told. And I only told her because she figured it out. I thought if I explained it to her, she'd understand. But she didn't. Wasn't long after that everybody knew. My father was so pissed, I think he wanted to just get rid of me somehow. He wouldn't look at me for days, weeks, and then it was like he had an idea. But it wasn't his idea."

"You think it was Savanna's?"

"Yeah. I *know* it was."

"Why?"

"Because my father's an idiot. He doesn't think of ideas. Savanna, though . . ." She trailed off.

Rufus looked down at the river again, as if there would be some guidance there, some hint of how to navigate this new and treacherous territory. He saw the tiny rocks that had probably chewed up those two Indians so long ago. He didn't like hearing bad things about Savanna. As much as he felt Harriet had been mistreated, Savanna was . . . God, his mind went blank when he thought of her. She was so beautiful, everything Rufus had ever wanted but had never known.

"Savanna's a good person," he said quietly. He would believe that.

"That's what everybody says," Harriet replied.

"Maybe they say it because it's true."

Harriet ignored him and pushed on. "I need somebody I can be honest with."

"You can be honest with me."

"I'm trying to be."

"I don't understand," Rufus said again. And looking back on it, he saw he was a fool in so many different ways, that sitting there on the rock beside Harriet, he'd actually believed he had a better grasp on not just the situation but the *world* than she did. He actually believed she was just confused, not gay, that the whole thing was just the product of some obscure envy she felt for Savanna. But he'd been so wrong, so devastatingly wrong.

"I am a lesbian," Harriet said. "I'm gay. I like women."

"No," Rufus said. "Don't say that. You aren't those things."

She just looked at him. "You really don't get it, do you?"

"Get what?"

"I like women. I want to kiss them. To touch them the way you do."

Rufus shook his head. "You're confused."

"No. I'm not."

Rufus stood up. "I think you are." He wasn't being purposefully obstinate. The idea was so foreign to him then, so outrageous to his sensibilities, that he just slipped back into his past, toward the stuff he knew best, the lessons he'd learned at the Holy Flame under RJ Marcus. Even though he'd renounced all of those beliefs, his subconscious self, when faced with something he'd not had time to truly consider, still returned to those teachings.

That was the only way he could explain it to himself later.

"I'm not confused. Please, Rufus. Don't do this. I need somebody to accept me. I need to know I'm not alone here."

Rufus backed away. He felt weird, as if everything he knew about the world had been wrong. It was scary and he didn't like it. The world was just straightening itself out for him, and now this? It couldn't be happening.

"Look," Harriet said. "You don't have to understand it, okay? I just need a friend, okay?"

"I think maybe you're just jealous of Savanna." As soon as he said it, he realized it was the worst thing he could have said.

"I might as well jump," she said.

"What?"

"I'm thinking about jumping across."

"To the other side?"

"Why not? The Indian did it."

"That's just a story."

"And this is just life. Stories are truer than life."

"You don't believe that."

"Yes, I do."

"You'll never make it. You'll die."

"I'm already dying."

"No, you're alive. You're here, right now."

"You've got a lot to learn."

He sat down again. He reached for her hand and turned to face her. "Promise me you won't hurt yourself."

She met his eyes but said nothing.

"You can't die, okay?"

"Okay," she said.

At the time, he thought he'd gotten through to her. It was only later that he realized how much it had actually been the other way around.

29

A knock on the barn door interrupted Rufus's story.

He gasped, sucking his last word back in.

"Who's in there?" The voice was female.

Rufus raised a single index finger to his lips, gesturing for me to not say a word.

"I know you're in there. I see the damned truck at the road. I'm opening the door, and I've got a gun."

Shit. I turned to look for Rufus, but he was already gone, faded into the back corner of the barn.

The door swung open, and harsh light nearly blinded me. I stepped out into the sun and saw the woman did indeed have a gun. It was a shotgun, actually, and she had it aimed right at me. She squinted at me and motioned for me to step off to the side, away from the door.

"You alone?"

"Yeah."

"Don't lie to me."

"I'm not. Listen, could we go inside and talk for a minute? I'm a private investigator. I wanted to talk to you about someone who used to live here."

"My father lived here until he died ten years ago, and I have no desire to talk about him. Especially not to a man who doesn't know how to knock before he goes snooping around private property."

"Again, I apologize. I just . . . I didn't think you were home."

"Doesn't matter if I was home or not. This is my property. You got no right to be here."

"I apologize. Truly. Sometimes, in my line of work, it's easy to forget my manners." I reached back and pulled the door shut behind me. "Anyway, it's not your father I want to talk to you about. It's your sister."

She lowered the shotgun, nearly dropping it.

"Which sister?"

"Harriet."

"Harriet's dead."

There it was. The conclusion to Rufus's sad story. It wasn't too surprising. Rufus's face had told me that much. "That's what I want to talk to you about."

"It looks like you were here to snoop inside my barn."

I shook my head. "No, I just . . . I'm sorry. Like I said, I didn't think you were home. Could we possibly talk?"

She was silent for a moment before raising the gun again and aiming it at my head. "Sure, but I'm keeping this with me the whole time."

"Fair enough," I said and followed her up to the house.

* * *

Sometimes the seeds to the way a story will turn out are contained in the very beginning. That was what I had to assume with Harriet. I'd already learned she was dead. The next leap wasn't a big one: she'd tried to jump across the ravine and failed.

We sat in the den, her in a large rocking chair with the gun across her lap and me on the couch, right across from the fireplace. The mantel above the fireplace was covered in framed photographs. I was too far away to get a good look, but I assumed they were pictures of her family.

"Are you married, Ms. . . . ?"

"It's Duncan, and no, I've always been single. But I thought this was about my sister, not me?"

"Well, I'm getting to that. Sorry. Just trying to get oriented. One more question. Harriet had two sisters. . ."

"I'm Lyda, the eldest. Lord knows where Savanna is these days." She shook her head. "Frankly, I'm glad she's no longer in my life."

"Savanna? Not Harriet?"

"Of course. Harriet was a soul in pain, but she wouldn't hurt a fly."

"And Savanna would?"

"I have to say, Mr. Marcus, you are trying my patience more than a little. First, you don't have the common decency to knock, and now I have to ask myself what your real motives are. You said you wanted to talk about Harriet, not Savanna."

I studied her closely. Once she had certainly been attractive, but time had done a number on her. Her face was pitted and scarred, her eyes dull and washed free of almost all their green. She was older than I'd expected, too, or maybe that was an illusion brought on by the perils of a hard life.

And she was right. I had told her this was about Harriet, and it was. I needed to focus. I just couldn't help but be curious about Savanna. It was obvious Rufus had a thing for her. And based on the way Rufus had reacted when the knock came on the barn door, he must have believed she lived here. He hadn't had time to finish the story, but it was clear it must have ended badly. Love stories were like that. You always knew the ending. If it had ended well, they would still be together.

"Okay, let's talk about Harriet." I paused. The trouble was I didn't know exactly how to ask about Harriet. Her story was much more complex. "I'm investigating a death out at the Harden School, and I was hoping to find out about your sister's time there."

"You're talking about the kid who jumped recently?"

"That's right."

"Well, for starters, I think it's a lot like Harriet."

"Right, which is why I wanted to hear from you. How do you see the deaths as similar?"

"Harriet was gay. At one time, she wouldn't admit it to anyone, but most people who knew her understood it. She liked other girls. That's pretty much why my father sent her there. To make her straight. Paid his brother-in-law a lot of money to do it, too." She shook her head. "Sometimes humans are so stupid. I mean, the idea you can change someone from something they have no control over to begin with."

"And you think that's why she killed herself?" I said.

"Of course it's why. She wrote me letters. They were torturing her. Calling her names, telling her she was worthless. *Spitting* on her. Grown men spitting on a girl. And there was more too. Stuff she wouldn't even tell me in the letters. Stuff that gave her panic attacks to even think on. She never explained, but I feel certain it was sexual abuse."

"Do you still have these letters?"

"No. They were lost."

"How?"

"I feel like I'm being put on trial here. Do you not trust me, Mr. Marcus?"

"I apologize again. I'm just trying to gather all the relevant details."

"I don't see how me losing the letters is relevant. They're gone, lost in a fire a long time ago. My life hasn't been easy."

"I understand, but the letters are relevant because they could directly link her death to abuse. What gave you the sense she was being abused?"

"Harriet told me once that at the end of each day, a counselor would come into her room to 'test' her. She never went into details about what these tests were like, but I know there was one particular counselor who she dreaded more than others."

"What was his name?"

"Harriet never told me."

"That seems odd."

She shrugged. "Not really. I don't think it's odd at all to be reluctant to name names when you've been sexually abused."

"It's just a name. Surely—"

"Have you ever been sexually abused, Mr. Marcus?"

"No."

"Then you wouldn't really be an expert on this, would you?"

I shook my head. She was right. I was pushing too hard. No, it was more than that. I was being an asshole. My natural state these days, it seemed.

"Okay, so did the letters say what it was about this one counselor she dreaded?"

"His test methods, best I could tell."

"Go on."

"I think he might have forced Harriet to have sex with him or someone else."

"And you feel confident about this?"

She just stared at me, expressionless.

I tried again. "So, it's your belief that Harriet decided to jump because of the bullying and abuse she received at the Harden School?"

"I'm almost positive of it."

"Did you try to get the police involved at the time of her death?"

"I was shut up."

"How so?"

"My father. He didn't believe women should become involved with matters such as those."

I nodded. Not surprising. It was the same way my father had treated women—as if they had a narrowly defined role that began and ended with pleasing the men in their lives.

"Ms. Duncan, would you be willing to testify to what you are telling me in a court of law, or at least make a statement to the police?"

She was silent, obviously thinking over her options. She bit her lip, tearing a small piece of flesh from it with her teeth.

"The men you are dealing with will stop at nothing to protect their good names."

"Is that a yes or a no?"

"It's a no."

"Which men are we talking about? Harden? Blevins? Or maybe Deloach?"

"Deloach is dead. I don't know Blevins, nor do I care to."

"So, Harden then?"

She shook her head. "This is hard for me for a variety of reasons."

I leaned back in the chair, stretching my legs. I felt as if she was telling the truth. There was something guileless about her, as if she was both sad and surprised to be asked these questions, to be here now talking with me about something she'd obviously tried hard to put behind her.

"Can I give you a piece of advice, Mr. Marcus?"

"Of course."

"Next time you want to interview a woman about the past, make an appointment. Better yet, do a little research of your own. The Harden School is an institution that has survived tragedy after tragedy, not to mention many controversial situations that would have taken other schools down. You and I aren't going to be able to affect change there. If I thought we could, I'd throw caution to the wind and do whatever you asked me to, personal consequences be damned, but I don't believe we can change it. It's like trying to move a stone that weighs so much more than you do. The harder you work, the more likely it is you throw out your back. Why do that when you know you can't move the stone?"

"I'm here to help you," I said. "We can move it together."

"You're not as strong as you think," she said. "None of us is. Especially compared to her."

"To who?"

She gave me a look that suggested I was an idiot for not keeping up. "Savanna, of course."

"What does she have to do with Harriet's death?"

"I wish I knew."

"You're not making sense."

She shrugged. "The world doesn't make sense."

"Right," I said, "but it's our job to make sense of it."

She just looked at me as if I were a child, uninitiated into the ways of adulthood and the hidden forces at work in this world.

Maybe if I hadn't just come off the breakup with Mary and the binge-drinking episode that had nearly killed me, I would have pressed her, maybe I would have demanded she explain to me about Savanna, but instead I let it go, afraid that in doing so I would have to face the inevitability that she was right, that the world wasn't something that was ours to understand.

* * *

In the end, I felt like Rufus would be able to put my conversation with Lyda Duncan into context, and if he couldn't, he would at least be able to finish his story, and I'd be able to go from there. I thanked her and left her my card, pleading with her to call me if she came up with anything else more concrete. I wasn't very optimistic. You can always tell if someone is eager to work with you by how they react to your card. If they reach for it, that means they're interested. The ones who plan on throwing it away as soon as you leave usually let you just lay it on the table. It's as if they think touching it obligates them to use it in the future. She didn't touch it. Hell, she hardly even looked at it.

I figured Rufus would be in the truck and was more than a little surprised when he wasn't. I glanced around, thinking maybe he'd wandered past it, confused. *That* didn't sound like Rufus, but he was blind, for God's sake. Surely he had to make mistakes sometimes?

Maybe he was still in the barn? I didn't want to risk going back. If Lyda saw me snooping around there again, she'd certainly peg me for some kind of criminal or, at the very least, a nut job. I chuckled. Too late. I was pretty sure she already thought I was a nut job.

I headed for the barn again, moving quickly. Once inside, I called out his name.

No reply.

I looked up into the loft. He wasn't there.

I called his number, pretty sure he hadn't brought his phone. He never did. It rang several times before going to voice mail. I didn't leave a message.

I jogged to my truck and scanned the road. Nothing, just a shimmering haze in both directions.

Shit.

I drove slowly on my way home, keeping an eye out for him walking along the road, but I didn't see him. Could he already be home, back at the old church? Not likely. Feeling a little anxious, I reminded myself that Rufus was capable despite being blind. Hell, he might have decided to take a shortcut home instead of walking along the road. That actually made more sense. In some ways it was safer for Rufus to stay off the road, considering he couldn't see traffic.

By the time I reached Riley, I'd just about talked myself out of being too worried. What did I think had happened, after all? Rufus had gotten lost? That was laughable. Even blind, Rufus knew this area better than anyone. So, what then? Was I really going to consider the possibility he'd been picked up, taken away by someone? Nah. The truth was somewhere in between, I convinced myself. Rufus had thumbed a ride back to the old church on Ghost Mountain.

But when I pulled up to his place, I began to doubt my own logic. I checked inside the church and found it empty. I checked around the graveyard and the creek again but found no sign of him.

How was it possible for him to just vanish?

I wasn't sure, but I needed to talk it over with somebody. I glanced across the creek and saw Ronnie and his friends working on the studio. They'd framed the whole thing out now and were busy hanging sheetrock. It wasn't very large, but I figured it would be plenty big enough for them to practice and record. I couldn't help but feel my spirits lift a little looking at Ronnie's progress. Somehow, Ronnie seemed to be doing better than anyone these days, and it was just another one of life's inexplicable blind curves that you could never see coming no matter how careful you were, how hard you tried to be ready.

I took a deep breath and walked across the creek toward just about the steadiest influence I had left in the world.

30

It took a lot for Rufus to get disoriented. He liked to tell people he just knew where things were. He explained it this way: he'd tell people to think of the place they knew better than any other. He'd tell them to imagine being there with their eyes closed.

"Would you still know where you were?" he'd ask.

"Sure," they'd answer.

"Could you find the door?"

"Yeah."

"Of course you could, because you know the place. That's what it's like for me in these mountains. I just know them."

He wished he could see people's expressions when he told them this. He imagined they were either amazed or just disgusted because they thought him a liar. The comparison was patently ridiculous. A room was nothing like the mountains that made up the Fingers. A room was a few hundred square feet, while the Fingers were miles and miles of rough terrain, riddled with rocks and snakes and deadfall, but somehow it didn't seem to matter. He found his way. The sun helped. He could get his bearings by feeling it on the side of his face or the back of his neck. The slope of the ground helped too. Generally, that would tell him which way the mountains were.

Still, there were times he'd get turned around, have to backtrack, retrace his steps to the last place he'd had his bearings. But completely disoriented like he was now?

Not often.

The only thing he knew for sure right at this moment was he was inside a vehicle, moving down the road, the sun on his right shoulder, which meant he was heading south. But beyond that, he was utterly confused.

He'd heard the vehicle coming toward him as he made his way out of the barn toward Earl's truck, but he'd assumed it was just a random vehicle on the highway and it would soon fly past. But it slowed—he heard the brakes grabbing the tires and the engine downshifting—and turned into the driveway. He stepped off into the grass hoping to give it room to pass by, hoping whoever it was wouldn't stop and ask him what he was doing there. But he also couldn't help but wonder who it might be. Lyda? Mr. Duncan? Savanna, God forbid?

He'd never in a million years thought anyone would still be living here. Jesus, if he'd only known. He would have stayed home. Opened some beers, told Earl everything from the safety of the Fingers.

The car coming down the drive stopped, idling nearby. He kept walking. A car door opened. He waited to hear it shut. The sound didn't come.

He tensed, listening closely. He heard the wind, the sound of an airplane passing overheard in what he believed to be the northeast quadrant of the sky, an insect—maybe a dragonfly—buzzing in high grass off the road. But nothing else. Whoever had opened the car door had yet to move from inside the vehicle.

He continued to walk, listening closely.

Still nothing. The airplane droned away, trembling and fading. The dragonfly buzzed closer. He felt it clip the seat of his overalls. The wind stopped. He smelled something like aftershave, except sweeter, nearly rotten.

"Who's there?" Rufus said. An alarm had begun to rattle inside him. This was the sixth sense, if he had one, the sure knowledge that the person—represented only by the sound of the car door opening and the smell of the menthol from the aftershave—meant to harm him.

But there was more than that, wasn't there? The person's silence, their absolute stillness, spoke to him as much as any sound or smell. This was a person who understood that Rufus wasn't to be taken lightly. Which meant he'd had an encounter with them before. Either that, or they'd been made aware through someone else that he wasn't any ordinary blind fool.

"Have a good day then," he said, and started on toward the road. He walked alert, every muscle as tense as his senses that waited for the first indication—be it sound or smell—that the person was coming for him.

He made it to the road and turned left, walking toward the setting sun. He felt it on his face. Three steps, four steps, five. Was he going to make it? Had the person just given up that easily?

Just when he almost believed it had all been a false alarm, he heard the seat squeak inside the car and then a boot heel came down on the gravel. Rufus picked up his pace, walking faster. The boot heels began to crunch loudly now. Repetitively. He ran.

The boot heels stopped. A whistle came from his pursuer, sharp and long, like one of those wolf whistles men used to do when a pretty woman walked by. The kind that showed appreciation but also something darker, suggesting the woman wasn't just relationship material but also a kind of potential prey. In that way, it was the perfect sound.

Rufus ran faster, staying on the side of the road, where he felt like an oncoming vehicle would have plenty of room to avoid him. It was only when he left the ground, flying into the dark horizon, briefly, like an airplane with no windows, that he understood the whistle had not been for him.

It had been for whoever tripped him.

He hit the asphalt hard, his right elbow taking most of the force. Better than his face, he thought, as he felt hands on his back. They raised him up powerfully. No sooner had he begun to struggle than he felt the gun muzzle jammed into the middle of his back.

Still no words spoken. The gun said everything he needed to know.

Part of him considered fighting. He doubted whoever it was would shoot him out here in the middle of the road in broad daylight, but he decided against it. He didn't even know who he was dealing with, which meant making a bet like that was foolish for sure. Instead, he let his body go limp to indicate he had given up.

"Who are you?" he said again as the man (it had to be a man, didn't it?) physically wrenched him around by the shoulders and began to walk him toward the car, the gun still pressed into the middle of his back. It was right against his spine, and Rufus felt like that was another sign. Whoever it was knew what he was doing.

And they also knew enough not to speak. Silently, the man guided Rufus to the car, where he was pushed into what he quickly realized was the back seat.

Leather. Clean. New-car smell. Power locks from the sound of them all clicking down at once.

"Can you at least tell me where you're taking me?" he said.

No answer. The car pulled out of the driveway and turned to the right. East.

He was sure of that much.

*　　*　　*

But now, after what he guessed had been nearly two hours of continuous driving, which included several endless doughnuts in a field to disorient him, he wasn't sure of anything. His mental radar was off-line. He was truly, truly in the dark.

The men in front were so steadfast in their silence, he gave up trying to engage them and instead focused on other details that might help him make some determination about where he was and whom he was with.

Initially, he'd suspected it might be a sheriff's county vehicle, but after touching the man's hair in front of him, he knew there was no glass separating him from the front seat like there would have been if it was a sheriff's vehicle. As soon as he touched the man's hair, his head moved. Rufus reached out again, trying to feel the head again, but instead all he felt were two large hands around his wrist. They flicked his hand back on itself, bending his wrist at an extremely awkward—and painful—angle. He gasped and settled back in his seat.

The message was clear. Hands to yourself.

"Asshole," he said.

No reply, just the thumping of irregular pavement under the rolling wheels.

Wait. That was something. Irregular pavement. He focused on the pattern of thumping. Maybe if he could memorize it, he'd be able to recognize the pattern again. Of course, that assumed he ever escaped his captors. He had a sinking feeling they might be taking him somewhere to kill him.

He wasn't ready to die. Hell, he hadn't even fixed himself yet. He still needed more time to figure out how to live with what he'd done, how to simultaneously move forward *and* never let himself forget the guilt, because forgetting was its own kind of guilt, happiness its own accusation.

But why? Maybe that was the most important thread he needed to follow. Had Harden connected him to Earl? Was it possible he was one of the two men in the front seat? Possible, he supposed, but unlikely. Harden would be in his seventies now, too old to be chasing people around the county.

But if not Harden, who? Who else would have reason to do this? Who else might feel threatened by Rufus?

There was Jeb Walsh, or course. He'd held a grudge against Rufus and Earl since the day they had greeted him outside the library in downtown Riley nearly a year ago. Of course, *greeted* wasn't really the word for what had happened that day. A better term might be *accosted*. Rufus had seen Walsh's descent on Riley and the Fingers coming and had had no intention of sitting by idly and just allowing him free rein. Walsh wasn't the kind of man who was used to being challenged directly and had been trying to exact some revenge against Rufus and Earl ever since. Kidnapping Mary had been his first failed attempt. Why wouldn't he try for Rufus next?

The answer wasn't clear. But one thing was. All of those possibilities were preferable to who Rufus believed was behind his abduction: Savanna.

He wasn't ready to deal with her again. He wasn't sure he'd ever be ready for that if he lived a million years.

31

I waited until midnight to call 911. I couldn't fool myself any longer. I was deeply worried about Rufus. I'd spent the afternoon and early evening with Ronnie, driving around the county looking for him, but we soon realized we were going to need some help. He wasn't at any of his old haunts, nor was he walking along any of the roads he would have taken to get home. I needed help. But I didn't call 911 because I expected any help. No, I called because I knew it was the first step, something to cross off the list before deciding what to do next. I knew I'd be patched through to the sheriff's dispatch, and at the moment my list of suspects who might have done something to Rufus was headed up by the actual sheriff. There was always a chance I'd get a friendly deputy instead, though I wasn't sure how much faith I had in any deputy that hadn't quit on general principles when Argent took over.

The dispatch operator took down my information and said a deputy or the sheriff would be in touch.

I put down the phone and walked over to the refrigerator for some whiskey, only to remember I didn't have any. This realization hit me hard and fast, and all wrong.

The goddamn nerve of Ronnie and Rufus to take my whiskey.

What followed could best be described as a tantrum. I lost my shit. Not just because I was out of whiskey. That was part of it, but the main part was the realization of how much I actually *needed* it.

That realization caused me to pick up a plate in the sink and fling it across the kitchen. It crashed into the wall beside the door and shattered. That felt good, so I found another plate and did the same with it, grinning savagely as it exploded against the wall.

I went for the table next, knocking it sideways, but that wasn't good enough. I got down low, palms against the flat underside, and flipped it. It slid across the linoleum, crashing into the side door of the kitchen.

The chairs came next. Then the microwave, the coffeemaker, more dishes, and the knives in the drawer. Soon I was in such a state of blind fury I couldn't see straight. Even so, I didn't stop. The outburst felt too good. It was the first time in weeks I felt the pressure in my head being released.

At some point, I made my way into the den. I was basically destroying the house on autopilot now. My mind had drifted away to some place of bliss where thoughts of Mary's absence or Rufus's disappearance couldn't reach.

"Are you okay?"

Later, I'd wonder just how long she'd been standing in the doorway watching me. Long enough, I was pretty sure, for her to think I'd lost my mind.

I stopped, aware suddenly of the candlestick holder in my hand. I'd been using it to bludgeon a mirror Mary had set up for me when I'd first moved in. It was splintered all to shit now, but I saw my reflection clearly enough. A man I barely recognized stared at me. He clutched the candlestick holder with a bloody hand. His face was crooked in the splintered glass, his eyes red and filled with a shimmering madness.

Standing behind him was the woman who'd started all of this. Daphne. I seethed, staring at her. I wanted to throw the candlestick holder at her. I wanted to curse her for what she'd done.

No, I thought. It wasn't her fault. It was no one's fault but my own.

I dropped the candlestick holder onto the floor and turned around.

"I heard the commotion from my place . . ." She stepped into the room. "You know, I messed up before. And it's caused you pain."

"Nah," I said, and surprised myself by smiling at my own joke. "What would make you think that?"

She smiled too, but it was a sad smile, and somehow, against all reason, I felt for her. Stupid, I know, but there it was. She had made a mistake, but how could she have known what it would unleash? That was the way life worked, it seemed. Every decision, no matter how inconsequential—or consequential—was filled with a dread potential, and you couldn't know for sure how your life would be able to coexist with that potential once it was free and able to squirm around the world.

"I know it sounds crazy, but . . . well, you seem like you're going through some shit, shit I caused, and *I'm* going through some shit maybe some other people caused too. Maybe we could be there for each other?"

For a moment, what she was saying didn't register with me. I was still in a state of shock from the tantrum I'd just pitched. How in *the* hell had I managed to drag the refrigerator into the den?

"Hey," she said. "Over here."

I looked at her. The words she'd said previously registered somewhat dimly inside my head. I thought of whiskey and I thought of her, and they seemed pretty close to the same thing at that moment. Salves, both of them, but not salvation.

* * *

Like the whiskey I craved so much, the sex with Daphne was good—no, great—until it wasn't. The moment of change was almost indiscernible, hidden inside the ecstasy of our orgasms. She peeled herself off of me, and as soon as her body lost contact with mine, I felt more alone than I ever had in my entire life.

She shivered. "Got a chill. You running the air?"

I shook my head, looking at her nakedness, trying to make myself care about her again to stop the pain.

"I'm sorry," I said.

"For what?"

"This is a bad idea."

She grabbed her panties, balled them in her fist, and wiped her crotch with them. Then she shimmied into her blue jeans. "Nah. It's a great idea. You're just a man. Women don't matter to you after it's over. Give your body time to build up some of that love juice and I'll be the best idea you ever thought of."

"No," I said, horrified at everything that statement revealed about her and most of all about me. Because she was right. And it hurt me to know how right she was, how wrong my behavior was.

"Don't look so pitiful, okay? I owed you one for screwing up things with your girl. Besides, you didn't take advantage of me. I liked what we just did. Hell, I could go again, but something tells me, at your age, I better check with you tomorrow."

I rubbed my face. We *were* both adults. We both had our eyes wide open. At least now we did. I'd been a little late to the party, too blinded by my need for a little soothing to see she wanted the same thing. Yet I still felt bad. Sick, even. Maybe because it put what I'd had with Mary in such sharp relief. *All* of it was ecstasy with Mary. The dance before *and* after the act. Our lives commingled with the kind of rhythm that made every moment special. And now I was searching for even one moment of special. No, not *special*, just a moment of nothingness that sex could provide.

"I'll see you tomorrow," she said.

"Don't," I said.

She put a finger to her lips. "Shh."

* * *

I got the call a few minutes after she left. I picked up my phone, praying it would be Rufus. Instead the screen said *Incoming Call Coulee County Sheriff*.

"Hello?"

"Well, if it ain't Mr. White Guilt. To what do I owe the pleasure?" It was Argent. Of course, it was Argent. Who else would it be?

"I explained it to the dispatch already," I said.

"Well, explain it again. My eyes are bad. Reading those notes makes my head hurt."

I thought about just hanging up. I might have, too, but then I realized if I was ever going to bring Argent down, I'd need ammunition. Reporting a missing person he wouldn't even bother to look for could be that ammunition one day.

"My friend Rufus Gribble is missing."

"Let's see . . ." he said, speaking in a slow, exaggerated drawl. "Spell that."

I spelled it through clenched teeth.

"Gribble. Now, that's an unusual name."

"Aren't you going to ask me where he was last seen?"

"Huh?"

"Last known whereabouts. Ask me *something*."

"I'm sorry, are you the sheriff?"

"Fuck you."

He laughed. "Last time I checked, I'm the one with the badge. I'm the one who the good people of Coulee County have entrusted to do this job the right way."

"This is a waste of time."

"You might be right about that. I tell you what I'm going to do, Mr. White Guilt. I'm going to make a report on this call. I go by the book, you know? In that report, I'll note that Mr. Gribble is a blind man and has been known to wander these hills alone. The report will show, in my personal opinion, that Mr. Gribble has become lost. I'll explain, of course, that we sent some deputies and dogs out to his favorite haunts and turned up nothing. Then I'll file this in the missing persons file. End of story."

"I want to be there when the dogs go out."

"Sure."

"When will it be?"

"Now, take it easy, Snowflake. I've got to dot all my *i*'s and cross all my *t*'s. This job is about methodology, following procedure. Whew, it is a good thing you didn't win. I can't help but think you'd be cutting corners all over the place."

"Just tell me."

"Sure."

I waited.

"Well?"

"Oh, I can't tell you until I know."

"When will that be?"

"Maybe the end of the week. Or early next week. Well, the fourth is next week, so maybe I better not promise what I can't deliver. That's policing 101, you know?"

"Go fuck yourself," I said.

"Now, that's no way to talk to a law enforcement officer."

"Yeah, well, it's a good thing I'm not talking to one then. I'll find him myself."

"Now, let me advise you not to do something rash, something that could get you hurt. I mean—"

I ended the call. I couldn't take it anymore. There was no way I was going to get anything out of him, which meant I was on my own again. Seemed like that was a recurring theme in my life—being alone. I couldn't help but wonder if maybe there was a reason for it.

32

Rufus staggered out of the vehicle into cool weather. Cool weather meant nighttime. In July the mountains stayed hot until dark; then the heat liked to slip away in a quick burst as the temperature caused the mercury in the thermometer to freefall. Night in the mountains in July made the hot days almost seem worth it.

Silent men grabbed each of his arms. How could two men say so little? he wondered for what seemed like the hundredth time. He felt a kind of begrudging respect for them now. These weren't your ordinary hillbillies. Their discipline had already caused him to rule out Sheriff Argent. Maybe he had a deputy that could pull this kind of disciplined work off, but Argent himself was too much of an asshole to do it.

So who then?

He thought of the Hill Brothers. They'd certainly be able to handle themselves well enough to pull this off, but he wondered what possible motivation they could have. Rufus didn't know them personally, but from what he'd ascertained, they didn't seem the type to be motivated by money.

He shook his head, frustrated.

The answer was as dark as everything else.

A door opened in front of him. The smell of dust and mildew hit him hard enough to make him hold his breath. He heard a light switch flip. One of the men let go of him. He was almost positive they were both men. He could usually smell the difference between men and women pretty easily. He felt like they were men. Neither stunk exactly, but as the day wore on, he smelled them both, a sweaty, earthy smell barely masked by strong deodorant and aftershave. Old Spice or something similar.

He heard the man who'd let go rummaging for something on the other side of the room.

Meanwhile, the other man stood with Rufus, his hand around the crook of his elbow.

There was a click. Rufus thought it was the sound of a flashlight being turned on. That meant the light they'd turned on earlier didn't work. Burned out, or maybe the place didn't even have power. He was pushed forward again. A hand pressed into his back. Then both men turned him and guided him down into a chair by his shoulders.

Outside, another vehicle pulled up. The engine idled softly for a moment before going silent. Footsteps on gravel. The door swung open again.

"What's wrong with the lights?" a female voice said. Her voice was familiar. Instantly, Rufus felt his body go rigid. He knew that voice but didn't want to accept it.

Silence.

"You can talk," she said. "He's never going to leave here."

"Needs a new bulb," the man to his right said. His voice wasn't familiar.

"You didn't bring any?"

"No."

"Stupid."

Neither man spoke, but Rufus felt them on either side of him, their presences somehow diminished in the proximity of the woman.

"Who are you?" Rufus said. "And why do you want me?" But he knew the answer already; he just couldn't bring himself to admit it.

"I'm disappointed in you, Rufus. I would have thought I'd have made a greater impression."

"Savanna," he said.

"That's more like it."

"Why?"

"Why not? You've been lucky I've left you alone this long."

He felt her coming closer. Smelled her now, that cloying sweetness he remembered from many years ago. Despite all his best intentions, he felt himself stirring, his dick hardening. It was what she wanted. Savanna used sex as a weapon. She could disable you with it just as easily as she could use it to threaten, coerce, or murder you.

He felt her straddling him in the chair. She was wearing a skirt, and he couldn't tell through his overalls what else. But when she ground down on him, pushing her soft places against his hard ones, he remembered the bliss he'd experienced with her so many years ago.

"You want me," she said. "After all these years, you still want me. Well, how about that? Can't even see me anymore and still wants to fuck me."

"Get off me," he managed.

"What if I told you I was fat now. If I had a potbelly and a big ass. Would you still want me?"

Rufus turned his face from her. He didn't want to breathe any of her, not her words or her scent.

"Well, don't worry. I still look good. Damn good. I'm fifty-two this month, and I can still get any man in the county, but right now, I've got Rufus Gribble."

"Please," he said. "I just want to be left alone."

She slid off, giggling wickedly. "You don't mean that, Rufus. You want me to fuck you. Deep down, that's all you've ever wanted, Rufus. Men are all the same. So, I'll make you suffer."

"What do you want with me?"

"I need to know where Harriet is."

"Harriet is dead. I watched her jump."

"That's what I thought too, but there's been rumors. And after the last kid died out at the Falls, I've got to make sure."

"Harriet's dead," Rufus said again. "Let me go."

He heard footsteps. She was coming toward him again. He put his hand up just in time to block the blow. Not only that, he managed to get a pretty decent grip on her wrist. She tried to pull away, but he was too strong.

"She's dead," he repeated, this time through clenched teeth.

He let go of her wrist, but not before he felt the blow from his right side. Knuckles to the jaw. He groaned at the pain, opening and closing his mouth, testing to see if his jaw still worked. Not broken. Busted up, but not broken.

"We've had reports," she said. "People have seen her. I think maybe you have too."

"I watched her jump," Rufus said.

"You and her were . . . you were trying to fuck her too, weren't you, Rufus?"

"No."

"There's nobody here to impress, Rufus. You can tell the truth. You don't have to hide the fact that you got off on thinking about doing two sisters."

"She wasn't into men."

"Oh, right. She had to be different. Had to be a lesbian. Well, I've eaten pussy before too, but you don't see me trying to make a statement about it. Jesus. What a drama queen." She stepped forward again. He braced, wincing against the blow he knew was coming.

But nothing came. Instead, she seated herself on top of his lap again. This time he felt her hands at his zipper. She found his penis, still achingly hard, and pulled it out.

"Stop," he groaned, but somehow, against all odds, he didn't mean it.

He felt himself slide into her, and instantly he was taken back to the night in the barn when she'd first approached him, when he'd still believed in love.

She began to ride him, slowly at first, but soon she was picking up the pace, bucking and moaning, her hands on his chest, her lips whispering around his neck.

"You need to tell me the truth," she said.

"I have. She's dead. Please stop."

"I can't stop until I get what I came for." She picked up her intensity, gripping him more tightly than before. "Friends don't let friends jump off bluffs."

"I tried to stop her."

"That's not the way I heard it."

He felt his body go stiff. "You don't know anything."

"I know a lot, actually. I know the entire school turned on her, that everyone, *you* included, participated in a hazing ritual, a ritual designed to embarrass and abuse her."

"Not true. You wanted me to do that, but I tried to help her."

"You *tried* to help her? Well, that didn't go very well, did it? Maybe your heart wasn't really in it. Maybe you weren't as different as Harden and

Deloach after all. Poor Deloach. Now, that's a man who's really dead. But Harriet? The jury is still out on Harriet."

He couldn't hold out much longer. He was going to explode. He didn't want to. It felt as if his physical body had separated from his spiritual self and was acting on its own . . .

It was going to happen. Jesus Christ, it was . . .

She stopped, sliding off him.

"Ugh," he moaned. "Don't . . ."

"Tell me the truth. Tell me where she is and I'll let you come."

"Thank you," he said.

"For what?"

"For stopping. I never want to touch you again."

He felt a sharp pain in his groin as she slapped his erect penis. Now she gripped it again, bending it to one side.

"Tell me, you piece of shit."

Rufus said nothing. He would endure the pain. He'd endured worse. What he couldn't endure was the pleasure, and the guilt he felt because of it.

She let go. "I don't want to hurt him too badly. I'll need him again when I want to get off."

"Fuck you."

She giggled. "Funny, that's exactly what I had in mind."

"You're evil."

"But evil never felt so good, am I right? I suppose I'll just have to get it from your friend. He's got issues too. You know I can't resist a man with issues."

"Don't you fucking dare go after Earl."

"Too late for that. I've already got him exactly where I want him."

"Bitch."

"Keep going, Rufus. You're turning me on. You know, as soon as I heard you were blind, I knew what happened."

"You don't know," he said.

"Sure I do. You could never keep any secrets from me."

"You don't know," he said again, trying to convince himself, not even sure why it mattered to him so much.

33

The next evening, I arrived at Jessamine's an hour before the Bluegrass Mountain Cult was scheduled to begin. Ronnie was at the bar, drinking a beer with a woman I didn't recognize, so I sat down at one of the tables and ordered a Coke.

Jessamine's was *the* place to come for night life in Coulee County. By day, it was a meat and three style diner, but at night they cleared out most of the tables, opened the bar, and turned down the lights, converting it into one of the loudest—and most dangerous—honky-tonks I'd ever had the pleasure of visiting. It was still relatively early, so the place was mostly empty except for the band and a few other folks.

The waitress brought my Coke, and I looked at it, disappointed. Would a beer hurt? Probably not, but I didn't want to risk it. Not with Rufus being gone. I needed to be alert. I needed to think. Unfortunately, at this moment, I wasn't feeling up to either one. All I wanted to do was have half a dozen beers and enjoy a night of what I hoped would be good music.

I nursed the Coke as the band began to set up and people gradually filed in. I recognized a lot of them, from Jessamine herself—she sat over by the window with her husband—to Mindy, the secretary from the Harden School who sat at the bar alone. I was on my way to join her when the mood shifted almost imperceptibly in the bar. The place, nearly full now, went quiet. I looked to the door and saw Jeb Walsh coming in along with Sheriff Argent and Mayor Keith. They settled into a table in the corner, removing the large sign from the tabletop that said *Reserved*.

Argent was dressed in stiff, dark blue jeans and a short-sleeved button-down. He wore his badge attached to his belt and a holstered .22 on the other side of his waist. He looked around the room with a self-satisfied grin.

Walsh sat down across from Mayor Keith. They were dressed almost identically: tan slacks, golfing shirts, and brown loafers. Walsh nodded to Argent and pointed at the bar. Argent took their orders like he was a waiter instead of the sheriff.

I sat down next to Mindy and turned away from Argent. "Hello," I said.

She looked a little confused, but then she recognized me and smiled. "Bob Jenkins, right?"

"That's right."

"You caused quite a stir the other day."

"I did?"

"I overheard my uncle telling Mr. Harden about it. Said you were snooping around upstairs."

I shrugged.

"Is it true?"

Before I could answer her, I felt a tap on my shoulder. "Excuse me," I said. I turned, expecting it to be Argent with some smart remark, but instead it was Ronnie.

He embraced me tightly, patting my back. "Thanks for coming, Earl."

I hissed at him, trying to warn him Mindy was there and he was blowing our cover, but Ronnie didn't catch on.

"I'm dedicating our first song to the one and only Earl Marcus," he said.

"Wait a minute," Mindy said. "Earl Marcus?"

I sighed and sat back down on the barstool. Ronnie said, "Oh. Shit. My bad."

I held my hand out to Mindy. "Earl Marcus. Private investigator. Nice to meet you."

* * *

After that, the night went well. Surprisingly so. At least for a while. The best part was that Argent and Walsh kept their distance. If they noticed me at the bar, neither showed any sign. Nearly as good was Mindy's reaction to me being a detective: she was fascinated.

By the time the Bluegrass Mountain Cult played their first song—a raucous number with a call-and-respond chorus that sounded like *you got yours, but I got tore up* repeated over and over again—Mindy and I were deep into a conversation about the school.

She wanted to know what I was investigating. I told her about Weston Reynolds, being careful to leave out anything that might relate to Joe.

"I've been wondering about that too. Why the secret identity, though?"

"I've got a reputation around the county," I said. "There are some powerful people who don't like me."

I had to resist the urge to turn toward Walsh's table when I said it. Mindy nodded. "Right. Well, what can I do to help?"

"Have you seen or heard anything about the boy's death?"

"Just rumors," she said.

The Bluegrass Mountain Cult ended the song with a sudden crescendo of guitar, drums, and driving bass, and the bar erupted in applause.

"Thank you," Ronnie said. He was sweating, and somehow he'd managed to get his Rolling Stones *Steel Wheels* T-shirt tangled up in his guitar strap, exposing his tattooed stomach. "That was for my buddy, Earl Marcus!" The crowd cheered. "Stand up, Earl!"

Mindy clapped and said, "Go on."

Reluctantly, I stood. The crowd cheered again. Two things struck me then. One, Ronnie's band was good. The place was eating them up. Two, I felt better than I had in a while. Not great. Probably not even good. But alive. I felt alive.

I was sitting back down as the band launched into their next number when I noticed Walsh out of the corner of my eye. He was laughing and pointing at me.

"Excuse me," I said to Mindy.

As I walked across the crowded bar, I realized I was making a mistake. I realized how easy it would have been to ignore him, to pretend he wasn't even there. I could have gone back to talking to Mindy, and I might even have found out something useful. But I couldn't let it go. I hated Jeb Walsh. I hated him and what he was doing to this county. But that wasn't why I was walking over to confront him. I was walking over to confront him because of my pride. Because I had to prove he didn't frighten me, that try as he might, he would never intimidate me.

I had no idea if this was right or wrong, good or bad. I just knew it was what I had to do.

All three men saw me coming and began to smile. Walsh nudged Argent as if to say, *can you believe he's coming over?*

On the way, I grabbed an empty chair from a nearby table and lifted it high into the air to clear the crowd. It felt good to see Jeb flinch a little as I brought it down to the floor. He recovered quickly—a real talent of his—and pointed at me.

"This asshole's just going to join us, Press. Shouldn't that be illegal?" Mayor Keith laughed nervously. Argent smiled as if he wasn't sure how to take Walsh's statement.

"Evening," I said.

"We don't want any trouble," Mayor Keith said.

"Shut up," Jeb said.

Keith bristled as if he was going to object to being disrespected but in the end said nothing.

"What do you want?" Walsh said.

"Just thought I'd say hi. Haven't spoken to you assholes in a while."

Walsh picked up his whiskey and threw it back. He placed the glass on the table, lightly, before turning to Argent. "Want to go get me another? The service in this place sucks."

Argent hurried off for another drink.

"Now that the law is gone, I can say what I want to say."

Mayor Keith stood up suddenly. "I have to go to the restroom."

"Go already," Walsh said.

Once he was gone and we were alone, Jeb slid his chair around until he was right next to me. The music was loud, but he spoke right into my ear, and I heard every word.

"You been sniffing around some stuff," he said. "That's going to get you killed."

"Maybe so," I allowed. "But I'm not going to stop."

"Well, I wouldn't expect nothing less of a man like you. How's Mary?"

"Where's Rufus?" I said, purposefully ignoring his question about Mary. He just wanted to bait me.

"Who?"

"Don't pretend you don't know."

"You mean the old blind socialist?"

"Call him what you will. Where is he?"

"Hell if I know. Maybe you should report it to the sheriff." He nodded at Argent, who was leaning against the bar, leering at Mindy.

"I'm going to win," I said.

"I didn't know we were playing a game."

"Fuck you."

He laughed. "I heard the African Queen left you. I'll bet a pale hand like yours ain't no match for that tight little pussy."

This is what he did. Every fucking time. I stood up, fists clenched, ready and willing to punch him.

But I never got the chance. The song ended, and with it, the tension that had been building inside me drained away. Mary didn't need me to defend her. Not like this. The only way to defend Mary and all the women like her was to finally find a way to take Walsh down. Punching him would feel good, but it would only be for me.

So instead of punching him, I leaned forward and repeated what I'd said earlier. "I'm going to win."

I didn't wait for his reply. I walked out the door, into the night, and wondered how I'd ever win anything again without Mary, without Rufus, without the calming influence of whisky. Which is why I decided not to go back in. I knew if I did that I was going to get drunk, and if I got drunk, I might blow everything up.

34

The next morning, I woke before the sun came up, unable to shake the feeling I was living on borrowed time, that at any moment I could get a call from Argent, not about Rufus but about the dead body I'd buried. He'd have some questions, but he wouldn't really want any answers. They would just be foreplay, a way to set up the inevitable charges. Maybe they'd even have Chip Thompkins on board as a witness.

I wished he'd call me back and tell me something, one way or the other. I'd nearly called him several times over the last few days but had resisted because I knew too much pressure might scare him away.

Chip or no Chip, one thing was clear: I had no time to waste. There was nothing else for me to do but try to take down Jeb Walsh and, in the process, figure out what had happened to Rufus. It felt good, in a way, to be light, to feel clean, just a man on a single path. The problem was what the problem had always been: when the path ended, what was left? I couldn't help but think of Backslide Gap and that long dark fall.

I was about to head out when my phone rang. It was Claire.

"Did you find out anything on the credit card?" I asked, though I wasn't sure why. I already knew Joe's identity.

"No, but I did come across something I thought might interest you."

"What's that?"

"An article from an old newspaper. Remember how you asked me to look into the Harden School?"

"Yeah."

"Well, I came across this while I was searching. It involves your friend Rufus."

That got my attention. "When can you meet?"

* * *

Twenty-seven rings and no voice mail. If I'd been calling anyone else in the world besides Ronnie Thrash, I would have given up. But not Ronnie. With Ronnie, you never knew. Besides, I was pretty sure he'd gotten trashed last night.

"Earl?" he said, his voice surprised, as if he would never—not in his wildest dreams—have conceived that he might get a call from me.

"Can you go see if Rufus made it home?"

"Ugh. What am I, his babysitter?"

"Just do it, okay? I've got a lot on my plate."

"Yeah, I noticed you didn't hang around very long last night. Hell, you missed our best stuff."

"I'm sorry about that, Ronnie. I had to get out of there or I was going to hurt Jeb Walsh."

"All the more reason to stay. Hang on."

There was a loud clatter, as if the phone had been thrown against the wall. I waited for nearly ten minutes, still sipping the last of my coffee, watching the slow spread of the yellow and orange turning the sky from black to purple to clear blue through the kitchen window.

"He ain't there. Fuck. You know I'm not going back to sleep now."

"Give it a shot anyway. I want you well rested."

"Why?"

"So you can go with me to the school early tomorrow morning."

"School?"

"The Harden School."

"What are we going to do there?"

"Hopefully get there early enough to get in."

"I don't understand."

"You don't have to. You in or not?"

"Okay. Whatever."

I was silent, thinking.

"You there?" he asked.

"I'm here."

"Well, shit. Say something."

"I think somebody kidnapped Rufus."

Now it was Ronnie's turn to be silent. I wasn't sure what I expected him to say. He and Rufus hated each other, or at least made a good show of hating each other.

"So, you think his disappearance has something to do with this school?"

"It's the only theory I've got."

"Last time I helped you, I went to Hays for eight months."

"I know."

"You ain't even going to try to promise me that won't happen this time?"

"No. I'd like to, but I can't."

Ronnie didn't speak. The moment felt odd. Bizarre, haunted somehow. Ronnie always had something to say.

"You there?"

"I'm here," he said. "I just . . . well, I guess I just respect the hell out of that."

"Out of what?"

"You being straight with me."

"Does that mean you'll help?"

"Of course I'll help. I was just trying to make you sweat. You think I'd turn down a chance to get the team back together? Now, let me go to sleep so I can be there with bells in the morning." Somehow I could hear his grin through the phone. Ronnie was the consummate no-regrets kind of guy. Maybe that more than anything was what drew me to him. My whole life was regret, meted out minute to minute, hour to hour, season to season, a cycle of pain that always came back to me, haunted me. Ronnie's pain could smack him in the mouth over and over again, and he'd never worry about it, at least not until he felt it hit him the next time.

* * *

My plan was simple, but risky. If Ronnie and I could get to the gate early enough to catch Mindy as she started through it, we could plead with her to let us in. Seeing her at the bar the other night had given me some hope she might be persuaded to help me. I had nothing concrete other than my gut to make me think this, but it was just about the only way I could imagine getting inside those gates again.

Once inside, I wanted to talk to Edward Walsh, and possibly some of the other boys. I wanted to get them on tape, telling me stories of abuse, of the cruel methods used inside. Once I had that, I'd have one more bullet in my cartridge that might convince Chip Thompkins to write the story.

Bonus if I could find a way to trace it all back to Jeb Walsh. But that was for tomorrow. Today I had to meet with Claire and hopefully find Rufus.

35

Frankie's Beans had gone through at least five iterations since I'd moved back to North Georgia from Charlotte. New managers, new names, new signs, but I was hoping this one was going to stick. I liked the new manager, a long-haired kid name Theo, who had a master's in philosophy from some school down in Florida. He wasn't a hippie—at least not in the traditional sense of the word—but you'd be forgiven for thinking he was. The long hair and unshaven face masked a sharp mind, one more interested in questions of metaphysics than psychedelic drugs. We'd spent many an afternoon in the spring talking about the world and the way things always seemed to go wrong. And damned if he didn't make a good pot of coffee.

I waited in the back for Claire, hoping I wouldn't see anyone I knew, especially not anyone who might ask me how Mary was doing. I didn't need anything else to remind me of her, not with her face already constantly swimming into my consciousness. Between that and Rufus's absence, I'd started to feel like the protagonist in a Greek tragedy.

When Claire did finally come in, I did a double take. She was more attractive than I'd remembered. Maybe it was her outfit, a short skirt and a tight blouse, both of which accented ample curves.

She smiled and sat down across from me. "Thanks for meeting."

"Can I get you a coffee?" I said, taking her hand.

"An iced coffee sounds perfect. This heat is insane."

I waved at Theo, and he came over, grinning.

He shook my hand, glancing at Claire but not speaking. "How's Mary?" he asked.

"We broke up," I said.

"Oh, shit. I'm sorry, man." He glanced at Claire awkwardly. "Is . . . is this . . ."

"No," I said. "This is business."

He nodded, pale faced.

"She did want an iced coffee. And I'll have some ice water."

"Coming up, Earl. Listen, if you need to talk . . ."

"I'm fine, Theo. Really."

"Should we meet another time, Earl?" Claire said.

"Nope," I said. "This is perfect."

Theo left to grab her coffee.

"You broke up with your girlfriend?"

"Yeah."

"I'm sorry. Are you okay?"

"It's okay. *I'm* okay. It was totally my fault."

She reached across the table and took my hand. I let her. Of course I did. I was a glutton for a woman's touch.

"I'm sorry, Earl."

Theo returned with the iced coffee and put it in front of Claire.

"Put it on my tab?" I asked.

"On the house. I feel bad for interrupting."

"Not necessary," Claire said, producing a small purse and putting it on the table. She opened it up and pulled out a five, which she handed to Theo. "Keep the change."

"We'll catch up soon, Theo" I said.

When I turned back to Claire, she was holding a photocopy of an old newspaper article.

"I found this after talking to Susan. I hope I didn't overstep my bounds." She pushed the article across the table. "I think you'll recognize a name in there."

The article was from a Chattanooga paper, and it was dated August 3, 1986. The headline read *Missing Woman Ruled Dead*.

Twenty-one-year-old Harriet Duncan of Brethren has been missing for three days, but Sheriff Hank Shaw is calling off the search. According to Shaw, the troubled woman committed suicide.

"*Unfortunately, she had some emotional issues that likely caused her to make this decision,*" Shaw said in a press conference.

Though not a student, Duncan was a resident of the otherwise male-only Harden School, where she was undergoing an extensive emotional evaluation. According to several students, Duncan was obsessed with the waterfall at the rear of the school.

"*She used to go out there and sit all the time. And she was always saying how she was going to jump across the ravine,*" 10th-grader Chris Marsh said.

At least one counselor witnessed the leap. Rufus Gribble, who helps with discipline at the school, was with her three nights ago when she told him she was going to jump across the ravine.

"*She'd been telling me for a while she was going to jump to the other side and never come back. I told her there wasn't any way to make it. I think she knew it too. It was just what she said because she didn't want us to know she was trying to kill herself,*" Gribble commented.

Sheriff Shaw claims she would not have been able to make the jump. "*Unless she's Superwoman, she's dead.*"

"*I tried to physically restrain her, but she slipped free,*" Gribble continued. "*She leapt into the darkness. I couldn't see, but I heard her scream. When I called out to her, there was no answer. She was gone.*"

Duncan's older sister, Lyda, has asked for a full investigation into the school, claiming the methods used by the administration were abusive, but according to Gribble, that just wasn't the case.

"*Mr. Harden and Mr. Deloach did everything they could possibly do to help her. She just didn't want help. I'd say if she hadn't come to the Harden School, she would have been dead a long time ago.*"

Randy Harden, the school's founder and headmaster as well as Harriet's uncle, echoed these sentiments. "*I took Harriet in as a personal favor to my sister, and we did everything within our power to save her, but sometimes you have to want to save yourself. She just didn't.*"

Later in the interview, Harden asked if he could make a statement to the community.

"There is nothing more disturbing than seeing a young person take their own life, but I would like to point out there is some light within the darkness. Rufus Gribble, a young man from the Fingers area, should be commended for his commitment to discipline and education of the students here. I just hate that he's finally getting the recognition on the back of this tragedy. Rufus is going to be a wonderful teacher when he gets his degree."

Despite not yet finding her remains, a funeral will be held for Harriet Duncan on Friday, May 17, at the Ponder's Funeral Home.

I wasn't sure what to make of the article. Did it happened like Rufus said? If so, what did it mean for what I was investigating now? Not much, I decided. I'd already determined Harriet was dead.

Still, there was something about the article that didn't sit right with me. When I looked up at Claire, she was studying me closely, leaning across the table, her eyes big and brown and filled with light that beheld landscapes I couldn't quite map.

"He's your friend, right?" she said.

"Yeah, how'd you know?"

"Susan told me. Did you ask him about this?"

I shook my head. "Rufus is missing."

"Missing? You're kidding, right?"

I shook my head. "I wish I was."

She touched my hand. "What do you think happened?"

"I think it goes back to this."

She looked down at the paper and read it again. I watched her, trying to read her thoughts.

She looked up after a time. "It feels off."

I felt the same thing but decided to play dumb. "How do you mean?"

"Well, the part at the end where Harden praises Gribble. Seems almost like a quid pro quo to me. Rufus says the right thing, and Harden praises him in the paper."

"So, you don't think it was suicide?"

Claire shrugged. "I'm not the detective, but something's off here."

"Explain what you're thinking."

She leaned in, her lips curling into a smile. "Okay, you're going to think I'm crazy, right, but what if Harriet's not dead? What if that's why it feels off? What if that's why Rufus is gone right now? Maybe he knows where she is. And somebody doesn't want that info to get out."

I couldn't help but see the possibilities in what she was saying. It actually jibed pretty well with what I knew about Joe. Perhaps Joe had known the truth about Harriet too and that was what he'd been wanting to tell me, in hopes that I would be able to help him do something about the school. Either that or because he wanted my help protecting her.

"It's a good thought," I said. "Something to look into." I didn't want to seem too positive about her idea because it might make her suspicious about the other stuff I already knew.

She shrugged. "What else could it be?"

I just looked at her, trying to figure out exactly who I was dealing with. I'd certainly been down on the idea of working with an armchair detective at first, but I had to admit, she was making some sense. Knowing Rufus like I did, I couldn't help but see something was *way* off about the article. And now Rufus was missing.

"What are you thinking?" she said.

"I'm thinking that you may be right, but I don't know what to do about it."

She clicked her red nails on the table. The more I was around her, the more attractive she became. She had a kind of knowing sexuality, very different from Daphne's. Daphne's hit you like an avalanche, obscuring your thoughts, your judgment, all rational thought. Claire was much more subtle, and I found myself becoming more alert to each small gesture, the curl of her lip, the sweep of hair off her forehead, the way her eyes shined a liquid silk beneath her glasses.

Focus, Earl. I took a deep breath. It worked. I was done with women for the foreseeable future. The emptiness of my last encounter with Daphne still lingered fresh in my mind, as did the disappointment on Mary's face when I'd told her about what I'd done. Those two feelings alone would be enough to make me keep my dick in my pants for many years to come.

I hoped.

But then Claire smiled at me and reached over to my touch my hand, and I felt myself stir. Goddamn it all to hell. I was nothing if not weak.

"I don't know what to do about it either," she said, responding to my earlier question. "I figured that was your thing." Her fingers snaked up toward my wrist, just her nails grazing the back of my hand, my knuckles, the fine hairs of my lower arm. It was exquisite.

I closed my eyes and made myself see Mary's face. And I felt better. The sad truth was, I still needed her to save me.

* * *

When I left the coffee shop, I couldn't help but notice two men standing listlessly down the street in front of the library. The Hill Brothers. One of them saw me but didn't move or wave or acknowledge me. I lifted a hand to him, but he turned away.

36

I dreamed of a sky filled with nets and moons, and each moon was a pale version of the future, hanging on unseen strings. I was lying in Ghost Creek, looking up, baptized by the future and the past, lost to the present.

Lightning cracked the cloudless sky, and when it did, I saw all the strings, crisscrossed along their competing trajectories, like a dense net, and it lay over top of the world, transparent yet still heavy. Each moon could be me or Rufus or Harriet, but then I looked again and saw there were some moons that had become fully realized and shone bright enough to shred the ropes of the surrounding nets.

And then I woke, throwing my covers off, believing momentarily I was submerged in Ghost Creek. Goose, who was in the bed with me, snuggled his warm nose into my naked underarm and whined. I stroked his head with my hand and wished for a simpler mystery, but there was no such thing.

* * *

The tatters of the dream stayed with me as I made coffee, scrambled eggs, and fed Goose. By the time I made it to Ronnie's, the sun was almost up and the dream had been replaced by Claire's knowing eyes. How had she intuited that the article was off? It was something to meet another person with an intuition that matched your own. Sort of like looking into a mirror and seeing someone else who shared your features but wore them differently, with a kind of grace you believed you lacked.

Ronnie was still asleep, so I let myself in and sat down next to him on the couch. He was lying with one leg propped up on the back of the couch and the other on the floor. A thin sheet lay across his body. He was snoring.

I asked myself what I was doing. What was the plan?

The simple answer was that I was going to talk to Edward Walsh about Weston Reynold's death. The more complicated one was that, somehow, I wanted to see the falls again, the gorge, and the possibility of making the leap across. I wanted to stand where Rufus and Harriet had stood, to see if there was some entry point into the mystery of Rufus's unfinished story.

Was taking Ronnie even necessary? I wasn't sure. I had the sudden urge to just get up and leave, to go it alone this time. To live or die, sink or swim, fall or climb on my own merits. No Mary, no Rufus, no Ronnie.

Still, I hesitated. Ronnie had helped bail me out of so many binds in the past. Was there truly some benefit to doing it alone, or was I simply trying to play a game with myself, trying to manipulate my own consciousness into believing I'd found redemption at long last?

I wasn't sure. What I was sure of was this: I was stepping into enemy territory. The chances were good I wouldn't come out unscathed. But, most importantly, I didn't believe I could live with myself if something happened to Ronnie again.

I stood up, and Ronnie stirred. "Earl?"

I walked away, toward the door.

"Hey," he called. "I had a dream."

I stopped at the door.

"You were falling."

I stepped outside. "Go back to sleep."

"Hey, aren't we supposed to head out to—"

I shut the door and moved swiftly to my truck. I was already across the creek when Ronnie came out, wearing a pair of stained white briefs and nothing else. I was glad I'd let him be. It felt like the right decision.

This was my mystery to unravel.

* * *

But Ronnie didn't see it like that. Thank God for Ronnie Thrash. He chopped mysteries down by force of will. He exploded them from the inside out with the raw fury of his personality. He didn't solve them, he *banished* them in a way I'd never be able to.

I noticed his truck just before turning onto the long mountain road leading up to the school. I pulled over and waited on him to do the same.

"You can't bring that piece of shit up the mountain," I said. "They'll hear you coming."

"Well, move over then."

"I need to do this one alone," I said.

"Ain't nothing a man needs to do alone 'cept shit and play with his pecker, and hell, the last one is optional."

See? Fucking banished. Poof.

He climbed in beside me and slapped me on the shoulder. "Let's roll."

He'd thrown on an old Incredible Hulk T-shirt and a pair of gray sweatpants along with some flip-flops. He pulled out a cigarette and lit it. He grinned, stuck it in his mouth, and blew the smoke sideways, his mouth a constricted snarl.

"You better go move your truck," I said. "If you leave it there, everybody and their mother will know what we're doing."

"Sure, Earl. Can I just say, it's good to have you back."

"Back?"

"Yeah, working again. I was worried about you for a while. Just sitting in the yard, staring into space. I thought you'd given up."

"I think maybe I did."

"What changed?"

I shook my head. "I guess I need to find Rufus."

He blew a line of smoke out the window. "That old bastard can take care of himself and you know it. What really changed?"

I wasn't sure how to answer him, but just before he got out of my truck to go move his, I saw an image from the dream. It was the sky with all the moons, except this time I focused on just one of them, and it was my moon, not the one I was destined for, but the one that was me, deeply and truly me.

37

Rufus could pinpoint four pivotal moments in his life. Each of them was filled with equal parts dread and exhilaration. As if the only moments in life that could truly be transcendent had to strike a balance between despair and hope. There was the moment he had walked away from the church, when he had flung the snake at the stained glass, cracking it open. That moment had cracked him open too. He'd been a solid, hard-shelled egg before that. But when the shell cracked, light was able to come inside, but other things slipped in too, including other influences. Influences like Harden. Friends like Harriet. A dream like Savanna.

Moment number two came after he'd been working at the Harden School for half a year. It had happened during what Harden called "free physical time." Harden had a lot of goofy names for things at the school. "Free physical time" was just recess with more violence.

This particular incident happened on a cold, slightly damp day in February, and Rufus was the only adult riding herd on the thirteen boys and Harriet. Lately, Harden and Deloach had insisted she join the boys for free physical time. Rufus was pretty sure the idea was that if Harriet wanted to like girls, she should be forced to play with the boys. Harden and Deloach encouraged fighting, wrestling, showdowns between the boys who held grudges, even group punishment for boys who got out of line. Rufus's only real job was to make sure no one was seriously hurt (bloodied noses, black eyes, and painful kicks to the groin didn't qualify) and that the boys were active. Any of them who were caught sitting around were to be sent directly to Harden. Rufus never had to take any to Harden. One thing was clear in the school: no matter how badass one of the boys thought he was (or really was), none of them wanted to cross Harden.

On this particular day, the boys had brought out the football, and instead of picking teams, they began to play something called "Smear the queer." The game was one Harden would have loved. One boy took the ball and spiked it on the ground. As soon as it hit the ground, it was live. The boys would scramble madly to pick it up, and whoever snagged it first became the "queer." The ball carrier attempted to stay on his feet as long as possible before eventually being "smeared" by the other boys. There was no scoring, no winning, no point really that Rufus could see other than being an outlet for the boys to take out their aggression. And maybe that wasn't so bad. These boys certainly had enough aggression pent up, and despite the violent and seemingly pointless nature of the game, he could tell the boys were having fun. Not only that, there seemed to be an odd camaraderie that arose out of the game. After a ball carrier would get absolutely rocked by three or four tacklers at once, it wasn't unusual to see the tacklers helping the ball carrier up and patting him on the back.

Harriet stood by and watched, as was her custom since she'd been forced to join the boys in free time a few days earlier. So far, the boys had accepted her presence without too much rancor. Occasionally one of them might shoot her a stern glare and mutter something, but for the most part, they quickly became engaged in pummeling each other and forgot she was there. But that all changed when the ball popped loose from Andrew Shanck's hands and rolled over to her feet.

"Shank," as the other boys called him, was the first to make it to the ball, but instead of picking it up, he stopped, holding his arms out like guardrails to keep the other boys back. All thirteen boys stopped behind his arms and watched.

"Hey," he said. "Why doesn't the dyke play?"

"We're not going to call her that," Rufus said. It was a mantra he repeated over and over again, but none of the boys listened. Why should they listen to Rufus when they'd heard both Deloach and Harden call her the same thing?

"If she can eat pussy, she can play football," another voice said. Rufus wasn't sure who.

"Enough," he said sharply. It was the voice he saved for the most urgent situations, the ones when he knew violence was close at hand. Usually, the voice worked. Rufus had a kind of gravity, even then, that was tough to ignore. It was the kind of gravity that pulled you into his orbit and made you compliant with his will. But not this time. This time, the boys had created their own kind of force, a centrifugal counter to his will. It was a wild thing, formed out of the primeval past, the kind of charging of the atmosphere that could only occur when hormones and angst bounced off each other and dispersed into the very air.

The impending violence was so thick, Rufus could smell it.

Shank picked up the football and handed it to Harriet. She held it for a moment, and the chant began from some unknown place, a mouthless voice that soon formed a chorus of real voices.

Smear.

Smear.

Smear.

The.

Queer.

Smear.

The.

Queer.

Smear. Smear. Smear.

The.

Queer. Queer. Queer.

The boys had formed a circle around Harriet, who stood awkwardly holding the football, like it might be filled with poison and if she gripped it too tightly it would spill. The boys continued the chant as they closed ranks on her.

"Hey!" Rufus shouted.

But his voice was drowned out by the chants. The first boy had reached Harriet now, and instead of tackling her, he swung at her, a wild haymaker that landed with a devastating crack. Rufus froze. It was like watching an explosion happen from a safe distance. It was instantaneous, and dreadful. All of the boys began to strike her, to push her, to beat on her. Somehow— and this is something Rufus would think about later—Harriet held onto the ball, squirming free of the initial assault, keeping her feet, breaking out of the circle, scampering and bouncing from body to body like a pinball. The chant subsided as the circle turned inward, stretching itself like a rubber band in her wake.

Two of the boys spread out wide, flanking her on either side, while Shank—one of the fastest boys—ran her down from behind. Shank caught her first and jumped on her back, dragging her down. The other two boys piled on, one kicking her in the face and the other grabbing a handful of her hair and yanking it up as hard as he could.

Somehow, Harriet still held onto the ball, and Rufus understood it was her way of fighting back. She'd never beat all the boys, never outrun them, but she wasn't going to drop the ball. Dropping the ball was quitting; dropping the ball was giving up, saying *no, I am not a queer.* Holding it was saying *yes, I am, and you will not smear nor erase me no matter how hard you might try.*

Rufus finally reached the fray. He didn't bother to speak or yell or do anything except grab boys by the shoulders, arms, the neck, and pull them off, slinging them like discarded clothes. His strength amazed him. He dug through to the last boy—Shank—still on top of her.

Rufus grabbed him and ripped him away, tossing him across the grass. Shank landed, scrambled to his feet, glared at him.

"What are you doing?"

"I'm stopping you from killing her," Rufus said.

"I'll kill *you!*" Shank shouted. That was Shank. He was the kid with the loudest mouth, but he also had the biggest muscles, hands like boulders, knuckles for inflicting punishment on faces. He spoke without thinking, but sometimes he acted without thinking too. He kept the other boys on edge. Rufus swore sometimes even Harden treated him with a kind of respectful deference.

"Bring it on," Rufus heard himself say. And that was how it was too. He didn't so much as actually consciously say it. His body was reacting, working through this situation without him.

Shank swung at him and Rufus took the full brunt of the punch on his left jaw. It felt like a damn rocket had exploded in his head, but Rufus clenched his jaw hard, regained his balance, and sent a return shot back at Shank's right eye. The boy fell to the ground.

Everyone was silent now, except Harriet, who lay on the ground still clutching the football, whimpering.

"Every one of you will do morning time with Deloach," he announced.

"For what?" one of the boys said, his voice rife with the kind of smart-ass challenging tone most of these boys had mastered instinctually.

"For bullying," Rufus said. "For attacking her."

He turned to face the boy who'd spoken, a weasel-faced kid named Jake Sanderson. If Shank was the physical bully of the group, Jake was the mental one. He was a little kid, not just short, but so slight Rufus often wondered if there was some deficiency that kept him from putting on weight. His face was all bone and skin, the fleshy underneath stuff just wasn't there, and when the light hit him right, he was more ghoul than boy. Rufus tried not to hold his unfortunate countenance against him. Rufus was keenly aware (even if he'd been so unaware of other things at that time) that his own appearance often put people on edge. He suffered none of the same physical deficiencies as Jake, but he did have pale skin and hair so unnaturally dark that sometimes people assumed it had been dyed for effect. He was rangy and moved with uncanny lumbering motions he could quickly convert to more economical blasts of pure power when the urge took hold of him, as it had just done.

"We were just playing the game," Jake continued. He was smiling slightly, pleased with the way things had gone, the way they were continuing to go. It was all a show to him, Rufus thought. Goddamn entertainment.

He went on, his voice continuing to ease into a treacly innocence. "She was the queer, Mr. Gribble. We were just smearing her." A couple of the other boys laughed. Shank sat up, his eye already shiny and swollen. Rufus touched his jaw. Not broken, but definitely bruised. Chewing wouldn't come easy for a few days.

"Game's over," he said.

"So, what are we supposed to do?" Jake whined.

"You're supposed to step away from Harriet so I can check on her." The boys parted, letting Rufus through. He knelt beside Harriet.

She smiled at him. It was one of the saddest things Rufus had ever seen. "I should have done it," she said. "I should have already done it."

"What are you talking about?" he said, but Rufus already knew. She should have already made the leap. Whether or not she landed safely on the other side hardly mattered, did it? Either way she wouldn't be here, clinging to her identity like she clung to that damned football.

"Are you okay?" Rufus said, and put a hand on her back.

There was a laugh behind him. He was sure it was Jake. "Looks like Rufus has a thing for the dyke," Jake said. "Maybe he likes boys and she's the closest thing to a boy he can go for without admitting he's gay."

"Maybe they're both queer," a voice said.

"Who's the queer?" a deeper voice said.

Rufus turned and saw Harden approaching. He was grinning like it was all some big joke.

"Harry and Rufus," Jake said.

"Well, I knew about Harry, the dyke, but what's this about Rufus?" Harden said.

Rufus stood up, shaking his head.

Harden drew closer, getting a better look at the injured girl. "What the hell is happening here?"

"They were playing a game that singled out Harry, I mean Harriet," Rufus said. "They were going to kill her."

Harden spat on the ground, and then nodded. He stepped on the place he'd spit with his boot heel and drove it into the ground. "So, what's this about you being a queer, Rufus? You like assholes? Dicks?"

Rufus turned red as the boys laughed.

"No, sir."

Harden studied him for a moment. His eyes narrowed and his cheeks tightened around his jaw. Finally, he nodded slowly, as if he'd just arrived at some decision.

"Free time is over. Go back to your rooms."

Rufus tried to help Harriet up, but Harden said, "Leave her."

"I'm just helping her up," Rufus said.

"And I said, leave her there. You been spending too much time with her. Her queerness might be rubbing off on you."

"It doesn't work like that," Rufus said.

"The fuck it doesn't." Harden had turned suddenly aggressive. It frightened Rufus a little. It was one thing to stand up to the boys, another to stand up to Harden.

"Just leave her," he said. "Me and my niece need to figure some stuff out."

And there it was. The moment he should have acted. Rufus implicitly understood he should have stayed with her, should have defended her against Harden just as much as he had defended her against the boys, but he didn't. Goddamn, why didn't he? He'd known, goddamn it, he'd *known*. But knowing hadn't been enough, had it?

He'd nodded and walked away.

Looking back on it now, tied to the chair inside the cabin where Savanna had brought him, he realized the shadow girl had started that same night.

38

This time Ronnie and I parked about a half mile from the gate, leaving my truck hidden under the low-hanging tree branches a couple of miles from where we'd left his at the bottom of the mountain. We walked the half mile or so to the gate, staying in the woods as much as possible.

When we reached the gate, we settled in behind some thick trees off to one side. The sun was up by then, but it was still pretty dark under the shade of the trees.

"I could get over that," Ronnie said.

I turned to look at the fence, which was about fifteen yards away from where we crouched.

"Nah. It's electric. And there's barbed wire on top."

He scratched the side of his face, frowning. "Yeah." He thought for a little longer. "If we get in today, I could rig us up a way to get back in."

"How's that?"

"Well, I'd need some rope or line or something. But if I had that, I could find us a good tree on the other side. Tie one end of the rope to it, toss the other end over. Then when we left, I'd come around and find another tree on this side, tie it tight, with no slack. Then all you've got to do is climb the tree and work your way over."

It sounded a little farfetched, but I had to admit I was intrigued. The problem was, we didn't have any rope.

Ronnie seemed to read my mind. "That heavy-duty extension cord the kid was using for the Weed eater the first time we came should work."

"It would hold us up?"

Ronnie hesitated. "Fifty/fifty."

"I don't like those odds."

"Well, it'd give you a chance at least. Right now, you've got nothing."

"Actually," I said, nodding toward the road, "that's not true."

A Mazda hatchback was approaching the gate. Mindy was driving. "Let's go," I said, and pushed my way out of the trees, through the low-hanging branches, and began to wave my arms.

When she saw me, the look on her face told me pretty much all I needed to know.

Mindy didn't look angry. I could probably have worked with that. Instead, she looked frightened. Stunned, really. Too stunned to even let the window down as I approached the vehicle. She looked from me to Ronnie to the unopened gate, no doubt calculating if she could get it open, get her car through, and close it before we could slip in behind her.

I shook my head. "It's impossible," I said loudly. "Might as well talk to us."

Ronnie, thinking the same thing I was, stepped behind her vehicle, effectively blocking her from putting the car in reverse and escaping down the mountain. I felt a little bit like a thug, ambushing her this way, especially because she looked so afraid, but I didn't see another option. If I wanted in again, it was going to be through her.

I rapped on the driver's side window gently. "I just want to talk," I said.

She shook her head, and that was when I saw the cell phone. Jesus, she was going to call Harden. Or worse, she'd call Argent. Then Ronnie and I'd both be in deep shit. Argent had been just waiting for a chance to throw me and Ronnie in jail. He'd been fishing for something the night I'd found Joe in my yard and had come up empty. I'd been slightly surprised by how easily he'd given up then.

Something told me he wouldn't miss another opportunity.

But she was still dialing. I dropped to my knees, pleading with her through the glass.

She shook her head and put the phone to her ear.

That was when it happened. The rock—more like a small boulder—slammed through her back windshield with a crack and then a thud as it landed in the back of the vehicle. Ronnie didn't waste any time examining what destruction he'd wrought but instead climbed through the busted glass and swam over the seats until he had her cell phone in his hand. He ended the call and then tossed it through the broken glass and onto the road.

I wasn't sure who was more shocked, me or Mindy.

Then she started to scream, and I knew it was her.

"Open the damn door!" I shouted at Ronnie.

He reached across the seat, across her, still screaming at the top of her lungs, and lifted the lock. I opened the door and knelt beside her again. "Mindy," I said. "Mindy. Please. We're not going to hurt you."

But apparently the same couldn't be said of her intention toward me. She reached out, clawing me with one hand, raking her nails across my cheek, drawing blood instantly.

I put my hand to my bleeding face and wiped it away. She stared at me, no longer screaming.

It was Ronnie who broke the silence. "Sorry about your window."

* * *

It took ten minutes of me constantly reassuring her we weren't there to hurt her, that Ronnie wasn't some kind of Neanderthal (this was the toughest part), and that we'd both acted out of utter desperation.

Twice she tried to run, and I coaxed her back, telling her she wouldn't make it far down the mountain on foot.

"We're the good guys," I said for what felt like the hundredth time.

"Good guys don't have to attack young girls," she shot back.

"Yeah, I can see that. And maybe there was a better way to do this. Ronnie's a bit of a wild card sometimes. Actually, he's what I like to call a loose cannon. He just doesn't think before he acts, you know?" I glanced at Ronnie. He was smiling and nodding along eagerly, and I realized he was perfectly content. Hell, he was happiest when reveling in the mess he'd caused, like a dog proud of the squirrel he'd killed and dropped at your feet. No harm, no foul, right?

"What do you even want?" Mindy said with the kind of sigh that could tear a man down. She was beyond exasperated.

"We want to help the kids inside that fence. Based on our conversation the other night, I sort of thought that was what you wanted too."

"I don't think this is the way to go about it," she said.

"Do you remember our conversation about Weston Reynolds from the other night?"

Her expression changed. "Of course."

"What if I told you it wasn't suicide?"

She just looked at me. "The police said it was."

"Do you know who Jeb Walsh is?"

She nodded, her face tightening a little. "I know Mr. Walsh."

"What if I told you he owns everything in this county, from the sheriff to the district attorney to the mayor in Riley?"

She made a face. I couldn't tell if she was still with me or if she'd gone away, somewhere else.

Turned out it was both.

"I believe that," she said.

"What do you mean?"

"Mr. Walsh . . . he made comments to me."

"Comments?"

"Inappropriate ones. I told Mr. Harden, and he said that was just how Mr. Walsh was and to ignore it. I tried, but then he grabbed me."

"He grabbed you?"

Mindy looked straight ahead. "Yeah. And that's why . . ." She began to cry, softly. "That's why I was so freaked out when you did what you did."

I felt myself getting angry. "He *grabbed* you?"

"My ass. He tried to play it off. Like it was a joke. I told Harden again, and he said to call the sheriff. I did, and the sheriff basically said it was my fault. That Mr. Walsh was a busy man and he didn't need young girls throwing themselves at him, and how did I expect him to react with me being so young and pretty?"

Jesus Christ, I wanted to *hurt* Jeb Walsh *and* Preston Argent.

"So, I guess maybe I do believe you."

"Then you'll let us in?"

She hesitated. I was aware that the longer we sat here, the greater the chance we had of being seen. Ronnie must have felt the same pressure because he spoke up, nudging her slightly.

"He's a pervert," he said. "Here's your chance to do something about it."

"*You* seem like a pervert," Mindy said.

Ronnie lifted his hands, a gesture of supplication. *Can't argue with you there*, the gesture seemed to communicate.

"Take your time," I said. "Just remember, we want to help you and these kids."

She nodded. "I do worry about them. The students. They always seem so sad."

I waited. Even Ronnie had the sense to stay quiet for once.

Ronnie nudged me and jabbed his thumb toward more exhaust coming over the rise.

"Somebody's coming," Mindy said.

"Yeah, you'd better get inside. We're going to follow you, okay?"

She looked at the exhaust floating lazily toward the sky. It seemed in no hurry to get anywhere, swirling and dipping, reforming and then dispersing into the powder-blue morning sky.

"Mindy?" I said. "We don't have much time."

Our eyes locked. I saw in her gaze that she was going to trust me. I saw something else there too, something that nearly broke me. There was a transfer of power there. The power shifted over to me. She was giving me her trust. I knew I would never purposefully abuse it like some men, but I also knew I was a piece of shit who sometimes forgot others when my own interest reared its selfish and demanding head.

"Okay," she said.

39

Once inside the gates, Ronnie and I sprinted for the nearest cover, which turned out to be a small, well-maintained flower garden just off the drive. We knelt behind thorny rosebushes and watched Mindy's car disappear as she made her way around the bend and on up to the school.

A pickup truck materialized at the gate, and I squinted my eyes, but I couldn't see who the driver was. I did note that it was a tan Silverado with local tags.

"What's next, Earl?" Ronnie said.

I shook my head. I wasn't sure if I should be angry at Ronnie for busting Mindy's window or thank him. This was my natural state whenever Ronnie was around. His company pretty much ensured you'd be vacillating between utter frustration and complete awe, with a little gratitude thrown in for good measure.

"What?" he said.

I nodded at him. "That was quick thinking back there. I'm sorry about what I said. About you being a loose cannon."

"Shit. I can't think of nothing I'd rather be."

I waited for the punchline, but then I realized he was completely sincere.

"Loooooose," he howled a bit too loud for my taste. "Fucking loooooooooose!"

I didn't want to laugh. I *tried* not to. But in the end, it was just too much. I covered my mouth with my hand and gave in.

It felt good.

* * *

A few minutes later, we split up. Ronnie headed for a work shed we'd found on the right side of the school. He hoped to find his extension cord and create a way back in. I made my way around to the rear of the school, to the garden, and tried to find a way into the building so I could talk to some more boys, specifically Eddie. Either that or catch one of them outside. Failing both of those, I'd at least be able to take a look at the falls again. It might not help me figure anything out, but I had a powerful urge to visit them, to gaze across the ravine, to picture the place where so much had happened that was out of my reach now.

We agreed to meet at the gate in three hours at exactly 10:45. Anything more felt like we would just be pushing our luck.

"What if you're late?" he said.

I shook my head, feeling increasingly frustrated. Wasn't he supposed to be the loose cannon? "Then leave without me," I said.

"You know I can't do that."

"You can and you will," I said. "You have to promise me that, Ronnie."

He shook his head. "Naw . . ."

I stopped walking. "I'm serious. You've already done time for me once. At some point, you have to take care of yourself. Promise me."

"Sure, Earl. I promise."

"Thank you."

"See you in three hours," he said, and began to jog toward the work shed. I watched him go, thinking how my life had so rarely gone like I'd expected it to. When I'd met Ronnie three years ago, I would have bet the pension I didn't have that we'd never get along, that in fact I would always despise him. For about a year or so, I would have been looking good on that bet, but somewhere along the way, our relationship changed. I still wasn't sure if it was me or Ronnie who had done the changing. Maybe both of us. Maybe neither. But something shifted and Ronnie had become like blood to me. I didn't have to like him or tolerate him. I could curse him, even ignore him, but in the end, I needed him.

And maybe that wasn't so bad. To need somebody. Sometimes I thought it might even be a good thing.

* * *

I headed to the garden at the rear of the school and immediately had to hit the ground when I saw Dr. Blevins standing outside the garden with one of the boys. They were about a hundred yards from me and I had no cover, so I simply hit the ground and lay as flat as I could.

Dr. Blevins had his hand on the boy's shoulder and was talking to him with a serious expression on his face. The boy—tall, rangy, and dressed in the blue pants, blue shirt uniform—nodded along solemnly.

I watched as Blevins patted the boy's shoulder and then removed his hand. The boy hesitated for just a moment and then stepped out of sight behind a large plant in the garden maze. Blevins followed him, and then I was alone, lying on the grass, the blazing sun hitting the back of my neck. I rose up slowly and looked around. Something caught my attention on the second floor. One of the boys was in the window, peering down at me. I stood, dusting my blue jeans off, and then lifted a hand to him. But there was no response. The boy was gone. The curtains were closed.

Knowing my time was limited, I skirted the edge of the garden, and before reaching the entrance, I hoisted myself up on the stone wall and climbed over. I could hear voices as I dropped down behind a pot of large purple flowers.

It sounded like Blevins.

"She's going to meet you in twenty minutes. It's out of my hands now. Harden has stepped in."

There was no answer. I slipped out from behind the flowers and crept a little closer. A row of small trees separated me from Blevins now. I could see the back of his shoulders, his shiny bald pate reflecting the bright sun. I couldn't see if he was talking to the same boy or a different one.

"See," Blevins said, "this is what I'm talking about."

"What?" the boy said, his voice a high whine.

"*What?*" Blevins mocked, cruelly imitating the boy's high pitch. "To be a man, to be straight, you have to believe it first. You can't believe it if you keep talking like that. Talk like a man. I've studied this stuff. How do you think I cured myself?"

"Okay," the kid said.

"Say it again. This time like you're a man."

The kid said *what* again, this time with a gruffness that was almost comical.

Blevins said, "Just remember. Think like a man, talk like a man, and men like women. It's science."

There was no response.

"You got it?"

"I got it." The reply was deep, more resonant than before. I could see Blevins's shoulders relax. He was pleased.

"You better get on over there."

"I'm scared."

"Of course you are. It's normal. What you're about to do is the most natural thing in the world. God designed it. God wants this for you."

"I heard she gets mad if you don't . . ."

"Don't think about messing up. Just . . ." Blevins patted the boy's shoulder gently. "Look, sometimes I have to get myself started by thinking about . . ."

"About what?"

"A fantasy."

"But, that means . . ."

"Just try it. Then when you're ready, you'll see what you're missing out on."

"Will there really be cameras?"

"Don't worry about that."

That was when I saw Dr. Blevins do something that truly disturbed me. He reached a hand to the boy's face and caressed it like a lover might, his hand lingering near the boy's ear. It took all I had to keep from charging him right then and there.

Then the moment was over, and Blevins's hand was back by his side. "Go," he said. "I'll be there with you."

A moment later, I saw a different boy walk past me and toward the garden exit. This boy was pudgy and thick. Not fat, not exactly. His belly was flat, but he was chunky in other places—his face, his arms, his thighs. He had ruddy cheeks and light-brown hair.

He left the garden. I waited, staying perfectly still, listening to see what Blevins would do.

For a second, I didn't hear anything and I thought perhaps he was waiting me out too, that somehow he'd become aware of my presence and was biding his time to see what I'd do next. But then I heard his voice.

"Hey," he said. "Heath's on his way." I looked through the branches of the trees and saw him talking on a cell phone.

He nodded, listening to the person on the other end. Then he said, "Where? On the big rock."

The person on the other end said something else, and Blevins responded with a quick, "All right, copy that."

He walked off, heading toward the school.

I waited as long as I dared and then slipped out of the garden toward the lawn and the forest of trees that would lead me to the waterfall.

40

Two Indian Falls was more spectacular than I remembered. I arrived expecting to see someone else already waiting for Heath. I'd stayed off the path and had instead run through the trees, hoping I could get there before Heath did. It worked. I didn't see him anywhere.

I stayed in the cover of the woods, keeping an eye on the flat rock, where Blevins had said it would happen. I scanned the area for some type of camera but saw nothing. It was almost as if the entire conversation had been a fake, a setup to throw me off. Was it possible he'd been aware of me? I remembered the kid I'd seen in the second-floor window. Had he somehow alerted Blevins? Had he known all along I was listening to him? What if he'd directed me here on purpose? I felt a chill snake down my spine. It had a strange kind of logic to it. After all, wasn't this the very spot where Harriet and Weston had vanished? If they wanted to get rid of me, to remove me from the trail permanently, wouldn't this be the exact place where they'd make it happen?

I'd almost convinced myself it was all a brilliant trap when I saw Heath emerge from the trees. He stopped about ten yards away from me and looked around, paying close attention to the flat rock poised near the falling water. He seemed perplexed, unsure as to why he was still alone. He looked around, his eyes going right past me, not even noticing my presence.

I let out a breath and waited.

He climbed slowly to the flat rock and stood in the middle of it. I couldn't get over how vulnerable he looked standing there. It was almost as if he were some sacrificial goat from ancient times that had been pushed into the clearing before an angry deity.

The only sound was the water crashing over the falls. The sky was clear and blue, streaked by a single thin V of blackbirds flying toward whatever lay across the gorge. What did lie over the gorge? Was it possible the rocky bluff on the other side led to new life, to redemption? It was hard for me, even now in my fifties, some thirty-plus years removed from my father's teachings, to think about redemption in any terms other than the sacred. I'd grown up with redemption as a Biblical imperative, and because that imperative had ultimately lost all meaning for me, the word itself had become sort of hollow, a dead word that landed wrong against my ears. But seeing the gap, the churning water that filled it, with the possibility of escape forever foregrounding everything else these boys might experience, I was able to see the word in a new light.

Escape had been the thing I'd always wanted, and the thing I'd finally achieved. But there had to be more than just escaping a failed system of meaning, didn't there? That would be like attempting a jump across the gorge and falling to your death. The escape was achieved, but nothing else beyond it.

When I'd made my jump thirty-some years ago, I'd almost fallen into the gorge, but a small ledge had saved me. That had been Arnette Lacey, the black midwife who'd taken me in. But when I'd left her, I'd fallen again. I'd found life tough and had constantly eased it with whiskey, women, even violence. I fell for a long time before deciding I needed to look for a way to stop the fall again. I faced my father. I won. I vanquished him and kept from falling over the ledge with him thanks to Mary's outthrust hand. But again, she was just a ledge. The second she stepped away, I was falling again.

So what was the trick? How could I get to the other side when I was already in the gorge?

Maybe that was what redemption really was. Maybe it was learning to walk on the air, to levitate, or at least do the hard work of climbing out, hand over hand.

* * *

I waited for ten more minutes, just watching Heath standing there. On several different occasions, he appeared to talk to himself as he paced back and forth on the rock. I tried to read his lips, but I was too far away to have any luck.

When I decided to leave my hiding place and make my way over to the rock, he was facing away from me, near the edge of the bluff.

"Hello," I said.

Heath spun around, his mouth open in surprise. He held both hands up as if to ward me off. "What do you want?"

"To help." I stepped a little closer to the rock. He backed away. "Be careful. You don't want to fall."

"Just stay back, okay?"

"I'm a private investigator. My name is Earl Marcus. I'm here investigating the death of Weston Reynolds. Did you know him?"

Heath lowered his hands a little. "Yeah. There's only sixteen of us. Well, fifteen now. We all know each other."

"Mind if I come up on the rock with you?" I knew I was taking a risk because there really might be a camera, but I felt like it was worth it if I could get the kid to talk.

"Yeah. No. Stay right there."

"Okay. Mind if we talk?"

"We can talk, but don't come any closer."

I nodded. "Sure."

He cocked his head to the side, the way people do when they're trying to focus on a distant sound. He seemed to hear whatever it was he was listening for and lowered his chin, meeting my eye.

"Where is she?" he asked.

"Where is who?"

"Sister."

"Who?"

He cocked his head again. Listening. That was what he had to be doing, right? What else could explain it?

"Sister," he said. "I don't know her real name. People say she's somebody's sister, maybe Harden's. But she's terrible."

"Have you had to meet with her before?"

He hesitated, as if unsure how much he should say.

"It's okay, Heath. No one is here but us."

"I haven't met with her. But . . . but, sooner or later, everyone has to." everyone has to."

"And what happens when you meet with her?"

He shook his head, as if he couldn't quite believe I was serious. "You haven't gotten too far on the case yet, have you?"

I had to laugh. "I suppose I'm a little slow on the uptake sometimes." What I didn't say was I'd been slowed down by the investigation of my own life. That I sometimes had a hard time handling more than one mystery at a time.

"They also call her Evangeline."

"But I thought you didn't know her name."

"It's not her real name. It's a nickname. A handle. Evangeline, as in Evangelist."

"Why would people call her that?"

"Evangelists save people. They convert them. She's their go-to. If all else fails, they send us to her."

I was finally starting to understand, and the realization sickened me. It was nothing less than institutionalized rape. "You don't have a choice?" I said, wanting to pull the words back as soon as I'd asked them, because it was dumb to ask questions you already knew the answer to.

"They tell you there's a choice, that it's all aboveboard. It's voluntary therapy, they say. They wait until you're eighteen. If they still think you're gay, if their therapy hasn't worked . . . well, you get an appointment."

"What was the talk about a camera?"

He cocked his head, yet again, squinting in concentration. "I signed some consent, saying I didn't mind being filmed. I don't know where the cameras are. I also don't know where Sister is."

As he spoke, I'd gradually been moving closer, picking my way up the rise, rock by rock. I was nearly to the flat rock now, and I could see he was shaking.

"What happens if you say no?"

He looked around again, his nervousness on full display. His eyes settled on something behind me, high in the trees. I almost turned around to see what he was looking at, but then he met my eyes. "I think I've already said too much. It's all legal. I signed a paper. I want to get better."

I did turn around then, because I was sure someone must be behind us. What else could explain his sudden change of tone?

There was nothing behind us but trees. So what had changed?

"I'm sorry."

"What?" I asked. I turned but never got a good look at him. The rock in his hand was so large it blotted out the falls, the sun, the whole sky as it slammed into my field of vision and knocked me on my ass.

"I'm sorry," he said again, standing over me, holding the rock high.

"No," I said, not sure what he was doing or why, but I was utterly sure what would happen if he slammed that rock down on me again. I was a goner.

Then he cocked his head again to one side, and I realized this whole time he'd had an earpiece in his right ear. Someone had been coaching him, telling him what to say and when to pick up the rock. Suddenly I remembered the gentle way Blevins had touched his face. Except now I realized it hadn't been his face. It had been his ear. Blevins had inserted the earpiece.

I took advantage of the hesitation on his part and rolled away from him, toward the ledge and the long fall. He came after me, the large rock still raised over his head. He moved slowly, staggering toward the ledge, the weight of the rock throwing off his balance, his arms shaking from the effort. I began to fear he was going to fall.

"Stop!" I said through my swollen lips.

But he didn't stop. He kept coming. I could hear the voice in the speaker inside his ear now, or maybe I just imagined I could. I tried to scramble to my feet, but one of my feet was closer to the ledge than I thought. I stepped into nothingness. The feeling was disorienting, scary, heart stopping. It was worse than having the floor pulled out from under you. It was like trying to stand up and realizing there had never been a floor at all. My other foot, still on the rock, slid back with the weight of the rest of me, and for an eternal second I was balanced perfectly on the edge, the tip of my right boot all that was connecting me to anything solid. The rest of me felt the fear of nothingness grip me, and then the exhilaration, the raw *freedom* of the fall as gravity ripped me down into the gorge and the toe of my boot scratched the rock and then lost contact.

41

The falling was familiar.

In some ways, I'd been falling all my life.

It was all I'd known, and all I'd been waiting for. It was my past and my future, and it had found perfect completion in my present predicament.

As the sky ran away from me, I realized I would find out at last if there was a bottom, or if the fall just continued forever. Honestly, it felt like a relief.

Instead I felt the jolt of sudden reality as unexpected as a bolt of lightning. There was shock, too. It ran up through my back and into my neck and stuck to the roof of my skull. I expected to feel water or blood or the sensation of my body smashing open against the rocks, but there was just the shock. A single jolt that was somehow more than physical.

I wasn't falling anymore. The sky had stopped running away. It was there, growing darker by increments. I breathed. My heart galloped. I lay on my back, and one arm, my left, was free, hanging out over the gorge. The roar of the falls was louder here, like a drumline, thudding rhythmically. I sat up and saw I was on a small outcropping, the same one I'd noticed from my first visit to the falls.

I slid away from the edge and pressed my back against the stone bluff behind me.

My back and neck ached, so I tested all my extremities to make sure there had been no permanent damage. Everything creaked with pain, but everything moved.

Above me, I could hear the faint sound of voices. I couldn't make out what they said, but I assumed they were talking about me, trying to figure out where I'd landed far below. This ledge was all but invisible without leaning out into the void and tempting fate and gravity.

The voices eventually faded away. The only thing I was sure of was that there was one male and one female. Heath and Sister. Or was Sister even real? I remembered the earpiece Heath had been wearing. I began to breathe faster, creeping toward hyperventilation as I realized how close I'd been to dying, how while I'd been falling it had felt like something I'd been waiting my whole life to find. The bottom.

I closed my eyes, trying to clear my mind. Why was I panicked now that I was faced with life again when the prospect of death had seemed almost calming?

I knew the answer, didn't I? My life was a derailed train, tipped over into an endless gorge. Death was peace. An end to the falling at last.

I pushed myself to my feet and studied the wall. It was smooth rock, slick from the spray of the waterfall and covered in a coat of slimy green moss. No way I was climbing up that.

I tried to keep my mind off what I feared was inevitable. If I didn't find a way out of here, I'd be forced to call somebody to help me. Once I did that, I would be busted. Harden and Blevins could call Argent and have me arrested for trespassing.

There had to be a better way. But each time I looked at the long fall below me and the slick, straight wall I'd have to climb to get out of there, the more despair I felt. I'd have to scale at least fifteen feet of smooth rock. That wasn't happening. Not at fifty-three. Hell, that wasn't happening at any age. I wasn't even sure it was possible without some mountain-climbing gear.

I turned around and lay flat on my belly, craning my head out into the ravine. The drop was dizzying. Two hundred feet or more, if I had to guess. I supposed it was possible for a man to survive that fall if he hit the water just right, but the chances were extremely slim.

Unlike this side, the opposite bluff was replete with ridges and divots, overhangs and small, dark corridors that might or might not lead to bigger caves. If I could only find a way across . . .

As I studied the other side, I noticed a strange phenomenon, something I'd completely missed before. As the bluff grew out of the valley, it leaned across the river, as if it were trying to reach this side, to reattach itself and clog up the waterfall, sealing the river off from the sun. The slant of the other side came to its closest point about eight to ten feet below me. If I could get a running start, I might be able to make the leap to the small ledge jutting out from the opposite bluff.

I checked my feet. They were a good three feet from the edge. That wouldn't be much of a running start before I had to jump. But . . . I looked right and then left. If I could start my run next to the wall and gradually peel away as I angled my trajectory toward the other outcrop, I might have a chance.

The more I looked at the ledge on the other side, the more I thought I could do it. And then what? I traced a path from the opposite ledge, using nooks and crannies and small ledges up toward the top of the other side. I could make that climb.

Maybe.

I sat down, still staring at the ledge across from me. Was there some mirage at work here, something deceiving me, making me think I could do something I couldn't? Had the two Indian boys made the same mistake so many years ago? What about Harriet—had she tried this very same thing, only to fall to her death?

Maybe. Maybe she knew that to get across the gap, you had to plan your leaps just so, that surviving the fall that was waiting for us all took more than determination. It took careful planning, grit, and vision. You had to see the way first. And wasn't that always the hardest part? Seeing past the blinders society placed on us?

I tried to imagine a way forward, one without Mary, a way that didn't involve destroying my days with alcohol. I didn't quite see it yet. The picture seemed so bleak, so filled with utter misery.

The weirdest thing was, right now, on this ledge, looking at my situation, I felt okay. I was alone. The river was below me and the falls to my left. The constant tumbling of the water gave me strange comfort, and I felt more clearheaded than I had in a while.

What if it wasn't Harden or Blevins who was behind it all? What if it was this woman, this Sister? What if she was the one calling the shots? Ronnie had said something about the kid doing yard work mentioning Sister. I thought of Lyda and the strange thing she'd said about Savanna, something about no one being as strong as her. Was it possible Savanna was still around? Rufus had seemed frightened when we'd been discovered in the barn. Was it because he believed it was Savanna and not Lyda? Hadn't he said something about Savanna being different, being less than he'd hoped she would be? Or was it just the way all jilted lovers tended to look at their exes, with an eye that grew more critical over time and distance?

I looked around at the walls of the gorge, the spectacular waterfall, the deep-blue sky like blown glass, the breathless nose dive that was waiting just a step away. I felt very close to piecing the mystery together, but something told me none of the answers would come without a price.

42

Sometimes you have to move forward on faith. Rufus had taught me that. When I'd asked him once about getting around as a blind man, he'd told me a bunch of stuff about having a sixth sense I didn't really believe, but he'd also said something that had stuck with me: sometimes you just had to move forward, take a chance. Standing still didn't help you figure anything out. Moving did.

So, it was time for me to move.

I peered down into the ravine again and then at the small outcropping on the other side. The jump was doable. I'd have to fall about eight feet, and of course jump far enough to bridge the gap, but technically, I thought, it was possible. As long as my aim was good, I had plenty of room to land. Sure, I could bust an ankle or sprain my wrist, but not if I rolled with the landing. I'd spent over thirty years making dangerous leaps from trees, rooftops, and ledges, and so far I'd managed to walk away from every one of them. The only difference between this and leaping from the roof of a house or a tree limb was the small margin for error I had if I missed my landing. Two feet off to either the left or right would kill me. Not to mention I was taking it on faith that once I made it to that ledge, there would be another ledge I could use to make my way down into the ravine. Or up if possible.

I decided to buy some more time by calling Ronnie.

"Earl!" he said in a sharp whisper.

"Where are you?"

"I'm in a bad spot here."

"What's happening?"

"One of the kids spotted me and must of told somebody inside. These two jackasses are out here with guns. I found a tree to hide in. Hold it. They're coming."

I was silent, listening as the wind blew into the receiver, mixing with Ronnie's heavy breathing. I heard voices from far away, but I couldn't make out what they were saying. A long time passed like this, and eventually the voices faded away. Ronnie's breathing slowed. The wind died down.

"Earl? You still there?"

"Yeah, I'm here. You okay?"

"They're gone. Can you bring the truck to the gate and pick me up?"

"I'm sort of in a bad way myself. You may have to get out on foot and walk to your truck."

"Oh shit. Yeah. That's all the way down the mountain. It's a walk, but I guess I can do it."

"I'm about to go across a ravine."

"A what?"

"I'll call you when I get to the other side."

"I better come help you."

"No," I said. "Somebody needs to take care of Goose and keep an eye out for Rufus."

"You gonna be gone a long time, Earl?"

I looked down at the river. "Maybe."

"I don't like this."

"I gotta go, Ronnie. Take care of yourself."

"Earl?"

"Yeah?"

"Thanks."

"For what?"

"For caring about me."

I didn't know what to say, but I didn't have to say anything. He ended the call. I turned to face the ravine and realized I didn't have a choice now.

43

After the two silent men helped Rufus to the toilet, where they let him sit long enough to take care of business, they led him to the chair and tied him up again.

He wasn't sure where Savanna was, but he feared she might be out there trying to mess with Earl. He could only hope Earl would see through her, that he would recognize her as a predator, but he had no faith in that. Savanna was nothing short of brilliant when it came to weaponizing sex. Aim for a man's weak spots and dissect him piece by fucking piece.

Rufus wanted to scream, but he didn't. He didn't even move. He was tired. Tired in his bones. His lungs even felt tired as he breathed. But he wouldn't sleep. He couldn't allow himself to sleep. There was something waiting for him in sleep he simply wasn't strong enough to deal with.

He heard the two men shuffling around in the other room. They never spoke unless it was to answer a question from Savanna, and then they used only monosyllables, saying no more than was necessary. Despite how he should feel about the two men, Rufus found himself developing a kind of begrudging respect for them. They seemed more like objects than subjects, unable to do anything but react to the world they had been placed in, automatons who'd been cursed with a free will they did not know how to access.

They brought him food periodically, usually fast food. Burger King, he thought, which was telling, because the only Burger King in Coulee County was near Brethren, so he was assuming the house was in the mountains not too far from there.

It began to storm. Thunder rumbled dimly at first but soon grew stronger, rocking the cabin with devastating booms that might as well have been dynamite exploding in the front yard. The rain came next, pouring as if from a tipped bucket onto the tin roof. Rufus felt some on his face as it slipped through a leak in the roof.

Another drop hit his eye and he felt his lid flutter. He saw something, a bare bookshelf, nearly covered in a net of spiderwebs. His other eye opened as well and the bookshelf came into focus. A single spider skittered along its web, moving up to the top shelf and disappearing into a crack in the wood.

Rufus tried to blink again, tried to will himself back to the comfort of blindness, but he was incapable of doing so. Somehow, he could see again. Somehow, he was able to perceive the world as it was, not as it pretended to be.

He rolled his eyes, rotating them first to the right and then up to the left and back again. It was dark, but that didn't matter. He could still see the boxes pushed against the wall, stacked haphazardly like steps leading up to the watermarked ceiling. He traced the dark water stain to its source and rolled his eye up just in time to see another drop of rainwater falling. It landed in his open eye, and when it did, his peripheral vision grew. He saw everything then, a stone fireplace, cold and silent; a panorama of junk and cobwebs and bare hardwood floors littered with dust bunnies that appeared to be somehow alive and inanimate at once.

But it was the door that drew him. To the left of the bookshelf, slightly ajar, but not enough to see on the other side of it, was a brown, wooden door. A red ribbon was tied to the doorknob, and it fluttered in the breeze that came through the slight opening.

The rain had stopped. There was just that breeze from outside the cabin. He waited, riveted, unable to look away, as the door began to open wider and stronger winds rushed in from the wild places in the mountains. The red ribbon slipped free from the door knob and blew across the room, landing on Rufus's face, tickling his nose and cheek. He tried to reach for it, to pull it away, to scratch the itch, but he couldn't.

Your hands are tied, dumbass. But that wasn't it. Not quite. He couldn't even strain against the ropes. He was paralyzed. That was when he understood.

She was back.

A shadow covered the door. It was a narrow shadow and *not* a narrow shadow, because there were a dozen or more iterations of the shadow that shuttered off from the original, like flashes from a strobe light, except there was no light. Which was impossible. You couldn't see without light. Hell, he was blind, but he could still see, so nothing made sense in this world he'd slipped into.

The shadow girl stepped forward and all her iterations came together, closing rank until they snapped into a single image that squeezed through the doorway awkwardly. She was just the shape of a body, head, torso, and limbs, all featureless and dark, and she moved with a stuttering gait more like a wind-up toy than a person.

He couldn't look away as she stepped over, chopping her steps unnaturally. She made it close enough for him to touch her if he'd been able to move his hands to do so. Her body bent unnaturally until her face was a mere inch from his. Her face was a void, a horrifying nothing; looking into it felt like being more than blind; it felt like being dead and more than dead too. Looking into her face was like looking into something worse than death. It was looking into a life lived wrong.

Rufus tried without success to speak, to banish the shadow girl. He wanted to tell her she was dead and it was okay to be dead, that it was better than being alive, and if he could make this feeling go away by dying, he'd do it in a heartbeat. But he feared that wouldn't work, that this shadow girl lived in a place that would allow her to follow him anywhere.

So he did what he always did and wished he could go back and make a different choice.

That didn't work either. He was forced to stare into the void, the abyss, and like some famous philosopher had said, the abyss was staring right back at him.

* * *

The moment had come when he'd least expected it. The third thing that marked his life. The two weeks after the incident with the boys and Harriet passed in a muddy slog. Rain and more rain, falling from nearly sunless skies, accompanied his already dark mood. There had been a change in the students, too. Ever since the day he'd tried to help Harriet, the boys had treated him with subtle indifference. There wasn't outright defiance. No, it was more sinister, and somehow worse. They often smiled at each other knowingly when he was around. Sometimes one of them would pretend not to hear him when he gave instructions. He'd repeat himself, his voice louder, and only at that point would the boy feign ignorance and say with a half smile that he hadn't heard Rufus.

The weather grew darker as October turned to November. Rufus felt a shift in his relationship with Harden and Deloach. They seemed constantly disappointed in him. Much like the boys, neither man actually said anything directly, but it was what they *didn't* say that Rufus noticed. Gone were the pats on the back, the words of encouragement, the talk of him one day taking over for Old Man Irwin. Instead, both men barely acknowledged his presence.

At least until it happened.

It was something he had hardly even dared dream about. Sure, he found Savanna attractive. No, that wasn't exactly right. He found her more than attractive. She was intoxicating. Being around her was like being drunk. Sometimes he found himself forgetting all of his problems, all of his doubts, and just soaking her up. The smell of her, the way she seemed to appear more vivid than nearly anything else. It was as if the rest of the world were in black and white and she was in Technicolor.

The night had been rainy again. Lightning flashed outside and Rufus smelled wood smoke. Probably a tree struck somewhere. A shadow crossed the yard. He assumed it was Mrs. Duncan, bringing him leftovers. Except it was raining pretty hard, and she didn't always get out if the weather wasn't nice. She'd apologize the next day, and he'd tell her there was no need because he was a grown man and should be able to handle his own supper. But the truth was, he did sort of depend on her. He was usually exhausted by the time he returned to the barn, and she was a hell of a cook. Her leftovers were better than just about anything he'd ever eaten.

He sat up, unsure what to do because he was already in bed, wearing nothing but a pair of briefs, still wet from the long, soggy walk home in the rain.

He'd just have her put it on the table by the door, and then when she shut the door, he'd get up and retrieve it.

The knock came, a series of light raps.

"Come on in," he said. "Get out of the rain."

When the door swung open, Rufus did a double take. It wasn't Mrs. Duncan but her daughter Savanna. She held a covered dish, her hands and arms shiny with rain, her white blouse soaked so thoroughly it lay flat and translucent against her skin.

Rufus looked away, finding the barn rafters, the dark hollows where he sometimes heard something scurrying late at night, causing him to close his eyes and sink a little deeper under the covers. He felt like doing the same thing now.

Her breasts were plainly visible beneath the white blouse. Surely she knew this. Didn't she?

"I brought your supper, Rufus," she said.

"You can put it on the table there. I'm sorry you had to come out in the rain."

"It's okay," she said. "I like the rain. It feels good to get wet sometimes."

He wasn't ready for this. He let her last comment sort of hang but quickly realized that wasn't what he wanted to do. He tried to think of something to say, something that would smooth things over, make it all less awkward. "What's for dinner?" That was all he could come up with. Jesus, he was an idiot.

"Well, if you'd look, you would see it's your favorite. I asked Mama to cook it for you special."

He kept his eyes on the rafters. Maybe the rat would show itself. Maybe it would come scurrying out and end this moment of impossibility, break his trance, make the world go back to itself, because . . . because . . .

"Rufus?"

"What?"

"Look at me."

With a nearly agonizing slowness, he moved his eyes along the center rafter, toward the front of the barn. When he saw the front side of the barn, he turned his chin down, and his gaze followed, easing toward the door frame and where she stood, her blonde hair wet and frizzy around her plump face.

"Rufus," she said, stepping forward.

"What?" His eyes were on her face, nothing else.

"*Look* at me."

And he did. He took her all in, his eyes only lingering on her breasts for a second before he pulled back his gaze and framed her like a flower in a field, blooming despite the hard rain. She was soaked, but the rain couldn't keep her from being what she was, which was an undeniably sexual creature. Her back arched and his eyes were drawn to her breasts again, her wet flesh, the dark of her navel beneath the blouse, which stretched and pressed itself into her like a second layer of skin.

"I know you like me," she said.

"How . . . ?"

She held a finger to her lips and shushed him. "I never like talking to boys too much. Some of my friends, they go on and on about how their boyfriends won't talk to them, how they only want to . . ." She smiled slyly, nodding at him, as if encouraging him to finish her sentence.

"Only want to what?" he said, his throat dry, his voice hoarse and small.

"Only want to, you know." She stepped a little closer.

"I'm not dressed," he said.

"Oh, okay. Does it make you nervous I'm so close?"

"A little bit."

"I don't understand that."

"What?"

"Being nervous."

He must have given her an odd look when she said this. He couldn't remember his exact reaction, but her words had stuck with him for many years. He'd often wonder if that should have been his first clue. But the more he thought about it, the more he realized he'd been too far gone to recognize clues. There are times in life when you are oblivious to everything except that one person or thing in your field of vision. That person you can't erase from your memory no matter how hard you try. That person whose hold over you is purely physical, purely experiential, but so intoxicating that quitting them is worse than quitting smoking or drinking or even breathing.

"Well, I understand it," he said. "I feel it now."

"I can relax you," she said.

"How will you do that?"

"First, you got to look at me."

He looked at her again. Her hands were at her waist. She clutched the bottom of her blouse and tugged it upward, pulling it over her head.

"Keep looking," she said with a grin, "or you might hurt my feelings."

"I wouldn't want to do that," he said.

"No, course not." Her hands went to the front of her blue jeans, and she ripped all the buttons on the fly open in one swift moment. The next part wasn't so easy. She wore her blue jeans tight, and they were wet, so shrugging them off was like shedding a particularly tight skin.

When they were finally on the floor next to her blouse, she was standing right beside Rufus's bed.

"You ain't never done nothing like this, have you?"

"No."

That made her smile, and he remembered thinking how he'd assumed when girls found out he wasn't experienced, they would be put off. But not Savanna. He seemed incapable of displeasing her.

She reached for his hand and placed it against her belly. "Touch me wherever you want."

He started tentatively, but she began to grow impatient with him. "That's not the spot," she said. "Down there."

He moved his hand down and found her center. Her body reacted immediately, and the way she shook and moved in time with his hand was the most wonderful thing Rufus had ever experienced.

The rest of it happened as in a dream. She climbed onto him, and there was a kind of vicious bucking, her body riding his so fast and hard he almost stopped her because he wanted to slow down to feel her against him, to soak it all up, but it seemed she had other ideas.

She always had other ideas, he realized later.

44

waited on the wind, standing for a long time, looking directly at the ledge some seven to eight feet below me. When the wind shifted, I didn't hesitate. I began to run, veering off with each step toward the edge. I took the last step and pushed off into the open air. For a moment the wind seemed to hold me up and I floated, poised like a wingless angel over the ravine. While I was there, I felt a cold regret snaking under my skin, rippling it with gooseflesh. And then I fell.

There was just enough time to realize I had indeed misjudged the distance across the gorge. I stretched my body to its limits, swimming madly through the air toward the outcrop. My hands hit first, followed by elbows, and then my midsection. My legs dangled below me as I tried desperately to pull my full weight up and onto the safety of the narrow ridge. My hands and elbows were raw and I cried out with pain as I used them to hang on. With a great effort, I scuttled onto the ledge, collapsing face first and closing my eyes.

I was exhausted and hurting. For a long time, I didn't move.

The sun was on my back, and then I felt it shift, and more shadows crept over the ravine. I rolled over and looked up into a dark-blue sky. A large, black cloud hung over the waterfall and appeared in no hurry to do anything but linger. I looked at my hands and elbows first. They were shredded. My palms were raw with blisterlike wounds, and three nails were broken from trying to use them to gain purchase on the rocks. My elbows weren't much better. They were less skinned up, but my right one ached every time I straightened it. How had I misjudged the leap so badly? Was it simply an optical illusion that had fooled me? Or perhaps the wind had shifted, pushing back against momentum?

Either way, I'd dodged a bullet. If I'd jumped even a few inches less, I'd be dead right now, crushed on the rocks below.

Speaking of which, now that I felt steady on my feet, I looked over the ledge and saw nothing but a long fall beneath me. There wasn't another outcropping or ledge in sight, just the two sides of the ravine, smooth and hard, and the spray of water as it spilled over the lip of the gap, boiling endlessly.

What had I done?

I turned my attention to the rock wall behind me. It looked more promising than the first ledge I'd been on, which wasn't saying a lot. The first ledge had presented nothing I could grab onto or use to push my toes into for balance. On this side, there were a few fissures in the rock face, but most of them were oddly slanted, running almost vertically up toward the tree-lined bluff above me.

After looking around a bit, I noticed another smaller outcropping about ten or twelve feet above me. If I could somehow make it up to that—

I froze. Voices filtered into the gorge, quavering beneath the sound of the falls. I melted into the wall, pressing my body flat. I looked across the gorge to the bluff where Heath had hit me with the rock.

Squinting against the sun and the blinding white of the water spray, I could just make out Randy Harden and Dr. Blevins. Their words were garbled, but I was pretty sure I heard Blevins say the word, "Sister."

Neither one of the men glanced in my direction. Instead, they peered straight down into the ravine, as if trying to read the lay of the river or to glean the location of my bones, which they clearly assumed were smashed against the rocks below.

I didn't move. In fact, I barely even took a breath while they stood there. As long as they believed I was dead, I held an intrinsic advantage over them. All it would take to disabuse them of that notion was a quick glance in my direction. There was nowhere for me to hide. I was a sitting duck, but so far at least, I was a duck neither of them had noticed.

Harden said something and put a hand on Blevins's shoulder before turning and walking away from the edge of the bluff. That left Blevins on the rock, still staring down into the abyss, where by all rights, I should have been lying dead. There was something breathtaking and profoundly strange about seeing him standing there, looking out into the deep gorge, so sure I was dead. For a second I felt like Schrödinger's cat, both alive and dead at once. Maybe, I allowed, I *had* fallen to the bottom. Maybe this was the afterlife and I'd be forced to climb among these rocks, jumping back and forth from narrow ledge to narrower ledge, trying to find my way out of this purgatory.

Blevins looked up, and his eyes fell right on me. For a second I believed he'd seen me, but if he had, he gave no indication. Then, he turned and walked away.

I was truly alone now. Just the ravine, the falls, and the spirits of those who'd come before me, those souls who'd found this place as a beacon to their pain, or perhaps their escape from it. Or maybe, for some of them, it had been the place they made a new start. Endings and beginnings were always tied together intrinsically, like two strands of rope spliced into a single cord.

The dark clouds worried me. Rain looked inevitable, and a thunderstorm was a real possibility. I'd be exposed to the elements out here on this tiny ledge. Not to mention that a good wind could make things difficult for me.

I needed to get moving before the storm blew in. I faced the wall, running my hands across its maddeningly smooth surface, searching for a tiny nook or fissure that would accommodate my fingers. There was nothing.

I stepped back for a wider view. There, over to the right, I spotted an almost invisible niche in the rock. If I could reach it, I could use it to pull myself up to what looked like a small ledge about seven or eight feet above where I stood. The problem was, the niche I needed to get a hold of was a good three feet from the right side of the ledge. I was long enough to reach it, but I'd have to lean out over the gorge to do so. It I didn't grab it properly, if my fingers slipped or the rock crumbled under my weight, I'd fall to my death.

I pulled out my phone again and considered calling for help. The problem was anyone who came to help me would inevitably alert Harden and Blevins to the fact I'd survived the fall, jeopardizing everything I'd worked so hard for. That was part of the reason I didn't call, but I swear there was something else too, a feeling, an urgency I found hard to put into words.

Being inside the gorge, trapped between the two rock walls, was like being in a different world, one simultaneously less real and *more* real than the one I'd always known. What happened here happened on two levels, both moving me forward in the real world and somehow instructing me and readying me for my return to it.

I was ready. I stretched as far as I could stretch, leaning sideways out over the gorge. I couldn't quite reach the handhold. Standing on my tip-toes still wasn't enough. I tried leaving one foot on the ground and lifting the other toward the wall, digging the toe of my boot into the rock and finding just the tiniest bit of purchase. I pushed myself up, straining and reaching with everything I had. The fingers on my right hand found the small divot, and I held on for all I was worth as I continued to haul my weight upward along the rocky face. It felt almost as if I'd performed some kind of magic trick. I might have believed I was levitating if not for the way my entire body trembled, each muscle stretched to its limit.

Sweat poured from my forehead down over my eyes, burning them. I tried to blink away the sharp sting, but it only made it worse. I closed my eyes and reached with my other hand.

I felt nothing. The ledge I'd been heading for seemed to have disappeared.

Worse yet, I heard the first low rumble of thunder in the distance and lightning somewhere in the direction of the school.

45

was going to die.

The realization hit me about thirty seconds after the rain started. I couldn't see. Rain pelted my face and filled my eyes every time I tried to look up. I couldn't find the ledge. It was up there, I was sure of it, but no matter how many times I reached for it with my free hand, I found nothing but smooth (and now wet) rock. And to top it all off, I felt my fingers slipping from the small divot.

As the rain intensified, thunder boomed through the gorge, seemingly shaking the whole bluff. My fingers ached with the kind of pain that would have normally caused me let go instantly. But I still hung on. I had too.

One more time, I decided, forcing my eyes open against the onslaught of hard rain. I kept them open, searching the rock wall for the ledge I'd spotted earlier. Once I had it in my sights, I understood the problem. I'd been reaching high enough, but I needed to reach farther to the right.

With this new understanding, I swung my free arm up again, hoping to grab it and at least relieve some of the pressure on my right hand. I never found the ledge. Before I could grab it, the toe of my boot slipped down the wet rock, and the sudden shift in my weight was too much for my tired fingers.

I let go.

The inevitability of gravity hit me immediately. There was nothing I could do. I was going to fall.

I *was* already falling.

The only thing I had left was the ability to control how I fell. I pushed my body backward, as if doing the backstroke through water, and closed my eyes, bracing for impact.

Or worse—the *lack* of impact, which would mean I'd missed the ledge.

The impact came, this time on my side, and I rolled with it, coming to a stop on my stomach. A piece of the ledge broke, falling away into the expanse below. I watched it—my eyes finally clear from the rain now as I looked down—as it fell for a long time before landing on a rock and bouncing off into the river. It disappeared.

I pushed myself away from the side again, toward the safety of the wall. Once there, I huddled against it, wrapping myself in a tight ball, and didn't move for a long time.

*　*　*

The storm grew worse. Thunder rolled through the gorge, a continuous drone. Lightning decorated the dark canvas of the sky, and the sound of wood exploding from above filled my ears as trees splintered and broke. At one point, I glimpsed a tree light up with a pale fire before splitting into thick shards and falling into the river. It floated away on the fast-moving water.

The rain soon flooded the gorge. I watched in amazement as the river spilled out onto the rocks, eventually erasing them beneath murky waves. Still, the rain continued. I forgot what it was to feel dry, to not hear water and taste it, to not shiver under its constant assault. The afternoon washed itself into oblivion.

With the darkness came clear skies at last. It wasn't cold, but the storm had sucked up all the day's heat, leaving the temperature tepid enough to make me feel a chill in my wet clothes. I stripped out of all of them except my underwear and laid them out carefully on the ledge to dry.

At some point, I drifted off to sleep, only to be jolted awake by the sound of a wildcat screaming in the night.

It sounded as desperate as I felt, a lost soul betrayed by its very surroundings, its home, its kin. I lay there, listening for it again, hoping I'd hear its lonesome sound, because it was a comfort to know I wasn't alone in the world. But it didn't come. The night passed, its long hours stretching out painfully, relentlessly. I felt helpless, too tired to move, too alone to go to sleep.

But sleep came anyway, creeping up on me like the master thief it was.

When I heard the voices, I believed them to be a dream at first. There was laughing and murmured good cheer. Then an outburst of amazement, the boys' voices tenuous and in awe of the night.

I turned over, saw the glow of a flashlight from the other bluff. It drifted lazily skyward. I followed the beam, losing it among the stars.

Sitting up, I squinted into the darkness. I could just make out two human shapes standing on the very rock I'd fallen from. They seemed engaged in some intimate conversation, but try as I might, I couldn't hear what they were saying. The tone of the conversation seemed gentle and good-natured, wild and new, and I let the sounds wash over me so I could be a teenager again, a teenager on the pulse of a forbidden moment, filtered through with a kind of innocence a person can only know once.

Or maybe that wasn't true. I felt it again now, at least a little piece of it.

Eventually, one of them shone their light toward me. Not *at* me, but in my general direction. They seemed to be discussing something slightly above me, trying to pinpoint it with their light.

It crossed my mind to shout at them, beg them to go get me help, but I couldn't imagine them doing that without alerting Harden or Blevins. And once they were alerted, I might as well go ahead and take a leap from this ledge and hope for the best.

No, I wasn't about to call out to them. But I did slide out toward the edge of the outcropping for a better look at the place where they'd aimed the flashlight.

It wasn't too far above the ledge I'd been trying to reach earlier. What could it be? Some esoteric marking on the gorge wall or even a secret cave, an aperture that would lead me out of this trap at last? I had to hope it was; otherwise, what did I have left?

One of the boys laughed again, and I turned to see their silhouettes moving closer together. They embraced, and I felt a keen sense of joy, seeing evidence for myself that whatever nefarious techniques Blevins and Harden had inflicted on the boys, they had not worked. The boys—despite all efforts to change them, to make them be who they weren't meant to be—had been able to retain their identities. Daddy had always claimed the trick to redemption had been to be reborn, to change, but I could see now how wrong he was. Not changing—or at least not letting the world change you—was the real trick. It was more than a trick, though. It was the truth.

I lay back down and looked at the stars, feeling a strange peace I had not felt since I was a small boy, small enough to be oblivious to the way the world pushed a man places he did not want—or need—to go.

*　*　*

The boys left and the gorge fell silent, save for the constant drone of the falls, but that was so unceasing it barely registered anymore. I thought of Mary and wondered what she was doing. Did she think of me with any regret? Was there any small part of her that wished she hadn't acted so rashly?

I couldn't help but hope there was, even while realizing she owed me nothing. She'd never owed me anything but instead had simply loved me. I'd always seen her love as some sort of spectacular gift, salvation from myself, but maybe that had been the wrong way of looking at it. Maybe she'd just loved me and I'd loved her. Why was that so hard for me to accept, to understand, to believe?

I scooted out toward the edge of the outcropping and picked up my still-wet blue jeans. I dug my phone from the pocket and pressed the home button, sure it would be dead.

It wasn't. The battery indicator revealed I still had five percent battery life. I checked the reception bars, saw there were two, and decided it would have to be enough.

It was two AM, so eleven or midnight out in Nevada, I couldn't remember which. Either way, hopefully not too late for a call. I found her name and hovered my thumb over the call button. She could always ignore the call, right?

My thumb dropped and the call connected. I listened as her phone rang three times and she answered.

"Earl?"

"Yeah."

"It's late out there. Are you all right?"

"Yeah."

"Okay, well, I don't think I want to talk to you."

"I understand."

"Then I'm going to hang—"

"Don't. Please? This won't take long."

She said nothing. I took that as permission. Maybe it wasn't, but at least she was still on the line.

"I love you," I said. "I want you to hear that first. But I also want you to hear something else."

"Okay . . ."

"I screwed up our relationship a long time before I slept with Daphne. That was just . . . I don't know, my way of exploding the bomb I'd already set."

I waited for a response. There was none.

"So, I just wanted to tell you, I understand something now. About myself. I wanted you to save me. I thought you were so perfect, so good, so . . . Jesus, so beautiful, that being with you would be enough to make myself better. It wasn't, and it will never be. I think you understood that all along." I swallowed, feeling some doubt creep in. She was being so quiet. "Didn't you?"

"Yeah. I think maybe I did."

"Why did you stay with me then?"

"Because I loved you, Earl. I knew I couldn't save you, but that didn't mean I ever stopped believing you might save yourself."

"I'm going to do it," I said.

"Save yourself?"

"Going to try."

"Good. I just wish you hadn't done what you did to figure all this out."

"I know."

"Earl?"

"What?"

"What's that noise?"

"Noise?"

"In the background. It sounds like a waterfall."

I laughed. "Yeah. I'm in this gorge, on a little outcropping of rock, two hundred feet above the river. The waterfall is so close I can almost feel it. But I'm going to climb out. I see that now. I'm going to climb out."

"Earl, is that some kind of metaphor or something?"

I grinned. "I don't think so. Maybe."

"Well, good luck, and do me a favor."

I waited, sure she was going to ask me to call her when I found my way out, but like so many things I'd been so sure of, I was wrong.

"Don't call me again, okay?"

I moved the phone away from my face so she wouldn't hear me begin to sob. I let the first one out, then sucked all my pain in long enough to speak into the phone again. "Okay," I said. "I won't."

* * *

I got one more call out of my phone before it died.

It was from Chip Thompkins.

"Mr. Marcus, I apologize for calling so late."

"It's fine. I'm happy to hear from you."

"I've been up thinking."

"Yeah, me too. I'm glad you called. I hope it was to tell me something good."

"Good? You really think anything good can come from this situation?"

I paused and looked up at the dark sky. Now that the clouds had cleared, there were so many stars. I couldn't remember the last time the sky had been so full of them. It seemed like a good omen, but I didn't tell him that.

"Mr. Marcus?"

"Sorry. I was thinking. I guess I'd answer your question like this: will it be a net good? Maybe. Who knows for sure? But we might be able to even the score a little. Maybe not all the way, but isn't even a little bit worth it?"

Now it was his turn to be quiet.

"Redemption," I said. "Even a little bit goes a long way."

Despite the lack of context for what I'd said, he murmured something that sounded like assent.

"Is that a yes?"

"I'll look at your information."

"You'll write the story?"

"I'll look at your information. You said there was someone I could talk to?"

"Definitely. I've got several—"

"I'll give you until Friday."

"Okay. Great. Wait, what's today?"

He was silent.

"Don't hang up. I'm not crazy. I just . . ." I took a deep breath. "I'm actually working on the case right now, and I've sort of gotten myself stranded at the waterfall . . ."

"Maybe this was a mistake. I'm not sure I feel good about this after all."

"No, wait! I've got something for you. Start by calling Claire Bishop at Ghost Mountain Books in downtown Riley. Tell her I said you need to read the newspaper article she showed me. You're going to want that for the backstory. So you'll know about Harriet."

"Harriet?"

"Yes. Harriet Duncan. And also call Mindy Hanks. She works at the Harden School. Just call the school. She'll answer the phone. She's like the secretary there. She's got a story about Jeb Walsh. And Lyda Duncan. Get in touch with her too. She lives outside of Brethren. Are you getting this down?"

"Yeah, I'm getting it. What's this about Walsh? Did he rape her or something?"

"Yeah, something like that. Just talk to her. Get that stuff down. I'll get back to you before . . ." Damn it, what had he said?

"Friday. That's in two days, Mr. Marcus. Either put up or shut up. And I need something substantial. Not innuendos and rumors. I need evidence. Otherwise, I'm going to think you're playing some sort of cruel game with me."

"I'm not. I promise."

"I don't know if I believe you. Furthermore, I'm not sure any of this will work."

I didn't know what else to say. Hell, there was no way to convince him without something more concrete. I actually understood exactly why he didn't trust me. What I didn't understand was why he was even willing to give me a chance.

So I asked him.

"There's only one reason. And the second I don't have it anymore, we're done."

"What is it?"

"The possibility that you're telling the truth and can help me find Joe."

"I am," I said, wincing at yet another lie. But what choice did I have? Telling him that I'd hidden his boyfriend's body wasn't going to get me anywhere.

46

The sun burned my face and I woke, blinking at the brightness, the god-damn sudden *dryness* of the morning. The rain might as well have been a dream. Even my clothes had mostly dried, the exception being the cuff of my blue jeans and a damp section around the waistband.

How long had I slept?

I picked up my phone and wasn't surprised to see that it was finally dead. Well, at least I'd gotten to talk to Mary one last time. At least Chip Thompkins was on board. Now the pressure was really on me to connect all the dots. I honestly had no idea how I would do it.

The sun was high in the sky, which meant it was somewhere around noon. How in the hell had I managed to sleep for so long out here on the hard ledge?

I dressed quickly and then examined myself, paying careful attention to the elbow I'd banged up yesterday afternoon. I could straighten it, but it felt unnatural, like bending a finger back in the wrong direction. I did it anyway, gasping at the pain when I finally got it fully extended. Back and forth I worked it, pushing out the pain with each contraction. There was some swelling, but there was nothing I could do about that.

The rest of me was okay. My hands were scratched up pretty badly from trying to grip the rock ledges, but all my fingers still worked fine. I'd just have to ignore the pain. The alternative was letting go. I'd been lucky enough to hit ledges two times already. I knew better than to count on it happening a third time.

Turning my attention again to the ledge above me, I reached for the small divot I'd clung to yesterday. I got a good grip on it and quickly dug the toe of my boot into the rock. I pulled myself up, ignoring all the pain in my joints, my hand, and especially my elbow as I reached for the ledge. Knowing exactly where it was helped this time. My left hand found it, and I locked my fingers around it. Now came the hardest part. I'd have to trust my bad elbow to hold me up while I brought my right hand up to the ledge.

Gritting my teeth, I made the move.

My eyes snapped shut. I saw red, tiny splotches burning against the back of my eyelids. I swear I heard something in my elbow creak as I hung there, and for a moment the pain was too much. I felt my hand beginning to slip.

Then I had the ledge with my right hand, and the pressure let up. The pain pulsed inside my elbow, but as much as it hurt, I was in no danger of falling, not with both hands on the ledge.

The toes of my boots clacked against rock as I sought some purchase. It was essential I find something. Otherwise, I'd have to pull my entire weight up with just my fingertips.

But try as I might, I couldn't seem to find a toehold.

I looked up for something else to reach for and saw the dark gap in the rocks. It would be barely wide enough for me to slip through sideways, but it still looked like heaven to me. If I could just manage to pull myself up a little bit, I could grab a chunk of misshapen rock that lay at the base of the opening.

With a great grunt, I strained to lift myself up, still kicking my feet for purchase. The opening of the gap drew closer, close enough to see that the rock was connected to the wall. I reached for it, grabbing it in my good hand, and pulled myself on up. I found the purchase I needed on the ledge with my other hand, and soon enough I was pushing my way into the gap, sideways, head and shoulders first, wriggling my body like some fish out of water or a snake, undulating forward.

It took a long time, but eventually all of me was inside the crevice. I lay there gasping, soaking in the cool air inside the cave.

I wasn't sure how much time passed before I moved again, but when I did, I realized the gap had widened. I was able to get to my feet and walk straight ahead into the dark.

* * *

I pulled out my keys and flicked on the penlight. Waving the light around, I was able to take stock of my situation a little better.

The corridor had widened considerably but would still barely accommodate two men standing shoulder to shoulder. The walls of the corridor were slick rock. Some of them were covered with moss and lichen, while other parts felt as if they had a thin sheen of damp dirt protecting their hardness from the rest of the world. I wondered when the last time was that human hands had felt these walls, or if they ever had.

The corridor curved sharply and narrowed as it rose. I trudged up the incline and came out into a wider space, a chamber or room almost. Moving the flashlight across the walls, I estimated it was no more than a twelve-by-ten area, but after being in the tight corridor, it felt palatial by comparison.

The penlight illuminated dark, mossy walls all around me as I turned in a circle, trying to take as much in as possible.

Something caught my attention. A series of marks on one wall stopped me. I aimed the penlight at one of the marks. It was a word.

dead

I moved the light to the left.

the

Only

My light flickered and came back on. The batteries were low. I moved it to the right again, reading the whole sentence now.

Only the dead are safe.

I scanned the rest of the wall and found nothing. What was I supposed to make of that?

I touched the writing, trying to determine what instrument had been used to scrawl the words. My best guess was whoever had left the message had simply picked up a rock and carved the words against the cave wall, in the same way teenagers often knife their initials into the bark of a tree.

But what did it mean?

It could mean just about anything, but there was at least one thing it meant for me. It meant someone else had been here before. And since I didn't see a corpse, it meant he—or she—had managed to escape.

Or maybe not.

Only the dead are safe.

It didn't exactly sound optimistic.

I made another search of the cave, scanning the ceiling and the floor as well as the walls this time. I found a backpack on the floor of the cave, just beneath the writing.

My hands were shaking as I opened it up. I felt as if I'd just unearthed some great buried treasure. Someone had definitely been here, and not only that, they'd left something for the next person, which was me.

Once I had the backpack open, I put the penlight in my mouth and shone the dim light inside. There wasn't much. A notebook, a couple of Polaroid photos, and a pen. I spread the photos out on the cave floor first and shined the penlight over them.

They could have been panels in a comic book. Each appeared to have been taken on the same day, with the same scenery in the background. One showed a young man who appeared to be in his early twenties. He was smiling, though I'd be lying if I said he looked happy. A better way to describe his expression would have been hopeful. Yeah, he looked like he wanted to be happy but wasn't sure if that was an emotion he could ever truly obtain.

I held the photo up, bringing it closer for a better look. The young man was handsome, with broad shoulders and straight black hair. He was tall, too, I realized, and long. Lanky. Rawboned, and the expression on his face—beyond the grin—was quizzical, determined, haunted, and most of all, I realized now, it was familiar.

I was looking at a younger version of Rufus.

It was disconcerting to see him before he was blind, and after he'd made his split with the church. The vulnerability in his eyes stood out. Somehow his blindness had made him more confident. Or maybe it had been all the years.

I couldn't stop looking at the photo. It was Rufus and it *wasn't* Rufus. I wondered, if I were to see a photo of myself from thirty years ago, whether I would recognize the person I once was, or if I'd be so different as to have become a stranger. Who knew? I couldn't imagine a single photograph of me in my twenties even existing anymore. I had been a nomad for many of those years, living on the road, my whole life stuffed into a small backpack. I hadn't owned a camera, nor had I known anyone long enough for them to want to take my picture. I felt a little jealous looking at the photo of Rufus because it was obvious he had known someone who had wanted to take his.

At long last, I put the Polaroid down and picked up the next one. This was not Rufus. This was a young woman, pretty, but not traditionally so. She looked like someone I knew, but then the feeling faded as I studied her closely. She had a pale complexion and straw-colored hair brushed straight back off her forehead. She was smiling, but if Rufus's smile had only looked hopeful, hers appeared to be some kind of awful paradox. The smile was forced, crooked, already collapsing at the moment the photograph was snapped.

I turned the Polaroid over, hoping there would be a name written on the back to confirm her identity. There wasn't, but it hardly mattered. Sure, it would have been nice to confirm what I suspected, but it wasn't necessary. This photo had to be Harriet, and this bag had to have belonged to her, which meant she'd made it across. I wasn't sure how she'd done it—if she'd done it the hard way like me, or the crazy way, which involved making an almost supernatural leap across the gorge—but she'd done it. That much I felt confident about.

The third photograph was the most interesting. I had to lean in closer for a better look. The penlight seemed to be dimming. I was pretty sure the batteries had to be close to running down. It appeared to be a shot of the very crevice I'd entered a few minutes ago. I squinted and saw there was writing on the photo. A blue, smudged arrow, nearly completely faded now, pointed to the crevice.

There was something else too. Barely more than old scratches on the photo. I had to turn it at an angle so the light would hit it just right in order to read what it said.

This is it.

I put the photograph down with the others and opened the notebook. My light went out. I smacked it against my knee. Nothing. I tried the palm of my hand instead, popping it hard enough to make me grit my teeth in pain. The force was enough to eke out a little more battery juice this time. The light came back.

The first page was filled with writing. And sketches. It appeared to be a journal dedicated to the gorge and possible ways to get to the crevice and this cave.

I skimmed it quickly because I was afraid my light would die again at any minute and I didn't want to miss anything essential. Two more pages of sketches and notes followed. At a glance it looked as if she'd taken a similar route to mine. I was most interested in what was on the next page. Here the writing got sloppier, the sketches rougher. Here Harriet wrote about being in the crevice itself.

Three days inside the cave. Light dead now. I fear I may die here. If so, then so be it. There are some things worse than death, some choices that make themselves. I do not regret giving up my safety for this chance. Safety is an illusion. Only the dead are safe. To live is to risk.

I looked up. The cave was so dark, but I felt as if I'd found the brightest lights in her words. *Only the dead are safe.* The words from the wall found their context, and Christ if they weren't true. I supposed in one sense I'd learned the truth of those words early in life. I rarely saw the point in being afraid of dying. But maybe there was a corollary for me. Sometimes I didn't see the point in embracing being alive. I didn't see the urgency to live on my own terms, without always looking for some other ledge to cling to. I understood now how Harriet, just a kid, had made it across. She hadn't picked, jumped, and climbed her way across with blood, sweat, and tears like I had. She'd just walked on the air.

The light went out. I didn't bother popping it against my palm this time. I didn't need it. I didn't need anything except this cave, and the comforting darkness I'd found.

I lay down on the bare floor and pretended to be blind, leaving my eyes open wide and unseeing in the total dark. I thought of Rufus, the pain he'd been in when he told the story. That seemed odd. He and Harriet had obviously been close, and I couldn't help but think she had left these things here for Rufus to find. Yet according to the newspaper, Rufus had watched her jump to her death. He'd claimed it was suicide, that Harriet had been depressed. The words I'd read in this journal didn't sound suicidal, though I suppose they could give one that impression if you were predisposed to view her situation a certain way.

Only the dead are safe.

It didn't sound like suicide to me. It sounded like defiance, like a woman who was ready to make a desperate jump. And weren't this journal, this backpack, and the damned Polaroids enough to prove she'd made it across?

I thought so.

But the question that still lingered, the one that was essential to my situation was, where did she go next? How did she make it any farther along than this small cave?

A terrible thought struck me. What if she was still here? What if she'd died inside this very cave, unable to find a way forward?

I sat up, reaching for the penlight again. My hand found my keys, and I picked them up and fingered the penlight, clicking it on. Nothing. I pounded it against the thigh so hard it hurt. It was dead.

Pocketing the keys, I stood up and walked down the narrow corridor toward the original crevice. As I drew closer, I could see the walls on either side of me more clearly. As I turned to the side to fit through the passage, I noticed something I'd missed before. Another passage so thin I wasn't sure I could fit. It was on my right, and it seemed to lead upward. Could this be the way to the top of the bluff, the way out?

Using both hands, I measured the gap, and found it dismally tight. I turned, sliding my shoulder in, and immediately found I was stuck. My chest was too big. An uneven piece of rock dug through my shirt and into my skin. I pulled away, feeling a moment of panic as the rock scratched me again, holding me between the two walls like I was prey caught in the jaws of some stone-toothed predator. I gasped as I slipped free.

I touched my chest, found it wet with blood. Maybe there wasn't a way through.

No, I refused to believe that.

I tried again, this time standing on my toes, stretching my body as much as possible. Now the piece of rock pressed into my belly, just below my rib cage. I sucked in my gut and tried to force my way through. The rock cut into me. I sucked in harder and leaned against the opening. The rock ripped my shirt again and ground itself against my bare stomach.

Just a little bit farther . . .

I gasped as I fell through into a much wider passage.

It felt even darker here. The light from the opening seemed far behind me, as did the backpack and the journal. Why hadn't I brought them with me? I immediately regretted not doing so. They would have been perfect for Chip and his article. It would have been concrete. I turned back, momentarily considering going through, but the thought of those stone jaws gripping my midsection again was too much.

Instead, I gritted my teeth and continued on down the ever-widening corridor.

47

Time fell away, lost in the darkness of the winding cave. I walked for a while and then grew tired and lay down on the cave floor and slept for some interminable amount of time. It might have been minutes or hours, or even days. The quiet inside the bluff got to me, made me paranoid, made me fear the slightest sound—the scuffing of my own boots against the rock floor once made me scream out in a sudden panic—and soon I began to move like a cat, slinking across the endless cave.

This is how it starts, I thought. This is how you lose your mind.

As much as the silence comforted me and the smallest sound disturbed me, I also began to feel irrevocably alone, as if I'd been condemned to live out the rest of my days in this stone prison, isolated from everything.

And everyone.

I lost track of what was and what was not. The invisible became the visible and I soon saw more in the darkness than I'd ever seen in the light.

Maybe I was asleep or maybe I was walking, but eventually I returned to the warm, silent place I'd visited on the suspension bridge over Backslide Gap. The dead place, where it felt too comfortable, where there was nothing to look forward to, nothing to strive against. I began to feel detached from my body, as if the whole of the darkness was me and my essence had been scattered across the vast universe of the cave. Size and shape were banished. Time slipped.

I was losing it. Losing it quickly.

I forced myself to keep going.

Why?

I searched my mind and realized I wasn't completely sure. Mary was gone. Rufus was gone. Ronnie? There was Ronnie, I supposed, but as long as I was in here, he was gone too.

What was left?

Me.

Nothing.

I felt as if I were floating. I reached for a wall, but they'd all somehow vanished. This was a dark world, a vast and unending universe. There was no way out.

I tried to quit, but something deep inside me, some spark of light, or of the divine, stopped me. My hand went to my mouth, and I pinched my lower lip, digging my thumbnail into the flesh. I kept doing it until I drew blood, until I could taste it. To escape the darkness, I had to endure the darkness. It was the only way.

It had always been the only way. There was no shortcut, no ledge. You fall, climb, or die. It was that simple.

As if I were a vampire, the taste of blood seemed to rally me. I was okay. I was fine. The darkness could not last forever.

Could it?

I walked again. I would walk until I found the edge of the world. I would touch the end and know the end and map the end, or if there was no end, I'd create a world within my mind, one I could carry with me forever and always, one that would keep me safe from the darkness to come.

A voice came to me from the darkness, from inside my head. Rufus. I couldn't make out what he was saying, but his voice was a comfort. He droned, the deep gravel of his voice scraping the bottom of my soul. One word came clear.

Blind.

I saw his face, sans the sunglasses, his eyes scarred by what appeared to be chemical burns. What had blinded him? And more importantly, what had he believed in to help him move forward? Not God. Rufus was what I called a conscientious objector to the divine. He wouldn't serve on principal.

What was I then? I was afraid of the dark. I was afraid of having nothing else to fear, nothing else to keep me moving, and nothing else to defeat me.

So I kept on moving, digging deeper into the spiraling heart of the mystery that would as soon devour me as reveal its secrets.

* * *

231

When I saw the light at last, I was moving blindly, one foot in front of the next, mentally checked out. I'd already resigned myself to spending the rest of my days in this maze of darkness, sure it was some punishment—some kind of hell—I was owed for my sins.

The light was dim at first, but at the first small hint of it, I picked up my pace, nearly running toward what I hoped would be an exit.

I wasn't disappointed.

The light grew stronger, blazing into my eyes, my skin, making me stumble under its glare. I picked myself up, dusted off my blue jeans and what was left of my shredded shirt, and kept on going, eyes shut, toward the glorious light.

Once I felt the sun on me, I opened my eyes in a squint and saw I was in a forest somewhere. Trees surrounded me on all sides, their branches parting directly above me to allow the bright light in. Birds sang, charging me with newfound energy. The warmth of the midday sun felt good on my skin, at least at first. It took no longer than a few minutes before I started to sweat and longed for the coolness of the caves again.

My best guess was I'd been inside the cave for about twenty-four hours, maybe a little less.

But where was I now? I walked a bit, noticing the land sloping downward gradually. The trees grew dense as I moved downhill. After walking awhile and finding nothing even resembling a trail, I turned and looked behind me. Through a gap in the trees, I could see the towering, rocky bluff. I'd been underneath this bluff, *inside* it. Like some dwarf in Middle-earth, I'd burrowed straight through the mountain instead of climbing over it.

I had to guess that was exactly what Harriet had done some twenty-eight years ago. And once she was here, she would have been free to go anywhere in the world. It seemed abundantly likely to me she'd done just that. Why stay in a place like Coulee County? As a gay woman—hell, as a woman period—I couldn't imagine her sticking around this godforsaken place one minute longer than necessary.

Then again, I hadn't been able to imagine myself as a seventeen-year-old straight male sticking around either, and I'd come back. Sometimes I wondered exactly why I'd done that. What had I been trying to prove?

The answer, of course, was that I'd been trying to prove myself worthy, first of this place, and later of Mary. But there was more.

I wanted to change my home, to make it all the things it could be. There was so much here to recommend it, so much beauty, so much ruggedness, so many hidden places that revealed themselves like slow-blooming flowers. And the people—the ones who hadn't been blinded by their own ignorance—were a people you could not find anywhere else. I wouldn't trade a thousand people from anywhere else for one Rufus, and as flawed as Ronnie was, I couldn't imagine a more loyal friend.

So, I was here for the long haul, with or without Mary, I realized. Great. That was one less thing to worry about, but the more pressing matter still remained: finding Harriet.

Finding her could be the key to Chip's article and the missing piece that might complete the picture of the school's—and, by extension, Jeb Walsh's—corruption.

Ahead, I noticed the first sign of what I took to be a trail. There was a stream curving along a tree line, and on the other side of it was another crevice, just a small niche in a wall of trees.

I followed it and didn't stop until I saw the ground had turned to gravel. I squinted at the sun's shimmering reflection off the aluminum siding of single-wide trailers.

48

An old man stood beside the banks of a muddy river, fishing with a push-button Zebco. He was black, and his skin shone in the bright sun. He had deep creases in his face, seams in old leather, and he wore a pair of athletic shorts, oversized fishing boots, and nothing else. A scar ran across his chest, all the way down to his waistband, where it vanished underneath his mesh blue shorts.

He saw me coming and nodded, his face contorting into something like surprise. It was a likable expression, and I decided this was the kind of man with whom you could spend an hour with and wonder where the time had gone. His surprise opened up into a gap-toothed grin, and he turned the crank on his Zebco, reeling in nothing, just a dangling hook. He caught the hook expertly, pinching it between his fingers before sticking the pole between his legs and bending to pick up a live worm out of his bucket. He stabbed it, pressed the button on the rod, and threw a beautiful cast out onto the slow-moving river.

"You'll have to forgive me," he said, "I thought you was a wolf."

"A wolf?"

He nodded but didn't explain.

"I'm just a man," I said. "Didn't know there were wolves around these mountains."

He shrugged. "They come and go."

I grunted, not sure how to respond to that.

"Why you coming from that direction without no gun?"

I shook my head, really confused now.

"You ain't been hunting?"

"No sir. I've been in the cave back there."

"The cave, oh boy, that cave is a killer."

He was reeling his line in again. This time, I thought he might have a fish. He popped the line and turned the crank faster.

"Goddamn it," he said as the hook came out empty again.

"What do you mean, the cave is a killer?"

He leaned his rod against a nearby tree and turned to look at me. "It ain't safe for no man. It's where them Wolf Brothers go."

"Wolf Brothers?"

He nodded. "You might have seen 'em. They run all over these mountains like they got a fire stuck up their asses. Used to be you'd see 'em once or twice a year, coming to try to pluck some virgin out of one of them trailers, but lately them boys have been on a mission."

I thought of the Hill Brothers. Was it possible he was talking about them?

"Why do you call them that?"

He shrugged. "Gotta call them something. They weren't born with no mama, no daddy. Folks say they raised themselves up in some barn. Had to kill mice and birds and ate 'em raw. Nowadays, they just come out of the mountains like spirits, or maybe demons. Yeah, they come out of the dark hollows like demons, that's what. People say they're the sons of Old Nathaniel. You know Old Nathaniel?"

"Yeah, I know Old Nathaniel."

"Then you know the kind of evil I'm talking about. Say, you still ain't told me what you were doing in them caves."

"I'm looking for somebody."

"Somebody in the caves?"

"That's right."

He whistled, seemed to think it over. "What did you say your name was?"

"Earl Marcus." I held out my hand, realized it was still beaten up pretty badly, and wiped it on my torn shirt.

He took it anyway, not squeezing too hard, which I appreciated. "I'm Zachariah Eason," he said. "Who you looking for?"

"Her name is Harriet Duncan. It's sort of a long shot. She would have been last seen in this area twenty-eight—"

"Don't know her."

"Oh." Why had he cut me off? "Well, it's been a while. Maybe there's someone else living around here that might—"

"I don't think so."

I studied him closely and felt pretty sure he was lying to me.

"I gotta get going," he said.

"Did I say something wrong?"

He shook his head. "Nope. Just can't help you. Never heard of Harriet Duncan."

Except he had heard of her. I was sure of it. Zachariah was a bad liar.

"Has somebody else been around asking for her?"

"Nope." He picked up his fishing rod and nodded at me. "Nice to meet you, Earl. I'd stay away from them caves."

"Thanks for the tip," I said. He hurried off, heading toward the wooden bridge that crossed the river and led to the trailers. I watched him go. When he made it halfway across the bridge, he looked back. I waved, but he didn't return the gesture.

49

followed Zachariah to his trailer, keeping my distance in case he turned around, but he didn't. He kept right on going like somebody had told him there was a fire that needed putting out. He lived near the front of the trailer park, close to a highway I didn't know. As I lingered a few trailers down, standing in the shade of a large pickup truck, I realized how hungry I was and how long it had been since I'd last had anything to eat. When he went inside his trailer, I looked around for what I hoped might be a kind face.

I didn't see one. Hell, I didn't see anybody. It was too hot to be outside. There was a single dog lying under a makeshift wooden porch that had been attached to a single-wide. He eyed me with disdain and growled. I waved at him and decided a dog was as good a sign as any in this kind of place. I walked across the dirt path and stepped onto the wooden porch. The dog bristled again but didn't show himself. Too hot, I figured.

Just before I knocked on the door, I heard a door close to my right. A young girl stepped from the trailer and out into the muddy road. She shaded her eyes from the sun and looked around.

When she saw me, her face changed. She smiled.

I smiled too. Here was a friendly face after all.

"Virginia Thrash," I said.

"Mr. Earl!"

She ran over to me, and I stepped off the porch to meet her. She gave me a huge hug, and I hugged her back. It hadn't even been a year since I'd seen her last, but it felt much longer than that. When we broke the embrace, I stepped back to get a look at her. In just a few months, she'd changed a lot. She looked less like a child and more like a teenager. She also seemed more confident, less sad than she had before, and that made me feel good. I wanted to believe what I'd done for her had played some part in her improvement, but I was wise enough to realize she was a special kid, resilient and strong in ways I'd never be able to truly comprehend.

"Do you live here?" I asked her.

She nodded. "Yeah. For about the last few weeks."

"What about Roscoe?"

Roscoe was her little brother. They were Ronnie's niece and nephew, and they'd had a hard time because their mother had been addicted to drugs. I'd helped get them into foster care, but something told me—based on the condition of this trailer park—that they might be back with their mom, which was probably *not* a positive development.

"Roscoe is with me. He's inside taking a nap. It's too hot to do anything else."

"And your mother?"

Virginia looked sad. It was her old face, the one she'd worn last fall when she'd told me how she'd witnessed lights in the cornfield, which had turned out to be Old Nathaniel and Jeb Walsh's camera crew trying to capture his violent acts for a snuff film. Yeah, she'd had a tough go of it for sure, but there was something noble about her, something transcendent, almost. Whatever it was made me believe she was going to make it. That she wasn't just going to make it, she was going to excel.

"She's inside. She's doing better."

"Better?"

"Yeah."

"Define better."

"She has good days and bad days."

"What happened to the foster family?"

Virginia shook her head. "It didn't work out."

"What happened?" I felt terrible. Had I somehow managed to make her situation worse?

"It's not like that," she said. "I wanted to come back. Mama needed me."

"But you don't need her," I said.

She smiled brightly. "I'll be fine."

"What about Roscoe?"

"He's doing well. I'm taking care of him and Mama."

I shook my head, dismayed and impressed at the same time. Just when you start to lose faith in human beings, someone like Virginia comes along and reminds you of the possibilities of love and sacrifice, of commitment and personal determination. I was in awe.

And now I needed her to help me, too.

"Could I ask a favor?" I said.

* * *

Roscoe wandered out of the back while I was dialing Ronnie's number. He saw me and started giggling and pointing. Virginia went over to him and picked him up, his curly black hair flopping as she lifted him into the air. She brought him over, and I offered my fist for a fist bump. He grabbed it with both hands and hung on. My heart swelled and I put the phone down on the table.

"Come here, big boy."

Virginia handed him to me, and he said, "Earl!" Damned if that didn't make me feel like there was something to live for. Damned if it somehow also didn't make me think of Mary. I squeezed him tightly and tried hard not to cry, but the tears came anyway.

Roscoe giggled at first, like he thought I might be pretending, playing a game, but when the deep sobs came in and racked me, he fell silent. Virginia came over and placed a hand on my shoulder.

"I'm sorry about that," I said, trying to suck the sobs back, but Virginia made a hushing sound and patted my shoulder again.

"Earl sad," Roscoe said.

I laughed. And cried. I did them both at the same time. It was the most alive I'd felt in a long time.

* * *

Ronnie picked up on the second ring. "What's up, Virginia?"

"It's Earl."

"What?"

"You heard me."

"What?"

"Where are you?"

"What?"

I sighed. "I made it across the gorge, found a cave and went through the mountain. I found this trailer park and ran into your niece. You knew she was out of foster care?"

"I just found out myself, Earl. Remember, I was in jail?"

"Right. Sorry about that."

"Fuck the apologies. I'm just glad you're alive. I've been calling and calling your phone. And don't worry, I fed Goose."

"Thanks. How did you get out?"

"Just what you said to do. I laid low by the gate and waited until Mindy was on her way out. Hell, she even gave me a lift. She's really cool . . ."

"Isn't she a bit young for you?"

"Look who's talking. How old was Mary?"

"Thirty-eight."

"And how old are you?"

"It's different."

"She's actually only ten years younger than me."

I realized I didn't exactly know how old Ronnie was. I'd assumed he was in his late thirties. Maybe I was wrong.

"Okay. So, did you find out what's going on out there?"

"I found out a lot. But I need you to come pick me up."

"I got the boys coming over in an hour to finish the studio."

"Cancel it. When this is over, I'll help you build it myself."

"Well, shit, Earl, I'd like that very much. Maybe you could be our manager."

"Maybe," I said, but I didn't really see *that* happening. I honestly didn't know what I'd do when I found Rufus and got to the bottom of Weston's and Joe's deaths.

"I'll be there as soon as I can," Ronnie said.

"Great. Meet me at Virginia's trailer. And Ronnie, could you bring me some lunch?"

"Big Mac or quarter-pounder with cheese?"

"Both."

"Jesus."

"Just hurry."

"Will do, and Earl?"

"What?"

"Looooose!"

I laughed and hung up the phone. Roscoe was sitting on the couch staring at me. "Earl happy?" he said.

"Yeah," I told him. "Earl happy." *At least for the moment*, I mentally added, and then walked over and sat down beside him, tousling his curly dark hair.

50

Ronnie's sister, Wanda, woke up and came into the den. She'd gained weight, and her eyes seemed more focused than I remembered. Good signs, I thought. She shot me a look filled with disdain.

"What are *you* doing here?"

"Just needed to use the phone."

"You're not here to take my kids away again, are you?"

"No. I'm not here for that."

"Good, because we're doing all right." She pulled up the sleeve of her sweatshirt, revealing a half dozen scars from the inside of her elbow down to her wrist. "See. Old. I haven't stuck a needle in this arm in nearly four months."

"I think that's great."

"Still drink, though. I guess you're going to tell me I can't do that too."

"No. I wouldn't ever tell you that."

"Well."

"Ronnie's on his way over to pick me up."

She nodded warily. "I guess . . . well, do you want a cup of coffee or something?"

"Water would be nice."

"You don't want to drink the water here."

"Why's that?"

"The well water is tainted."

"Do you have bottled?"

She rolled her eyes at this obviously unreasonable request but walked into the kitchen and returned with a warm bottle of Walmart-brand water. She tossed it to me, and I unscrewed the top and drank deeply.

"Damn," she said. "Thirsty man. What have you been doing? Some of that private investigating?"

"Yeah. In fact, I wanted to ask if you'd heard of someone."

"Who?"

I decided to start with the brothers Zachariah had mentioned. "The Wolf Brothers?"

She laughed. "I've seen them once or twice. Saw their handiwork, too."

"Handiwork?"

"Yeah, go on down to the end of the road and hang a left. You'll see what they done to Robert Jimmy's place."

"Robert Jimmy?"

"That's what I said."

"What did they do?"

"Knocked his trailer off the blocks. Took a sledgehammer to the outside of it, beat the hell out of it. Smashed the windows. Threw the furniture outside. Probably would have killed him, too, if Doug Farmer hadn't of showed up with a shotgun. People know Doug's just crazy enough to shoot a man without even thinking twice. I reckon the Wolf Brothers has got some human in them after all, because they seemed to know this too and left out of there. What I heard, anyway."

"Did anybody call the police?"

"Shit, are you kidding? The new sheriff is worse than the last one, and people say the last one wouldn't show his face out here except for to visit one of them prostitutes in the woods behind the park."

"Where is this?"

"That girlfriend ain't getting the job done?" She looked at Virginia and Roscoe, both watching her closely. "Take your brother out to play, Virginia."

"It's hot outside today."

It was odd. Normally a teenager saying something like that to her mother would have sounded like backtalk, but from Virginia, it sounded patient, almost loving. Definitely wise.

"Okay," Wanda said. "Go to his room, then. Let him build some Legos."

"Okay," Virginia said. She took Roscoe's hand and pulled him off the couch. He started to cry, but she bent down and whispered something in his ear. He grinned. They left the room.

Wanda sat down next to me.

"You really want to go to one of those skinny girls in the woods? Good way to catch something, you know? And I'll bet a man like you could find it for free if he had a mind to." She put a hand on my knee.

I slid over on the couch, causing her hand to fall away from my knee. "I'm not looking for *it*," I said. "I'm on a case."

She frowned. "Well, I reckon that woman of yours keeps you pretty satisfied, then."

I wasn't about to get into my breakup with Mary, so I ignored her and pushed on.

"I'm looking for somebody named Harriet Duncan."

She shook her head. "Never heard of her."

"How about a man named Zachariah?"

"Yeah. He lives just down the way."

"He always act funny?"

"Depends on what you mean by funny."

"Like his britches are on fire and he has to go somewhere fast?"

She shook her head. "I ain't never seen that man do nothing faster than it takes to catch a fish. He's about the slowest-moving man I ever saw."

"Yeah," I said. "That was the impression I had, too." I stood and walked over to the window, pulling down the shade for a look at his trailer. Was he still inside? The old truck was still parked there. I just hoped Ronnie was here before he got in it and pulled away. I had a feeling I might be interested in where he was going.

"So," I said, still looking out the window. "What else do you know about the Wolf Brothers?"

"Not a lot. Like I said, I seen them a time or two. They're always together. Look like they don't even know how to speak or nothing. I guess that's why folks call them the Wolf Brothers."

"Dark-haired boys, in their twenties, probably? One of them has a kind of bowl cut?"

"Yeah, that's them. You seen them before?"

"Yeah, up near my place in the Fingers. But folks up there call them the Hill Brothers."

"They get around."

"Any idea what their story is?"

She shook her head. "There's legends and shit. Hey, want to go for a drink?"

It sounded like the best damned idea in the world. Not that I had any interest in Wanda. The part that sounded great was bellying up to the bar with a kindred spirit and forgetting about the world for a while. God, just the thought of it and I could already taste the whiskey.

"You got these kids," I said. "And Ronnie's on his way to pick me up. My friend Rufus is missing."

"The blind man?"

"Yeah."

"Well, I reckon he fell into some gorge somewhere. The rain'll wash him out."

I shook my head. "He's alive. I think someone took him."

"Or killed him."

She had a point. Why was I so convinced Rufus was alive? If somebody needed to get rid of him because they thought he might know something about Harriet, then wouldn't killing him be the best way?

The door to Zachariah's trailer opened. He walked out, wearing a hat (and a shirt) and carrying a walking stick instead of a fishing rod. He looked around, almost as if checking to see if anyone was watching him. Then he headed down the road, back toward the river.

"Tell Ronnie I'll be back in a few minutes. Tell him to wait on me . . ." I glanced at the phone Virginia had let me use earlier. "Better yet, can I borrow that phone?"

"I don't think so," Wanda said.

I winced. I *hated* being the bad guy, but sometimes it just couldn't be avoided.

I let the blinds fall back into place, and I walked over and pocketed the phone. "I'll bring it back. Tell Ronnie to call me on this number when he gets here."

"Fuck off," she said.

"I probably deserve that," I said, and headed out into the heat of midday, still hungry, still tired, but at least I'd had some water. It would have to do for now.

51

Zachariah walked slowly now, carefully picking his way through the woods, taking trails that were barely trails at all, just footpaths worn into the dirt forest floor. I kept a good distance from him, and at least twice believed he'd spotted me, but each time he looked away and continued moving. Perhaps his eyes were bad?

Or maybe he had spotted me. Maybe he was leading me somewhere I didn't want to go.

It didn't matter. I'd never believed in shying away from a trap. Hell, I actually enjoyed the sensation of being led into danger. It was just the way I was built. People probably thought that was brave, but I knew better. I would have traded the ability to not be frightened by the bad guys for the ability to face everyday life alone in a heartbeat.

All told, I followed him through the woods for nearly an hour before the trees began to clear and I saw a tiny, weather-beaten shack situated at the edge of a meadow. A dirt road ran off through the woods in another direction, and a few pickup trucks had taken it to get here. They were parked off in the grass a few yards from the shack's shady yard. Two women sat in chairs under the shade tree, drinking from Dixie cups. They smiled at Zachariah like they knew him. One of them was wearing earbuds, and she pulled one out to listen to what he said.

I watched from the edge of the trees, taking the women in. I was pretty sure they were prostitutes. Had I followed the old man all the way out here just to watch him get his rocks off?

He spoke to the women for a few moments before one of them pointed off to the left of the trailer. I followed her finger and saw a woman I'd failed to notice earlier. Like the women in the chairs, she was seated, but her seat had wheels. She was about my age, maybe a little older. She had long blonde hair and wore no makeup. Her face was lean and pretty and slightly bird-like. She saw Zachariah and waved at him. Zachariah hurried over to her and leaned over so they could embrace.

I stepped out of the woods and headed toward the woman in the wheelchair. One of the women at the table—she was a blonde, about thirty, with bad teeth but surprisingly good skin—got up and stepped in front of me.

"Hey. You looking for an hour? Maybe two?"

"No thanks." I tried to step past her.

"She doesn't work here."

"I'm not here for sex," I said, and continued to walk toward Zachariah, who saw me coming and said something to the woman in the wheelchair. She nodded and reached for something underneath the chair. When she straightened up, she was holding a sawed-off shotgun. She aimed it right at my face.

"Who are you?"

"That's him," Zachariah said. "Must have followed me here. I'm sorry."

"I'm Earl Marcus," I said. "I make no secret of my identity. I'm looking for a woman named Harriet Duncan."

Zachariah shook his head. "I told you I ain't never heard of no Harriet Duncan."

"What about you?" I said to the woman in the wheelchair. "Have you heard of her?"

She lowered the gun slightly. "What do you want her for?"

"So you have heard of her?"

Zachariah stepped forward. "Hey, leave her alone. She just wants to live her life and not be bothered, okay?"

"You're Harriet?" I could see it now. The photo of the smiling and sad girl came back to me, and I saw that girl hidden inside the aging face of the woman sitting before me.

She said nothing, but she didn't have to. She lowered the gun completely, laying it across her lap.

"What do you want?" she asked.

"I need to talk to you about your time at the Harden School."

She frowned. "That's not happening."

"It's urgent."

She looked around, lifting her hands to the sky. The heat had settled into this place, giving it a languid, almost sleepy feel. The women were sitting at the tables again, drinking and smoking. Zachariah stood off to my right, a single bead of sweat tunneling into one of the deep creases on his face.

"I don't see any urgency," she said at last.

"Sometimes appearances can be deceiving. Why all the secrecy, anyway? The Wolf Brothers are looking for you, aren't they?"

"You know the Wolf Brothers?"

"I know of them."

She rolled his eyes. "Everyone knows *of* them. You can't live in this godforsaken county if you don't know *of* them. I'm talking about actually *knowing* them."

"Do *you* know them?"

"I'm going to have to ask you to leave, Mr. Marcus. I'm not sure what you're trying to dig up, but I'm very happy here. The girls take care of me. Say what you want about the whore-with-a-heart-of-gold myth, I believe it. The girls that have worked in that trailer over the years come and go, but there's always one or two willing to take care of me." She glared at me, the sadness I'd seen in the Polaroid now charged with anger. "It ain't every twenty-year-old who's willing to help a stranger to the outhouse. Those women are some of the finest people I've ever known."

It was time to pull out my ace card.

"Did you know Rufus Gribble?" I said.

Harriet was still, her eyes focused on something far away, off in the trees behind me, and I thought maybe hearing the name had peeled back the curtains of her past.

"He's my friend too," I said. "And now he's missing. I was wondering if you might be able to help me find him."

One of the girls was coming over. A brunette this time. A pretty girl, and I wondered how she'd ended up here, helping to take care of a woman in a wheelchair and servicing other men for money. How did any of us end up anywhere? It was easy to think that all was random in the universe, but whenever I thought that, I felt like giving up, buckling under to the dense mass of cosmic nothingness, and giving up had never been something I'd been able to do for very long.

No, we were all here because this was where we'd put ourselves. There were forces, sure. They worked on a person like gravity and the burden of age, but if you fought back, you could move the needle at least a little bit. And that was why I was here. I'd been looking for the needle of justice, and it had led me to this hollow in the woods with these people, broken and dismayed. Now, maybe if we all put our backs into it . . .

"Rufus is still alive?" she said.

"Yeah. Well, as far as I know. The last time I saw him was at your sister's house."

"My sister? Which one?"

"Lyda. The older one."

"What did she look like?"

I shrugged. "Dark hair. Some wrinkles. Probably in her sixties."

"Good. Savanna is blonde. Unless she dyed her hair to fool you."

I shrugged. It hadn't looked dyed.

"I'll talk to you," she said.

Zachariah stepped away from me, shaking his head. "You sure about this, Harriet?"

"I'm sure. It's past time. Besides, I know who took Rufus."

52

I followed them even deeper into the woods, toward the cave I'd come through, to a tiny one-room shack with an outhouse about twenty yards away. A well-worn path led to it, and I imagined the struggle Harriet had to go through just to take a shit, and felt the whole of the cosmos pushing down on me again. I stood up a little straighter and kept walking.

Inside the shack, Zachariah and I sat across from Harriet at a wooden table.

Zachariah asked if he could make coffee, but Harriet told him to get the whiskey instead.

"You don't mind sharing the same bottle, do you?" she said. "I never did get around to getting any glasses."

"I don't mind."

The bottle made its way around the table twice before Harriet asked the question I'd been waiting for. "How'd you find me?"

"I followed Zachariah."

"How'd you find him?"

The bottle came back to me, and I allowed myself a small sip. "Luck, I guess." I laughed. "It started out as bad luck, there was some scary stuff in the middle, and then I got lucky again."

"He just come up on me while I was fishing. He came from the caves, Harriet, just like you." Zachariah shook his head when I passed the bottle to him. Harriet reached for it and held it.

"You came from the caves?"

"That's right. Maybe I should back up."

"Go for it."

I tried to think where to start. That was the problem with mysteries. The real ones were like circles that defied time and space.

"A couple of weeks ago, I found a dead man in my front yard." That was how I began. I didn't leave out anything, except for the stuff about Mary and Daphne. That seemed like a different mystery that had somehow gotten wrapped up in this one. I told her about coming to the school and finding out about Eddie Walsh. I had to break the narrative there to go back and explain the nature of my relationship with Jeb Walsh and Sheriff Argent, and how that was the reason I hadn't reported the body in the first place. When I got to this part, Harriet shook her head in disbelief.

"I wouldn't put it past Harden."

"Wouldn't put what past him?"

"Killing."

"You think he killed the man in my yard?"

"I wouldn't put it past him," she repeated.

"I wouldn't put it past Jeb Walsh, either," I said.

Zachariah nodded and murmured something I could just make out. It sounded like "Birds of a feather . . ."

"Go on," Harriet said, her voice steady, determined.

I tried to remember where I'd left off.

"You were going back to the school," she said. "A second trip."

"Oh, right. Well, this time I witnessed something disturbing. Very disturbing." I told her about the kid who was supposed to meet Sister to have sex with her.

"Sister?"

"That's right. Do you know who that could be?"

"It's got to be Savanna."

I nodded. "That's what I'm beginning to think, too."

"How much did Rufus tell you about her?"

"Not enough."

"Not surprising. He never wanted to hear the truth about her."

"The truth?"

She nodded. "Finish your story. I'll tell you then."

"Well, the rest may be familiar to you. See, it turns out I was set up. The kid had an earpiece and was being fed lines from somewhere. He got the jump on me and knocked me off the flat rock near the waterfall, the same one where you jumped."

"Yeah. But you got lucky. You landed on the ledge."

"That's right. And I don't need to tell you that once you're on that ledge, there's no way out, at least from that side."

"You made the jump?"

"I did. But I wasn't the first, was I?"

"No."

"What happened to you?" I nodded at the wheelchair. "Where did it happen?"

"I got lost in the cave. Did you come through the crack?"

"Yeah. I had to turn sideways and suck in my gut."

She nodded. "Exactly. Somewhere after that, I fell into a pit. Landed on my neck. Couldn't feel my legs. Haven't felt them since."

"But how did you get out of the pit?"

She held up her arm and pointed at her bicep. "Used these to drag myself out."

Zachariah jumped in. "When I found her, she was pulling herself through the woods with her hands, grabbing roots and clawing the ground."

She pulled up her sleeves to reveal deep scars running from her elbows to her wrists. "I was bleeding pretty bad when Zachariah found me." She reached out and patted her friend's shoulder. "This man is a fucking prince. He didn't ask questions. He didn't care I was a lesbian. He kept my secret. He fed me. He wiped my ass and bathed me when I was too weak to do it myself, for God's sake." She pointed at the bookshelves along the wall. "He brought me every last one of those. Those books have become my life."

I looked at Zachariah, who lowered his eyes, obviously uncomfortable with the praise. He mumbled something under his breath. It sounded like "Friendship goes both ways."

I didn't know what to say. I couldn't get past the determination it had taken for Harriet to get through that cave, how easy it would have been for her to just lie there and die.

"Everybody thought you were dead," I said.

She nodded. "I was fine with that. All I ever wanted was to be myself. To live unashamed of who I was." She paused, screwing up her face as if to keep from weeping. "You ever read Joyce?"

"A long time ago. Don't remember much."

She nodded. "My favorite line in all of Joyce applies to my situation, well, maybe to all situations. I can quote it: 'When the soul of a man is born in this country there are nets flung at it to hold it back from flight. You talk to me of nationality, language, religion. I shall try to fly by those nets.' I didn't discover that until fifteen years ago, but when I did, it immediately became my favorite line. This world around us wants to hold us down, not from success. Success is fine with the powers that be. The world wants to keep us from being who we are. I've flown over the gorge. I broke my back, but my spirit remains intact. Am I making sense, Mr. Marcus?"

"More than you'll ever know."

"Good. Now, I need to tell you about my twin sister."

53

Rufus woke to his blindness, and had never been more thankful for the dark. The shadow girl had plagued him for hours, her presence so close to his face, like the regret that had crowded around his heart.

"Gotta piss," he said.

He waited for the sounds of the men shuffling out of their room. They never complained, never grumbled. They came silently as ghosts and untied him without fuss. But not this time. This time, there were no footsteps creaking, no doors swinging open. He was alone.

Rufus pulled against his restraints until he felt like he might pop a blood vessel in his forehead. He stopped, breathing deeply, trying to think. His hands and feet were bound, so his options were pretty limited.

He rocked the chair back in frustration. The wooden legs creaked, and an idea came to him. His feet were tied to the legs of the chair. If he could somehow break the chair, he might be able to disentangle himself from the ropes. But how could he break it when he could barely move? He leaned forward, placing all of his weight onto his feet. Nudging himself forward with a great effort, he managed to get the chair legs off the ground. He was standing on his own two feet now. Well, standing wasn't the right way to put it. He was still sitting, but the chair legs were in the air behind him and he had some limited mobility now. *Very* limited mobility. He moved one foot forward about half an inch, all the ropes would allow, and then slid the other foot up, closing the small gap. His legs ached from the pain of holding his body in such a contorted position, and he let the chair legs touch the floor again. He relaxed.

The problem was knowing where he was going. He needed to move toward something solid enough to break the chair. If he could get close enough, he thought he might be able to generate enough force to slingshot himself forward and crack the chair apart.

When his eyes had been opened during the visit from the shadow girl, he'd seen a stone fireplace to the right of the bookshelf. It was a good ten feet away from where he sat. If he could work his way over, get his chair turned around properly, he might be able to crack the chair against the stone hearth.

He took several deep breaths and leaned forward again, feeling the ache in both of his legs. This time, he managed to move his feet only an almost imperceptible amount before he shifted his weight back to the chair legs. He groaned as every muscle in his thighs and calves caught fire. He'd have to rest.

Rufus did really need to piss. He called out again. "I gotta go, assholes! Somebody going to untie me or not?"

But there was no response. He settled in, leaning his head back, and thought about the shadow girl, and how she had begun and how he had stopped her at least for a little while.

*   *   *

As the torture of the shadow girl had begun to take over his life so many years ago, the pleasure with Savanna intensified. Though, looking back on it now, Rufus had a hard time seeing it as pleasure. There was the thrill of anticipation, sure, and there were the lost moments of head-exploding orgasms, but afterward there was always the inversion of the orgasm, a lingering meaninglessness, a kind of fervent disappointment that haunted him. It was as if he'd finally discovered the secret of human relations, and at its core was a hollowness so profound he could hardly bear it.

Worse still, he had found himself craving more of her as soon as the hollow feelings subsided. In that way, Savanna became a kind of drug for him. After weeks of nightly sex with her in her family's barn, he began to feel guilty, to think he was somehow flawed, that he could only connect to a woman sexually instead of on a deeper, healthier level.

At work, he was doing better, at least on the surface. He wasn't sure how, but both Harden and Deloach knew about his encounters with Savanna. Deloach claimed he "had the look of a new man." Harden said he had a "sixth sense about these things."

They both started patting his back again, and to his surprise, both men asked him for details of the encounters, pressing him to push her to do wilder and wilder things. He never felt comfortable doing that, thank God, but eventually Savanna seemed to grow bored with their sex and told him she wanted to "spice things up a bit."

Rufus, having no previous experience, thought this might be fairly normal and went along with some of the violence she introduced, but he drew the line when she said she wanted him to harass Harriet.

"It turns me on," she told him. "To see that bitch suffer."

He shook his head, more than determined not to give in. He'd realized by this point that there was something deeply wrong with Savanna. Maybe there was something wrong with him, too. He wasn't sure about anything except that Savanna was, in some fundamental way, broken.

"I'll make you hurt her," she said. "I can make you do anything."

"No," Rufus said. He realized he wanted her to leave him alone.

"Oh, you'll see," she said. "I'm not like other girls, Rufus. I eat men. Or I control them. Which kind do you want to be?"

"Neither."

"Neither is not a choice." She reached for him and leaned in to kiss his face.

"Don't," he said.

"Not a choice either," she said as she grabbed his balls, squeezing just hard enough.

And to Rufus's disappointment, she was right again. He didn't seem to have a choice. Once again, he found himself in bonds, tied down by chains he couldn't even see.

54

Harriet drank some whiskey and closed her eyes. She seemed almost to pray, her face tensing and then relaxing before she opened her eyes again, and within them was pure determined calm, as if her very survival depended on not giving in to the emotions she felt. I had to guess it was something she'd had a lot of practice with.

"Savanna wasn't like me," she said. "I understood that from the beginning, and by the beginning, I mean the very beginning. Even as a small child, I understood she was a different kind of creature from me. She knew how to make the world work in her favor. We were twins, but you would never have known it. I was ugly and meek. She was beautiful and strong."

As she spoke, I glanced at the bottle of whiskey on the table, now half empty between us. Zachariah still hadn't partaken, and I envied his self-control. Somehow I envied Harriet too, a ridiculous emotion for me to feel toward a woman who was condemned to a wheelchair, but it didn't matter. That was just one limitation, and it seemed incongruous to the rest of her, which was anything but broken. She was self-assured, smart, kind. She was a woman who needed very little in her life, and that seemed the highest compliment I could think of.

"I remember vividly when we were nine years old. We were outside, playing in the backyard. There was a cellar door there. Stone steps dug into the ground led to the base of the house and to the door that in all of my later memories remained locked. But not on that summer day. Savanna dared me to go open it. She was always daring me to do things, and even at that early age I'd developed a sort of sixth sense about her dares. They never worked out well for me. Somehow she always managed to make me feel like a loser if I didn't do them, and if I did . . . well, that was sometimes even worse.

"'We're not supposed to open the cellar door,' I told her.

"'That's because it's where they keep the other kids,' she said. I swear, she could be so convincing. She had this way of always making her lies sound like the other things she said. There was no way to tell the difference. And if you questioned her, she'd get so angry. Maybe it was her being my twin, but I loved her. I *needed* her to love me back, and sometimes she gave me just enough of that love to make me think she was normal, that *we* were normal.

"I asked her what she meant by the 'other kids.' Her answer still haunts me."

Harriet picked up the bottle, studying it, before handing it to me. I took a sip and put it back on the table. Zachariah cleared his throat. A quick glance told me he knew what was coming, that he'd heard this story before.

"She said the other kids were the ones our mother and father had murdered. She said they kept their bodies in the cellar.

"Of course, I immediately said she was wrong, that she was lying to me.

"'Go see for yourself,' she said.

"'I don't want to,' I told her.

"'You have to. If you don't, you'll never go with me.'

"I asked her what she was talking about, and she said they were going to kill us when we turned ten too, and that I had to see if for myself. If I didn't, I wouldn't have the courage to leave with her, to run away." Harriet shook her head and laughed ruefully. "I was nine. I was gullible. I went to the cellar and opened the door."

"What happened?" I said.

"I felt her push me and slam the door behind me. It was so dark inside that cellar, I panicked. I'd never been down there before, and I didn't know where anything was. I knocked over a tool cabinet almost as soon as I tried to move. It fell, blocking my path back to the door. Outside, I heard something else fall. It sounded like an avalanche. I worked my way over to the cabinet, cutting open my heel on a screwdriver. I tried to open the door, but it wouldn't budge. Something on the other side was stopping it. I pushed and pushed, but I couldn't move it."

"Jesus," I said. "What was the sound?"

"That's what I find most chilling now. Sometime or another, she'd discovered that the heavy cinder blocks that lined the steps were loose. She just gave them a good shove and down they went, essentially locking me in. All told, I was there for four days. My parents grilled her on my whereabouts, but she never told them anything. Search parties looked for me day and night. All the while, Savanna knew exactly where I was. I yelled and screamed and pounded on the stone walls, but no one ever heard me. If it hadn't been for my father going down to the cellar to find another flashlight, I would have died there."

"But you told your parents what happened when you got out, right?"

She nodded. "I did."

"And?"

"They refused to believe she'd done it on purpose."

"I don't understand."

"Me either. Well, I do because I know her. She was more believable when she lied than when she told the truth. And she could cry on demand. When I told my father what had happened, he called her into the room, and she immediately fell onto the floor and began to cry. She confessed it all, except the part that she'd done it on purpose. Instead, she made up a story about me begging her to stand guard outside the door while I went inside to see what was there. She said she stood on the rocks and knocked them loose by accident. She tried to move them to help me, but they were too heavy. She said she was too scared to tell anyone because she thought I was dead and it was her fault."

"They bought that?"

"Every bit of it. That's not all. A few days later, she elaborated on her original story, telling my parents I'd wanted to go in there to do 'dirty things' to myself. I didn't even know what masturbation was. But she did. I think I might know why."

"Was she abused?" It would, perhaps, be the only thing that could explain such vile behavior. Maybe she was simply acting out on her own victimhood at the hands of a monster.

"I think it's a possibility, but I'm not sure. I am sure she knew things I didn't. And she was sadistic. A few months later, after a period in which she'd been nicer to me than she had been in a long time, she quietly took me aside, my hand in hers, and told me she was actually glad I was still alive. Her exact words were, 'It's more fun to have you around, because once you're dead, you can't suffer anymore.'"

"Psychopath?" I said. I was no expert but had dealt with one or two people over my career as a private investigator who I thought might fit the bill. Neither of them held a candle to what Harriet was telling me about Savanna. And Rufus had been in love with her? Jesus.

"I've read a little on the topic." She gestured to her books again. "If you put a gun to my head and asked what's wrong with Savanna, that would be my answer." She shrugged. "It hardly matters what you call it. Her actions were evil. They didn't get better with age, either."

Harriet went on to tell me about their teen years, during which Savanna discovered a compelling power over boys at their school.

"They'd do anything for her, including break the law. In return, she'd have sex with them. She used it as a bargaining chip, or to get close enough to someone so she could hurt them. I watched as she went through boy after boy, literally tearing them down, reducing them to nothing more than rubble.

"I was sixteen when I had my first sexual encounter. It wouldn't be until years later that I would understand she'd orchestrated it. She'd long suspected—probably even before I did—that I was gay. Turned out, she found another girl at our school who was gay too. She paid her to come on to me in our barn. Then she spied on us while we . . ."

Harriet shook her head, and I saw how painful these memories were to her.

"My sexuality became a new toy for her. She tortured me over it endlessly. Anytime I didn't do what she wanted me to do, she threatened to tell our father. It was the only thing I dreaded more than her torture. If that doesn't tell you the agony gay teens go through, I don't know what will. I was literally more willing to be tortured by a psychopath than let my father know I was a lesbian."

"But eventually he found out, right?" I asked.

"Sure. When she tried to make me kill the neighbor's dog."

"What?"

"Every day it was something new. 'Do this, or I'll tell Dad.' Sometimes it was just stealing something. Sometimes she asked me to take pictures of her. Inappropriate pictures. She would send them in the mail to random men she looked up in the phone book. But I couldn't kill the neighbor's dog. So she told Dad. After a few months of Dad not speaking to me, she offered a solution."

Harriet drummed her fingers on the table and looked at me as if she couldn't quite decide where I'd come from, what strange wind had blown me into her life.

"You already know the solution, don't you?"

I nodded.

"Harden is my uncle. I'd known about his school for as long as I could remember. It was honestly the one place I thought I'd never end up. Turns out both he and my father thought me being gay was about the most troubling thing either one of them could imagine. That's where I met Rufus, of course."

"I hope he at least treated you right," I said. I felt confident he had. Rufus was one of the most vocal supporters of equal rights I knew. He actually attended meetings at a local progressive church to discuss how to combat issues of hate and violence against members of the LGBTQ community. Despite this, I felt less confident about my assumption when I saw the look on Harriet's face.

It was a sad look, not so different from the one she'd worn in the Polaroid from so many years ago. Except this look was less hopeful, more resigned. It seemed to suggest a kind of forbearance or miserable tolerance for a past that could never change.

"Go on," I said.

"There's not much more to tell. I would have killed myself if it wasn't for Rufus. He was the only person who was decent to me, who treated me as if I didn't have a disease." She shook her head. "In the end, they got to him, of course, but maybe I shouldn't be angry. They get to everybody. The nets are strong. It's so easy to get tangled up in them, to fall without even realizing it."

"But you didn't fall," I said. "You jumped over."

"Are you familiar with the term hyperstition?" she asked.

I shook my head. "Is it anything like superstition?"

"Maybe a little. It's the idea that something from art or from the imagination can become real, can manifest itself in the world in powerful ways."

"Okay . . ." I had no idea where this was going.

"I found an old book, hidden in the little one-room library at the school. Well, maybe not hidden, but it was on the very bottom shelf. I think it was where the legend about the Indians started. Have you heard it?"

"Yeah. Two Indian Falls?"

"That's it. It's a novel, and it's actually set somewhere in Illinois or something, but it hardly mattered. The two boys in the book, they wanted out. The only way out was across the gorge, just like our gorge. The boys waited on the wind and jumped. One made it, one didn't. A tragedy that stayed with me a long time after reading it, but something else stayed with me too. One made it, but he wouldn't have made it if he hadn't tried. It all came together for me then. I'd been contemplating suicide, but the *real* suicide was not living as myself. That was my choice. I figured that out almost as soon as I arrived. Harden wasn't going to let me go if I didn't change, if I didn't betray who I was. So I planned it out. I even told Rufus what I was planning. He helped me survey the gorge, looking for a way across. When we spotted the ledge, it felt like salvation."

"So, he knows you're alive?"

"I'm not sure if he does or not. It was dark when I left. He went to the waterfall with me, but after the first ledge, I purposefully didn't answer any of his calls. I wanted him to think I'd died."

"Why?"

"I couldn't trust him. As much as I wanted to, I'd learned not to trust anyone." She glanced at Zachariah and reached over to pat his hand. "It took me a long time to learn to trust people again."

Zachariah cleared his throat. "You done what you had to do, lived the way you had to live." Zachariah's eyes were tearing up, and he laughed as the tears began to fall. "And you done more. You made your life your own."

A title of a Flannery O'Connor short story I'd read a long time ago came back to me. It was called "The Life You Save May Be Your Own." I'd read the story and liked it, but the title hadn't held much resonance for me until this very moment. We were all obligated to save ourselves, I decided. If you didn't, then who would?

55

"What now?" Harriet asked, wheeling her chair away from the table to open a window. Mercifully, the day was cooling off with the incoming dusk, and a breeze filtered through the window. I was suddenly aware I'd spent an afternoon sitting here, just listening to her talk. If nothing else worked out for the good, I was at least glad to have met Harriet Duncan. Her story helped me put my own story in perspective.

"Well, I was hoping you might be able to help me find Rufus."

"Whoever took him must have done it because they were afraid he knew something, most likely about me," she said.

"Do you think he really did know you were alive?"

She shrugged. "Not sure. As far as I know, he didn't. Zachariah brought me the newspaper articles after it was over. I didn't like Rufus saying I'd killed myself, but I understood that was the best thing for him to say."

"Where do you think Savanna is now?"

"Not sure, but she's back in the area."

"Why are you so sure?"

"The Wolf Brothers."

I remembered the thread we'd started to pull earlier, out in the yard. Suddenly I had a thought. Was it possible . . . ?

"They're her heavies. When they get active, it means she's around."

"Does she manipulate them in some way?"

"Yeah, something like that." She glanced at Zachariah, who chuckled and said something under his breath.

"What?"

"He said she's been manipulating them since birth," Harriet said. She wasn't laughing.

"I don't understand."

"They're her boys. Her sons."

"Oh . . ." I said, suddenly remembering the way they'd dealt with the overdressed kid at the little bar Eleanor Walsh and I had visited. The cold, almost nonchalant way they'd been moved to violence. It wasn't like most people I knew. Most people, you could see the transition from calm to violent; there was an interval in between. Maybe it was God's way of letting folks know somebody was about to go off. That didn't seem to exist for the Wolf, er, Hill Brothers.

Or maybe I should just think of them as the Duncan Brothers now.

"I only know about them from Lyda. Yes, we've been in touch, but she'll never talk to anyone about me. That's one good thing about her fear of getting involved. Anyway, according to Lyda, after I made my grand disappearance, Savanna started to show. She never told anyone who the father was, and honestly, there are any number of candidates. By the time I started my 'therapy' at the Harden School, she was having sex with relatives, friends, and random strangers. Her pregnancy, according to Lyda, was an embarrassment to my parents, so they began to talk of sending her way. She beat them to the punch and left. She came back several months later with no child and a story about losing it in childbirth. Later she'd admit to Lyda that she'd had them, twins, that she kept them in an old shack in the mountains, visiting them once a day to feed them and not even that as they stopped needing breast milk. By the time they were four or five years old, they basically lived alone in the mountains, foraging for food wherever they could get it, looking forward to her rare visits when she'd drop off something to eat or the occasional toy." Harriet closed her eyes again, and I couldn't help but think it was a prayerful gesture.

"It's odd to think I'm their aunt," Harriet said, "but it's true. They'd just as soon kill me as acknowledge me, from what I can gather. I don't blame them, though. They're *hers*. I doubt they are as evil as she is, though. But can you imagine having a mother like that? They have a lot to process."

"Any idea who the father is?"

She laughed. "Lots of possibilities there."

"Why does Savanna want to find you so badly?"

"Because she's decided I'm a loose end that needs to be tied up. Good thing she can't find me."

"But can you find her?" I asked.

She looked down at her useless legs, the spoked wheels that rose up from the floor surrounding her like shields. "No, but I can tell you where to start."

*　*　*

"Savanna eats men alive," she said. "But there's one that always seemed special to her. I'll bet he could lead you to her."

"Okay," I said. "Where can I find him?"

She jabbed her thumb toward the rear of the cabin. "Up that way. At the school."

"The school?"

She just looked at me, waiting for me to catch on.

"Oh shit. Harden?"

"That's right. I have no real evidence, but I think the man abusing her from a young age was good old Uncle Randy, the same uncle who told me if I didn't figure out how to stop liking girls, he'd introduce me to something long and hard that would change my mind." She laughed bitterly. "And *I* was the pervert."

I didn't know what to say. It was one of the first families I'd encountered that seemed worse than mine. Hell, they were worse than Ronnie's family. I'd always *thought* such a thing might be possible, but now I had the hard evidence.

Zachariah sighed. "Maybe we should wrap this up."

"It's okay, Zac. I want to help Mr. Marcus."

Zachariah bristled. "You don't need this stress."

"I'm sorry if I've caused either of you pain."

I looked at Harriet. Her eyes were tired, the kind of dog-tiredness I used to see in my mother's eyes after she'd come home from working two jobs and then cleaning my father's office and the sanctuary at the church. The difference being I still saw light in Harriet's eyes, while Mother's had been dimmed long before, crushed beneath the force of my father's cult of personality.

"One more thing. How can I get in touch with you again?"

"Zachariah can give you his number. You can call him."

I glanced at the older man. He didn't look happy about it, but he nodded. "Sure."

"Thanks." I turned back to Harriet. "Is there anything you want me to tell your sister if I find her?"

She thought about it for a long time, so long I wondered if she'd heard me. Then she nodded, her face as serious and sure as any face I'd ever seen, and said, "Tell her I made it. I'm free and she isn't."

Part Three
The Life You Save

56

It wasn't until I'd made the long walk back to Virginia's trailer that I remembered I'd called Ronnie earlier. His truck was parked outside and he was sitting on the steps smoking a cigarette while Roscoe played in the mud near his boots.

He saw me coming and waved but didn't speak.

"Sorry about that," I said.

"I was beginning to think that call was just a figment of my drug-addled imagination," he said. "But then Wanda told me you'd stolen her phone. Too bad you didn't think to look at the damned thing once."

"What?" I pulled it out of my pocket and saw there were twelve missed calls from *Ronnie*.

"Damn, Ronnie. I'm really, really sorry."

He waved me off, blew smoke up into the brilliant afternoon sky, where it mingled with the light breeze and was whisked away into the hidden corners of the trailer park. "I didn't mind too much. Me and Roscoe was catching up."

Upon hearing his name, Roscoe looked up and grinned at his uncle. "Ron Ron!" he shouted.

Ronnie stuck the cigarette in his lips and grabbed the boy, swinging him around. The moment felt near enough to perfect, what with the bright blue of the sky, the breeze like the very breath of God touching my neck, my heart full of second chances, new philosophies, fresh starts. But I couldn't enjoy it. There was still Rufus to think about. Not to mention Joe and Weston.

"What's the plan, boss?" Ronnie said as he put Roscoe—still giggling maniacally—back on the ground.

"Recon."

"Please don't tell me you want to go back to that school?"

"Okay, I won't tell you that."

"Shit. That means we're going, doesn't it?"

"Sort of. I think the only way to find where Rufus is being held is to watch the place, follow anyone and everyone who leaves."

"I'm down for that."

"I'm not asking you to come."

He ignored me and said, "We can grab your truck too, boss."

"Boss?"

"That's you."

"Well in that case, I want you to stay here. Visit with these kids. I'll go by myself. That's the boss's orders."

Ronnie laughed and looked a little hurt. "That's a joke, right?"

"No."

He shook his head. "Well, too bad. I'm coming anyway. Give me a minute to tell Wanda and Virginia bye. Last time I helped you out, I ended up in prison for eight months. Hell, I better say my goodbyes, let them know I love 'em and what not."

"You don't have to come."

Ronnie put a hand on my shoulder and looked me in the eye. "Nobody *has* to do anything, Earl. We all do what we want and live with the consequences. Least that's the way I've always seen it."

I nodded at him. He let go of my shoulder and started toward the trailer. I scooped Roscoe up and followed him.

57

We managed to pull Ronnie's truck into the trees beside mine. It was a tough squeeze, but after getting out and looking at it from the winding mountain road, I felt like it was hidden well enough. We got into mine, and I backed it out, repositioning it so that we could watch the road and see vehicles coming and going from the Harden School.

We waited with the windows down, watching the road.

Ronnie smoked and drummed his fingers nervously on the dash. "What are we doing, exactly?"

"Well, I'm hoping we can catch either Blevins or Harden leaving for the day. And then I'm hoping one of them might head over to visit the woman I believe abducted Rufus."

"Lots of hoping."

"Just requires patience," I said. What I didn't say was that I felt completely frustrated. Patience be damned. I was ready to move, to do something. Yet, I knew from experience, sometimes waiting was all there was.

"Okay," he said. "Let's pass the time. Tell me the damned story."

"Excuse me?"

"The story. You've been holding out on me since the first time we came here. All of it. From the beginning."

"Okay," I said. Hell, I owed him that much, didn't I? What right did I have to keep asking for his help and not tell him what was going on?

Time slipped away as I spoke. By the time I'd finished, it was late afternoon, getting close to six thirty. Dusk.

"So, the dead man . . ." He snapped his fingers, trying to remember the name.

"Joe," I said.

"Right. So, Joe's boyfriend is going to write the article? The one you hope will take down Walsh?"

"Yeah. That's the plan. Hopefully, he's already contacted Mindy and Lyda. Maybe even Claire."

"Okay, but to bring Walsh down, won't you need some hard evidence?"

"Yeah, probably. But I can't worry about that until I get Rufus back."

"Yeah, I guess that makes sense. Look, I'm tired of waiting."

"Me and you both."

He flicked his cigarette out the window. "Let me see your phone."

"Why?"

"Do you have Blevins's number?"

I started to say no, but then I remembered I'd called him several weeks back after finding his number in the letter he had written to Joe. "Yeah. I got it."

"Pull it up."

"Why?"

"Just trust me."

"I don't know . . ." Trusting Ronnie wasn't always a wise decision. In fact, it could often be the opposite.

"Come on. I can do this."

"Do what?"

"Make a call. Fool him into leading us to her place."

"How?"

"Okay, he's not afraid of the police, right?"

"Why should he be?"

"What about the Georgia Bureau of Investigation?"

I shrugged. "GBI? How would we get them involved?"

"We don't have to actually get them involved. He just has to think they're on to him. You told me about Sister. That's got to be Savanna, right?"

I sighed. It didn't *have* to be. I mean, I thought it was, but who could be sure of anything?

"Just go with me on this, okay, Earl?"

"Okay."

"So, if that's Savanna, then wouldn't Blevins or Harden keep her abreast of what was happening with the authorities?"

"I suppose so, but there isn't anything actually happening, is there?"

"Not yet, but there will be when I make the call."

I was starting to understand what Ronnie had in mind, and as much as it surprised me, I thought it might work.

"You can pull this off?"

"Are you kidding me? I've been pretending to be people in authority since I can remember. Dial the number."

I scrolled through the recent calls on my phone, hoping it hadn't been too far back to be considered "recent." Luckily, I didn't use my phone very often, so it was still there. I pressed call and handed it to Ronnie.

"Put the speaker on," I said. "I want to hear it."

We waited for Blevins to pick up. It went to voice mail. Ronnie ended the call.

"What now?" I said.

"Wait a few minutes and call again. He probably thinks it's a spam call."

"Right."

But before Ronnie could call again, the phone rang. "It's him," Ronnie said.

"Well, do your thing. And turn the speaker on."

"North Central GBI," Ronnie said.

"What?" The voice on the other end sounded angry.

"This is the GBI, Mr. Blevins. We've been following up on some reports about your school. Some parents have contacted us directly hoping to get our support."

"Who called you?"

Jesus, he was buying it. I had to give Ronnie credit. He was *selling* it.

"I can't reveal those names, sir. I apologize for the lateness of the hour, but I felt like it was only right to give you a heads-up. We know all about Sister and what she's been doing with the boys. We'd like to bring you in for a conversation in the morning, see if you might be amenable to working with us. We're trying to nail down some details about Sister. Would you be able to help us with that, Mr. Blevins?"

Damn, he was good. There was no trace of Ronnie's usual hillbilly drawl, the cagey way he talked like he was always expecting somebody to contradict him and he had to keep his guard up. This was matter-of-fact talk, fast and grammatically correct. I'd had no idea.

273

"What's your name?"

"Agent Pete Nichols. Keep in mind, Mr. Blevins, that a refusal to cooperate will likely mean you'll be indicted along with Sister. We only extend this invitation out of deference to your and Randy Harden's relationship with Mr. Walsh."

"Jeb? He knows about this?"

"We're trying to keep him out of it, actually. We can keep you out of it too if you cooperate."

He was silent for a moment. The whole world was silent, waiting. Everything seemed to hinge on his response. When it came, I felt my heart sink. "You ain't got nothing. If you did, Jeb would have already told me about it."

Damn, he was right about that. I waited to see what Ronnie would do next, but he played it cool.

"Well, if that's the way you want it. Fine by me. We'll get what we need on Sister eventually, and when we do, we'll remember that you refused to cooperate."

There was a silence followed by the sound of someone typing on a keyboard.

"Mr. Blevins?"

"Give me a sec."

"I have other calls to make."

More typing. Deep breathing.

"That's what I thought," he said at last.

"Excuse me?"

"Who the hell is this?"

"I've already told you—"

"Fuck off with the GBI. I just looked up this number. It belongs to that detective, Earl Marcus. Only I don't think it's him, so who the hell are you?"

"I'm the man who's heading to Sister's house right now. Going to get my friend Rufus back, and kill your girlfriend," Ronnie said, and his drawl was back, never missing a beat.

"You fucking try it, asshole. Just go on and try it."

"We'll talk later," Ronnie said. "After she's dead."

He clicked off.

I turned on the interior light to see him better. "Nice work," I said. "Do you think it'll draw him out?"

Ronnie handed me the phone. "Time will tell."

58

Rufus woke to hands on his shoulders, shaking him.

"Bathroom," one of the men said. The other one was already untying him. Once his feet and hands were free, he stood up and stretched his aching torso to his full height. Before falling asleep again, he'd been working the chair across the room. He estimated he was only a few feet from the hearth now. That is, assuming the hearth was even there to begin with. He was blind, for God's sake. There was no way he could know what was in the room. Except somehow he did. He'd seen it.

On the way to the bathroom, he stuck out his left hand.

"What are you doing?" one of the men said.

"Getting my bearings. I'm blind, if you hadn't noticed."

"You don't need bearings," the man said, and pushed his arm back down, but not before he'd touched the stone around the fireplace. It was there. He had a way out. He had an escape.

When they brought him back from the bathroom, they sat him down in the chair and retied him. He waited until he felt the rope tighten around his ankles and grimaced. "Ow, that hurts. Could you loosen it just a tad? Look, I ain't going nowhere, all right? I don't even know where the fuck I am."

Neither man responded, but Rufus noticed the rope around his ankles was left alone, not loosened, but not tightened either.

"Where you boys been? I was hollering for you a while back. Like to piss my pants."

No reply. Of course there wasn't.

"Listen, before you go, I want to ask what she's got on you. Savanna, that is. If it's sex, just run as far as you can. Get away from her. If it's something else, maybe you want to talk about it? I could help you."

He didn't expect an answer; in fact, he was just talking now because he was starting to go crazy being alone so much without anyone to talk to. He was about to ask another question he didn't expect an answer to when one of the men spoke.

"What did you say?" Rufus was so stunned he couldn't process the words.

"I said, there's nobody that can help us."

"Now, that's not true. You boys Christians?"

"No."

"Well, I can't fault you there. I'm not much of one myself. Don't believe in all that heaven-and-hell stuff. But I've always liked Jesus. Can't imagine he was perfect like they say, but he definitely had the right idea."

"Hell's real."

"Come again?"

"You heard me."

That hit Rufus pretty hard. Maybe it was real. Weren't his moments with the shadow girl evidence enough of that? If that wasn't hell, what else would you call it?

"You boys got names?"

"No."

"That can't be right. Everybody's got a name."

"We don't."

He nodded. "Well, that must be terrible."

Neither man spoke. Rufus took the silence as agreement.

A few moments later, he heard them retreat to their room.

He leaned forward, putting his weight on his feet, lifting the chair. The ropes weren't as tight as they'd been. He slid one foot forward and then the other. His legs screamed in pain, but he didn't stop. He made it three more steps before putting the chair back down to rest.

When he did, he saw the face of Harriet standing beside the falls, her hair blowing in the wind, the determination written on her face.

"When I'm gone," she said. "Tell them I'm dead. But tell them *why* I'm dead. You have to promise me."

He had promised her. Of course he had. He was a fool who didn't understand his own role in her torture, how working for the very system that denied Harriet her right to be herself was just as evil as the men who'd

276

started that institution, just as evil as the woman—Savanna—who'd spent her life capitalizing on it.

"Please don't do it," he said. "There's another way."

She was a pale wisp on the rock, the moon illuminating her marionette body, strings gone, burned in the long sun, now fading. Such an insignificant figure in the night. She could never make it across. And if she did, then what? There was a single ledge, an outcropping of crumbling rock she pointed to as her destination. Wouldn't it be easier to climb the fence?

"What about going out the front?" he said.

"They'll track me down within twenty-four hours. Blevins knows this mountain better than anyone. He'll track me down and humiliate me. This is the only way. You know the story."

He did know the story. Two Indians. Both lost. Except Harriet somehow believed one of them had made it, and if he'd made it, so could she. Rufus had to stop her. He stepped onto the rock with her.

"I've changed my mind," he said. "I'm going to tell them the truth. I'm going to tell them to come look for you."

She slid away from him, closer to the edge. The moonlight hit him then, and he felt lifted by it, filled with some kind of magic light he wished could carry him on from here forever. If he could feel that moon glow on him, if he could keep it in his breast, he would be able to do anything, live through and beyond any challenge.

He reached out his hand. "Let's sit and talk. We can look at the moon."

"I want to look at the moon as me," she said. "Surely you can understand that."

She never gave him a chance to reply. She stepped off the ledge. He scrambled after her, peering down below. He saw her one ledge down, still ghostlike, still almost unreal. It all felt unreal. Just a few months ago, he'd been the good son, the good Christian, worshiping the fundamental tenants of RJ Marcus's mountain faith. He'd managed to escape that and now he was here, trapped between heaven and hell, trying to find out who he was, and how he might move forward.

"This is it," she said from the ledge below. "Now it's time for me to go."

He opened his mouth to respond, but the words stuck in his throat as he watched her begin her sprint. She leapt. Her body made it halfway across the void before it seemed to reach up and envelope her. She vanished. The world went dark, much like it would some weeks later when the shadow girl revealed she would never stop visiting him without a sacrifice.

*   *   *

The next morning, he stood with Deloach and Harden on the flat rock, looking down into the ravine.

"She did it because of the way she was treated here," he said again, determined not to let them change what he knew was the truth. "It's not right to treat someone like that."

Deloach cursed again. He'd been cursing since he'd shown up ten minutes earlier and Rufus explained what had happened. Harden said little, standing with his arms crossed and spitting into the ravine occasionally.

"That's fine," Deloach said, "but if you fucking tell any of this to the media or the police, you're done here."

Rufus nodded. He'd expected that. In fact, he was done here regardless. For the life of him, he couldn't figure out why he'd stayed on as long as he had. Savanna, probably. He'd been caught in her web, somehow, and it had taken this to get him out of it. He just wished he knew if Harriet had made it or not. After the second leap, he'd called out to her, begging her to give him some clue that she was still alive, but there had been no response. He'd squinted into the darkness, trying to find her against the other wall of the ravine, but found nothing but formless shadows. He couldn't help but think she had not made it, that she'd never truly intended to make it. He'd stayed on the flat rock until the sun rose and he could see for himself that there was nothing in the ravine. She was gone. One way or the other, he doubted he'd ever see her again. All that was left was for him to do the right thing.

"That's okay," he said. "I quit."

Harden cleared his throat. "You can quit, Rufus. I understand that. You feel like you've betrayed your personal values. That's a bad place to be. You want to start over. I want that for you too."

Rufus stared at Harden. Was he being serious? "Thanks," he said, still wary.

He had a right to be. What Harden said next changed everything. Everything.

"Of course, if you do decide to go that route, you'll need to face up to your other sins."

"Other sins?"

Harden shrugged and spat again. The wind blew some of the spittle onto Rufus. He ignored it.

"Well, I wasn't going to make a big deal about what you did with my niece, but since you aren't willing to help us out, maybe I shouldn't help you out."

"What are you talking about?"

"You didn't have sex with Savanna?"

"I did, but that's not illegal. What's your point?"

"Well, it might actually be illegal. Hell, it might be very illegal. See, the story she tells is that you raped her. Repeatedly. That she'd come to bring you food at night and you'd lock the door behind her and take what you wanted."

"That's ludicrous."

"Is it? You're a big man, Rufus. She's just a little slip of a thing. And maybe you've noticed . . . she can be very convincing."

Rufus felt like he'd been deflated, like someone had popped both of his lungs and he couldn't get any air. His instinct was to go to Savanna to see if she would really do this to him, but he realized he didn't have to. Of course she would. It was probably the reason she'd had sex with him to begin with.

He looked at Deloach, as if for some help. Surely one of these men had some sense of right or wrong, but Deloach was smiling, happy as a lark. Rufus sat down on the rock. He looked at the sky. The moon was gone. The sun was so bright, he couldn't see. He closed his eyes.

* * *

The rest had felt inescapable. He knew now, of course, nothing was inescapable. Sometimes it was painful, but there was always a way out. Harriet had taught him that. Perhaps she *was* really alive. Savanna certainly seemed to think so.

He leaned forward again, wincing at the pain in his thighs. He stepped forward five times, quickly, bearing the pain. On the fifth step, he felt something rough and hard in front of him. The hearth. Escape was always possible.

He didn't hesitate. He didn't think. He could see it in his mind's eye. None of this was possible, he knew. Yet it was happening. He'd seen the hearth in his dream, except he'd never believed his sleep paralysis was a function of dreaming. He didn't give a fuck what the science said. The shadow girl was real, and he'd seen her in this room.

He pivoted the chair around, then shifted his hips as hard as he could, smashing the legs into the hearth. Again and again, he swung the legs, until he heard them splinter. He stood, his hands still bound around the backrest of the chair. But his legs were free now, the rope around them slipped away, and he stepped from the hearth carrying what remained of the chair.

He heard the bedroom door open as he slammed his body into the door leading to the outside. It popped open and he fell into the grass, rolling. He smelled honeysuckle, felt the hot sun, the wet grass, and he was happy for just those small things. He did not want to die without feeling them again. The men shouted for him to stop, but he just continued to roll down a hill. Rocks cut his arms and tore his shirt. The backrest of the chair was pulverized, and his hands were freed.

He stood up, stumbling forward. Something was wrong. The ground gave way beneath him. He walked on the air.

And then he fell.

59

We didn't have to wait long. A Cadillac drove by about a half hour later. It was nearly dark now, but I kept my lights off as I pulled into the road behind it.

I followed the Cadillac down the mountain and east along 52. By the time the Caddy pulled off the main road and onto another mountain road, it was completely dark. I kept the headlights off and maintained as much distance as I dared, focusing on the tiny red taillights in front of me.

The road rose in front of us, narrowing and turning like a snake. Off to our right, I saw the lights of the small town of Brethren. We continued up the mountain.

Over my many years working as a private investigator, I'd followed a lot of people in this same way, headlights off, chasing their red taillights, but I'd never done it on a twisty mountain road like this one. Eventually I felt Ronnie growing tense in the seat next to me, especially when we caught a glimpse of what was coming in the glow of the Caddy's headlights. The road wrapped around a rocky bluff, tightening itself like a belt. There was barely enough space for a vehicle on the road, and any mistake would cause a long plummet into a dark valley and an almost certain death.

The taillights disappeared around the bend.

"Turn your lights on now. He's on the other side of the mountain," Ronnie said. "He won't be able to see them."

I considered doing just that, but then thought better of it. Any inkling the driver of the Cadillac had that he was being followed would be a problem.

"Open your door," I said.

"Why?"

"So you can see the ledge. Tell me if I get too close."

Ronnie did as I asked.

"Can you see anything?"

"Maybe. It's so fucking dark. Where's the moon when you need it?"

"It's too cloudy. Give your eyes time to adjust."

While I was waiting for that, I drove slowly, my foot just barely touching the gas. I rolled down the window on my side and stuck a hand out, feeling for the stone wall. Once I touched it, I cut the wheel to the left, inching even closer to the wall, hugging it until I heard the scrape of the side mirror against rock.

"You're good over here," Ronnie said. "Just don't straighten it out, or this tire will be in the air."

Eventually, with me touching the wall on my side and Ronnie looking out on his, we made it around the bend. The taillights were in front of us again, far away, and much higher than we were. If I hadn't known better, I would have thought the Caddy was on a totally different mountain, but that was just the way the road rose. I dropped the truck into second and started to make the climb.

We followed the Caddy like this for about twenty minutes. I became more convinced that the driver was either Blevins or Harden himself.

I was beginning to wonder if we'd ever get there when I heard Ronnie whistle.

"What?"

"Slow down."

"Why?"

"Somebody's in the road."

I squinted hard as I slowed the truck. Sure enough, two figures stood in the road. One of them was smoking a cigarette.

"You think it's the Hill Brothers?" Ronnie asked.

"Yeah, Blevins had to have called ahead."

"What now?" Ronnie asked.

"We pretend to be lost," I said.

"And then what?"

"We go back."

"But we ain't even seen it yet."

"I know, but we're close, right? We have to be if these guys got here on foot so fast. Just let me handle it."

One of them—the one without the cigarette—was heading this way.

With my window still down, I could hear his boots crunching on the gravel. He was moving slow, cautious. I could hardly see him at all, just a shape—a shadow—floating this way. The only corporeality that emanated from the shadow was the sound of the boots on the gravel.

Ronnie gasped.

"What?" I said, but I'd barely felt the word slide past my lips when I saw it too. Another shadow in his hands. A rifle, or shotgun, it hardly mattered except it was aimed right at me.

I slid down in the seat as the first shot hit the windshield, splintering it into bladed pebbles. The night came alive with sound and light.

More shots hit the vehicle. I was down low, my body twisted under the steering wheel, but I managed to reach up and put the truck in drive.

"Hold on," I said, and put both hands on the gas pedal. I slammed it to the floor and felt the truck lurch ahead, spinning gravel out behind us like machine gun fire. I felt the truck lift, rising with another hill, and I pulled myself out of the floorboard, cutting my hands and wrists on the broken glass. I ignored the pain, grabbed the wheel with one hand, and flipped on the headlights with the other. The road ahead was suddenly awash in my headlights. Another bend lurked, this one as tight or tighter than the last. I slammed my foot on the brakes, but there was no stopping. I'd have to take the turn. Ronnie, still in the floorboard on the passenger's side, screamed out, as surely as if he'd seen the same thing I had. He must have intuited it somehow. I cut the wheel, and the back end of the truck began to slip out to the side, toward the long fall into the dark nothingness.

I let off the brake, tried to center the truck, but now my front end was threatened by the yawning pit. The front right tire slipped off the ledge and Ronnie screamed again. I felt my body tense as I ripped the wheel left again, flooring the vehicle.

Somehow the other three tires found their purchase, and with a great bump and hop, we were back on the gravel road—the now *straight* gravel road.

"You okay?" I asked, bringing the truck to a stop.

"Yeah. Cut up a little, but I ain't shot. That was some hellacious driving back there, Earl. Never knew you had it in you."

"Me neither," I said. I looked around. The road continued up a long winding rise, at the top of which was a lone cabin with a single light burning inside. The Cadillac was parked in front. "Get out," I said.

"What?"

"Trust me. I've got an idea."

"I thought you said we were going to come back after we had the lay of the land."

"I got the lay of the land, and there ain't no point in putting off the inevitable. Besides, this might be the only time those brothers are behind us. Hurry, before they catch back up. Oh, and look in the dash. There's a gun for you."

Ronnie opened the dashboard and pulled out my spare gun, a 9mm.

Then we were both jogging up the rise, toward the cabin and whatever waited inside.

60

felt the light on my back as I ran. I managed to get down before the first
rifle shot rang out. A bullet nearly grazed my ear and pinged into the
door of the Cadillac.

I rolled away from the light, toward some trees. Two more shots and
the door to the cabin swung open. I looked for Ronnie. He was coming
my way, crouched over, the 9mm in one hand. He hit the ground next to
me and lay on his belly. I swung around and aimed at the flashlight one
of the brothers was holding. I fired. Ronnie fired twice. The light went
out.

The night was silent except for the long echoes of the gunfire, gradually
diminishing in waves of eerie dissonance.

"You think we hit him?" Ronnie said.

"I doubt it. Otherwise he would have dropped the light instead of turning it off."

"Good point."

I turned my head to get a look at the house, but it was gone now, as
dark as the rest of the night. Someone had come out of it moments before.
We had attackers on both sides of us we couldn't see.

Footsteps on gravel. Coming from two, no, three directions. One up
the hill, in the direction of the cabin. A second from downhill, to my right.
That was the brother with the light. The third was the closest of all, just off
to our left.

I nudged Ronnie and whispered to him. "Watch your left. I've got the
right side."

"What about behind us?"

I didn't answer. What could I say? There were only two of us, after all.

My feeling was that the brother with the light would turn it on again at some point. Otherwise, they were as blind as we were. As long as that was the case, we were all handicapped.

Something moved to my right. I pivoted slowly, irritating the wounds on my stomach as I slid it over the dirt. I held my .45 in both hands. I'd never been what you'd call a crack shot, but I'd also never thought that part mattered much. Most people could hit a target within thirty feet. The problem was most people had a hard time doing it when the target was more than just a target. When it was an actual person. For better or worse, I'd always been able to shut that part of my brain down. Hell, I'd say it was for the better, because if I hadn't been able to do that, I'd probably have been dead by now.

The thing I couldn't do, the thing I'd never been able to do, anyway, was shoot an unarmed man. I remembered the opportunity I'd had to do just that last fall when Jeb Walsh had stood in front of me at gunpoint. God, if I'd just pulled the trigger, would we even be here right now? I had to think we wouldn't be.

The life you save may be your own.

Except when the life you save is some asshole who can't help getting his dirty fingerprints all over the damned county.

I felt the light before I saw it. Right on top of me. I rolled over, aiming the gun up, firing wildly. I rolled into Ronnie, who cursed and squeezed off a shot too.

The ground exploded beside my shoulder, and we were both showered in dirt. The light went crooked and aimed toward the sky, making a full moon in the branches of the trees.

Someone groaned. I got to my feet.

Ronnie clutched at my ankles, trying to pull me down. "What are you doing?" he hissed.

"Going to get that light. Cover me."

I was almost there when I realized it might be a trick. The light still lay aimed at the tree branches, and I could see the dark casing of the flashlight, still in the man's hand. I raised my gun for what I hoped would be kill shot when the light shifted, flashing in my eyes, causing me to lose the target.

Someone fired. In my blinded state, I couldn't tell where the shot had come from. But I didn't feel hit. And the light fell away. The groan was different this time. The groan was misery, the kind from the depths of hell that pricks you inside and makes you regret everything all at once.

Except being alive to feel regret. Not that.

I blinked several times, trying to get the spots out of my vision, but they lingered. A hand fell on my back. I jumped, screaming out, and Ronnie hushed me.

"We got to get down on the—"

Shots came from two different directions. We fell, rolled onto one of the brothers. I heaved his body over top of us to use as a shield.

"You hit?" I asked.

"Yeah, I think maybe I am," Ronnie said.

"Shit. Where?" I'd no more gotten the question out than the headlights came on. A car was coming toward us, its high beams freezing us where we lay.

"What now?" Ronnie said.

"Where are you shot?"

"Leg. No, hip. Maybe thigh. Everything hurts."

"Can you stand?"

"Nah. That ain't happening."

"Okay." I swallowed hard. The car was still coming toward us. If I timed it just right . . .

I stayed still, waiting, hoping the driver—Blevins or one of the brothers or even Savanna—would assume us all dead and stop the vehicle.

The headlights stayed on us as the car crept steadily forward. I'd have to act soon.

My fingers tightened on my .45 caliber, and I thought again about last fall, the chance I'd had to take Walsh out. Would it really have kept me from this moment? Maybe. Or maybe I would be in prison right now. Still, when it came down to death and prison, there was no real decision to be made . . .

I waited until I heard the engine rev before shrugging the dead Hill brother off me and standing up. I couldn't see because of the high beams, but I held the gun steady and squeezed the trigger until it was empty. The car swerved just before hitting me, hitting *us*. I watched as it slid down the hill and into a bank of trees before coming to a stop.

Before I could head down to check it out, I heard another vehicle start up. I spun toward the cabin in time to see a small car darting away. Its headlights illuminated a man—the other brother. He stood there, passive, unafraid, just standing there, as the car slowed and the driver said something to him.

My gun was empty, so I went to Ronnie and asked for his. He handed it to me, grunting from the pain, but by the time I got the gun up, the brother was gone and the car was moving again. I squeezed off two shots, but I didn't think either one of them hit anything. The taillights vanished around the bend.

As far as I could tell, we were alone. I looked up at the cabin. The single light burned inside again. Somehow I doubted we'd find Rufus there.

61

Two days later, Ronnie and I checked into the Wildflower Motel on the west side of the county. We took possession of a spartan room with two double beds, an old box television with a button on the remote that said *press for adult only content*, a framed watercolor painting of the ocean at sunset, and a bathtub with a broken drain. The best part of the place—other than it being far enough off the beaten path to let us avoid being found—was the back window that looked out onto a meadow dappled with wildflowers and rolling hills, hence the name of the place. Ronnie and I both commented that the view alone was worth $18.99 a night.

Mindy and Chip were in the room right next door. It had been Chip I'd called first when Ronnie and I finally made it to my place and I'd had a chance to charge my phone.

"Where are you?" I'd asked him.

"I'm safe," he said. "And I've talked to Mindy. In fact, she's here with me."

"You're still interviewing her?"

"Not so much. She's worried, though, because her mother overheard her talking to me and called her uncle."

"Okay, that's good. I'm glad you're both all right."

"What about you?"

I looked at Ronnie. I'd helped him out of the truck and onto the couch at my place. He was still in a lot of pain, but the bleeding was under control. He'd live as long as the wound didn't get infected. Despite my best efforts, he would not hear of me taking him to the hospital. "Bad news," he'd said. "That's how Argent finds out where we are."

I would have made him if I'd thought he was in real danger. Still, it wouldn't hurt to get some antibiotics in him just in case.

"We've been better," I said.

"Did you find what I needed?"

"Not yet. I'm still working on it."

"Are you safe?"

"Far from it."

"Come stay with us."

Once he explained where they were and how he'd only seen a few people since being there, I agreed that Ronnie and I would stay there for a few days until I figured out what my next move was. Except I thought I might already know.

We'd been at the Wildflower less than two days when Chip asked me to come over to his room for a talk.

Mindy was around back with Ronnie, the two of them sitting in the grass, watching the sunset. We could see them through the back window of Chip's room from where we sat across from each other at the small round table, the same round table that was in Ronnie's and my room. He had his laptop out and told me he'd gotten in touch with Harriet that morning.

"Her story is quite compelling. I think I've got something here. The one thing I don't have is something that connects Jeb Walsh to it all in a concrete way. Do you really think he was behind the death of that boy?"

"Absolutely," I said. "But that happened a while back. There's no way to know for sure."

"I'd like to interview his son."

"That's going to be tough."

He shrugged. "You found Harriet. After talking to her, I understand that was no easy task. This whole story is coming together, but there are still some missing pieces I need you to fill in."

I knew he was right, but I didn't have many options available to me to fix the problem. Well, maybe one, but the truth was, I'd been putting it off. Ronnie needed me, I told myself. But that wasn't it. Mindy or Chip could have taken care of him fine. The real truth was I was still pretty depressed over Mary, and now Rufus.

When we'd gone inside the house at the top of the hill, after all the shooting, we'd found no sign of Rufus whatsoever. I searched the place for as long as I dared, looking for anything that might prove to me he'd been there. I didn't find it.

But I did find something. Well, a couple of somethings. One was a mini recorder with a missing battery door. I rewound the tape and pressed play. I heard my voice and Claire's as we talked that day in the bookstore. But how and why had the brothers known to follow me there?

I could think of only one reason. They'd been the ones who'd killed Joe.

The other something I found was sitting on the kitchen counter among a veritable mound of other dirty dishes.

It was a red cooler just like the one Daphne had filled up at my house.

* * *

Was it possible it was just the same kind of red cooler but not Daphne's red cooler? Sure, anything was *possible*. In fact, it might even have been likely. But it got me to thinking about Daphne and Savanna and how the clues had been there all along.

First and foremost was timing. A few short days after Claire and I had been recorded in the bookstore, Daphne had shown up. Second was my own arrogance. It was actually quite astonishing. I'd been willing to accept that this woman had just come out of nowhere to fuck me. That I was just so damned attractive—at fifty-three, for God's sake—that she literally couldn't keep her hands off me.

And then there was the car. She drove a little Toyota Corolla. When Savanna had made her escape—with or without Rufus—she'd been driving a small car, roughly the size and shape of a Corolla.

The red cooler just snapped all of this into focus. The one thing I couldn't get my head around was why. If I'd been a threat—and obviously I had been, since she'd felt the need to put her feral sons on me early—why not just have those same sons eliminate me? The only answer I could come up with was that sex was a luxury she believed she had, like a cat toying with a mouse before killing it. This seemed to fit with Harriet's narrative of her sister.

So, that left me with one more thing to do, and that was wait. But I had to make sure I was waiting in the right place. I had to go home and hope she showed up, hope she was willing to play cat-and-mouse one more time. And this time, I had to make sure I was the cat instead of the mouse.

I walked to the back window and raised it. "Come on in," I said. "I need to talk to both of you."

Ronnie and Mindy turned as if embarrassed, as if I'd caught them in the middle of something they didn't want me to see. I felt a flood of emotions as I realized they were falling for each other. On the one hand, I couldn't help but think of Mary and how much I missed her, and that made me hate both Mindy and Ronnie just a little bit. On the other hand, I'd come to love Ronnie like a brother—imagine that—and my heart felt full seeing him so happy.

The world was made of mysteries, I decided, and sat down at the table to think about how I was going to solve one of them and come out on the other side unscathed.

Except I'd faced enough of the world's mysteries in the past to know that wasn't going to happen. This wasn't a gentle world. It always left a mark.

62

I decided to head home and wait her out. My logic was that, sooner or later, Daphne would come looking for me. She had to know I was the one who'd killed one of her boys, not to mention whoever had been driving the Cadillac.

I spent most of the day sitting outside, pretending to read, waiting for the sound of her car coming up the road. I kept my phone beside me in case someone called. But the car didn't come and the phone didn't ring.

Two days passed this way, with me checking in with Chip and Ronnie on a daily basis. They both begged me to come back to the Wildflower where it was safe, but I told them I knew what I was doing. I sounded confident when I said it, but in reality I was growing less and less sure of myself with each passing day.

Eventually I decided I might need to be a little more proactive. An idea began to take root, and the more I thought about it, the more it made sense. I was in the midst of contemplating the best way to initiate it when the phone rang.

I didn't recognize the number and wondered if it might be Savanna. I picked it up, ready for anything.

It was Claire. She wanted to meet me somewhere to talk about "the case." I almost told her no, but I decided it might not be wise to exclude anything at this point, so I agreed to meet her.

"Where?" she asked.

"I'll get back to you."

"Okay, but don't wait too long. I want to know what's going on!"

"Sure," I told her. "I'll call you back."

The reason I wanted to wait on where to meet was because of the idea I'd had. I needed to check on a couple of things first.

I found Eleanor Walsh's number and dialed it. She picked up on the third ring.

"Mr. Marcus, I thought you'd fallen off the face of the earth. I've tried to call you several times. I even left a voice mail. Did you know Dr. Blevins was missing?"

"I'm sorry. I've had a hard couple of days. Haven't even checked my voice mail yet. And no, I hadn't heard about Blevins. What happened?" I decided playing dumb was the way to go here.

"Randy Harden was quoted in the newspaper as saying he'd last seen him on Sunday night when he made his 'lights out' rounds. In the morning, his Cadillac was gone, and no one has heard from him since."

"Interesting."

"Do you know anything about it?"

"I wish. I'd love to catch up with him."

"I was hoping you'd killed him."

"I'm a PI, not a mercenary."

"Well, as a PI, have you found out anything else on the Weston boy?"

"I'm still working on it. In fact, that's what I called you about."

"Oh?"

"Well, I was wondering about that bar we went to a while back. The one where the kid got beaten up?"

"Oh, yes, Livingstone's place."

"Is that the name of it?"

She laughed. "Not really. It doesn't actually have a name. But Livingstone is the owner, so that's what I call it."

"How about a number? I need to talk to him."

"Yeah, I think I've got that somewhere. What's this about?"

"I think I might know who the woman is that's abusing those boys."

* * *

I called Livingstone, hoping he was open, hoping for a break. He answered almost immediately. "Bar, what's up?"

I heard voices in the background and the plucking of an acoustic guitar. Sounded much busier than the time Eleanor and I had been there.

I told him who I was, reminding him of what had happened that day with the Hill Brothers. He remembered. "Eleanor's friend, right?"

"Yeah. And I'm not sure if I told you that day, but I'm a private investigator, and I'm looking for one of your regulars. She goes by the name Daphne or Savanna? She's the one that comes in with those brothers."

"I don't know that woman's name, I'm sorry to say. Could be Daphne. Could be Savanna. She hasn't been in yet today, but she's been showing up a lot lately."

"With or without the brothers?"

"Depends. Sometimes with. Sometimes without. But I always get the sense they aren't too far away, no matter what."

"I'm heading your way," I said. "Do me a favor. When I get there, act like you've never met me before."

"You ain't planning on starting any trouble, are you?"

I paused, not sure how to answer that.

"No," I said at last. "I'm planning on ending it."

* * *

I called Claire back and asked her if she knew where Livingstone's place was.

"Sure. I know it."

"Meet me there in half an hour?"

"Sound good. First round is on me."

"Okay. Claire?"

"Yeah?"

"I'm happy to talk, but I'm also working. If a certain person comes in, I may have to go pretty quickly."

"Ooh . . . sounds fun."

"So you don't mind?"

"Do what you have to do. I'm just excited to be a part of it all."

I told her I'd see her soon and hung up. Then I went inside to grab the recorder I'd found at Savanna's house. There was still plenty of room left on the tape. I slipped on a light jacket and put it in the inside pocket. Goose was watching me closely. I shrugged and stared back at him. "I don't know any other way," I said.

63

Livingstone's place was different at night. As soon as I pulled my truck into the dirt lot, I saw how he stayed in business. It was nine thirty on a Tuesday night, and damned if there weren't fifteen cars in the lot and not a single space left for me. I made a three-point turn and worked my way back out to the road, where I parked in a little gully and walked back up to the small, well-lit shack, feeling slightly naked without my gun.

I had decided to leave it in the truck. Daphne wouldn't go anywhere with me if she saw the gun. I had to get her away from the bar before I could do anything else.

Now that it was dark, I could see Christmas lights strung around the shack, dangling like moss from the eaves of the small porch, where five people stood, clutching bottles of beer and wiping sweat from their brows. Of the five, three were women. The other two were young men, no more than thirty, wearing five-o'clock shadows and tight-fitting blue jeans. They eyed me as I approached, and I wondered if I was going to be pressed into some trouble. Ordinarily, I wouldn't even have bothered trying to avoid it. My dirty little secret was that I often relished these kinds of situations. Fights had never particularly scared me, and as I've said many times, this was both a blessing and a curse. Tonight, it was definitely a curse. I had to make sure I assumed the right posture as I moved past these two muscle heads. Not only that, I needed to be sure I didn't accidentally ogle one of the women. Not that they were my type anyway. Far too young for me.

I slipped by them cleanly, not even bothering to turn around when I heard one of them mutter to his friend that it must be "hillbilly hour." I kept my cool, no easy feat.

The inside was even more crowded. There was no space at the tiny bar and no tables available. I pushed through the crowd of mostly men— old-timers and burnouts—and motioned for Livingstone, who did exactly as I'd requested and pretended he didn't know me. I noticed he had about a dozen bottles of whiskey sitting behind the bar this time and wanted desperately to order one of them, but it was going to have to be beer tonight. My life might literally depend on it.

He opened a bottle of beer for me, and it was as cold as I remembered. I drank it quickly, fast enough to feel the buzz I'd been missing, to calm me, to make the room settle down around me just a little bit. Leaving the empty bottle on the bar, I looked around, searching for Daphne or Claire, and found Claire already seated at a small table in the back of the room.

She was dressed in a short skirt and a low-cut blouse. She wore sandals wrapped around her ankles and lower calves, accentuating the tone of her muscles. She wasn't wearing her glasses, and her hair was different. I couldn't help but notice how attractive she seemed. Each and every time I saw her, she looked a little different. It was amazing. The first time I'd met her, she had seemed older, bookish, not unattractive, but nothing like she appeared now, either. Now, she was . . . wow. That was the only word I had for it.

I sat down across from her, and she grinned. "Tell me everything."

"Everything?"

"About the case. Did you find Rufus yet?"

"No."

She frowned. "Well, maybe he's still out there somewhere."

"Can I buy you a drink?" I said.

"No, remember I said they were on me?" She stood. "What do you want?"

"Just a beer."

"Can or bottle?"

"Can."

"Be right back."

I took the opportunity to look around a bit. No Daphne. But it was early still. I could pick Claire's brain, maybe get some insight into the situation. She was smart enough. And attractive. Jesus. She seemed like the kind of woman I would like to pursue, but not now, not with the pain of

Mary still lingering. Not with the uncertainty of my future, my ability to just live still up in the air.

There was a line at the bar. Claire waved at me. I waved back. The door to the porch opened, and the kid who had messed with the Hill Brothers last time I was here waltzed in. He was dressed to the nines again, and from the looks of him, he'd already forgotten the broken nose the brothers had given him, which was amazing, because it was still visibly crooked. He called out to Livingstone, and the old man ignored him. The kid pretended not to be bothered and reached inside his sport coat for a couple of twenties, which he held up for Livingstone to see. He slapped the money down on the bar and walked around back for a bottle of whiskey. Livingstone scowled at him but was too busy with the other customers to do anything about it.

The kid began to drink straight from the bottle. A middle-aged woman with platinum-blonde hair and a painful-looking sunburn sat on one of the stools next to him. He leaned over and whispered in her ear. She shrugged and reached for the bottle. He pulled it away from her, lifting it up into the air, showing her he wanted to pour it into her waiting mouth. She gave him a look. It was a look of resignation. She knew who she was dealing with now, but he was offering free whiskey. I could relate. Sometimes I felt like I wanted it bad enough to let the kid pour it into my mouth, too.

I watched the woman open her mouth up, and the kid stood up and tipped the bottle over. She accepted it eagerly and without shame. He leaned forward, trading his mouth for the bottle, and she kissed him even though her face registered nothing but disgust.

I felt an overwhelming urge to go over and tell the kid to get lost, but I couldn't. Not tonight. Tonight, I had to stay contained, stay within myself, and wait.

Patience had never been a virtue for me.

*   *   *

Claire was on her way with my beer and a bottle of whiskey when the door opened and one of the men who'd been trying to start something with me outside came in. He held the door open, a drunken and self-satisfied leer on his face. He looked like a man who'd found the golden egg and was confident he would be rewarded for it later on. He ushered Daphne in with a hand that fell a little too close to her ass, but for her part, Daphne didn't seem to mind at all. She was dressed in a low-cut blouse and cutoff blue jean shorts that left little to the imagination. Her boots came up over her knees and there was a dazed look on her face, as if she'd entered some kind of primal state, as if she were on the precipice of a sexual ritual that was both familiar and intoxicating.

Most women her age would never have attempted those shorts, but she pulled them off without a hitch. Hell, you could feel the room turning to her, the collective gaze of every man in the small room, laser focused on her midsection where the blouse failed to meet the top of her shorts.

She didn't see me at first, which was to the good, because it gave me an opportunity to watch her, to observe how she worked. It was easy to see her in a different light like this. It was easy to be sympathetic. Wasn't she doing the same thing Harriet was doing, that I wanted to do? Wasn't she living her life free of restraint? Hadn't she thrown off Joyce's nets Harriet had spoken about?

Yeah, I guessed she had, in a way. But here was a case where some restraint was needed, where a net might do its job and keep her from hurting others. There was a difference. Some people just wanted to be themselves. Others, like Daphne/Savanna, wanted to be more than themselves; they wanted to inflict their own lives onto others, to suck out the souls of men and women alike and crush them for sheer pleasure.

Jeb Walsh was like this too, I realized, but somehow he managed to stay above the fray, to work at a distance, pulling strings and levers, the wizard from Oz, the man behind the curtain. Was he a psychopath too, or did such a designation even exist? Maybe we were all psychopaths, driven by genes and past experiences utterly beyond our control.

Like me, for instance. I was running on instinct now, sure something would happen, one way or the other. I just hoped I'd come out on the other side able to really live my life. Because that was the secret, I realized. Not the highs or the lows, not the tragedies, the trials, the vanquishing of foes, but simply the everyday routine of living with yourself, with the one person you could change, the one person you could save.

"Hello," Claire said. "I'm right here."

I turned to her. "Sorry. Thanks for the beer."

"No problem. Drink up. And talk. Who are you here to stalk?"

I nodded at Daphne. "See that woman?"

"Yeah. You think she's hot or something?"

"Something. I think she's the woman who kidnapped Rufus."

Claire just stared at me. "You can't be serious. Her?"

"I don't know. I'm still trying to figure it out."

"Did Harriet tell you how to find her or something?"

"Sort of."

"So you found Harriet?"

"Hmm?" I was focused on Daphne. She and the asshole were having a really good time. I was hoping if I went up to her, she'd drop him and take a walk with me. We'd walk out to Backslide Gap. Once I got her on the swinging bridge, I'd be able to get the information I needed from her.

"I talked to your reporter friend," Claire said. "Not sure I was much help, but I told him what I could. He asked about Harriet. I didn't know what to tell him. Did you find her?"

"Yeah," I said. "Look, I've got to go."

"Uh, okay."

I stood, taking my beer with me, and walked slowly toward the bar.

Daphne and the man had found a spot at the end of the bar. He wore a pair of dark blue jeans that looked new along with a white button-down shirt tucked in crisply. His boots were new too and looked like real leather. He was bald, but handsome in a tough-guy kind of way. He saw me looking at him, and his eyes lingered on me briefly before settling on Daphne's cleavage.

I stood behind them as they ordered beers, and Daphne laughed at the man's joke. He put his arm around her, and she snuggled in close to him, whispering something in his ear. He smiled and nodded, whispering something back. I decided to make my move.

I leaned in on Daphne's right as if to order another beer. "Hey, you," I said. "I was hoping for another visit."

Sometimes you can catch a person without their mask on. Sometimes, briefly, you can see their true self. In my experience, the true self of most people can be an ugly thing, and at the least disconcerting. People wear masks for a reason. Underneath, they are lonely and disturbed. But Savanna/Daphne's true self was neither of these things. What I saw in her moment of unguardedness was pure hurt, as if she she'd been self-medicating through her behavior. But then the moment was gone, and she smiled at me, fluttering her eyelids and turning her cleavage to me.

"Well, I came by for a shower and you weren't there, so I had to make do without you. A girl can do a lot without a man's help, but there's some things a man is really good for."

The man she was with cleared his throat and craned his head to look at me. "Who are you?"

I stuck out my hand. "Earl Marcus. Me and Daphne are old friends."

"Well, she's on a date right now. So get the hell out of here."

"Hey, weren't you one of the assholes on the porch laughing at me earlier when I came in?"

He nodded. "Yep. So what?"

"Well, I was wondering what was so funny."

He shrugged. "I guess you were."

I nodded, trying to decide how far to take this. Why not all the way? After all, I didn't need her trying to decide between the two of us, did I?

"I think you and your asshole buddies need to learn some respect for others."

He stood up, and when he did, there was a shift in the mood of the bar. I felt it but didn't participate in it. I felt fine. Hell, there was definitely a part of me that was broken, because I actually felt better than fine. I felt like all was right in the world at that moment, and the anticipation of the coming violence was like a relief. Assholes like this one always took me to the same place. It was a place I'd regret later, but much like getting drunk, I'd enjoy the hell out of the actual time spent in the zone.

He reached over and grabbed the front of my shirt. I just looked at him, not moving, not reacting at all. I was still clutching my beer bottle, and I remembered the way that Hill Brother had smashed his bottle into that kid's face a few weeks ago.

"Let go," I said.

He laughed and tried to pull me away from the bar, away from Daphne so he could begin to pummel me, I suspected.

I let him pull me to the side before slipping out of his grasp. He stepped toward me, grinning like I was going to be easy, but I had just enough time to see his grin change, to crinkle and then spread into something like the shape your mouth makes when you say *oh shit*, and then the bottle smashed him there, shattering against his teeth. He staggered back, wiping blood from his lips, spitting out a tooth, moaning in pain.

I watched him for a minute as he fought the pain and tried to remain on his feet. He got his legs under him again, wiped his hands on his jeans, and came with a haymaker, fresh blood cascading from his knuckles as he wound up. I sidestepped, caught the back of his neck, and slammed him to the floor.

Damn, it felt good. The air in the bar returned. The man groaned but didn't try to get up. People began to talk again. I turned to Daphne. "Want to go for a walk?"

I was reaching for her hand already when I heard her answer. It caused me to do a double take.

"No," she said.

"Excuse me?"

She was looking at the man on the floor in horror. "What is wrong with you?"

"I . . ." I shook my head.

Something was wrong. Her eyes . . . her face . . . she was horrified.

I'd misjudged the situation. The red cooler had been a coincidence. I saw that clearly now. Daphne wasn't Savanna. She was just a woman who self-medicated with sex. She was actually a lot like me. But not as bad as me. Because . . . I looked at the man groaning on the floor and up to her horrified face.

Livingstone came over. "You better go."

I nodded. "I'm sorry. I misread the . . ."

But Daphne was already crouching on the floor next to the man.

I walked out of the bar in a daze, trying to determine where I'd gone wrong.

64

"Wait up," Claire said.

I turned and saw her exiting the bar, holding a bottle of whiskey.

"Sorry," I said. "I was kicked out."

"Yeah. I, uh, noticed. What happened in there?"

"Mistaken identity. I'm going to head home."

"Sure you don't want to take a walk?" She held out the whiskey.

I grabbed it and took a swallow. It tasted good. "I better not."

Claire reached for my hand, squeezed it. "She wasn't the one, huh?"

"No."

"What made you think she was?"

"It's complicated."

Claire grinned at me. "I hate when things are complicated. Things don't have to be complicated."

"What are you talking about."

"Let's go somewhere. Somewhere private and I'll show you."

She was clearly coming on to me. I felt intrigued. Not so much by the possibility of sex. Well, that *was* intriguing, but what was even more intriguing was Claire. This was a side of her I hadn't seen.

"And you never told me about Harriet," she said. "Where you found her."

She tightened her grip on my hand. The night seemed to darken and tilt. I was in freefall again. I was dying. I was in the creek, looking up. I was in the gorge, climbing. At the top I saw Claire's face.

"Hey," she said. "I'm serious. Let's go."

I wasn't sure what was happening. The red cooler was a coincidence, a red herring, nothing more. I looked around and saw all I needed for confirmation. The remaining Hill brother stood on the porch, watching us closely. Even Joe had been to the bookstore where Claire worked before coming to see me. Hell, he'd probably been bringing me the bookmark so I'd be sure to know where to find her. Everything snapped into focus. The unseen visitor in the bookstore when I'd first met Claire had to have been one of her sons. And hadn't I also spotted one of them lurking around the coffee shop when we'd met not too long ago?

I looked away quickly, pretending not to notice him.

"Okay," I said. "Let's walk."

She squeezed my hand and nestled herself against my right side. "Where are we going?"

"I know a place," I said. "It's where I learned about living and dying."

* * *

We walked up the mountain and down an old trail I remembered exploring as a kid. I knew the trail would eventually lead us to Backslide Gap, the same place where I'd almost killed myself during my misery binge after Mary ended things with me.

No, I reminded myself. Mary hadn't ended the relationship. I'd done that when I decided to take comfort in the bed of another woman. I cringed, thinking about what I'd done and how I'd also misjudged Daphne. I'd confused her need for sex with a need for pain. Ultimately, she was just a female version of me. And now I was holding the hand of the real sociopath, a woman who I had also severely misjudged. I wanted to let go, to wipe my hands on my jeans, but that would have broken the spell. I couldn't afford to let that happen.

"Where are we going?" she asked again.

"I know a place not too far from here." I squeezed her hand. "You'll like it."

She smiled, but I could tell she wasn't sure what to think. She was trying to read the situation, trying to determine if I knew who she really was. My job was to make sure she thought I was oblivious, to make her feel overconfident, like she was still the one in the know, the one in the position of power. Meanwhile, I had to hope she actually wasn't. As we walked, I continued to watch the trail behind us for signs of her one remaining son. I didn't see him, but I knew better than to draw any confidence from that.

"I can't believe you found Harriet," she said, fishing.

"She's doing great," I said, not missing a beat.

"Is she hidden in a cave somewhere?"

"Somewhere," I murmured.

"That's not very specific."

"Let's not talk shop." I stopped, reached for her shoulders, and turned her until we were facing each other. I leaned in and kissed her neck. She shivered slightly, giggling.

"I've been waiting for that," she said.

"I'm sorry. I don't always read the signs."

"And you call yourself a detective."

I laughed, playing along.

She reached for my groin.

"You're not hard," she said, disappointed.

"Well, shit. Give me a minute."

But I was just buying time. As attractive as she was physically, learning what I'd learned about her made it difficult for me to become aroused.

But Claire wasn't patient. That was something we seemed to have in common.

She dropped to her knees and unzipped my blue jeans, working my penis through the opening at the front of my briefs. It was still flaccid.

She looked at it, disappointed. "Let's see if we can work on this a little bit." She shrugged her purse from her shoulder, and when it hit the ground, I noticed the gleam of metal in the moonlight. A gun. All it would take was for her to get me wrapped up in the pleasure of the moment, and she'd be able to grab it and shoot me. We were far away from the bar now, far away from nearly everything. She took me in her mouth, murmuring, as if she'd never done anything before that brought her as much pleasure as what she was doing to me right now. She was the consummate actor, and somehow, feeling her mouth on me, listening to the murmuring noises she made as she eagerly worked on me, I overcame my disgust with her and was aroused.

"There he is," she said. "Now, close your eyes and just enjoy it. This one is on me. We can get you going again when we reach wherever it is you're taking me."

I pushed her head back gently. "I don't think so. Save it. The place we're going is special." I took a chance. "It's dangerous. You like dangerous, don't you?"

She grinned and nodded. "Okay, just as long as you let me finish what I started when we get there."

"Of course." I zipped up and took her hand, helping her to her feet.

"I like danger," she said, "but I'm not an exhibitionist. I want to be somewhere private."

"This place is the most private in the world." There could be no doubt what she was planning now. Had there ever been? All along, I'd believed she'd been planning for this moment. Why hadn't I seen it before? She wasn't an amateur detective. She was a psychopath trying to find her sister.

As we walked, I decided to take another chance. It was a big one, but if I didn't try it, I'd risk having our confrontation without getting any of the information I needed.

"I heard a rumor."

"You did?" She seemed genuinely curious, but I couldn't dismiss the possibility it was all part of the act.

"Yeah. Just a rumor. You know how those things go. Maybe nothing to it."

"Well, what did you hear?"

"I heard that you and Randy Harden used to see each other."

The pressure on my hand shifted slightly. If uncertainty was something you could feel through a person's hand, I felt it. She was waiting for more, for the other shoe to drop. I confess, I let the moment linger, savoring it. It was still too early to lay all my cards out, though, so I held the other shoe back for a little longer.

"My buddy Ronnie said he saw the two of you together. He's a little bit of a loose cannon, so maybe he was mistaken. He said, 'Hey, Earl, I saw your bookstore woman, Claire, out with Randy Harden the other night.' Pissed me off a little. I mean, that you'd never mentioned it when you knew I was investigating his school."

She let go of my hand. I turned, watching her, ready for her to make a sudden move to her purse, but she didn't. Instead she stood on her tiptoes and kissed me hard.

"I think your friend is mistaken. I was dating a man a while back. Must have looked like Harden." She grabbed my crotch. "I'll tell you one thing, none of the men I've dated have anything on you."

I moaned, playing the part.

She slipped out of my arms, and I kept my eye on her. The purse stayed on her shoulder. "Want me to carry that for you?"

"No thanks. I hate when men carry their woman's purse. It's such a turn-off."

We walked some more. The landscape changed slightly as we neared the gap. The ground rose sharply beneath our feet, steeper with each step, while the branches of the trees above us twisted together, creating a false ceiling and the sense we were in our own private world, sheltered from the sky and its vastness. The path narrowed, growing more rocky, and I remembered hearing Rufus's story about his mother and how as a girl she'd been up here near Backslide Gap, watching Rufus's aunt, who was born with water on the brain. She'd been sitting near the swinging bridge and had lost track of the sister because she was focused on a boy she liked. The girl had fallen to her death, and Rufus's mother had lived the rest of her life with that seed of hard regret buried inside her heart. It had bloomed there, blowing the pain outward like exploding glass.

As the dark gap came into view, I believed I saw the young girl standing beside the swinging bridge, her form translucent and shiny, generating light where none should be, a star stolen from the sky but still burning. And I understood she would never stop burning until there was no one to hold her in their heart anymore. Until someone forgot or at least let go.

"Oh," Claire murmured when I clicked on the penlight to illuminate the dark scar running through the mountains, the slender and shaky bridge strung across the scar.

I aimed the light on the bridge. "I dare you."

"What, to go out there?"

"Yeah. All by yourself."

"It won't be fun without you."

"Well, if you went out there naked, I might be persuaded to follow you."

She grabbed my hand. "No, we go together." She started to pull me toward the suspension bridge, but I stopped short.

"You're not taking your purse, are you?"

"I got protection in it. For you."

"I brought my own," I said.

"Well, look at you, Mr. Prepared. I might want a cigarette after," she said, holding it close to her.

"I didn't know you were a smoker."

"Lots you don't know about me."

We stepped to the bridge. "Ladies first," I said.

"I'm scared. You go and let me hold on to you."

I'd had a feeling that was coming. "Okay. Grab my waist with both hands."

She did as I instructed, and I stepped out onto the bridge. It wobbled, and I held onto the ropes on either side. As long as both of her hands were on my waist, she couldn't shoot me. And I didn't believe she was strong enough to throw me over the side.

We were about a third of the way out when I decided to begin.

"Do you know Rufus?"

"Of course. He's your friend."

"But do you know him? I remember when you brought him up, I'd never mentioned him to you before."

"Oh, I doubt that. I don't think we've ever met."

"Really? I was sure you two knew each other."

"No, but you're starting to scare me a little bit."

I laughed. "You scared of heights?"

"Just smart. I don't see how we'll do it out here. It's so shaky."

"Oh, I've done it with lots of women out here. You're in front . . ." I turned and put my arms on her shoulders to slide her past me, but she stiffened.

"I'm ready to go back."

"Well, shit. That's no fun." I turned all the way around now, facing her, my hands still on the ropes, hers on my waist. "But I understand. Go on back. I'm going to hang out here for a little bit. It's the only damn place you can see the sky."

"Okay," she said, and I made myself remember the way she'd done Harriet when she was only nine, locking her in the cellar. I thought of what she'd done to Rufus, and what she'd do to me if given the chance. I thought of the way she'd treated her own sons, abandoning them, making them fend for themselves like dogs. I thought of what I had to do, and how I had to do it right now.

She turned away from me and her hands found the ropes. I retrieved the penlight from my pocket, holding on with one hand tightly because the suspension bridge was wobbling more than usual. Our movements were out of sync now.

I held the light up and saw she'd barely moved. I still had time. With a lunge, I could grab her. Still, I hesitated.

Maybe it was because she was a woman. I'd never raised a hand in violence toward a female before. It was one of the few things in life that truly seemed forbidden to me. Not only that, it felt unnatural, like something I couldn't fully comprehend.

She was too far away now. I'd have to go after her and risk alerting her. She'd have to get the gun, but maybe . . .

I reached into my jacket and pressed record on the mini recorder.

I stepped forward, holding on with one hand, aiming the flashlight with the other.

She stopped. A hand left the rope and dug into her purse. She spun around, shaking the bridge wildly. We both careened to one side, and I dropped the penlight.

Somehow I still saw the gun, a dark bird wheeling madly through the night. She got it level, under control, just as I lunged hard against the rope, rocking the bridge and sending us sideways.

The gun went off, and the echoes of its retort coursed through the gap with a thousand tiny answers.

Time to let go, they seemed to say. *Time to let go.*

Her body landed on mine, and I held on with my right hand and grabbed at her with my left hand, snagging a large clump of her hair. The rest of her rolled off me and out into open space. Her weight tipped mine, and together we twisted the bridge over on itself. I held onto the rope with my right hand and her hair with my left. The rest of us hung in the gap.

Above us, I felt the moon come out from behind the clouds, as if awaking from a long sleep, pleased to find the drama unfolding beneath its solemn gaze.

65

"Please help me," she said. Her voice was cracked and strained with pain and fear and something else, something I believed was indignation. It was as if she couldn't fathom how all of this had happened. There would be no remorse, no regret from her, I reminded myself.

"I want to help you," I said, "but first you have to tell me the truth."

"I'll tell you anything."

"Where's Rufus?"

"I don't know. God, he escaped, okay?"

"I don't believe you."

"Fuck you. It's true. Please, you're not a killer."

"I've been reborn," I said. "I can be whatever I want to be."

"Be a savior," she said.

"I've already done that."

She whimpered. "It hurts so bad."

"Tell me where Rufus is."

"I don't know. The day before the shootout, he escaped. My boys chased him. He fell off the ridge. He's probably dead. But I don't have him."

"Which ridge?"

"Right by the door. He rolled down the hill, stood up, and walked off the ridge. He's dead."

I believed her. "What about Jeb Walsh? I need to know if he killed that kid."

"What kid?"

"The one who jumped at the falls."

"He had him killed."

"Who did it? Who pushed him?"

"It was one of his thugs."

"I don't believe that. I'm getting tired of holding you. All I need is to think you're lying one time, and you get to take the fall."

"Okay, I pushed him. It was me. But I only did it because he made me."

"Now we're getting somewhere. Reach up and grab my wrist with both hands." She did as I told her, and I let go of her hair.

She groaned. "Thank you."

"Now, how does the dead boy fit in? The one in my yard? What's Joe's connection?"

Somehow, against all odds, she laughed. "Joe? You mean the queer? I had a good time talking to his boyfriend. You should talk to him."

"I want to hear it from you, or I'm going to drop you." I pulled my arm up, causing her hands to slip down my wrist toward my hand.

"Please," she said. "Don't let me fall."

"You'd better talk quick, then."

"He went to the Harden School. He wanted to hire you to help him find me. I guess he got his wish after all."

"Who killed him?"

"You really don't know?"

"Your boys?"

She grimaced. "Yeah. Pull me up, okay?"

"Who told them to do it?"

"Me," she said. "Blevins didn't like it, but he's a queer too. I tried to tell Randy not to hire him. Pull me up and I'll tell you everything."

"You can tell me as you fall," I said, and tried again to pull my arm away from her, but she was too strong. She held on, even reaching for my elbow with one clawlike hand. Her other hand followed, and then she was squeezing my bicep and reaching for my shoulder. I used my now free hand to reach for her face. I placed my palm over her eyes and slid it down against her nose, smashing it nearly flat. There was a crack of cartilage, maybe bone, and then she screamed. But she didn't let go. I pushed her head back, bending her neck unnaturally.

"If you let me up," she gasped, "I'll tell you how to bring down Jeb. I know . . . all . . . his . . . secrets."

One of her hands slipped and I shrugged her other hand off my shoulder, and for a moment I was free of her weight. But only for a moment. I felt her grab my shirt now. The fabric tore, a loud hissing sound that filled the gap. Her hands scrambled for my belt, and she dug her fingers underneath it.

Before I had time to follow up on what she'd said about Jeb's secrets, the moon reemerged from the silk clouds and I saw a man standing on the other side of the gap, holding a rifle. He was tall and lean and still. The rifle bucked in his hands and the night shook. The suspension bridge exploded into bits of rotted wood and fibers of rope. The knuckles on my right hand felt hot and then hotter. Finally, the pain came. I let go, keeping only my left hand on the rope.

I was only dimly aware of Savanna as she climbed up me again and shouted for her one remaining son to kill me.

66

He certainly tried to do just that. The rifle coughed and sputtered bullets, spraying them everywhere. I felt them whiz past my head, my torso, and one hit the bottom of my boot heel as it dangled over the gap.

Backslide Gap, I thought. What a place to die. It was the place where young boys who'd turned their backs on God had gone to die. It had haunted so much of my childhood, because like all the things that haunt a person, I knew it was something I wanted. To backslide, that is, to push all the stuff that scared me way down inside and not think about it again. Now I wondered if backsliding might be the only way to truly be saved. The world demanded so much. It was only when you stopped listening and let yourself fall into who you were really meant to be that salvation was possible.

Savanna was screaming now for him to stop. He didn't hear her or didn't care to listen, because the bullets kept coming.

Miraculously, none had hit me, though I gritted my teeth in anticipation that one would.

Finally, the gun fell silent, but the gap didn't. It was filled with the echoes of the past, reverberating from wall to wall, seemingly stuck there like a lump inside the throat of a great and eternal beast. I wanted to expel all of the past that had built up inside me, that had led me to this moment where I was truly, truly alone. If I could have made a different decision at some point, learned to live with myself better, not been so damned desperate for a few fleeting seconds of pleasure, maybe this moment would have been a dream or a scene in some book instead of my life, my reality, the crushing present that would not ever go away because the past trailed it around like mud on the underside of death's old shit-kicking boots.

The remaining Hill Brother—as nameless as he'd ever been—was shaking the bridge now as he came out onto it, his face hidden by the night, his body luminescent in the moonlight until he was nothing more than a ghost of a man, a boy disregarded by his mother and unknown to his father, a wolf, a hill, a forlorn wind twisting through hollows that would never be fully mapped.

But not a man. A grotesque specter from the feral past. He came on, resolute and unblinking, and I thought of Old Nathaniel again, the masked phantom. If I died right now, I'd never know his real face. Maybe it had been this brother all along, or maybe it was the other one, or maybe Old Nathaniel was their father and they were the product of some unholy union between their flesh-and-bone mother and a spiritual manifestation of evil that was the thing that stalked the corn.

But I didn't think so. There was something deeply human in the Hill Brothers, something sad and broken and something stuck, hanging just like Savanna and I were hanging, sinners all of us over an endless abyss.

I started pulling myself up, and my muscles ached with the effort, but I didn't stop. Muscles were tissues that felt the past keenly, but they only worked in the present. I worked them like there had never been a past, like the now was everything and always, and by the time I was almost up on the shaky suspension bridge, I realized I'd found a truth right there.

Savanna still clung to me, holding on to my boots with everything she had left. I could see she'd been shot. Well, I couldn't *see* it, but I could sense it. Her breathing had turned ragged, there was the smell of blood in the air, and the unmistakable sense of gravity pulling her down.

With a great effort, she pulled herself up my legs and to my hips. I was partially lying on the suspension bridge now, and I thought about how our lives were too often spent in a gap, trying to balance on a suspension bridge, trying to avoid the fall, but sometimes it was better to get to the other side and never look back.

She reached out a hand for me to take, and I did. I pulled her up until I could see her face. The bridge wobbled and shook as her son approached. He shouted something. It sounded like *Mother*, and the sound of it touched me greatly. I felt a great respect for the primal things of this world, the bonds between mothers and sons, but then I remembered his brother, and

I met Savanna's eyes, now filled with moonlight. She could have been beautiful, I thought, if she'd had any light in her at all.

"I've got to let go," I told her.

Her eyes grew wider. "No, you don't. I'll tell you everything about Jeb. You can take him down."

I was running out of time. The brother was getting closer now. I needed to make a decision.

"I already know about him," I said. "And I know about you."

Her eyes understood before I think I did. They went dark, flushing the moonlight out, repelling it. There was emptiness inside her, and when I let go, I felt like I was dropping a shell of a person. She fell, screaming, and I watched her as long as I could before the darkness ate her and a new silence settled over the mountains.

67

pulled myself up to safety just in time to get knocked back down. The Hill Brother swung the stock of the rifle hard, and it landed against my jaw. I dropped to wooden planks, scrambling to hold on to something to keep from sliding off and joining Savanna in the fall.

"You killed my brother," he said, and drove the stock of the rifle into the center of my back. My body lit up with pain that flashed outward to my extremities. Fingers, toes, even my teeth hurt.

"Why did you kill my brother?" he asked, and I swear it wasn't rhetorical. He expected me to answer, but I had no answer. *Why* was the toughest of all the mysteries. Even *how* couldn't come close.

"I don't know," I moaned.

He sucked in a breath, and I understood he was raising the gun again. I waited a beat before kicking his shins with both of my boots. He gasped in pain and dropped the rifle onto my back. I screamed as the pain came back, like a flame that ran along my nerve endings. The bridge rocked as he fell.

"Help," he said. Gradually, I worked myself up to my knees and turned to see that he'd been pitched headfirst off the bridge, and somehow his leg had become twisted in the rope. The rest of him dangled headfirst over the dark gap. It was the same way I'd hung as a boy, so many lifetimes ago.

I slid over on my knees and examined the situation. I could easily let him fall by simply pulling up on the rope, releasing the snag that had saved him.

"What's your name?" I asked.

He said nothing, his arms spread out like he was ready to embrace the darkness.

"It's okay," I said. "I'm going to help you." I just didn't have it in me to watch somebody else disappear into that darkness. I just didn't. Besides, maybe he still had a chance now that his mother was gone. Was being put in a shed in the woods when he was a small child his fault?

"You wearing a belt?" I asked.

"Huh?"

"If you're wearing a belt and can take it off, then you could toss it up to me. I can hook it to my belt, and then you can get a hold of it. Then I can let your foot loose and pull you up."

He reached for his midsection and unbuckled his belt. Once he'd pulled it through the loops, he let it dangle in his hand, holding it by the buckle.

"Are you ready?" he said. I realized I'd never heard him speak in a normal voice before. His voice was low and gravelly, almost poetically powerful. Calmer than I'd expected.

"I'm ready," I said. "Make it a good throw."

He swung the belt up and let go of it. The buckle gleamed in the moonlight. It was a bad throw, and I had to lunge to get a hand on it, disrupting the balance of the bridge again. I caught the belt and landed flat on my belly, my arms and head out in space. The rope his boot was tangled in shuddered, and he slipped down into the gap two or three inches before it snagged him again.

I unhooked my own belt and then spliced the two of them together. I held onto one buckle, sliding it over the middle finger of my right hand. "Here it comes," I said, dropping the rest of it into the open gap. "Can you reach it?"

He didn't have to answer. I felt the tug on the belt. "Make sure you've got a good two-handed grip. When I undo this boot, everything is going to change."

"I got it," he said.

"Okay, here goes."

He said nothing.

I lifted the rope with my free hand. It was harder to lift than I'd expected, but eventually I created enough space and his boot slipped free. I felt the sudden weight of the man just an instant before I doubled up my grip. I was dragged forward with him as he started his fall, but when I got two hands on the belt, I was able to curl my arms up, to fight against gravity again, to make my muscles forget the past and live in the now.

Together we worked to get him up to the bridge. I lay there on my back, panting, and a memory I'd lodged inside the blacked-out places of my mind came back to me suddenly and vividly.

This was where I'd lain drunk, looking up at the stars, and decided there was no point in continuing to try. Hell, I was so done with life, I didn't even have the energy to off myself. I just wanted to go to sleep and let the chips fall where they fell, which I was quite sure would be in the gap my father had once promised me would by my destiny.

But my destiny was still writing itself. The past isn't set in stone even if we want it to be, because it's a living, fluid thing, open to a thousand interpretations and evaluations, influenced by the present as much as the other way around. Destiny and the past are intertwined because they can both be manipulated by the present.

And right now, I felt like a man who'd done a hard day's work, and a man who still had a few jobs to do, but I'd have to do them after I rested a bit. But just before I faded off, I heard the Hill Brother speak.

"What?" I asked the dark.

"It's Jeb," he said. "My name. It's Jeb Junior."

*   *   *

I dreamed of my father and Mary and Rufus. Ronnie was by my side and we were in the woods, on some island in the middle of some river. My father was a ghost we saw on the path, and Mary lived in a small hut beside a small stream where she made moonshine and happiness, just not the kind that could do me any good. We encountered Rufus last of all, lying faceup in a stream that looked a lot like Ghost Creek. He was naked except for the tattoos on his chest. They shimmered in the clear water and came alive in the radiant light of a moon brighter than any I'd ever seen.

On his chest was a road map tracing the path of his life from the Holy Flame to the Harden School to Two Indian Falls and then back to the church. It was a circle, and I was struck by the strength of the circle, the way the present ate the past and subsumed the future. I reached a hand out to him, and he opened his eyes and saw me. I helped him out of the stream, and that was when I realized my dream had played a trick on me in the way dreams sometimes do: Ronnie had vanished and in his place was Joe. I patted his shoulder and pushed him toward the creek. And now Rufus had been replaced by Harriet and her wheelchair in the creek. She extended a creek-dirtied hand, and Joe took it.

Harriet closed her eyes again and nodded. Above us, the moon went dim, and then all of us were as blind as we'd been in the womb, the last safe place before death.

68

Rufus hurt, but he was alive. He could move, but what was the point? His blindness had finally beaten him. He had no idea where he was. To walk was to fall. To rise again was to tumble into a void. Why shouldn't he just stay put? Stay put and die.

But dying wasn't as easy as it seemed, and after what seemed like hours of lying in the same spot, Rufus dragged himself up and began to move forward, away from the slope of the hill, away from the mountain. There were trees in every direction, pine mostly, but some that felt like maple and oak as well.

There was deep shade here, but periodically he stepped out of the cover of the trees and felt the sun on his face. The day was hot and he began to sweat. Wiping it away with one hand, he wondered where he'd find water, and if he didn't find it soon, when he'd begin to feel the effects of dehydration.

If he just had some idea where he was. He needed a landmark, but there was nothing, just random trees, a pitched forest floor, occasional sun.

He sat to rest, listening closely to the woods. Birds sang in the trees. Wind blew branches like silent bells, ringing whispers all around him. Was there a sound beyond that, something faint, like silk pulling away from silk?

Wiping the sweat from his forehead, he rose again and began to walk toward the sound. It was barely there, beneath the wind, and occasionally when the wind stopped shaking the tree branches, he heard it more clearly. Smooth and soft. Eternal. It was a stream or maybe a river, water caressing rocks, grooving its way through the land. He kept going.

The sound got louder, more clear, more like a river, and he knew he was going the right way. Fifteen minutes later, his hands raw from stumbling into trees and over deadfall, he knelt and scooped the water into his mouth and drank. It tasted like life itself.

An image came to him then, the last one he'd ever seen before the world went dark. It was of the milky-white substance floating away in the stream not too far from the Duncans' farm.

Mr. Duncan had given him a month to get out of the barn when he'd told him he was quitting. "Take your time. Randy says he hates to lose you. Maybe you'll change your mind. I also want to thank you for trying to help Harriet. You didn't have to do that, and I appreciate it."

Rufus didn't even attempt to tell him how he hadn't helped Harriet at all, how he'd actually betrayed her.

It was funny how quickly things had changed after Rufus said what Harden wanted him to say in the newspaper. Not only was Mr. Duncan offering to basically let him stay for free, but Harden and Deloach acted as if there had never been any conflict with him, as if he was one of them again. He wasn't fooled. He was done being fooled. And he was done caring about men like Deloach and Harden. Once, when he walked out of RJ Marcus's church, he'd believed he had the world figured out. Now he knew he had nothing figured out, which was why he'd never trust a man selling something again, be it religion, a way of life, or just plain hatred.

He'd made a clean break from all that. Well, almost clean. He still had to live with the regret.

Savanna had moved away, and for that he was thankful. There were rumors she was pregnant, but Rufus didn't imagine it could be his. He later learned she'd been having sex with multiple men, including Deloach. Maybe he would make it after all.

The shadow girl showed up again on the second night after he quit. He was terrified, but it was just a strange dream, he told himself, not the same thing that had happened to his mother. Just a dream.

Three nights later, he realized how wrong he was. It was no dream. It was Harriet, and she wasn't going to stop coming for him. Each night, she drew a little closer, and each night he tried not to sleep, but eventually he succumbed anyway. He soon understood there was a pattern. Eventually she would get close enough to reveal her face. And once he saw her . . . he couldn't properly explain what dread the thought of seeing her did to him. It broke him. It made him not want to live.

The idea came to him easily, the way a person might see a bowl of sugar on the table and decide it would be good in a cup of coffee. It was just a thought at first, but it grew inside him in a way that felt like a solution, a final answer to all his problems, a way to live in the face of his regret.

The drain cleaner was under the sink in the Duncans' kitchen. The heavy-duty, industrial kind.

He left it alone for a week, while he looked for a new job and packed his things. He didn't sleep much. Whenever he did drift off, the shadow girl was there to greet him, and then he was stuck, facing down the regret he'd created during his waking hours. He hadn't killed her, but he hadn't saved her. Worst of all, he'd smeared her legacy to save himself. It was an act, he came to understand, that had condemned him. The only way to save yourself was to live your life for others. Short of that, there was damnation. The hell of the mind was so much more brutal than that of the body.

The next time he saw the drain cleaner was during dinner with the Duncans. Lyda, the older sister, was home, and she'd invited him to eat with them. He liked Lyda, wished he'd met her before he'd become so broken, before the regret had infected him. He tried to be polite, to answer their questions about his future, but he didn't feel polite. He didn't feel like he had a future.

When Mr. Duncan stood and went to the sink, Rufus watched him. He opened the cabinet under the sink, and there was the drain cleaner just waiting for him.

After dinner, everyone moved into the den for coffee. He sat next to Lyda but couldn't relax. She asked him about Harriet and seemed to be under the impression he had somehow been kind to her sister instead of betraying her. When it became too much, he excused himself to go to the bathroom.

The bathroom was off the foyer. He walked right past it, turned into the dining room, and slipped past the laundry room back into the empty kitchen. He was moving as in a dream. In fact, he wondered if it all hadn't been a dream as he opened the cabinet and picked up the drain cleaner. He walked back the way he'd come and out the front door. He didn't pause at the barn, not to get his things or for a moment to say goodbye. He knew he would never be coming back to the barn again. At least he didn't plan on it.

He made it to the road, crossed it, walked into the trees that soon turned to woods. He walked in the darkness for most of the night, looking for the right place. When he finally found it, morning had come, and the sun was bright on the water. He didn't know the name of the river, but the best he could tell, it flowed down from the Fingers, gathering all the streams and rivers into this body of slow-moving yet resolute water. It seemed appropriate that this be the spot.

He never hesitated. It was as much about penitence as it was about putting a stop to seeing the shadow girl. He lay down with his head hanging off the bank, looking up at the sky. He unscrewed the top of the drain cleaner and held it up like an offering. In a way, he knew that's exactly what he was making. His sight for his life, his sight for the regret that ate at him, his sight for a second chance to be himself without the rest of the world trying to hold him back.

He tipped the container over, and the nearly clear white liquid spilled out, hitting his rapidly blinking left eye. The burning was instantaneous and exquisite, but he didn't scream. Instead, he felt pure exultation as the cleaner filled his eye cavity, as he switched to the right one, careful to keep his hand steady as he poured it drop by drop into his pupils.

Once the burning had filled both eyes, he turned around and dropped the container in the river. The excess drained from his face into the water flowing away from the Fingers. He watched it go downstream, a white mess he hoped was his penitence. He watched it until it faded away, not around the bend or out of the range of his vision but gone forever, replaced by a darkness Rufus hoped would somehow save him.

69

When it was all said and done and the article was typed and printed, I asked Chip for a copy. He gave me one and asked me what I was going to do with it.

I'd been worried about this part, but I just came right out with it.

"I'm going to use it to blackmail Jeb Walsh."

"Good," he said. "But we're going to print it, right?"

"Maybe."

"What do you mean, maybe?"

"Well, I'll have to see what he says."

"I want to come."

"I don't think that's wise. In fact, I was going to mark through your name. He's not an enemy you want to make."

We were at the Wildflower, sitting in Chip's room with Ronnie and Mindy. Still no Rufus.

I'd been looking for him nearly night and day while Chip got the article ready, but I'd found nothing. He was gone. I wouldn't stop looking. I knew that. I'd look for the rest of my days if I had to. But first, I had to take care of Jeb Walsh. I owed it to Harriet, to Rufus, to Eddie, and even to myself. Hell, I owed it to Mary.

"I'm willing to take that risk," Chip said. "For Joe."

Joe. Jesus, I hadn't even gotten around to telling Chip about Joe yet. It was coming. I thought it best to do one thing at a time. First, Jeb. Then I'd deal with Joe.

"What are the terms?" Chip said.

I nodded. I'd been thinking about the terms a lot lately. "Well, we start big. He has to resign his run for Congress."

"He won't do that."

I thought he was probably right. Jeb would just as soon fight a media war than do that. He could call "fake news" and hope for the best. It was the new trend for politicians these days, especially the ones of Walsh's sniveling and selfish ilk.

"Well, if he won't do that, we'll go for the next best thing."

"And what is the next best thing?"

I shrugged. "Close the Harden School. Demand Sheriff Argent's resignation. All charges against me dropped."

"What charges against you?"

I paused, struggling to think of a way to cover for my mistake. Was now the time to tell him about Joe? I decided it wasn't. I needed to keep him on board until I talked to Walsh. After that I'd come clean.

"You know I had to break the law to find Harriet, right? Not to mention what happened on the bridge with Savanna."

"Oh, right."

"Yeah, and maybe there's some other stuff too. A lot has happened."

"Right." He hesitated. "We still need to find Joe."

"We will," I lied. "We will."

*　*　*

The day felt tropical by the time we arrived at the gates of Sommerville Chase. We took Chip's car, a late-model Taurus with a broken air conditioner. We kept the windows down, but it made little difference. The day was filled with a dank humidity that seemed to permeate everything from my clothes to my thoughts.

A white-haired gentleman stepped out of the guard's station at the front gate. "Hot one," he said.

"Yes, sir," I said, relieved he wasn't one of the guard's I'd dealt with—and lied to—last fall in order to gain access to the exclusive neighborhood and film director Taggart Monroe's massive home. "I'm heading to Jeb Walsh's place. He's expecting me." It was true. I'd asked for a meeting, and he'd agreed without hesitation. It was almost as if he'd been waiting for this.

The guard checked his clipboard. "Name?"

I leaned over so he could see me from the driver's side. "Earl Marcus."

"Got you right here, Mr. Marcus."

"He sent me a code," I said. "You don't need it?"

"Nah. His secretary called and said to be expecting you." He looked at Chip. "Didn't say anything about another man coming. He your driver or something?"

I laughed, but then realized it was a serious question. This was the kind of neighborhood where people had personal chauffeurs. "He's with me. Jeb's going to want to talk to him too."

The guard looked unsure, but ultimately he looked *more* like he just didn't want to deal with it.

"Great."

The gate swung open, and we drove inside, following the directions from the robotic voice on Chip's phone. The voice led us through what had become one of the most desirable neighborhoods in the entire Southeast, at least according to the Southern Living article Mary had shown me in the spring. We'd both spent a few minutes marveling at the incongruence of such an award going to a neighborhood in the same county where people literally couldn't afford to buy shoes for their kids. Driving through the neighborhood now in broad daylight made it clear to me there were two Coulee Counties. The one I'd grown up in where wealth was a distant star that had burned out a long time ago, and the other one that was separate, fenced off, and filled with (mostly) white men who demonstrated a special kind of willful privilege. Walsh was one of those men, and Sommerville Chase was the perfect place for him. It existed within Coulee County, but most of the citizens of the county would never see it. You had to have an appointment or you had to have money. Everybody else was shit out of luck.

I was surprised when we took a sharp right that led us away from the neighborhood along a ridgeline covered with dandelions. We drove for about a mile on the ridge before descending into a ravine. The land eventually flattened out and a large wooden fence emerged, so high I couldn't even see over the top.

A few hundred yards later, I saw a side road that led up to yet another guard's station. This guard was young, fit, and appeared to be put off by my presence. "License," he said.

"What would cause a man to need a fence inside a fence?" I said as Chip handed him his license.

He ignored my question and studied Chip's license like he was a criminal. He kept glancing at him and then down at the photo. Finally, he nodded and handed the license back.

"Follow the road all the way to the house and then go around back. Mr. Walsh is on the porch."

"Thanks," I said. "Have a good one, bud."

He just looked at me as if I was a fool. Perhaps he was right.

*　*　*

Walsh's home was the kind you see in magazines but rarely in real life. His expansive yard was lined with well-groomed hedges and flower beds and studded with live oaks. The driveway was clean of any debris and paved with gleaming red bricks. A porch began in front of the large home and wrapped around the right side. The brick drive opened up into a parking area close to the white three-story home. The place screamed wholesome privilege, the kind of house where you'd expect to find a well-heeled couple with two kids grilling out and eating watermelon on the back porch while a friendly golden retriever lay respectably nearby.

Chip parked next to an expensive-looking European sedan, and we had no more exited the vehicle when a woman appeared in the driveway. She was in her thirties and wore a pair of blue jeans and a long-sleeved blouse. Her hair was pulled back into a ponytail. She beamed at me as if we were long-lost friends.

"Mr. Marcus. Thank you for coming. And who did you bring?" She sounded slightly put out by Chip's presence.

"A friend. He actually wrote the article we're going to be sharing with Jeb today."

"Mr. Walsh is on the back porch. This way."

We followed her onto the front porch, and my boot heels echoed loudly on the wooden planks as we made our way toward the side of the house, where the porch continued. Before we could make the turn, we were accosted by two large men wearing dark suits. Both men wore oversized sunglasses and had the same crew cut style hair. Neither spoke. The woman put a hand on my shoulder. "I'm sorry for the bother, but Mr. Walsh requires his visitors be searched. Do you mind? Mr. Walsh has a thing about guns."

"Is it absolutely necessary?" I asked.

"Mr. Walsh won't see you if you don't submit to the search."

Chip spoke softly. "Just let them. Get it over with."

"Fuck's sake," I said, and held my hands up. One man stepped forward and patted me down. When he felt the .45 in my waistband, he withdrew it and stepped away. The other man continued where the first had left off. Luckily, neither man found the small mini recorder I'd taped behind my knee. They turned to Chip next. I grimaced as the two goons put their hands all over him. When neither found anything, one of them pulled out a two-way radio and pressed the call button. "One forty-five-caliber hand-gun. That's it."

A voice on the other end said, "Send him on."

"You'll be able to retrieve your weapon when you leave," the woman said.

The two men walked away quickly. I watched them, trying to deter-mine which one had my gun, but he'd obviously already tucked it away somewhere.

"Assholes," I said to the men's backs, but neither one acknowledged I'd spoken. As pissed off as they made me, I couldn't help but admit they seemed professional, which had to be setting Walsh back a pretty penny. That he had that kind of wealth made him even more dangerous than I'd previously thought.

"This way," the woman said, smiling again, as if there was nothing more pleasant than being patted down before paying someone a visit.

When we finally reached the back porch, I saw the pond first. It was a good-size fishing pond with a small dock and a rowboat, which someone had out in the middle of the water. Walsh sat in a rocking chair, looking out at the pond, at the rowboat with its single occupant, who appeared to be fishing.

Walsh didn't stand when he saw me approach. He didn't even speak. Nor did he look in my direction. Not at first. Instead, he kept his attention on the boat in the little pond. The woman who'd led me to Walsh nodded to the rocking chair next to her boss. I motioned for Chip to sit, but he shook his head as if to say, *this is your show.* I sat down.

"Drinks, Mr. Walsh?" the secretary said.

"No, this won't take long. Give us complete privacy. Don't let anyone outside the house. If Donna asks where I am, tell her I'm not here. But like I said, this shouldn't take long."

I didn't like this already. He was asserting his authority by establishing parameters on the meeting. I needed to do something or this would get out of hand quickly.

"Yes, sir," the woman said, and walked to the back doors. She closed them behind her and we were alone, save for the solitary figure on the pond. I thought the person in the boat was male, but I couldn't even be sure of that from this distance.

"I'm glad," I said.

"Glad of what?" He still hadn't looked at me.

"That this is going to be quick. I'm afraid if I spend too much time alone with a man like you, I might resort to violence."

He laughed. It was a genuine laugh, as if he was actually taking joy in what I'd said, and this caught me off guard a little bit. "You don't seem like a man who ever has to 'resort' to violence. It seems as if it comes rather easily to you, Mr. Marcus. And my guess is you're the one behind some of the bodies of my friends that have been showing up lately."

"I wouldn't know anything about that. Besides, I don't really believe you have friends."

He laughed again. "Everyone wants to be friends with a man like me."

"Well, almost everyone. Your son isn't a fan of yours."

He nodded at the boat on the pond. "You mean Eddie? We get along great. We understand each other. It took a while, but he came around. He's sixteen tomorrow. You don't have children, do you, Mr. Marcus?"

"No. I figure some people aren't cut out for kids."

"Some people like me?"

"Exactly."

"Fair enough. You're right. But what may surprise you is that I love him."

"I don't think you're capable of love."

Walsh turned to look at me for the first time then. He nodded in what appeared to be agreement. "I didn't think I was either. But then he came along, and I realized I was capable of the emotion in certain situations.

329

And when those situations arise, I can be downright vicious about protecting those I love."

"That's not love. It's possession," Chip said.

He looked at Chip. "And you must be the reporter who is going to bring me down."

Chip scowled at him. "You brought yourself down."

"Call it what you want. Here's the point. Earl knows things about me no one else does. He's witnessed things. And you've even written them down, whatever your name is. I'm not going to insult your intelligence and try to defend them, though I think if you'd walked in my shoes, you might not be so different than me. Nevertheless, I am what I am. A bad man? Maybe so. But I'm still a man. And as a man, I will protect the sanctity of my family and my campaign with every fiber of my being. I never quit. I never stop. Consider that a warning."

"You talk as if you think we're here to blackmail you," I said.

"Oh, of that I have no damned doubt."

"Tell him," Chip said.

"Yeah, tell me, Earl. What do you have?"

"We know you had Weston Reynolds killed. That you put Savanna Duncan up to it."

He shrugged, neither denying nor admitting anything. "Can you prove it?"

"Chip lays it all out. Quotes from your wife and from Savanna."

"Savanna would have never admitted that."

I handed him the article. "People tend to talk when they're hanging on for dear life. You should read this."

He pushed it away. "What else?"

"You're not going to read it?"

He waved me off. "I'll take your word for it. Either way, it's just hearsay. You don't have any hard evidence."

Here it was. The moment I'd been waiting for. I let his words linger long enough to make him do a double take, long enough for him to suspect something was up.

I rolled my blue jeans up enough to reach the recorder. I ripped it away from my leg, wincing as the duct tape snatched the hair from my skin. I held it up. "This belonged to your girl, Savanna."

He stared at it for a moment. I thought I saw something like fear on his face. It was, quite honestly, a terrible thing. It wasn't like an ordinary person's fear. Walsh's fear was tinged with indignation, anger, violence. It was a reactive fear, the kind that would always wound others. He simply could not bear the fear alone, and I realized in that moment what he was: a frightened, small man. Nothing more. But with his privilege and the force of his personality, it was enough to wreak havoc on the world.

I clicked play.

His face grew red when he recognized Savanna's voice, and redder still when she said Jeb had instructed her to kill the boy.

"Turn it off," he said, his voice trembling.

I ignored him, letting it play until the part where I asked about Joe. I didn't want Chip to find out about his boyfriend like this, so I fast-forwarded a little and hit play again. There was a near silence as the tape squeaked. Then the sound of gunfire made the soundtrack explode in a clatter of distortion.

"Your son," I said. "He missed me completely. And I'm beginning to think I know why."

"My son?" Jeb looked offended. "What do you mean?"

I nodded out at the boat on the lake. "I heard Eddie's a good boy. Andy? Not so much. But this is one of your other boys."

"You're a liar. I don't have any other children."

I held the recorder up, hitting fast-forward again.

My timing was nearly perfect. Jeb Junior's voice was the first thing we heard. "Jeb Junior," he said. "My name is Jeb Junior."

Jeb Sr opened his mouth to speak, but nothing came out. He coughed, seemingly choking on his own words.

I clicked stop.

"No one will believe him. He's a Neanderthal, a damned wild animal."

"He's your wild animal. And I was surprised at how eloquent he was. And the best part is he's still out there somewhere. I think he's sort of pissed about his brother, and since his mother's gone, the only other person who ever showed him attention, no matter how pitiful . . . well, since she's gone, he's somewhat of a wild card."

I'd found a sore spot, and I wasn't about to let it go, especially if he wasn't even going to read the damned thing.

"What do you want?" he said.

"End your campaign," Chip said.

Jeb said nothing, and for a brief and wonderful instant, I believed he was considering his request. Then he shook his head, perhaps realizing he was nothing without his campaign, without his constant quest for power.

"Fuck that. I'll fight you before doing that. I'll fight all of you."

I looked at Chip. We'd expected this. And truthfully, we could have fought him. But I didn't think we'd win. We had all the evidence. We were on the side of good. But none of that mattered against Walsh. He had proven himself to be a slippery man, capable of wiggling out of the most precarious traps.

"We figured you'd say that. We have some other requests, however," I said though gritted teeth. I hated giving even the smallest amount of power to this asshole. But what choice did I have?

"I'm waiting."

"Preston Argent steps down."

"Let me guess, you're installed as sheriff?"

"Nope. I can do more good outside the law."

He grinned. "What else?"

This was good. He'd breezed right by Argent stepping down.

"The Harden School closes."

"I have nothing to do with that school." He nodded at Eddie out on the boat. "As you can see, Edward is home with us now. He'll be returning to Coulee High next fall."

"We all know that's a lie. Chip covered your ties to the Harden School in the article. In detail. And even if you didn't have ties, you have influence. If you're willing to exert that influence, you can have the school closed. At the very least, Harden resigns. A new admin is put in place that doesn't target gay kids."

Walsh gave me a look I believed might have been begrudging respect. "Okay, but that's all."

"No," Chip said. "It's not all. Before Argent steps down, he has to clear Earl of all charges that might come up because of the investigation."

He laughed. "Fine. I don't care."

"You'd better make sure it happens," Chip said. "If it doesn't, I send this article to every major newspaper in the country."

"Along with the tape," I added.

"Right," Chip said. "And I should also mention that my paper, *The Birmingham News*, is already in possession of a copy of the tape and the article. In the event that anything happens to me or Mr. Marcus, they will publish both."

"How will I know they won't do that anyway?" he asked.

"Because if they do, it'll be on me, and you'll feel free to retaliate," Chip said.

"That's the last demand," I said.

"Excuse me?"

"A peace treaty. Between you and me."

"We're not at war."

"True, but if you stay in the county, we will be. I want you to go somewhere else."

"That's ridiculous."

"Is it? Okay, Chip, let's go. We'll publish it. Get your lawyers and PR people ready. This is going to be a nightmare."

I stood up, feeling slightly dizzy. I hadn't planned on asking him to move. Maybe it was too much?

"Okay," he said.

I stopped. "You'll move?"

"This county is dead to me anyway. Once I'm elected, I'll be in Washington most of the time, so . . ." He shrugged.

"And you're dead to it," I said. "Oh, one more thing."

"What?" He looked as angry as I'd ever seen him, though he was trying hard to hide it, to appear in control.

"You've got two weeks."

"Two weeks?"

"Yep. Or the article goes out."

"You don't make de—"

"I just did," I said. And with that, I rose, nodded at Chip, and we started toward the front of the house. We'd reached the end of the long back section of porch when Walsh called out.

"Hey, asshole."

I turned.

"This isn't over."

I nodded. "If that's the way you want it."

"It's the way it has to be."

Chip grabbed my arm and pulled me around the corner of the house before I could respond. When the two men stopped us on the way out to give me back my gun, I offered them a piece of advice. "If I were you, I'd start looking for another gig."

It felt good, even if it was hollow. The truth, I realized as we walked to the truck, was that Jeb was still going to be in Congress, and we'd only moved the tumor that was his presence to a different part of an already ailing body.

But damned if it didn't still feel good.

70

Later that afternoon Chip informed me it was going to be his last night at the Wildflower before heading back to Birmingham. I asked him if he minded taking a ride with me.

"A ride?"

"Yeah, I'll drive."

"Fine with me. Where are we going?"

"Just get in. There's something I need to tell you."

Mindy and Ronnie had already checked out that morning, and now it was just the two of us at the motel. When we left, his Taurus was the only vehicle parked outside the long strip of rooms. It felt like the end of something, like we were on the edge of a long story, like a page was about to turn.

We made small talk as we drove up the backside of Ghost Mountain. He told me about his dog, Sam, and how he couldn't wait to see him when he got back to Birmingham. I asked him about his job at the paper, his plans for the future.

"I want to make a difference," he said.

"You already have."

"I know. It felt good. I don't want to ever lose that."

I understood. What I wanted to tell him was that he would eventually lose the feeling. He'd lose it to the mundane drone of routine and its sometimes insurmountable roadblocks. But I decided not to ruin his day. He deserved to feel good. And, who knows, maybe he wouldn't be as broken as me. Maybe he'd be able to know the feeling of redemption, of salvation, and hold on to it. Maybe I'd be able to do it too. It was a nice thought.

"You know," he said. "Walsh scared me."

"He has that effect on people, but you're safe now. We've got the tape and the article."

"That's just it," he said. "I think he knows."

"Knows what?"

"That I was lying about already sending it to the *Birmingham News*."

"You were lying about that?"

"Yeah. Truth is, I've got the only copy with me now. By the time I mailed it, I could just take it myself, which is what I plan on doing after this."

I had to admit, hearing this made me a little nervous, but in reality I didn't think it changed much. Jeb might suspect he was lying, but he'd have to be a fool to try to do something to either one of us. If he even believed there was a small chance Chip had been telling the truth, he'd be wise to just stand down.

In the end, I just couldn't get too worked up about it, especially not in light of what we were going to do, what I was about to tell Chip.

When I came to the creek and the road shifted steeply uphill, I told him we'd have to get out and walk. I was buying time now, afraid of saying the words swelling inside me.

We made it to the top of the rise, both of us sweating, breathing hard. The field opened up in front of us, and I saw the single oak out in the middle where I'd paced off my steps before burying Joe. The sun was setting behind the tree, and strands of brilliant orange were ensnared in its massive limbs. The tree appeared to be on fire, the leaves lit with a green-orange cast that was nothing short of breathtaking. A wind swept across the flat field, rustling high grass, cooling our skin from the heat of the day.

We stood there, taking it in, and I found myself thankful we'd arrived when we had, at dusk, when the world settles and cools, when new possibilities arise out of the remnants of past fires, where the present has no choice but to linger and reverberate.

"It's beautiful," Chip said.

"I need to tell you something," I began.

"You already said that at the motel."

I nodded. "It's not going to be easy."

"It's about Joe, isn't it?"

I turned and looked at him. He read the answer in my eyes. I reached for him, praying silently, reactively, that he would let me hug him, let me apologize. He did, and then I told him everything.

When I finished, the sun was gone and the stars were out. I thought of Harriet, of James Joyce and his nets, of Rufus. I thought of Jeb Walsh and all the sacrifices it had taken to finally penetrate his armor, even the slightest bit.

But most of all, I thought of Mary and how I needed her. I needed her right here beside me. I needed her to see this field, this fallow and beautiful soil that no one was left to tend. But then a voice came to me, a whisper, and I knew it was right.

Time to move on. Time to forget. Time to start climbing out of the past.
So I did.

* * *

The next morning, after I'd said goodbye to Chip, Rufus showed up at my house. He was more gaunt than usual and he had a busted nose, but otherwise he looked fine.

I embraced him, squeezing so hard he grunted that he couldn't breathe. I let go, grinning at him.

"Got a sandwich or something?" he said.

We went inside, and he sat at the kitchen table letting Goose lick his hands and wrists. His shades were gone, and the chemical burns around his eyes were visible. He seemed lost in thought, so I let him be while I made the sandwich.

"Here," I said, putting it in front of him. He ate greedily and drank four glasses of water.

When he finished, he slid the plate away. "Tell me she's dead."

"Yeah," I said. "She's dead."

"Thank God." And then he put his head down on the table and began to weep. When he finished, I told him everything that had happened while he was gone, careful to leave out the parts about Harriet. I was planning a more dramatic reunion, and I didn't want to spoil the surprise. He frowned the whole time until I got to the part about blackmailing Jeb Walsh. It was only then that his tight, down-turned mouth loosened and curled into something resembling a smile.

* * *

A little while later, Rufus and I went for a ride out to the east side of the county.

It was a cool day for early August, and I thought I sensed a whiff of the coming fall in the air. It made me feel hopeful, like there was a chance for redemption after all. The summer would die with dignity, as it had lived. There was a lesson there, I thought.

We took 52 east, the road virtually empty except for a beat-up pickup truck in my rearview, three men squeezed into its cab. They looked tired and dirty after a hard day's work. I guessed they were construction workers or maybe carpenters.

I was working on how to begin what I needed to tell Rufus when he spoke.

"I blinded myself," he said. "Out of guilt."

I kept driving, saying nothing, waiting for more.

"When Harriet jumped, I wasn't sure if she was dead or alive, but I was sure she'd jumped because she wanted to live, not because she wanted to die. Do you see the distinction?"

I might have if I'd been able to focus better. Hell, I'd hardly heard him. The words *I blinded myself* were still rattling around in my head. I was trying to make sense of them. It would be a long time before I ever did.

"What?"

"Sometimes being willing to die is the opposite of wanting to. Living ain't living when you spend your time trying to keep your head down, trying to be somebody you ain't."

I nodded. That made sense.

"I'm trying to get it right. *Say* it right." He shook his head. "There's a way to live, and you can't be afraid of dying."

"Only the dead are safe," I said.

"Exactly."

I glanced at him and could tell he was pleased with the phrase.

I still wasn't ready to tell him where I'd found it, though.

"I have dreams. My mother called it 'getting rode by the witch.' Scientists call it sleep paralysis. Both of them are right and both of them are wrong. What it really is, is something worse. It's the past pushing its way into the present."

I'd heard a little about sleep paralysis, enough to know it could drive people insane.

"Is that why . . . ?"

"That's why I did it. I thought if I couldn't see anymore, it would stop."

"Did it stop?"

He nodded. "For a while, but I don't think it was because I was blind. I think being blind just gave me something new to focus on, something for my subconscious to work out, to make sense of. The shadow girl came back recently. Even blind I saw her."

"Shadow girl?"

"Yeah. That's who I see. Her face is always hidden, though."

"Who do you think it is?" I asked.

"I know who it is. It's Harriet. It's her damned ghost."

I was about to tell him he was wrong when the truck behind us made a move out into the left lane to go around me. I slowed down, letting it pass. As the truck pulled up alongside us, I glanced over. The man nearest the passenger side door glanced at me and looked away. He looked familiar.

In fact . . .

I sped up a little, trying to get another look, but the truck sped up too and kept just a little ahead of me.

"What?" Rufus said as the truck finally created enough separation to merge in front of us. I tried to see the man's face through the back window of the cab, but I just couldn't make out any details.

"I'm not sure," I said.

"Not sure about what?"

"A truck just passed us. I think I may know one of the men inside it."

"So?"

He had a point. What exactly was the big deal? Coulee County was really small, and you were bound to run into the same folks over and over again. I mean, hell, the whole sheriff's department was made up only of the sheriff and a few . . .

"Shit," I said.

"What?"

I reached for my cell phone and found Chip's number. He'd be in Birmingham by now, I thought. It rang five times before going to voice mail. I swallowed hard. It didn't mean anything.

Did it?

"Will you please tell me what's going on?"

"One of the men in the truck is a sheriff's deputy named Hub Graham."

"So?"

"He's dressed like he's coming from a day's work. And I can't get in touch with Chip . . ."

It didn't take Rufus long to catch on.

"You think Walsh has already gotten to him?"

Before I could answer, the taillights of the truck in front of us came on. I slammed on my brakes, but I wasn't in time. I plowed into the back of the pickup, pushing it across the road for several dozen feet until both vehicles came to a stop on the shoulder.

I reached across Rufus for the glove box and my pistol as the doors of the pickup truck flew open and the three men spilled out. I did a double take when I saw that one of them was Jeb Walsh.

He held an AR-15 in one hand as he stepped out into the road. The third man was none other than Jeb Junior. He, too, carried a high-powered rifle. Only Hub carried a handgun.

I managed to get my own pistol and shout at Rufus to get down just before the front of my truck was obliterated by gunfire.

It lasted all of fifteen seconds before the silence settled over us. I forced myself to look at Rufus. His blind eyes were opened in a parody of shock while his lips worked spasmodically as pain racked his body.

Before I could ask, he said, "I'm okay. Just grazed my elbow. Focus on them."

"Okay," I said, but what could I do? Two high-powered rifles and a pistol against me and my .45? We were both dead men.

I heard footsteps on the asphalt as someone widened out, flanking the driver's side door, most likely looking for a better angle or to at least ascertain if we were alive.

I was just about to come out of the floorboard shooting when Rufus hissed at me.

"What?"

"Listen."

I tried. I heard nothing, which was somehow more frightening than the footsteps had been. I suddenly realized I did not want to die. Not like this, not without figuring out how to live with myself. And certainly not at the hands of Jeb Walsh. I was already on my way up, ready to fire through my own window, when I heard it.

The rumble of a coming vehicle.

I stayed put, realizing they'd have to take cover, and that if the driver stopped, Jeb and his two men would have to deal with one more person. At least.

I heard boots on asphalt again, then the sound of brakes.

A car door swung open. I decided it was now or never and raised myself up, sliding my ass back into the driver's seat. What I saw chilled me to the bone. It was a young boy, and it took me less than a second to guess it was Eddie Walsh. Yeah, based on the forlorn expression on his face and the way he was looking directly at Jeb, I had no doubt. Jeb aimed the AR-15 at his boy from where he crouched near a cluster of honeysuckle vines. Hub was nearby, and Jeb Junior . . . I didn't see Jeb Junior anywhere.

With Jeb's attention on his son, I had a clean shot at Jeb. I tried to get the window down, but the power wasn't working, either from the wreck or the barrage of bullets. I opened the door and stepped out onto the road. That was when Jeb saw me and fired.

I managed to step back just before he shot, and I used the open door as a shield. The sound of gunfire was eclipsed by a mighty scream.

It was Eddie. He was waving his arms and shouting at his father.

Jeb stopped shooting. I chanced a peek around the door and saw Eddie walking toward his father, shouting at him.

Jeb's voice cut through the noise. "Get out of the damned way."

"I followed you," Eddie said. "Because I knew this was what you were!"

I glanced at Hub. He was aiming his gun at Eddie too.

I stepped out into the road and fired, hitting Hub in the chest. He fell to the ground. Eddie, completely blocking his father from me, stopped and looked at Hub.

He didn't even bother to look back at me. Instead, he kept walking, heading for his father.

"Get out of my goddamn way," Jeb said as he tried to step around his boy for a clear shot at me, but Eddie was too quick. He moved with his father, the two of them caught up in some primeval and instinctual dance that only fathers and sons know. That was when I heard Rufus hiss at me.

"To your right."

I turned and saw Jeb Junior, still carrying the assault rifle. He wasn't aiming it at me, though. Instead, he had it aimed the other way, at either his father or his half brother, I couldn't be sure which.

By this point, Eddie had reached his father and was trying to embrace him, but Jeb was having none of it. Instead he sidestepped his son and fired several quick rounds in my direction. One of them hit me in the shoulder, pinning me back against my truck. Despite the pain, I was able to see what happened next.

Eddie reached for his father's arm and tried to pull the gun away. But instead of separating the arm from the rifle, Eddie only managed to turn the rifle toward himself. A single shot rang out.

I closed my eyes and my knees went weak.

When I woke up again, the world had changed.

* * *

With what felt like superhuman effort, I opened my eyes. I saw Rufus on one side of me. I turned and looked to the other side and saw Ronnie.

I closed my eyes again. It was good to have friends.

Sometime later, a doctor came in and told me I was going to live. I thanked him profusely and asked for more pain meds. He obliged.

It was only when I woke up again that I remembered I didn't know. I sat bolt upright in the bed, and the pain flashed through my shoulder like someone was running a razor blade across my nerve endings.

"Take it easy, Earl," Ronnie said.

"He probably wants to know what happened," Rufus said.

"The kid?" I managed, but I wasn't sure which kid I meant, Eddie or Jeb Junior. Okay, it was both. Somehow Rufus understood.

"The young one filled me in. Said, just after you got shot, Daddy was about to shoot him. That's when the Hill Brother stuck a bullet right in Jeb's eye." Rufus chuckled, and it was a dry, crackling sound, like a fire that might burn on a cold winter's night.

"Dead?" I said, realizing as I said it that I'd never wanted anything more in my life. Well, that wasn't quite true. I'd wanted Mary Hawkins more, and maybe I could want other things too if I played my cards right, learned from my mistakes, caught a few breaks . . . like this one. Lord, please give me this one.

"Naw, but he ain't never going to be the same. Besides losing that eye, the bullet blew out the back of his skull. He's in a coma, and the doctors ain't sure he'll ever come out of that, and if he does . . ." Rufus shrugged. "Then he's going to have a hard row to hoe."

I nodded, not sure if feeling excited about that made me a bad person or not, but I was pretty sure I didn't really care.

"Chip?"

Rufus winced. "They got to him."

I felt like I'd been gut-punched. I closed my eyes, knowing I'd have to find a way to absorb that blow, a way to catch my wind again, to keep moving forward.

"What about Jeb Junior and Eddie?"

"Jeb Junior?" Ronnie said.

"You haven't caught him up?" I said to Rufus.

Rufus smiled. "I don't care to talk to him, if the truth be told."

It sounded like the old Rufus, the one I used to know, but it also sounded like he was joking. Sort of. Either way, Ronnie laughed, and that made me feel a little better until I remembered I still didn't know what had happened to the two boys.

"They're okay," Rufus said. "Well, I reckon as okay as they'll ever be."

Ronnie snorted. "Ain't that the way it is for everybody?"

"No," I said, remembering suddenly what I'd been about to tell Rufus before I realized that the men in the truck weren't who they were pretending to be.

"You said you thought the shadow girl was Harriet," I said.

"I know it is," he said.

"You're wrong about that."

"How would you know?" he said.

"Let me get out of this hospital bed, and I'll take you to her and you can see for yourself."

Rufus was silent, his face opening up into a sense of serendipitous awe. Ronnie giggled. "He ain't going to *see* shit."

Neither of us commented on Ronnie's dumb pun. We'd both realized, I felt sure, that real seeing didn't require eyes as much as it required the truth. The truth of who you were and what you'd done, and the truth that the present mattered far more than the past or the future, the truth that we were all hanging over an endless and empty void, our feet snagged in the ropes of a suspension bridge that just got shakier as the years went by. The truth that hanging on was all there was, and all there had ever been, and you could always hang on longer than you thought if you had somebody there swinging out over the void beside you.

Acknowledgments

Thanks are due to my agent, Alec Shane, and the fine people at Writers House. A hearty appreciation also goes to Faith Black Ross, Jenny Chen, and the Crooked Lane crew. I was lucky indeed to find such a wonderful publisher. I'd also like to recognize some people who have always been there as readers, mentors, and friends: Kurt Dinan, Sam W. Anderson, Jamie Nelson, Bracken MacLeod, Paul Tremblay, Karim Shamsi-Basha (for the use of his office), and William Richardson. Finally, all of my love and thanks go to my patient and gorgeous wife, Becky.